I0664469

Also by Kelly Peasgood

Druid's Daughter

Spirit of the Stone

In Dreams We Live

The Forgotten King (The Forgotten: Book 1)

The Forgotten Magic (The Forgotten: Book 2)

god-touched

Kelly Peasgood

A Kelly Peasgood Publication

Cover art by Janet Christie

ISBN: 978-1-9991149-0-9
ISBN eBook: 978-1-9991149-1-6

This is a work of fiction. Names, characters, places and events are fictitious, and any resemblance to any persons, living or dead, or any events and locations, is entirely coincidental.

A happy shout-out to Jen, who read it first, and Paul, who has a good eye for details.

Many thanks to my editor Noah Chin, who knows his stuff.

A big thank you to Janet Christie for her amazing cover art design. Better than I'd hoped!

And as always, to Mike, who listens to my ideas even when they make no sense, and encourages me to write anyway :)

Anstore
Islands

Formorket
Enger

Merveah

Trandee

Hada

Danvers

Granbon

Ferna

Kemta
Bay

Hamiqa

Fyvm
Oasis

Gobani

Kahf
Alramal

Chapter 1

Jal's eyes raked across the myriad stalls set up in Ferna's market. One could find everything from pots and jewellery and tapestries, to livestock and fruit and fish in such markets. Boots and rucksacks nestled next to saddles, tack and horse blankets. Large hard-eyed men armed with cudgels watched over swords, daggers and light bits of armour displayed by both the merely competent and the most highly skilled of blacksmiths.

Every colour of the rainbow—and some harder to come by in nature—vied for attention amid the overwhelming scents of produce, people, and animals. Occasionally pleasant, often pungent, the combination wove together with the unfamiliar brine from the nearby bay to sting Jal's nostrils.

Used to more arid conditions where the clean bite of sand borne by desert winds dried one's sweat before its odour could offend a companion's unprepared nose, the golden-skinned Gobani girl did her best to ignore the tangle of aromas while keeping a sharp eye on her surroundings. The din of traders and those who'd come to purchase their wares, the clashing colours of displays and attire, the mix of races she knew from similar market places back home, all vied for attention. The pervading humidity and air heavy with the stink of salt and fish took some getting used to, even after four months skirting the edges of Merveah.

Born in the Gobani desert, the third of five children, Jal,

once named Ajala, had always known she didn't want a typical desert life. Nomadic, yes, but not one tied to a man's family, expected to play the role of a docile and subservient wife and mother. Her father, recognising her martial rather than marital leanings, had supported her, promising that she would follow in the ways of a warrior and not a wife. Both her sisters had little desire for anything beyond the womanly arts, and Jal's training with sword and arrow, spear and pike, saved Father from the necessity of setting aside a third dowry.

But Father had died, and her elder brother Olbaehn made his displeasure with his middle sister known. He wouldn't accept a woman nearly twenty summers old living without the influencing hand of a man. Her elder sister Zania, oldest of the women of the family since Mother's death seven years ago, couldn't gainsay Olbaehn's decision to wed Jal off to another tribe in return for payment. Zania had no power over Jal's future since her own marriage nearly four years ago.

Jal's younger sister Teagan certainly had no say, nor any interest in the fate of a sister who didn't aspire to matrimony as she did. And Nolbaehn, the youngest, though he would have sided with Jal in almost anything, had no authority over their brother. While Jal and Nolbaehn had trained together since Nolbaehn could hold a weapon, he had barely seen fifteen summers. Although strong and well on the way to becoming a fierce warrior, Nolbaehn couldn't stand up to a brother full grown and eight years his senior.

But in the end, Jal didn't need anyone to fight her battles for her. She had outstripped Olbaehn's prowess in arms by her last name day. He could overpower her with brute strength, but she had better technique and far more cunning. So when Olbaehn came to her with an ultimatum, Jal had simply stopped by her tent long enough to gather her weapons, pack some clothing and a bit of food, taken the monies Father had given her in the event that Olbaehn tried to force her hand, and walked away. Leaving Nolbaehn behind remained her only regret.

She did not regret changing her moniker to Jal.

With her rusty shoulder-length hair worn in a tail and a simple helm to hide her features, coupled with her warrior's clothing cloaking a well-muscled, athletic build, Jal could pass for a man. Only her short stature and slightly curved chest gave her away. Her breasts she could hide with padded armour; her short height she suffered with stoicism. Not that such a simple disguise would fool Olbaehn should he come looking for her, but she expected the expense and hassle of chasing his errant sibling would curb any such efforts—assuming he bothered to search at all. Jal didn't think he would. He had, after all, declared her outcast.

Still, she carefully surveilled her surroundings wherever she went, even now in far off Merveah, north across the briny sea from the Gobani desert. Olbaehn could never force her back home, but she had no wish to encounter her brother—or anyone he might send—unprepared.

Add that to the care one must take in any town, keeping light fingers away from coin pouches and travelling bags, watching for those who would prey on the weak or solitary traveller, Jal cast a wary eye over everyone and everything to stave off unpleasant encounters.

The clash of swords rang over the cacophony of the market in Ferna, drawing Jal's attention. Stowing the food she had just purchased in her pack and securing it over her shoulders, she followed the din of battle to an open square. The locals used the space to display livestock, the raised wooden platform at its end used in the barbaric northern practice of slave trade, both thankfully empty at the moment. In front of this ugly platform, ringed by curious onlookers, Jal watched the unfolding of an uneven sword fight.

Two men with fair skin—one tall and brawny with pale hair, the other shorter with light brown hair escaping from its loose tie—faced six dark haired, swarthy sell-swords, enough alike to share a similar heritage. Their two opponents—perhaps ten or twelve years her senior—fought as one, negating the advantage of numbers of their foes with superior skill.

Jal pushed to the front of the crowd and watched in fascination the ease with which the pair held off their attackers, seeming almost bored in their easy defence. She had seen enough fights break out in such trading villages, confrontations often turning deadly when tempers soared, and as now, the northern penchant for turning the possibility of seeing bloodshed into an entertaining spectacle instead of running for cover surprised her. This fight, however, deserved some appreciation.

The six men foolishly thought they had the upper hand judging by their exuberant expressions and fierce assault. Jal snorted at their misguided arrogance. Numbers didn't always matter if met with true skill, and the two fair-skinned men seamlessly wielded their weapons in a beautiful dance, deflecting blades and not causing any real harm. They clearly had a gift.

She wondered if either might deign to train her when they grew bored with the six amateurs stumbling over themselves in their haste to feel the blunt edge of a sword smack against arm, leg or, in one case, backside.

A slight breeze caressed Jal's cheek as the light around the larger man shifted, growing somehow more dim and yet also gaining a shimmer. Jal blinked to clear her vision, surprised to see a mirage so far from the desert sands, but the shimmer didn't fade. It grew to encompass the man, and Jal heard a woman's voice—low and sensuous yet cold and deadly—emerge from the eerie light, her words reverberating with awful strength and hatred.

"Here your glory ends, Phatomar. I will not allow you to take our due. You will not supersede our powers."

Jal glanced to her neighbours, but no one paid any heed to the voice from the light, focused only on the spectacle of the fight.

"I take from you your most cherished gift," the voice continued, drawing Jal's attention back to the strangely glowing man. *"I take your courage."*

Again, a breeze brushed past Jal, one which, she noted uneasily, touched no one else. She shivered as the tall man suddenly lost focus, his pale eyes growing wide as his movements turned sluggish. A second, more sonorous voice thundered from the dim light, this one belonging to a man.

"And I take your identity. Your memories of past deeds belong to me now, as does your name. A trifle soon forgotten in this world."

Their laughter mingled in malicious amusement, then faded, as did the glow surrounding the warrior, who even now began to tremble, his sword lowering and leaving him open to attack. One of the six men, seeing his confusion, sprang forward, sword raised. The smaller man blocked the thrusting blade and pushed the man away, sparing his stunned companion.

He called out something to his friend, though Jal only caught the words *Phatomar*, *Dearn* and *sword*.

Phatomar—his name had a familiar weight, though Jal didn't place it immediately—stared in horror at the weapon shaking in his fist, then at the men confronting him. His sword fell to the ground with a dull clatter. He could no longer fight, not without courage, or the knowledge of how to wield a blade. Jal realised that his shorter comrade didn't understand the new danger; no one seemed to. Why no one else heard the voices, she didn't know.

She acted on instinct, refusing to let thugs slaughter a frightened man that no one else knew needed defending. Reaching over her shoulder to the sword strapped to her back, Jal wrapped calloused fingers around the hilt and drew her weapon, leaping in front of Phatomar in time to deflect another strike. Phatomar dropped to a crouch, arms hugged protectively around his legs and head hidden against his knees. His sword lay abandoned at his feet.

His enemies, faces briefly lit by elation, now blinked in consternation at the new warrior added to the fray. Phatomar's companion stared in surprise and mistrust. He couldn't miss his friend's distress, though he knew not the cause.

"I saw hills to the north with plenty of brush for cover," Jal said as she defended herself and the man cowering behind her.

"Who are you?" The shorter man parried a vicious sword thrust from another adversary, his voice strangely accented. "What are you doing?"

Jal shook her head. "No time. Take your friend and go. I'll hold them back."

"We will *not* abandon a fight," he hissed in indignation.

"You can't fight them alone, and your friend can no longer hold a blade."

"What are you talking about?" He barely sounded winded despite his continuing dance.

"He's had his memory and his courage stolen," she said. The man gave her an incredulous stare while still managing to defend against his attackers. Jal shook her head. "I'll explain later. Just get him to safety."

Their opponents moved to circle them, hoping to cut off their retreat. Jal wanted them to rethink that. She raised her sword high, spun it twice, and brought it down in a wide arc while screaming a rough battle cry. Showy and not terribly efficient, but she had seen intimidation work before. The men paused and stumbled to a halt, drawing closer together as though seeking safety in numbers.

She knew what they saw, the image she had cultivated. Her slightly curved sword, favoured by the tracker assassins of the south, fit smoothly in her strong and capable hand. The long knife still sheathed in her belt, its leather casing worn yet well cared for, matched the dagger strapped to her thigh. Her dull bronze helmet, unpolished so that it wouldn't glint in the sun and give away her position, hid her eyes enough to mask her full expression, though her scowl showed hard-jawed determination. Her tunic, with its loose sleeves and cinched cuffs, designed to fade into the desert sands—protective in the bright sun yet warm in the cold nights—flowed around her without ceremony, utilitarian rather than flashy. She looked like a warrior, and despite her height, she knew how to hold her own in a fight.

Phatomar's companion, not much taller than her, grinned at her audacity. Instead of retreating with his friend, he came to her side and bellowed a battle cry of his own. The thugs jumped at the sound, which angered them.

Anger made them more careless, and with Phatomar obviously unable to help himself as he shied away from the noise, his companion lost all compunction of civility. He blurred into motion, and blood soon flew. In an instant, three of their dark haired opponents had gashes. Jal scored a few hits of her own, and the thugs found themselves retreating. With a final scream and lunge, Jal's new companion made the men stumble over each other as they fell back.

The shorter man then turned, grabbed Phatomar beneath the arm, and hauled him to his feet, pushing him along the path of least resistance toward safety. Jal had a second to blink, then, with practised efficiency, thrust her sword into its sheath on her back. She scooped up Phatomar's weapon, both larger and heavier than her own, and raced after the retreating pair. The gathered crowd gave a smattering of

6

applause at the unplanned spectacle, then turned to their own affairs, somehow managing to get between those fleeing and those who might follow given the opportunity.

Jal ran after Phatomar and his companion, the large man's unfamiliar weapon an added hindrance to her speed. Not the fastest runner at the best of times, Jal soon fell behind, her breathing laboured, but she pressed on, keeping them mostly in sight. Until she rounded the corner of the inn on the outskirts of town and met an empty street.

The road had split. She stumbled to a halt, her lungs bellowing as she wheezed for air, staring up each road and wondering which path they had taken. She knew how to read desert sands, but not hard-packed roads, and she feared she had lost them. Jal stared morosely at Phatomar's sword in her hand, lamenting the lost opportunity. She would have liked the chance to master the northern way of fighting as those two had. And perhaps to learn why she heard voices others didn't, and what made Phatomar special enough to torment so.

A piercing whistle had her whirl to locate the source, heart tripping faster as her blood surged anew. She swung Phatomar's weapon before her, anticipating a renewed attack. To her astonishment, Phatomar's companion swept out from the inn's stables on the back of a blond horse. Atop a chestnut horse next to him came Phatomar, tears streaming from his closed eyes and knuckles bloodless from his intense grip on the reins as he crouched low over his mount's neck. Jal gaped at the pair, and before she could even think to move, the smaller man reached over the side of his horse, took Jal's unresisting hand and, in a maneuver she didn't understand, hauled her up awkwardly behind him. She barely managed not to cut him or herself with her borrowed blade, and clung to his waist with her free arm as he sped eastward.

They didn't go far—a couple of miles only—before the man turned his horse up a rutted path that led to an odd building which resembled a shed, though it lacked full walls. The horse came to a halt, and at the man's impatient glare over his shoulder, Jal gently dropped Phatomar's sword to the ground, then wriggled around enough to slide off the beast's back.

She had ridden horses before, but rarely, more accustomed to the camels that journeyed between oases. Even those she seldom rode, as her tribe used such creatures mainly to transport goods, not people. She knew how to dismount, just not with any finesse, and she stumbled before finding her footing. She almost didn't notice Phatomar's clumsy dismount as he flinched away from his animal and cowered.

When she turned around, she found the brown-haired man right at her back, Phatomar trying to hide in his shadow. She didn't have to look up very far to meet his hazel-eyed glare. He stood quite a bit shorter than Phatomar, but he made up for that with a ferocious expression which she withstood by sheer force of will.

"Who the hell are you, and what have you done to Phatomar?" he demanded.

"I saved his life," she retorted, matching his heated tone.

The man crossed his arms and did a credible job of looming over her.

"That's not what I meant," he growled. "You said his memory and courage were stolen. Explain that."

How? she wondered. Saying she had heard voices upon the wind that no one else had would make her sound crazy, but what other explanation did she have?

"During the fight," she began, hating the hesitation she heard in her voice. "A glow surrounded Phatomar, and then I heard voices speak from above; one female, one male, both full of hate. The woman said she took his courage, and the man said he took his memories. They laughed, and Phatomar stood helpless." She shrugged. "No one else paid the words any attention, or they didn't hear them as I did. Had your friend not dropped his guard, I might have thought I'd lost my mind. But he just stood there defenceless with a sword coming at his throat. I couldn't stand by and let that happen."

After a long moment of silence, the short man spoke. Jal couldn't identify the thoughts clouding his eyes.

"Do you hear voices often?"

Jal snorted and shook her head. "As I said, if he hadn't lowered his guard at that moment, I'd have doubted my sanity."

8

He glanced over his shoulder at Phatomar who cringed, then turned back to Jal, slowly unwinding his arms.

"Who are you?"

"Ajal—" She bit her tongue. She may have taken a shortened name, but she hadn't had to share it often. "Jal," she said. "My name is Jal. Who," she countered, "are you?"

He stared at her, a light brown eyebrow raised.

"I am Eamon, son of Branon. This is Phatomar, son of Gordukah."

Jal blinked, the name finally finding resonance in her mind. Even in the Gobani, they had heard tales of the mighty son of Gordukah and his stalwart companion, Eamon. Phatomar, strongest and most fearless warrior in all of Merveah. Some said in all the world. The most gallant of men, matchless in courage and honour, his prowess unquestioned and envied. And right now quivering with barely restrained panic in the protective shadow of Eamon, a man with his own share of accomplishments and accolades.

"What's going on?" Phatomar asked now, a deep voice that should have held quiet strength, instead trembling in fear. Jal couldn't even begin to imagine his terrifying inner struggle.

"I don't know, old friend, but we will find out," Eamon answered with tender concern. His gaze sharpened on Jal. His head tilted to the side just a bit, a new concentration and consideration bringing out a stronger hint of green in his hazel eyes.

"Take off your helmet, Jal."

"Why?" she asked, resisting the urge to step away from him.

"I like to see who I'm dealing with, meet them eye to eye. A helm conceals too much information."

Exactly the point, she thought. But she wouldn't shy away from the truth. *A warrior, not a wife,* she reminded herself. If these men rejected her for her gender, then she didn't need their company.

Jal reached up and removed her helmet, shaking her head to dislodge rusty strands of sweaty hair that had escaped their tail and now clung to her forehead. She tucked the helmet under her arm and stared at Eamon, waiting to hear what he had to say.

"So, you *are* a woman," he said.

9

"And you're a man," she retorted, eyes narrowing.

Eamon raised a hand. "I meant no disparagement, Jal; just an observation. Are you god-touched?"

"Am I—what?" she asked, certain she had misheard.

"God-touched," he repeated.

Jal shook her head. In the desert, the closest she had heard to the term suggested someone overexposed to the sun and suffering hallucinations. "I'm not crazy."

Eamon's brow quirked. "That's not what I—" He paused and shook his head. "I don't know where you're from, but here in Merveah, god-touched refers to one blessed by the gods, gifted with powers beyond the average person. With the exception of Phatomar, I've mostly encountered women touched by the gods. It might explain why you heard what no one else did."

"God-touched." Jal didn't know whether she felt amusement or concern at the term. Olbaehn would laugh himself silly at the thought of his stubborn sister having any favour with the gods. She wondered what Father might have thought.

"Either way, it's a mystery we must solve, and quickly." Eamon looked back to Phatomar as the large man flinched from the shadow of a bird flying overhead. "If news of his predicament gets out, Phatomar will have far too much attention levelled at him and no way to defend himself." Eamon's intent stare returned to Jal, and she swallowed back her unease.

"So where do we go now?" he asked her.

Jal gaped at him.

"We?" she managed to say.

"You're the only link I have to what happened to my friend. Until we learn who stole his courage and memories, we're not leaving your side. Help me restore Phatomar to his former self and I will give you anything you ask in return."

Jal had left the desert and her homeland to make her own way in the world, but she didn't have a plan beyond that. Her knowledge of cities came from maps, not experience, and she had no idea where to find answers regarding strange voices from the sky that could steal a man's memories. Nor what tomorrow would bring, let alone next week or next year. Why not tie her future to something that might matter in the world?

"Will you teach me to fight like you?" she asked.

Eamon's head twitched. Jal suspected she had surprised him.

"Is that your price for helping us?"

"It is."

"Then I will do so, and gladly." He held out his hand to seal the bargain. Jal took it.

"As to where we go now, I don't know your lands or customs. What do you suggest?" she asked.

"Perhaps the temple in Grandon. If they have no answers, I'm of a mind to seek out an oracle."

Jal nodded, though she didn't know the term *oracle*. *Not likely the last new thing I'll learn on this journey.*

Chapter 2

Eamon led the horses as they walked. Phatomar had flat out refused to take to the saddle after their hasty retreat from Ferna, and without the incentive of fleeing from armed men, Eamon couldn't cajole his friend onto the back of the giant stallion (giant to Jal; the perfect size for Phatomar) again. So they walked. Lacking her own mount and far more used to travelling on foot anyway, Jal hadn't complained, especially not with Eamon's horse now carrying her belongings in addition to his own equipment.

"Tell me again what these voices said."

She repeated what she had heard in the market place, word for word this time rather than merely conveying what she felt had the most bearing at the time. Eamon listened with a frown furrowing his brow.

"*I will not allow you to take our due.*" He pondered the woman's phrasing. "What due or powers does she imagine Phatomar usurped? Some form of worship?" He chewed at his bottom lip in thought.

"How does someone take such a specific group of memories?" Jal wondered. "Let alone steal so defining an aspect of a man as his courage?"

"The gods are a capricious lot," Eamon muttered, his gaze distant.

"The gods," Jal scoffed, then came to an abrupt halt when she saw Eamon meant what he'd said. He continued without pause, Jal jogging to reach his side again. "The gods?" she ventured, shuddering at Eamon's serious expression.

12

"But—" She swallowed. "Gods? I heard the voices of gods?" She'd thought he'd spoken facetiously of being touched by gods earlier, not an actual interaction with otherworldly beings.

"That's my guess," her companion said with a shrug, as though he dealt with gods all the time. Phatomar, walking on Eamon's other side, offered no comment. From his darting eyes and tense shoulders, Jal wondered whether he followed their conversation or if he simply kept his feet moving alongside theirs in the hopes that they would keep him safe. *What a horrible situation for a hero,* she lamented.

"Why?" she asked Eamon, not even certain what she questioned: why would gods interfere in the affairs of mortals; why did she hear celestial beings; why did a good man suffer when so much stood wrong in the world?

"That's what we need to find out," the short man replied, an answer fit for all her questions. "With luck, one of the priests in Grandon can help." He looked at Jal. "They have a temple there dedicated to Dearn, god of warriors. Phatomar stands as a prime example of those whom Dearn loves; I can't imagine the warrior god would do anything to harm one of his own. But what other gods might believe Phatomar turns worship away from them and onto himself? Why would a god think Phatomar has taken any aspect of what we owe to them?"

"How many gods do you northerners follow?" Jal asked.

"We have the major gods of course, plus a plethora of lesser gods, and any number of demi-gods begat on elementals and humans. Too many to count, really. Which gods do you worship in the south?"

His query had more than one layer. Though her skin had deep tones of gold, it also carried a darker hue than either man's, and their eyes held more roundness than hers, further outlining their differing origins. Her own comments had marked her as from somewhere south, and distant enough to not recognise the same deities. Eamon offered her the opportunity to explain her heritage, but the decision of how much to reveal remained with Jal. She could appreciate his discretion, though she knew, in his place, her curiosity would beg for answers to her ignorance. Having nothing to hide from these northerners, she gave him the information he'd

13

only hinted at wanting.

"I come from the Gobani desert, and we have only five deities to placate. God of the sun, goddess of the moon, god of sand and wind, goddess of water and the oases, and the hermaphrodite deity of the hunt. As far as I know, none of them have spoken to mortals since the sun first rose from the sands."

"Huh," Eamon hummed softly in his throat. "Do they have no names?"

"We don't invoke their names unless in dire need. We don't want to draw unwanted attention."

They both glanced over at Phatomar.

"I can understand that," Eamon muttered. After a few paces in silence he spoke again. "We also have a god of the sun and a goddess of the moon, the god of day, with his counterpart, the goddess of night. Then there's the goddess of earth, and the god of sky, the god of storms and winds who governs the waters, the god of warriors, and a goddess of the hunt whose son watches over the animals. We know the goddess of love and the god of death, the goddess of fertility and birth with her handmaids who watch over the harvest and marriage—"

The list staggered Jal. "And some of these beings altered Phatomar?"

"Or one of the lesser deities, or any number of their servants. Some follow the ways of order, others the paths of chaos. We need to determine who might benefit from Phatomar's predicament. As I said, I don't see why anyone associated with Dearn would wish to cause him harm. Nor those affiliated with love or poetry, as so many tales and songs about Phatomar's deeds have filled the land. Perhaps one of the gods of death? Phatomar fights so well that he only sends the most vile to the underworld, helping the misguided find a better path. But then why take his courage, why not his conscience instead? The nature gods don't pay much heed to mortals; I don't know why they'd single out Phatomar. And the Elder gods Night and Day, Sun and Moon, Earth and Sky have little to do with mortals. They birthed the Younger gods, like Dearn, who then fashioned life such as ours, but they don't interact with their children's creations."

14

"Are those their names? Or do only the Younger gods have names?" Jal asked, overwhelmed by his tirade.

Eamon frowned as he glanced over at her.

"Who?"

"Night and Day, Sun and Moon, Earth and Sky."

"No, no, that's just a description." He considered. "Do you want to know their names?"

"Perhaps later," hedged Jal with a quick shake of her head, already having trouble keeping so many celestial beings straight. "After we know who—and what—we have to deal with perhaps. Until then, I hardly think it matters."

Eamon shrugged and they marched on in silence for a few minutes. Occasionally one of the horses would nicker, or a bird would call as it winged through the currents overhead. The wind whispered amongst rustling leaves as the three wound through wooded areas, the gentle sound accompanied by the frenzy of small animals scurrying through undergrowth and deadfall, such lush surroundings still amazing to one born in the desert. Oases had an astounding abundance of life, but nothing compared to the verdant vibrancy she had seen in Merveah.

The steady padding of their boots on the hard-packed road made a soothing counter-rhythm to the clomp of the horses' hooves, and the hitching of Phatomar's breaths as he cringed from every strange or loud noise broke up any monotony, at once comforting and annoying.

Jal snuck glances at her companions, wondering how she had managed to get caught up with them, trying to decide whether happy fate or frightening folly followed on her heels. She found herself in the company of legends, one willing to help her with her weapon skills, and the other now unable to wield a sword and requiring constant attention. If gods stalked the pair—or trio, if she counted herself—then they stood in the sights of powerful beings, a thought that made Jal less than pleased. And if not gods, then what? Sorcerers? Shamans? Men and women of unspeakable magicks? Definitely not beings sensible people tangled with, not if they wished to live for very long.

So how did Eamon, short of stature yet large in generosity, continue to move forward with such grace, as though he faced the supernatural all the time? He found their predicament a nuisance, yes, but not terrifyingly unusual. Jal found herself reconsidering some of the more fantastical tales of his and Phatomar's feats—stories she and her siblings had enjoyed hearing, fully aware that the tinkers who brought them embellished their words to entertain children.

Yet Eamon spoke so casually of gods and why one might wish Phatomar ill; perhaps not all of the fireside tales exaggerated their deeds. Did creatures like centaurs and dragons truly exist then? *Had* Phatomar vanquished giants? Did his strength and skill come from physique and practise alone, or did gods truly gift him with other powers?

Did it matter? On the one hand, most definitely. On the other, not at all. Phatomar now stood helpless and Eamon had requested help to cure his friend. Jal found herself in a position to offer such assistance, and she had done so with few reservations, rewarded with the promise of learning to fight from one of the best. That she might have to face entities beyond her experience—perhaps beyond her current belief—merely added some challenge.

I'll certainly learn things I never would have among the desert tribes.

A quick study of the two men's attire—they wore simple tunics and breeches, although fur lined their vests and boots—suggested that Jal might want to consider obtaining something warmer than her tunic should the days grow cooler. She wondered whether Grandon had more than temples to cater to travellers' needs and what, if any, supplies she might want to procure.

It will depend on what the priests can tell us, she decided. *Perhaps they'll have our answer.*

But if not, she'd have to coordinate with Eamon in case their travels took them any great distance, or spanned multiple seasons. She understood the weather fluctuated a great deal more outside the desert, and had seen the inklings of such in the few southern portions of Merveah she had travelled. She might even need to find her own horse.

"I wonder if one of the messenger gods wants retribution?" Eamon said suddenly.

Jal jumped nearly as much as Phatomar at Eamon's voice, then smiled sheepishly at her reaction. Eamon grinned at Jal, reached over to pat Phatomar's shoulder in comfort, then slipped back into brooding silence.

Jal hoped it didn't take long to reach Grandon.

***

The name Phatomar sat strangely in the mind of the man walking next to Eamon. Eamon's voice as he spoke with the desert girl soothed him with its familiarity when so much else left his heart thundering in panic. He tried to pay attention to the conversation, but every sound, every slight bit of movement caught from the corner of his eye, brought renewed tremors to overwrought muscles.

Focus, Phatomar ordered himself, searching for some semblance of normalcy. *What's normal?* a tiny voice shrieked in his head. He blinked at that, nearly tripped over his own feet when the startling slap of the scabbard strapped at his waist tapped his thigh, drawing his attention.

The sword Jal had returned to him made his stomach churn in a most unpleasant way. The calluses on his hands told the tale of a familiarity with such weapons even though his fogged brain didn't remember ever clutching the hilt.

How can I have such calluses, such a breadth of muscles, yet the sight of a sword, the thought of drawing forth its wicked edge, leaves me weak with terror?

Surely he hadn't always cowered thus at the slightest provocation. How could a man function with so much confusion and panic swirling in his thoughts?

Nothing makes sense, he lamented as the cry of a bird made him flinch, his eyes wide as they searched overhead for the predator he feared would plunge down to rake formidable talons across his scalp. *How can I know the difference between an eagle's shrill scream and that of a hawk, yet still have so distant a call nearly bring me to my knees, gibbering in fear?*

Beside him, his mighty chestnut stallion blew a gentle sigh through his lips, the sound startling Phatomar enough to put a hitch in the man's step as he stared at his horse. *Why do I recall endless hours of peace riding atop Croga with Eamon at my side on Cosantoir, yet the thought of mounting so large a beast now makes me quiver in dread?*

Phatomar hadn't noticed that his companions had lapsed

17

into silence until Eamon's voice speaking in Jal's language shattered the stillness. Phatomar nearly swallowed his tongue in an effort not to scream.

Eamon's hand on his shoulder helped Phatomar rein in his galloping heart, but it took an uncomfortable amount of time before his breathing slowed to something that didn't leave him gasping. *If I react so badly in the presence of my dearest friend, how much worse will I find myself surrounded by strangers in Grandon?*

Hopefully, they wouldn't find themselves running for their lives again. The memory of fleeing Ferna before the onslaught of men bent on causing harm—of Jal's sword flashing before his face as the girl stepped in to defend him—made Phatomar flinch all over again, and he shivered, wondering how anyone could bear so much uncertainty. That he didn't remember any of the events leading up to that rescue disturbed him, and confusion tripped over uncertainty in his gut, leaving him nauseated.

He feared for his sanity.

***

They reached Grandon two days later. They tethered the horses near the simple stone temple dedicated to Dearn, god of warriors. Phatomar did his best to hide his anxiety, but he crowded close to Eamon, shoulders hunched to avoid drawing attention.

Eamon could hardly believe the change in his dear friend and companion of six years. He thanked Dearn and whichever other gods cared to listen that Jal had—for whatever reason—heard the origin of Phatomar's plight and chosen to offer assistance. Others might have stood by gloating if only to relish in the downfall of a mighty icon, realising too late the vital service someone like Phatomar provided.

Together, he and Phatomar had saved whole villages from bandits, extortionist tyrants, and creatures no others could battle. When foes from other districts threatened to invade, rulers turned to Phatomar and Eamon to guard their borders. If foul weather struck and threatened a harvest or destroyed a town's infrastructure, Phatomar and Eamon would learn of it and help the farmers reap their crops, and aid the townsfolk in rebuilding their homes and shops. They had recovered scores of missing children, whether lost or stolen, defended countless travellers from thieves, shored up numerous bridges damaged by flood or fire.

But some didn't see a saviour when they looked at Phatomar, only a man doing what they would not in a chaotic world, and that bred envy. Phatomar's strength led some to fear, while his compassion and mercy often brought contempt. Phatomar didn't care; he would continue to do what he saw as right, regardless of outside opinion.

Seeing him quail now in Eamon's shadow nearly brought the shorter man to tears, but remembering Jal's fiercely protective expression in Ferna—and since whenever she witnessed another instance of Phatomar's fears—had brought him a measure of hope. *She* had stopped to help, and not because she thought she might save a legend. She had helped without knowing either of them, only seeing two men at a disadvantage against an enemy. That he and Phatomar could have easily overcome the thieves didn't matter—although perhaps taking the time to humiliate them, intent on teaching a lesson, rather than quickly subduing them had not, in retrospect, proved the wisest of decisions. But Jal had intervened when she had seen the danger which Eamon had failed to recognise.

Because she believed it the right thing to do, a true rarity in this world.

"You'll want to let me talk when we get in there," Eamon warned Jal as they left their horses behind.

Jal gazed up at the drab temple wall and scowled before turning back to Eamon.

"And why should only you speak?" she asked. "Does your Dearn not recognise women warriors?"

Eamon gave her a wry grin. "He does, but the priest might have a harder time understanding you than Dearn would."

She frowned, wrinkling the golden bronze skin between eyes tinted gold like a lion's. Before she could reply, Eamon clarified for her.

"They probably don't know the desert tongues here. Unless you know any of our northern dialects, you're stuck with me as an interpreter."

"Northern dialects? Like the words of traders and tinkers?" she asked. Then she spoke a few words in Eamon's native language. "Sword, trade, what food do you like, how much?" She switched back to her own tongue. "Is that the language of the priests?"

Eamon would have laughed if not for her earnest expression.

"It's the language of most of Merveah," he explained. "Some few know the language of the desert, like Phatomar and me, but most here, away from the trading towns along the coast, will only hear gibberish."

"You—" she sputtered, paused, tried again. "We speak my language now, but not yours? We don't even have a common tongue?"

"We don't," Eamon confirmed. He wondered where her tribe travelled that she didn't know this; how long she herself had spent in Merveah. She had a youthful face—*has she even seen twenty years?*—yet she bore herself with maturity and surety. In the two days it had taken to reach Grandon as they avoided roving bandits and other travellers, she had fit in to his and Phatomar's strange new routine seamlessly. At moments like this, though, her otherness became all too apparent.

He watched her come to a decision as she chewed on her bottom lip, staring at the temple in concentration. When she turned her tawny gaze back to him, determination again lit her features.

"I know a few of your words—enough to get by in markets and the like—but I will trust you to speak true, to both the priest and to me so that we may understand each other. I have no right to further burden our agreement, but—"

"I will teach you my language Jal, if you want."

She blinked at his interruption. Then a small smile stole across her lips.

"I would like to learn it," she said.

"Then let's be about our business." He forced a levity to his tone to mask his concern for Phatomar. He and Phatomar had donned hooded cloaks at the outskirts of Grandon, and Eamon pulled his up now. Phatomar copied him after a moment's hesitation. Jal had her helmet in place, disguising her features, and Eamon swept his hand toward the stone building, inviting Jal to precede him to the temple doors. He then took Phatomar's arm gently to follow.

"You could have told me sooner that I didn't even speak your language," Jal muttered irritably as she started walking. Eamon didn't think she had meant him to hear her complaint, so he kept his chuckle to himself.

The interior of the temple didn't boast many amenities. Apropos of a warrior's life, Dearn's temples lacked most comforts, although one could often find its adherents practicing sword work in the open spaces—minus any actual blades, which the trio deposited into the care of the Blade Keeper at the door—or discussing tactics and past engagements with comrades at one of the two stone tables ringed with simple stools in the far corner.

An altar stood opposite the entrance, its scarred top littered with tokens from both warriors and their families: flowers and food; stones and amulets; pitted blades and fine daggers; arrow heads, feathers, bow strings and broken shafts; coins. All manner of offerings meant to ensure safe travels (abroad in the land or to the underworld) and successful campaigns. An acolyte stood in attendance next to the altar, his sole duty to oversee the would-be patrons of the god, guarding the solitude of supplicants who wished to leave some sort of tribute.

Steering clear of the few other people in attendance, Eamon led them to the west wall, which looked barren though in truth it contained two well-concealed doors. He tapped on one gently, then pushed his hood back to reveal his face, standing back a few paces to wait.

After a moment, a slot in the door opened, revealing only a pair of brown eyes. The man studied Eamon briefly, swung his gaze to his still cloaked companions, then disappeared as the slot slid shut. The door opened a second later and a man in tan and black leathers stepped out, an amulet around his neck bearing the bow and dagger sigil of Dearn the only indication of his priestly status.

"Welcome to the Grandon Chapter, brothers," he said in a deep baritone. "I am Brother Cantastor. How may I assist you today?"

"We seek knowledge and advice, and I invoke Micah's Oath in doing so," Eamon announced in a quiet voice. Long ago, the great General Micah had established a system of confidentiality whereby warriors could seek advice and guidance from those who served Dearn without fear of compromise. Two opposing forces might even confide in the same priest without fear of betrayal. Dearn served harsh punishments to oath breakers, and unlike Jal's limited experience in this world, Eamon had seen the power of the gods on more than one occasion. The creative and terrifying forms of vengeance meted out by the god of warriors kept his priests in line.

By invoking Micah's Oath, Eamon wanted to ensure some measure of secrecy. The longer he could keep Phatomar's condition from reaching malicious ears, the safer he could keep his friend.

Brother Cantastor met Eamon's steady gaze before giving a solemn nod. "Micah guards your words," he said. "This way, if you will."

He led them to the second door, taking a heavy iron key from his pocket. He unlocked the door and pushed it open, revealing a windowless room beyond. Cantastor ushered them in. He turned to a table, lit the lantern sitting atop it, then sealed the entrance once more, leaving the three companions to sit in one of the six chairs around the table. Nothing else adorned the sparse room.

Once settled across from the priest, Eamon quietly instructed Phatomar to lower his concealing hood, and Jal her helmet. Cantastor watched in silence, waiting for Eamon to begin.

"Two days ago, my friend had something stolen from him," Eamon said, his hand first indicating Phatomar, then Jal as he continued. "Jal heard voices speaking from a cloud of light: a woman claiming Phatomar's courage, and a man taking his memories of deeds won through that courage. The voices contained the power and potency of gods."

Cantastor turned to Jal, examining her. Jal met his gaze without flinching. He looked back at Eamon.

"But you did not hear these voices?" Cantastor asked.

"I did not, though I bore witness to the result."

Cantastor inclined his head, inviting clarification.

"Phatomar and I had crossed swords with a group of thieves when suddenly Phatomar ceased fighting. Jal

22

intervened, saved him from a lethal strike. Phatomar has never backed away from a fight, and certainly wouldn't have shied away from such unworthy adversaries as these without cause. Having his courage ripped from him at such a moment constitutes such cause."

"Convenient timing, her appearance," Cantastor said. Eamon narrowed his eyes.

"Fortunate rather," he countered.

Cantastor raised a sardonic eyebrow and turned to regard Jal again.

"Did you bewitch this man?" the priest demanded. Although Eamon had suspected such a line of questioning—had briefly considered it himself when first Jal told her tale—it still irritated him.

"Jal doesn't speak our tongue."

Cantastor's gaze swept back toward Eamon. Eamon read both a hint of surprise and a note of superstition in his expression.

"Then how do you know what she claims to have heard?" he asked.

"Because I speak hers," Eamon answered. He looked at Jal and switched languages. "He wonders if you bewitched Phatomar."

"If I what?" she said in surprise. Then she scowled, her face flashing in anger. "He thinks I spoke some words of magic over him to make him helpless and then stepped in to help? Why would I do such a thing?"

"I'll ask his opinion," grinned Eamon. Jal's outrage somehow lightened his mood. He confronted Cantastor once more.

"She wants to know why you'd accuse her of spell craft."

"A woman pretending at being a warrior?" Cantastor scoffed. "Perhaps she wished to attach herself to a couple of mercenaries such as yourselves, looking for an easier road that she could manipulate."

Eamon stared at Cantastor, not sure what to take offense at first; his dismissal of Jal's skills, the derisive undertone that assumed armed women sold their bodies for protection, or his belief that Eamon and Phatomar would sell their swords to the highest bidder. The last, though not the most damning, gave Eamon the greatest pause.

"Before I correct your erroneous line of thought," he said in an even tone, though his jaw ached from clenching it too tight, "I must ask: do you not know of Phatomar, son of Gordukah?"

"Even the priests of Dearn can hardly keep track of all the warriors in Merveah," Cantastor said. His tone implied a growing impatience as no doubt the man wondered why Eamon had insisted on Micah's Oath for so paltry a discussion.

"What's wrong?" Jal whispered, reading Eamon's unease.

"He doesn't recognise Phatomar," Eamon answered.

Jal drew in a sharp breath.

"The god said he took his identity as well as the memory of his deeds," she said, echoing Eamon's thoughts. "I thought he meant just from Phatomar, but perhaps it's more insidious than that. But then, why do we still know of him?"

Eamon could only shake his head, having no answers. He stared at Cantastor.

"Phatomar has done mighty deeds," he said to the priest. "And I don't say that just to boast. He has served Dearn from his early years, a renowned and highly skilled warrior, blessed by the gods. Until two days ago, you would have rejoiced to have Phatomar grace the steps of your temple. Now you only see him as a nameless would-be hero, wasting your time. I ask that you consider what this means if we're right. If the gods can remove one of Dearn's most beloved disciples in such a way that no one—not even his priests—questions their actions, what's to stop them from doing so again?"

Cantastor frowned in thought, considering Eamon's challenge. After a moment, he looked to Jal, then back to Eamon.

"Yet the only evidence you have comes from this girl? She alone heard these voices speaking to your Phatomar?"

Though he knew the answer, Eamon put the question to Jal.

"He asks if you alone heard the voices speak to Phatomar."

"They didn't speak to Phatomar," said Jal. "They spoke over him. I don't think they intended *anyone* to hear them."

Cantastor nearly smiled at the distinction when Eamon translated Jal's words. His manner grew serious. "Why do

24

you bring this matter to Dearn?" he asked. "And why under Oath?"

"I hadn't considered you wouldn't know Phatomar, at least by reputation," Eamon admitted. "I believed if others knew of his impediment, they might try to take advantage, if only to claim the accolades of destroying a legend. With Phatomar's long and loyal service, I felt confident that neither Dearn nor his servants would have placed this curse upon him, and not knowing what other gods might wish him harm, had hoped a priest of Dearn would have deeper insights."

"And instead, I deride your company," Cantastor said. "Yet if you speak the truth, you must understand *my* predicament."

"I do," Eamon admitted with a heavy sigh. Jal gave him a questioning look.

"He's trying to decide if we tell the truth or have brought him a fantasy," he explained.

"Why doesn't he just ask Dearn?"

Eamon stared at her in astonishment, then blew out an incredulous laugh.

"What did she say?" asked Cantastor in a cautious tone.

"She wants to know why you don't ask Dearn what he thinks." At Cantastor's affronted expression, Eamon couldn't help another laugh. "You'll have to forgive her. Her gods are not ours, and until two days ago, she didn't believe the gods spoke to us. I have seen their work enough to know they exist, but even I have to admit they speak to us, though rarely. She will learn."

Cantastor's voice took on an eerie quality. *"You might learn a thing or two as well, young Eamon."*

Jal sat up tall, her hand jerking into a fist and her golden skin growing pale. Eamon looked at her in concern, but she kept her eyes glued to Cantastor.

"Did you hear that?" she gasped. "He spoke my language, but his voice...it suddenly has the same quality as the two from the market."

"This mouth does not utter your tongue, Ajala of the Gobani, yet your ears hear the words of gods. You have great perception, child, and a unique gift. One my brethren must not learn about."

Words of gods? Eamon wondered. *Brethren?* The blood drained from his face as Cantastor looked at him through

25

eyes the colour of darkest night—the fathomless eyes of a god.

"My lord," he stammered, half rising from his seat, unsure how to greet this unexpected visitor.

Cantastor's hand gestured him back into the chair.

"I know your deeds Eamon, son of Branon, valiant warrior and defender of Merveah. And I see many of the feats of your companion in your heart, though I see them not in his. This theft of valour and deeds displeases me.

"Know, however, that I cannot intercede. I can but point you in the right direction. It is for the three of you together to walk the path that might restore a warrior to their rightful place."

"And where does this path lead?" Jal barely breathed the question, her eyes wide.

The god within Cantastor turned his ebony gaze upon her.

"Into the unknown, as most paths do," he replied cryptically. *"It starts in the mountains at Hada. Many trials you will encounter, each vital to overcome if you wish to proceed. And at every juncture, you will face a choice; do you help this man, or do you leave him as he now stands?"*

No choice at all for Eamon. He had followed Phatomar to the edges of the underworld, why would he stop now? The Oracle at Hada might give them a clue to the riddle of the gods, but she would never find a reason for Eamon to abandon Phatomar.

"You may find those you seek at the end of your journey, but beware of calling attention to yourselves from my kin," the god warned. *"You are right to conceal your friend's condition and the cause of it. Do not trust in others lightly."*

Cantastor blinked, the flinty sight of Dearn leaving his eyes. Eamon tried not to let his frustration show. He bit back a curse, glancing first at Phatomar, then at Jal. They had learned all they would here, yet he wondered whether they had learned enough. He stood.

"Thank you for your time, Brother," he said to the priest. He wondered how much, if anything, Cantastor had experienced while a god rode his body. "We will keep you no longer."

Cantastor gave him a puzzled look as Eamon's companions rose to leave. Phatomar pulled his cloak's hood over his head and Jal donned her helmet. The priest simply nodded and moved to the door, allowing them to return to the main temple.

"Did you hear what he didn't say?" Jal asked softly once the three of them had retrieved their weapons and returned to the street. Eamon thought it a curious phrase, but then he believed he understood.

"That even if we find the answer to Phatomar's lost gifts, he might not get them back?"

Jal shook her head. "That Dearn didn't know Phatomar's name or achievements either. What kind of god can hide such a thing from another god?"

Phatomar shivered, a low moan caught in the back of his throat. Eamon agreed. *What kind of god indeed*.

Chapter 3

Jal understood bartering, and she could appreciate substituting coin for goods when you had neither products nor skill to trade. She had done the former in the Gobani and the latter at market places like Ferna. Yet neither experience had quite prepared her for the overwhelming depletion of funds that outfitting for the next stage of their journey entailed.

Without Eamon next to her, she suspected she might have parted with even more of the coins her father had left her. More than once, she had caught a scowl from her companion aimed at a vendor, which elicited a fresh round of bargaining. Jal didn't know whether the merchants had hoped to take advantage of her foreignness, her inexperience, her gender, or simply her need, but she found herself grateful for the man at her side who understood the language and customs of Merveah far better than she did. Not to mention his advice on what they might require to reach Hada and the Oracle there.

"You'll need a horse," Eamon had said after they left Dearn's temple. "I don't particularly want to walk all the way to Hada, and once we can get Phatomar used to the idea again, riding will cut days off our journey."

They found a horse dealer, where Jal learned that the temperament of a horse depended on more than how previous owners had treated it. A high-spirited beast like Phatomar's stallion Croga accepted Eamon's gelding Cosantoir, but might fight another stallion, so they needed another gelding or a mare who would neither fight nor cower. Age and breed mattered too, along with physical well-being. They didn't want anything too old and set in its way, nor too young and overeager. The horse would require endurance and a willingness to carry a rider, not a beast bred for work or show. A finely brushed coat and mane couldn't disguise bad teeth or poor hoof care, aspects that Eamon pointed out as Jal looked them over. None of these details had occurred to Jal, who had never owned a horse.

Thankfully, Eamon knew what to look for, so when Jal kept coming back to the little mare whose russet coat reminded Jal of her own hair, her companion confirmed the wisdom of her preference. Phatomar had even stood with commendable patience with Croga and Cosantoir while Jal and Eamon brought the mare over to see how the animals would fare together. Croga tried to assert his dominance, but the mare snorted at him as though in amused tolerance before turning her back and ignoring him. This seemed to confuse Croga, and Jal imagined she could see calculation and challenge in each animal's eye. It reminded her of her brother Olbaehn and how he had never managed to intimidate his middle sister despite his best efforts. After some consideration, Eamon had agreed that the three horses might get along, though he suspected Croga might lose his place as leader of the pack.

The purchase, however, set Jal back a goodly sum of money.

"We're heading into the high mountains," Eamon said later as they made their way north-east through a more run down village. It had supplies enough, but didn't boast much prosperity, and Jal didn't like the desperation and cunning she saw in some faces. "You'll need warmer clothes and boots." He warned her not to scrimp on those necessities. "We don't want to reach the Oracle only to have one of us succumb to frostbite or grow ill with more than the height."

"Heights don't bother me," Jal said. "We have many deep canyons and shifting sand dunes in the Gobani."

"Trust me on this," he replied with a solemn air rather than condescension. "You've not seen heights such as these, nor suffered the frigid rigours of the snow-swept landscape of the mountains that shelter Hada. Only buy the best quality gear."

So she had parted with more funds and now owned saddlebags full of equipment she had never encountered in the desert (*What* is *snow anyway?* she wondered). Eamon and Phatomar had similarly stuffed packs, so at least she knew her new friends had not exaggerated.

Each evening they stopped early enough to set up camp and train, choosing likely sites near the road yet far from any habitation to avoid unwanted encounters with ruffians and desperate farm folk. Eamon instructed Jal on his style of fighting, and she in turn showed him how it differed from her own.

The first evening out from Grandon, Jal noticed how Phatomar shied away from every perceived blow exchanged, yet kept careful track of each movement as he watched the two of them spar. The second evening, she watched his hand twitch and his shoulders shift along with the patterns Eamon demonstrated, as though his body wished to copy the motions, even though his mind couldn't remember executing the moves.

The third night, with the shadow of mountains smudging the horizon, Jal had suggested Phatomar join them. He had jerked violently and shook his head with a muttered, "No thanks."

On this, the fourth morning, Jal wanted to try to help engage Phatomar more. Eamon sat quietly, waiting to see how his friend would react to this overture, careful not to interject his opinions lest Phatomar mindlessly adopt them as his own. He and Jal had talked about this, and both felt Phatomar needed to assert himself more rather than allow him to continue letting others (mostly Eamon) dictate his future. Jal marvelled at the strength of Eamon's control, for she had recognised early on how much the smaller man longed to protect Phatomar, even if only from his own fear and insecurity.

Jal sat beside Phatomar in front of the small fire they had lit to ward off the chill of the morning. Phatomar glanced at her with wide grey eyes, and flinched when the wood emitted a sharp crack as it shifted in the flames. He looked over the camp with a frightened gaze before concentrating on a patch of earth between his knees.

"Tell me what frightens you," Jal urged, her voice gentle.

30

Phatomar flicked his eyes up briefly and then resumed his vigil of the ground.

"Do you fear what you see, what you don't see, what you hear?" she pressed, watching the fire rather than Phatomar.

"I fear everything," he whispered miserably.

She moved just her eyes, peering at him sidelong. "Do you fear Eamon?" she asked.

He looked at her in surprise, blinking rapidly.

"Of course not," he said.

"What about me?"

Phatomar shook his head, nearly making eye contact. "How about Croga and Cosantoir? Or Onoir?" Eamon had told her that Croga meant *valiant* and Cosantoir meant *defender*. When she had asked him the word for *honour*, she had found the name she wanted for her mare: Onoir.

"The horses don't frighten me like they used to," Phatomar admitted after a moment's thought. "Unless they run when I don't expect it."

Expectation, she thought. *The fear of not knowing what would happen, of not being prepared.* Perhaps they could overcome Phatomar's lack of courage to a degree if they could retrain him not to react so strongly to the unexpected. She hoped to start that process now, now that she had confirmed one of her suspicions.

"Will you let me try something?" she asked.

Phatomar jerked back, his gaze seeking the ground for support once more.

"Do you trust me not to hurt you, Phatomar?" whispered Jal. After a moment, the large man finally nodded, though he didn't glance up. "Will you look at me?" she asked. He tensed, then slowly pulled his chin up until he faced her, his eyes seeking refuge on her jaw. Jal nodded with a smile. "Thank you," she said, gratified to see a slight relaxation of his shoulders.

She turned to face him, sitting cross-legged before him, the fire warming her right side.

"Can you sit like this?" she asked. He hesitated, then turned to mirror her, left shoulder to the gentle flames. "Good," she encouraged. "Now, I want you to close your eyes."

Instead, his eyes widened even further.

"I won't let anything harm you," she assured him. "Eamon won't let anything hurt you."

Phatomar glanced across the fire to his friend, then back to Jal. With a deep but unsteady breath, he closed his eyes.

"Tell me what you hear."

"The breeze," he said. "The fire. I hear a bird singing."

"Can you hear your breath?" she asked, careful to keep her voice soft.

"Yes."

"Your heartbeat? The blood rushing in your ears?"

His eyes popped open. She smiled, then ran her hand lightly in front of his face as though to close them again, careful not to touch him. Obediently, his eyes slid shut.

"Listen for the rhythm of your heart, the cadences of your body. You can acknowledge the other sounds—the wind, the flames, the animals—but concentrate on finding the sound of *you*." She let him sit quietly a handful of moments, waiting for the instant when his face relaxed. With barely a whisper, she asked, "What do you hear?"

His lips parted on a sigh. "My heartbeat," he said, his voice low yet more sure than she had heard before. She could sense Eamon's acute interest rising from the other side of the fire, but kept her focus on Phatomar, on reaching a place free from fear. "Steady breaths: mine, yours, Eamon's." *His keen warrior senses.* Not lost; merely buried.

"Do you feel safe?" she asked.

"Yes."

She beckoned Eamon over. He approached on silent feet, crouching beside Jal.

"Hold that feeling, Phatomar," Jal said. "Remember it well. The next time something startles you, try to recall what you feel now. Can you try that?"

"I think so," he answered.

"Then open your eyes."

He did, saw Eamon where he didn't expect him, and thrust his arms behind him, ready to scramble away.

"Remember what you felt," Jal said quietly but with a sense of urgency. Phatomar stiffened, drew in a harsh breath, then a gentler one. She and Eamon watched the wildness seep from his eyes, the tension drain from his limbs. Both kept very still as Phatomar forced calm to overcome fear.

Suddenly he grinned.

"It worked!" He almost laughed. "I could feel my heart slow."

Eamon clapped him happily on the shoulder, blinking away the sheen of tears that hazed his eyes.

"I won't promise that it will work every time," Jal cautioned, amazed that he had responded to the technique so quickly. "But if you like, we can work on redirecting your fear in other ways too. It won't replace your courage—"

Phatomar inhaled with such depth of feeling. "If you can help me banish this constant knot of terror eating at me, it will suffice."

She hadn't heard so many words at once from the erstwhile warrior. She hoped the few meditative tricks she knew would prove equal to the gratitude he directed at her now.

"Then let's add that to the evening lessons," she suggested. Both men agreed.

When they put out the fire and started this day's ride, they did so with a greater sense of hope than they had felt since Jal first met this pair of legends.

***

Jal hadn't known so many different shades of green existed in the world until she reached Merveah. She knew a myriad of earth tones, but had only encountered the refreshing greens of the oases in the Gobani and the dull greenish greys of the stubby plants that clung to desert sands. Merveah had such a plethora of grasses and trees in every imaginable hue of green clustered together that it overwhelmed her senses. Indeed, the very idea of wide stretches of trees spanning as far as the eye could see astounded her, and traversing through such forests amazed her.

She would give much to see those swaths of green again, guiding her horse beneath the sheltering canopy of sun-dappled leaves rather than plowing her way on foot through the stark white of snow that nearly blinded her with its brilliance now.

She hadn't known skin could burn with cold, nor that

nostrils could freeze with arid iciness, making it as hard to breathe as in a sandstorm. She alternately shoved her mittened hands beneath her armpits in a futile attempt to find additional warmth, and found herself covered in clumps of the white menace whenever she lost her footing in thigh deep snow. Happily, the pack strapped across her back contained only the bare minimum (plus a small offering of food for the Oracle), thanks to Phatomar.

"I do not remember the exploits that Eamon does," he had confided when they had discussed provisions for this part of their quest. "But I remember many of the journeys which must have led to them. You don't want any extra weight in the mountains."

They'd left the horses and their swords in a small village stable the day before. Eamon wouldn't risk the beasts on the final path to the home of the Oracle. After scrambling up near vertical sections of cliff—sometimes bare rock, sometimes caked with snow and ice—negotiating between clefts barely wide enough for Phatomar to squeeze through, skirting strange cascades of ice formations which somehow encased the pressure of falling water—stray droplets making footing treacherous—and finally wading through drifts of snow taller than her, Jal completely understood his caution even as she lamented the loss of Onoir's heat and the strength of her mount's legs.

She gave thanks to whoever had constructed the simple plank structure they had sheltered under the previous night, something Eamon had called a pilgrim's hut. Marginally warmer than the exposed air, it warded off the frigid blasts of the wind and the sting of icy snow pelting from the sky, though the eerie howl of the gales in the night hadn't helped Jal sleep well. The fur-lined blanket Eamon had encouraged her to buy had at least brought some warmth, as had the proximity of her companions in the hut. Desert nights often grew cold (though nothing like these frozen peaks), so the idea of sharing body heat didn't sit as a foreign concept. The oddness of sharing that heat on a winter-swept mountain with men not of her family quickly faded as her shivers subsided.

That warmth retreated to a distant memory as the sun climbed overhead, grudgingly sharing its light between thick clouds. Jal could do nothing save plant one weary foot in front of the other and hope that they reached their destination before her straining muscles seized completely and she froze to death.

It had taken them four days to reach the mountains she'd first sighted on the horizon, their distance as deceptive as a mirage on the sands. Two additional days followed as they picked their way through steepening foothills before stabling the horses, and now this, a second day on foot. Eamon had assured her they would reach the Oracle before sunset, but Jal saw nothing beyond a swirling flurry of white flakes when the wind blew, facets of a blinding crust of unmarred snow glittering when the wind lay still, and the shape of Eamon trudging along ahead of her. She heard the creak and groan of Phatomar's boots as he crunched in her wake, occasionally swallowed by a whistling blast of frigid air as the god of sand and wind made his fury known.

Does my god have dominion over snow as he does over sand, or does he respect the boundaries laid out by the maps of men? Jal shook her head, such contemplation almost too much for a mind sluggish with cold.

Why anyone would make their home in such adverse conditions baffled Jal. Why would an Oracle—a woman of mystifying powers who could see and understand that which others could not, according to Eamon—ply her trade so far from civilization? How would she react to the three of them interrupting her privacy?

Even more than the cold and glaring snow, Jal found a tingling discomfort steadily growing, adding to her misery. An ache which had started just behind her eyes spread to encompass her whole head until the throb against her temples made her squeeze her eyes shut, trying to block the pain. Someone drummed inside her brain with mallets, threatening to pop her eyes from their sockets. Her chest felt full and heavy, yet strangely hollow, each breath taking more effort than the last until she found herself gasping with more than exertion. She swallowed once, twice, her stomach churning as her throat constricted, her last meal swirling as much as the wind, nausea demanding her attention.

When at last she discovered herself fallen in the snow again, clumps of chill wetness clinging to her cheek where her scarf had slipped down, specks of black dots dancing across her vision, and unable to move her body faster than quicksand, Jal admitted she had a problem. But she couldn't find her voice to call for help, nor muster enough energy to find this situation overly worrisome.

Then she saw the terrified face of Phatomar bent over her, quickly followed by the concerned visage of Eamon, his lips moving though no sound penetrated the roar in Jal's ears. She knew hands shook her only by the dancing of the clouds overhead, her flesh too numb to register any physical sensation. That brought a spark of fear into the desert girl, quickly swallowed by unconcern as cold oblivion sucked away even that emotion, easing her torment in its uncaring embrace.

***

Phatomar had spoken honestly when he told his companions that he didn't recall a single incident that Eamon claimed Phatomar had accomplished. Yet the tales his friend spun around the campfires at night aside—they couldn't *all* contain the absolute truth, could they? How did one even approach an angry minotaur, let alone wrestle it across the wastelands? And regardless of all his strength, surely Phatomar couldn't hold his breath long enough to evade a leviathan while rescuing a princess—Phatomar did remember that he had travelled long and far with this man.

They had seen the deserts of the south and the frozen wastelands of the north; the mountains in the east and the great forests of the west; multiple seas and plains throughout the lands. Phatomar could recount long hours of travel, though he seldom remembered the destination, and never what had happened at the journey's end.

Simple matters of daily life like cooking and eating, making camp, wandering the marketplaces, riding a horse—these he could perform without hesitation, though it had taken the steady patience of Croga's gentle manner with his master (if with few others) to ease Phatomar's trepidation about sitting in the saddle. Holding a sword, leaping over a narrow chasm that blocked their way, even speaking with strangers, all left him near incapacitation. He couldn't even imagine facing a real opponent with a blade in hand without coming near to wetting himself in gibbering fear. How had he ever accomplished even half of the things Eamon claimed?

Thankfully, the mutual respect and affection he felt for Eamon hadn't disappeared from his memories. Phatomar had no siblings, but Eamon had become his brother all the same. And now Jal had begun to feel like a sister, someone to care for and protect, someone who did the same for him.

When she collapsed into the biting snow and did not rise again, the fear of losing her pressed down on Phatomar like a lead weight, dropping him to his knees at her side. When Jal's eyes clouded over before slipping shut, he knew a moment of absolute terror. It felt different than losing his courage; more of a hopeless darkening of his soul than a confusing lack of strength, but it crippled him all the same.

Then Eamon spoke, breaking through Phatomar's black cloud of despair.

"Mountain sickness," he announced, concern roughening his voice. "We need to get her off the heights." Eamon frowned, his gaze following the trail to the temple, though only pristine snow lay ahead. "An hour to the temple and shelter where we'll find warmth, and where the priestesses of the Oracle may have a way to ease Jal's symptoms." He turned his head back the way they had come, studying the path they had already traversed. "Or hours back down the mountain to the pilgrim's hut where the elevation didn't affect her. Either way, Jal will suffer."

Phatomar stared at his friend, hearing the indecision. Eamon wanted to continue for Phatomar's sake, but he also cared enough for Jal not to want to risk her life. Dearn's words, spoken in Grandon, echoed in Phatomar's mind: *It is for you three together to walk the path,* and *at every juncture, you will face a choice.*

Phatomar took a deep breath, then another, Jal's voice in the back of his mind guiding him through his anxieties. Now, more than ever, he must force aside his crippling panic if he wanted to help his family. He made a choice, forcing the paralysis from his limbs. He leaned over Jal, wrapped his arms around her to cushion her in his warmth, and pushed to his feet, the girl held securely in his embrace.

"We can't run through snow this deep," he said, his voice rumbling as it cut through the wind, "but let's make what

37

haste we can."

"Are you sure?" Eamon asked.

"She won't thank us to give up." Phatomar managed a small smile. "And the priestess *will* cure her."

Eamon regarded him in silence but gave a grim nod and spun back to the path they had to carve ahead. A fierce sense of purpose filled Phatomar as he rushed his would-be sister toward the promised shelter, a spark of hope in the wilderness guiding his steps. He didn't need courage to save Jal; he only needed this little family he and Eamon had formed, and to reach safety before they all froze.

Despite his shorter stature, Eamon pushed through the thick crust of snow with grim determination, carving out a path for Phatomar and his burden. When he began to grow tired, Phatomar took Eamon's shoulder, entrusted Jal's limp form into his care, and took his place out front.

The pair soon glimpsed the grey shadow of the temple built into the mountain ahead. The wind picked up, swallowing the sparse sun with impenetrable clouds and gathering fresh snow from the heavens, stealing their view of safety. For the last furlong, they trudged through a blinding blizzard, reaching the stout doors of the temple by feel rather than by sight.

With Jal cradled in his arms again, Phatomar waited while Eamon pounded on the massive wooden entrance. For a long moment, nothing happened. They exchanged worried looks as the snow began to paint them in layers of white.

Just as Eamon raised his arm again, they heard the heavy groan of the door's seals being released. The wind pulled and pushed at them, plucking with icy and tenacious fingers at their clothing and forcing Phatomar to lean forward to shield Jal. They waited for the door to open just enough to admit them before stumbling into the lantern-lit interior. The door shut, and both Phatomar and Eamon leaned against it, helping to hurry it on its way, sealing out the frustrations of the storm.

They turned as one to face the brown-haired woman robed in silver who glided forward to greet them.

"Welcome to the Oracle of Hada," she said in a melodious voice, though her ice blue eyes remained oddly flat. "The Oracle will not speak today. When the storm clears, you will return whence you came." With that, she turned to walk away.

Phatomar stared after her in disbelief, as did Eamon.

"But we have to speak with the Oracle," Eamon objected. "Dearn himself sent us here."

The woman didn't stop, nor did she turn her head.

"Wait," Phatomar ventured, his voice cracking. "Please. Our companion suffers. Please, will you help her?"

Now the woman paused, turning her cold gaze in his direction. He swallowed the trepidation that stare engendered, again focused on breathing as Jal had taught, then spoke past his agitation. "She suffers from mountain sickness."

The priestess simply blinked, waiting in silence.

"You said yourself we cannot leave until the storm passes," Eamon added. "Will you at least allow someone to look at her, ease her pain?"

Those pale eyes didn't waver, and Phatomar suddenly wondered if she saw things of this world or another. Finally, she gave a nearly imperceptible nod and walked into the darkness.

Eamon made a sound of disbelief, but before he could voice a question or complaint, a young woman in a light blue gown stepped from the shadows to the right, a long black braid draped over her shoulder.

"Please to follow," she said in a heavy accent. She led them down a stone corridor and past several closed doors.

"What do we do now?" Phatomar asked Eamon quietly as they followed the acolyte.

"First we see to Jal," answered Eamon. "After that...I don't know. It seems unwise to force an Oracle."

The young woman glanced back at that, a small smile playing at her lips. She stopped and opened a door.

"Lay her within," she instructed. "One will come soon."

Without another word, she continued down the corridor, leaving Phatomar and Eamon behind. The men entered the room, finding a cozy chamber with a cot, chair, and a small table inside. The table held a lit candle and someone had folded back the sheet on the bed.

"The Oracle might not speak today," Eamon grumbled. "But I believe she has anticipated our needs."

Phatomar nodded, then laid Jal gently on the bed. They removed her fur boots, hat, and damp coat, tugged off her frozen mittens, then tucked the sheets up to her chin.

A wizened, grey-haired woman wrapped in a slate grey shawl arrived moments later, a basin of water in one gnarled hand and a basket of glass vials in the other. She shook off their offer of assistance and chased them from the room, firmly closing the door behind her.

Phatomar glanced at the empty stone hall, looked down at Eamon and shrugged.

"I guess we wait," he said.

Eamon could only nod in agreement. What else could they do?

Sliding down the wall, they sat outside Jal's room. Phatomar began to tremble, his fear rising again now that he lacked any sort of activity to mask it. Eamon looked over to his friend.

"Did I tell you about the time when we visited Leda's temple in Oren?" Eamon began, then regaled his friend with an improbable tale of heroic deeds that only Phatomar and Eamon could have accomplished, distracting them both from their concerns for the woman on the other side of the door.

Chapter 4

Jal floated in darkness, the pain and nausea which had stolen her senses held at bay by something that felt like a thick curtain laid over her body. Gradually, she became aware of a gentle light flickering beyond her closed eyes. Awareness flashed even as she realised she no longer lay in snow, but wrapped in warmth. Her eyes flew open and she pushed up on her elbows, her fingers brushing at her waist as they searched for the dagger at her belt.

A blanket covered her, but more than that, she no longer felt the heavy encumbrance of her fur-lined garments, nor the belt that should have held her weapons. She still had the use of her arms and legs so she didn't lie defenceless, but her ignorance of the situation left her vulnerable. A quick examination of her surroundings didn't clarify much. She reclined in a low pallet in a grey room, a chair and a small table holding a ewer, a basket, and a candle the only other furnishings. Despite the stark stone walls, the chamber held a comfortable heat. It did not, however, contain anything familiar, not even her clothing.

Jal pushed the blanket aside and tested whether the movement would bring a return of her headache and upset stomach. Her breath still came in shallow pulls, but the pain had retreated to a dull ache. *Good enough.* She swung her legs around and brought her stockinged feet to the bare floor. She still wore the tunic and breeches she had on beneath the winter gear, just none of the warm outer clothing.

The door opened and she stared at a wizened grey-haired

woman in a dark shawl, whose charcoal eyes stared back with a quiet intensity that bore hard-won wisdom. Jal's great-grandmother had had such eyes. Jal respected it now as she had then.

She opened her mouth to offer a greeting, but the stranger beat her to it. Only she spoke in the language of Merveah, and though Eamon and Phatomar had begun her language lessons, Jal had difficulty understanding anything beyond the woman's initial "how do you feel?"

"Better," Jal answered, keeping her words simple. "Head no bad." She raised a hand to her temple to demonstrate her meaning. "Here," a hand to her stomach, "better. This," fingers splayed on her chest over her lungs, "full." She shook her head, knowing she had the wrong word. "Short?" She tried again before growling her frustration. Then she held the woman's gaze and made a series of short, exaggerated gasps, winging her brows up as though to ask, *do you understand?*

The wizened woman nodded and spoke slowly as she approached the table, her wrinkled fingers pulling out a glass container from the basket. Jal caught the words *water* and *help*. When the woman lapsed into silence again, Jal could only stare helplessly at her. Did the glass contain special water, or did Jal need to mix its contents *with* water? Did she ingest it or spread it topically? Her great-grandmother had known medicines too, though Jal only knew enough not to experiment when wisdom spoke. She needed someone who knew the language.

"Where Eamon?" asked Jal. "Where Phatomar?"

Her companion cocked her head to the side as though listening to someone. She nodded, patted Jal's shoulder—that hand perhaps offering comfort, but definitely issuing a silent command to stay on the bed—then left the room, pulling the door to, though not completely shut.

Jal stared at the table and its contents as she waited, her mind spinning. Had they reached the temple of the Oracle? Had she just communicated with the woman they had come to see, or one of her priestesses? Had this Oracle restored Phatomar's memories and courage? Or had Jal's failure to keep up with the pair forced her friends to abandon their quest? She fervently hoped not, but couldn't dismiss the idea. That the woman had seemed to at least recognise her companions' names reassured Jal somewhat. They hadn't left her, but at what cost? She couldn't allow her weakness to deprive Phatomar of his chance to return to his previous life.

She didn't know how long she waited, caught in the hypnotic sway of the candle's flame, but footsteps outside her door drew Jal's attention as the door swung inward, followed by Eamon and Phatomar. Relief swept through her as the small room became crowded by the bulk of her companions. She offered a tentative smile which the men returned in full force.

"You look much better than when we brought you here," Phatomar said, his relief plain in the smoothing of the worry lines that had creased the edges of his pale eyes.

"How do you feel?" Eamon asked.

"Better, though it's still hard to get a full breath. The old woman tried to tell me about one of those medicines," Jal gestured to the bottles still on the table, "but I didn't really understand her."

"She wants you to drink some in water but suggests not to do so on an empty stomach."

Jal nodded, her gaze solemn as she held their attention.

"Did we reach the temple?" she asked. "Have you spoken to the Oracle?"

The men exchanged a glance that had Jal's stomach twist, though in anxiety rather than illness.

"She won't speak to us. They want us to leave when the storm passes," Eamon answered.

Jal frowned, perplexed now. "Why? Why wouldn't the Oracle speak with you after all the trouble to get here? I would think only those with a pressing need would venture through such torment to reach her home; can she just turn us away with no explanation?"

"It is her home," Eamon said. "And we guests who invited ourselves."

"They at least afforded us a place for you to recover," Phatomar said. His tone gave Jal the impression that such consideration had not come easily.

"Yet they still want us to leave without speaking to the Oracle," said Jal, a bitter thread of anger coiling through her.

"How do people usually arrange to see her, then? Do they have some kind of messenger birds that won't freeze in this barren landscape? Some intrepid villager to brave the mountain meant to act as a liaison? A guard or escort we missed? What protocol did we fail to observe?"

"I don't know how else one approaches the Oracle at Hada," Eamon admitted, rubbing at his chin. "I've never heard of any special stipulations, and Dearn certainly didn't give us any indication."

Jal narrowed her eyes in speculation, trying to tamp down her ire and think rationally. As Eamon had said, the Oracle hadn't invited them. To expect hospitality and immediate answers as they intruded upon her sanctuary only spoke to their own conceit. The Oracle owed them nothing.

"You know," she said slowly. "Dearn never mentioned the Oracle at all."

Both Eamon and Phatomar jolted in surprise.

"He said our path started in the mountains at Hada," she continued. "You assumed he meant the Oracle. What else lies in these mountains?"

"Only more snow and ice," Eamon replied, his focus turned inward as he also searched for answers. "But Hada doesn't name the mountain range, it names the temple. We stand in Hada, home of the Hada Oracle. If we're not meant to speak to her, then what?"

"Dearn also said we'd face many choices," Phatomar added, his voice barely above a whisper. "Perhaps whether we allow the Oracle to evict us without meeting her stands as such a choice. Or the choice might lie in us affording the Oracle her privacy, or imposing on her further. How can we know which path to follow?"

"We follow the path that best serves you," Eamon said firmly. "We're here to right the wrongs placed on *you* by capricious gods."

Jal snorted, suddenly hearing how arrogant that sounded. Yet what else could they do? Dearn had charged them with finding answers, even if he had only provided cryptic clues to guide them.

"This Oracle," Jal wondered. "You called her a woman of mystifying powers." Eamon nodded. "But definitely a woman? Not a god?"

44

Eamon cocked his head in contemplation. "Oracles are god-touched, able to see beyond and sometimes act as a conduit for higher powers," he mused. "But I've never heard one referred to as a god. Why?"

Jal answered his question with a question. "Does this one speak for one god or many?"

"Dearn warned us not to call attention from his fellows," Phatomar said, his thoughts clearly aligning with Jal's. "And not to trust lightly."

Eamon huffed. "And still he sent us here."

"To someone who may or may not know more than him," said Phatomar.

"But what answers might an Oracle glean that lie hidden from a god?" Jal wanted to know.

A rap on the door startled them all, and a black-haired woman younger than Jal and clad in blue bustled in bearing a tray laden with a bowl and a cup. She said something in the language of Merveah, to which Eamon nodded with a smile, taking the tray from her. The woman regarded Jal for a moment.

"Better," the woman said carefully, pinning Jal with disconcerting azure eyes flecked with streaks of silver. Jal blinked, the silver fading to leave bright blue orbs staring at her. "Eat," the woman said with a nod to the tray. "Back later."

When she left, Eamon handed the tray down to Jal.

"Best to listen to an acolyte of the Oracle," he said with a smile.

"Is that what she was?" Jal asked, studying the green leaves and handful of grains floating in an otherwise clear broth that filled the bowl. When she stirred it, she saw that corn bobbed beneath the leaves, and a light-hued shredded meat had sunk to the bottom. A curl of steam rose from the adjacent cup, its contents also packed with bits of green which slowly steeped the liquid within a yellowish-green colour.

She wondered how a place trapped in snow-bound mountains found any such food, for surely small offerings such as those they had brought wouldn't last long in isolation.

"She seemed young for a priestess, and too well-dressed for a servant," Eamon said. "If not an acolyte, then what?"

Jal shrugged, raised a laden spoon to her lips, and carefully tasted the soup. Oddly spiced but pleasant enough. She took a sip of the tea, finding the flavour slightly bitter, though not objectionable. She wondered what they contained. Eamon had said the old woman wanted her to take the medicine to help her shortness of breath on a full stomach, so she continued with her meal. Phatomar waved Eamon to the solitary chair while he lounged against the wall, the three trying to determine their next course of action while Jal ate.

With the soup gone, the tray perched on the edge of the table, and the nearly empty cup of tea held in her hands, Jal realised that her breathing had improved. Not completely, for she still felt a heaviness on her chest, but it became easier to draw air into her lungs. She stared into her cup with wide eyes, wondering if the acolyte had mixed some medicine in the tea.

"I can breathe." She caught Eamon's grin when she looked up.

"Coca leaves to combat the height," he said. "I didn't think to find any before we left, but the wise woman knows her trade."

The door then opened as the young woman came to retrieve the tray. Jal wondered how she knew Jal had finished, whether the woman had some ability to see like the Oracle. But before that thought could lead to others, another body squeezed into the room; the grey-haired old woman.

The youth gaped at her, then scowled and hissed something that sounded like, "Why are you here now?"

Wrinkles folding even deeper with an impish grin, the old woman surprised Jal with a wink as she shook her head and scooted the youngster out of the room with a firm hand to her back. She turned to Jal, giving a satisfied nod at the cup in her hand. Ignoring Eamon and Phatomar, she came over and stood before Jal, the back of her wizened hand first touching Jal's forehead, then turning so that her bony fingers brushed Jal's temples.

"Still good?" she asked.

Jal nodded, then placed her hand on her stomach, raised it to her chest. She smiled at the grandmotherly figure. "Good too." Jal drew a deep breath to demonstrate. Holding up the cup, she added, "Thank you."

The woman cupped Jal's cheek and whispered, "Good girl," with a fond smile. Then she turned to Eamon, who had moved out of the way near Phatomar as the old one studied Jal. She spoke too rapidly for Jal to follow. Eamon regarded their wizened host without expression when she finished. Finally, he nodded and thanked her. Jal thought she saw a sly smirk curl upon her lips as she withdrew, leaving the three companions alone again.

"What did she say?" Jal asked when the silence had stretched long enough.

"That evening draws in and night will fall before the storm slackens. She offered us food and lodging for the night."

"No mention of the Oracle, though?"

"None," Eamon confirmed. "Although she suggests we remain open to learning forgotten truths and helping all things find their proper balance."

"Huh. Nothing cryptic or oracular in that," Jal said. "I guess we're back to figuring out our next step." Eamon could only nod in agreement.

***

Jal didn't remember falling asleep, and though she dreamed, only the sense of deep frustration from chasing unanswered questions followed her into wakefulness. She blinked up at the stone ceiling, the final spluttering flickers of her candle causing shadows to dance madly above. In a room with no windows, the extinguishing of the tiny light would cast her into utter darkness.

She sat up and looked to the door, wondering whether to go to it now to seek more light, or merely mark its location so she could find it once the candle had gone out. How much time had passed? Did it lie closer to midnight or daybreak? Should she try to find more sleep, knowing they had to face the rigours of the mountain soon and so would need all her strength, or would leaving her bed now make for a better use of her time?

Having seen nothing beyond this room, Jal's curiosity got the better of her, and, feeling rested, she determined to explore a little. She pushed her covers off and rose from the

47

bed. A quick survey of the room confirmed neither her coat nor boots lay within. She shrugged, wiggling her toes within their woollen stockings. They would have to do to keep the chill of stone floors from numbing her feet.

Her fingers brushed the handle on the door just as the candle lost its battle and plunged the room into darkness. Jal pulled the door open and found, to her relief, another candle braced in a sconce in the hall beyond, lighting the corridor. She also found her boots sitting beside the door. Several closed doors lined the hallway, and Jal stood there in uncertainty for a moment. Left or right? Which rooms might house her companions, and which juncture might lead to something besides sleeping chambers?

How many live here? she wondered, leaving her boots to mark her room and randomly picking a direction. Her silent steps soon brought her to a wide octagonal chamber edged with stone benches, empty space holding the centre. A dark archway faced her across the room, and large tapestries covered the six solid walls, each bracketed by a lantern hung on a pole which brought to life the vivid colours of each canvas.

Jal moved closer to the middle of the room, turning in slow circles to take in as much detail as possible. Four of the tapestries, one adjacent to each entrance, depicted the elements. The browns and greens of gardens and forests held sway on the artwork to the right of the far archway, while the bright plumage of a myriad of birds soared through an iridescent sky on its counterpart to the left. Swirls of red, orange, and yellow flamed across the canvas to the right of the doorway she had just entered, balanced on the left by the blues, teals, and greys of the deep seas and the life therein.

Jal saw life and death face each other upon the final two walls across the empty room. Scenes of weddings, couples embraced, births, flowers unfurling in the spring, the sun cresting the horizon as it birthed the day; images of bloodshed and warfare, funerals, mourners kneeling beside graves, plants wilting and barren in the clutches of winter, the setting sun dragging its warmth into the underworld.

Each time she gazed upon a tapestry, Jal noted something different, some new detail or nuance she had missed the time before. She continued her measured dance around the room until she felt eyes watching her.

Dragging her study away from the incredible threads that painted the course of existence within an otherwise stark room, Jal met the unblinking stare of ice-blue eyes. It took a moment to see beyond those cold orbs to the silver-robed woman with unbound brown hair who now confronted her.

Not knowing the proper greeting to give a priestess of an Oracle—for surely such stood before her now, not a servant or pilgrim—Jal pressed a hand to her heart and bowed low at the waist as she would in the presence of a tribal leader. When she rose, she hesitated. Would this woman understand her words?

"My apologies if language stands as a barrier between us, honoured one," she said slowly and humbly, hoping the priestess would at least understand her tone, if not her words. "If I have offered offence for entering a place I should not have, again my sincere apologies. I wish to extend my appreciation for your hospitality, and for the care you have shown to me and my friends." Jal bowed again, this time with the first three fingers of her right hand pressed to her forehead. In the desert, the gesture spoke of gratitude and obligation. If it had any meaning here, Jal didn't know, nor did the priestess' lack of reaction offer any insight.

The two women stared at one another in silence.

Should I ask her about the Oracle? Would she understand me if I did? Jal thought not.

Jal tried one more time, bowing just her head this time. "Forgive me if I disturbed you." With a final appreciative glance at the tapestries, she turned back the way she had come. Before she set foot in the corridor, however, she paused. She had neglected one vital part of the desert greeting and felt compelled to provide it now. She faced the priestess again, who had not moved. Placing hand to heart, Jal maintained eye contact and spoke.

"I am called Jal, though my parents named me Ajala. This name I entrust to your lips."

"And you expect mine in return?" the priestess said, her voice light and musical. Jal gaped at her, astonished to hear her own tongue. She quickly shook her head.

"No, *shala*," she assured, affording her the rank of a shaman, not knowing what other title to use. "My name

49

stands in acknowledgement of my debt for your kindness."

"What kindness do you believe I provided?"

Jal studied her, thinking hard. Did she expect an empty platitude or the truth?

"You allowed us into your home," she finally answered. "You could have chosen not to unbar your doors, leaving us to the elements." Jal's hand rose to indicate the water tapestry now on her right. "Instead, you welcomed strangers into your home, knowing full well that the Oracle they had come to consult would not speak with them, risking both disappointment and anger. You allowed a potentially hostile force into your tent with no guarantee of your own safety and shared of your bounty, asking nothing in return. I call this kindness."

"Some might call that folly," the priestess said.

"Some might," Jal agreed. "But they don't stand here now."

The ghost of a smile brushed the priestess' lips, vanishing so quickly that Jal might have imagined it.

"Perhaps we will have words before you depart," she told Jal. "The storm has passed and the sun now lightens the sky. Aura will show you a place to eat where you will rejoin your companions, and Cleo will prepare you a tea to aid in your breathing. I entrust you, Jal, with the name Rachel."

With a regal nod, the priestess retreated into the dark recesses of the far archway, disappearing so quickly that Jal shuddered with the fancy that the blackness itself had swallowed her. An unexpected light step at her back had Jal spin around. The dark-haired girl smirked, gesturing behind her with an open hand.

"Please follow," she said. "Food is prepared."

"Thank you, Aura," Jal said. The girl gave no reaction to Jal knowing her name beyond a slight nod of the head. Jal's brow furrowed as she considered the gift Rachel had provided.

***

"Have you seen anyone other than the three women here?" Jal asked as the three of them sat together in a small dining area, porridge bowls empty and cups of tea half drunk.

Eamon shook his head. "No, why?"

"I'm not sure," she said. "But I'm trying to remember a tale a tinker once told me. Something about three mystical women working as one. A child, a mother, and a grandmother. Could a similar concept apply here? Three people working in concert to achieve one goal?"

"Jal," Eamon hesitated. "That could just as easily describe us."

"But we're not stuck here at Hada," she said, exasperated that she couldn't put her thoughts into better words. She tried a different approach. "Where is the Oracle? Does she have her own chambers? A place to meet supplicants?" *Like a chamber just beyond an octagonal room?* "Surely many seek the wisdom of such a god-touched being, yet only we three sit in her halls. Wouldn't such a revered person attract more than three followers? Shouldn't a place of this size have more retainers to attend to those supplicants and the Oracle herself?"

"Do you suggest they've deceived us?" Phatomar wondered. "That the Oracle is merely a myth?"

"Not a myth; just other than we expected. And perhaps tired of fulfilling the expectations of others."

A dry chuckle sounded behind them. They turned to see the old woman, Cleo, walk into the room, a small woollen bag tied with thread in her hand. Her dark gaze regarded Jal, then moved to include the men. She spoke briefly in Eamon's tongue, then waited while he translated. Eamon wore a puzzled expression.

"She says Rachel has discerned your language well enough to speak it, but Cleo herself can only understand what you say, not reply." He stared at Jal. "Who's Rachel?"

"The mother," she said, watching Cleo. Cleo's wrinkles creased even more with her grin and impish nod. She extended the bag to Jal, said something else.

"Coca leaves," Eamon translated. "For a final cup of strengthening tea once we reach the pilgrim's hut tonight. And a second bundle of leaves, should you ever encounter a Kursak in need. Well," he finished his tea in one last swallow, placing his cup carefully on the table before standing. "I don't know where we'd ever come across a Kursak, but it seems time to make our farewells."

They gathered their few belongings and followed Cleo into

the hall where Aura waited. The young woman turned and led them to the front hall, no expression betraying her thoughts. Cleo trailed behind them. Jal paused to walk beside the old woman, but Cleo waved her ahead, indicating that she would walk alone. When they reached the great wooden door, Jal glanced around, but she didn't see Rachel as she had hoped.

It seemed that they had made the trip to Hada for nothing. Eamon spoke, giving the women his thanks, though by the set of his jaw, Jal suspected he held in his frustration. He bowed, Phatomar echoing his actions. Jal quickly added her own thanks, but as Eamon and Phatomar turned toward the door—Eamon's grimace speaking to his discontent—Jal didn't move. She met Cleo's charcoal stare, Aura's azure one, and tried to pull the niggling feeling itching at the back of her mind into coherent thought.

If she and her friends walked out that door now, they would miss an important opportunity. But how did one properly approach a figure like the Oracle?

Without expectation, she realised, not sure whether the thought came from within or without. She looked over to Eamon.

"Eamon," she called. He stopped and turned to her. "What did you say to explain why we came?"

He blinked in surprise, exchanged a glance with Phatomar, then came to stand beside her again, all under the watchful eyes of Aura and Cleo.

"Rachel, I presume, told us the Oracle wouldn't speak to us before we could even explain our presence," he said. "I tried to tell her that Dearn sent us, but she didn't seem to care."

"She let us stay long enough to care for you," Phatomar added. "But none of them seemed inclined to listen to our pleas."

"So you really haven't had a chance to clarify why we made the journey?"

"The theft of Phatomar's courage and memories doesn't interest them," Eamon grumbled darkly.

"Nor should it," Jal replied. Eamon jerked back in surprise. His fleeting scowl made her cringe, and she pressed on quickly lest he think her uncaring of Phatomar's plight. "He's a stranger to them, one soul among many who has suffered an injustice. That others have wronged him, cheated him, stolen from him and made his existence terrifying just adds him to the untold number of people who find life unfair through circumstances beyond their control.

"Perhaps the Oracle doesn't need to hear his story," continued Jal. "She needs to understand *why* we would undertake the arduous journey in order to help him. We didn't come just because a deity suggested we do so, nor did we come only because of what the theft did to Phatomar."

She watched Eamon's hazel eyes fill with understanding.

"Then why did we come?" Phatomar asked, his voice that of a lost little boy.

Eamon turned to regard his friend. "Because we love you." Although they spoke the desert tongue for Jal's sake, a quick glance to Aura and Cleo showed Jal that they understood their words. "Because you're family, and family does everything it can to keep each other safe. And when that fails"—the shorter man placed a fierce yet comforting hand on Phatomar's trembling shoulder—"we find a way to do the impossible anyway. If we can't learn why the gods so altered your life, if we don't retrieve what they stole, by all that's sacred, it won't be because we stopped trying to find the answers."

"You may not like the answers you find," a new yet familiar voice said. The three companions watched Rachel step from the shadows and place herself between Aura and Cleo. When the trio stood shoulder to shoulder, a soft white light surrounded them, the eerie glow reminiscent of the aura which had encompassed Phatomar on the day that the gods stole from him. Jal wanted to ask the men if they saw the same thing, but feared breaking the spell woven by the Oracle. Instead, she raised a hand to her heart and bowed low, as she had when she'd met Rachel alone. Eamon and Phatomar likewise paid their respects.

The three women nodded as one, their motions synchronized as though one being. In a way, Jal believed the veracity of that thought; three aspects with a shared purpose, linked as one when the Oracle rose to share her wisdom.

"You have your own share of wisdom and insight for one so young, Jal, once named Ajala," Cleo spoke, though her words reverberated with an otherworldly power that combined all three voices. Jal found it difficult to differentiate between the three, watching as they formed one being with three shimmering bodies. She chose to concentrate on the central figure.

Rachel's face took on Cleo's wrinkles and Aura's bright unblinking eyes, her silver robe wrapped around Aura's blue gown, topped by Cleo's dark shawl, and her brown hair shimmered with streaks of Cleo's grey even as it took on the length of Aura's braid. Jal didn't dare look away, afraid of what else she might see.

The Oracle raised her resonant voice, the unearthly quality of the gods suffusing her proclamation.

"Three tasks you must accomplish," she informed them. *"Each will reveal part of the answer you need. One will give motive, one a location, one an identity. If you succeed, you will face one last challenge, and that, even I cannot foresee.*

"You have climbed to the heights; now you must look to the depths. In a cavern beneath the sands far to the east, you will find the Faqadat Alqalb, *the Heart Stone. This you must take to the Blackened Fields where ancient death engendered a tree of starry night. With a limb freely given, you might win free of its mighty reach. Limb and Stone will point you to the watery grave; do not shy from its liquid embrace.*

"You may find help along the way, and you will find hindrances. Do not judge too quickly lest you lose an opportunity."

A wave of prismatic light engulfed the Oracle. Jal blinked from the brightness, and when she looked again, the three woman stood shoulder to shoulder regarding them, their own selves once more. Rachel stepped forward, her eyes returned to an icy flatness. Aura stood behind her, head bowed and hands clasped. Cleo took a shuddering breath, her back slightly more hunched before she pulled herself erect.

"The Oracle has imparted what aid she can," Rachel said.

Aura looked up and stared at Phatomar.

"Know that what has happened to you, happened for a reason," she said, her accent heavy, though Jal found she understood the girl's words despite the fact she didn't speak in the desert tongue.

"Every action still has a choice," added Cleo. "Together, you will remain strong. Balance your strengths and weaknesses; do not lament them."

"Now we bid you farewell," Rachel finished. The three women nodded as one again.

Knowing they would learn nothing more here, the companions nodded in return and expressed their heartfelt thanks. They opened the doors of Hada onto a pristine snowscape of brilliant white, the glare blinding. The pale sun shone in a cloudless blue sky, beckoning them out into its chilly embrace. With scarf and hat pulled close, coat and mitts tucked tight, they left the warm halls of the Oracle. The door swung shut behind them, and Jal, Eamon, and Phatomar glanced at one another in silence, then set out through the fresh fallen snow; together, as the gods intended.

Chapter 5

The Oracle's riddle fresh in their minds, they discussed their options as they made their way back down the mountain. Jal felt surprisingly energised by Cleo's tea and had only to contend with the rigours of the exhausting pace rather than any lightheadedness or shortness of breath.

"I think the Blackened Fields might refer to the Formorket Enger in the north-west," Eamon said as they descended, the still air easily carrying his words to his companions. "Long ago, the volcanoes left vast swaths of black soil and barren rock strewn across massive fields. Though I've never ventured into those wastes or any forests it might contain, I suspect we might find this tree of starry night somewhere in the Formorket Enger. Sadly, I don't recognise the reference to the cavern beneath the sands far to the east."

"I do," Jal replied. "Or rather, I've heard of the Faqadat Alqalb. Beyond the deep deserts that border the Gobani lies rumours of vast treasures, the Faqadat Alqalb chief among them. It's said that death stalks any who seek to claim what does not belong to them. A few have attempted to find the Faqadat Alqalb as a means to win glory or honour. Those who seek it for selfish reasons never return, while those who undertake the journey for the experience alone come back with awe and horror in their eyes."

"So, an Oracle bidding us to take the Faqadat Alqalb puts us where?" Eamon wondered. "As one of the selfish or those who seek an experience?"

"I don't know." Jal shrugged, a sense of overwhelming

circumstances beyond their control settling around her. "It feels like this task the Oracle has set for us reaches farther than just restoring Phatomar's courage and memories, though I don't understand how. I can't believe one man's restoration to wholeness should require such extreme measures, no matter his legend. But where our journey will lead us, and what answers we may find, let alone the purpose behind the Oracle's riddle, I cannot fathom."

Jal couldn't shake her disquiet at the thought, an uneasiness that didn't fade as they travelled further from Hada and eventually back to the stables where their horses and weapons awaited them.

As they journeyed south toward warmer lands and Jal swapped her fur hat for her helm, Eamon brought up the subject of their destination again. "If this cavern beneath the sands that holds the Faqadat Alqalb lies somewhere beyond the Gobani, then it lies a long way off indeed. A sea voyage past the Gobani to the ports of the east will save us time, though it would take us through dangerous waters."

"I don't know much of the lay of the land in Merveah," Jal said. "But I know travel through the deep desert kills the unwary. If we can skirt most of it by taking to water instead, it might behoove us to do so. Better dangerous waters than the scorching sands."

"Obviously, you haven't sailed through treacherous waters," Eamon said, but they eventually agreed that a sea voyage would avail them best, continuing south and east to reach the distant waters.

They encountered various other travellers during their month-long trek; villagers journeying from one town to the next on market day, farmers and tradespeople travelling in groups for safety, a merchant train, a couple of sell-swords. They even accompanied a bard and his lyre player for a few days, enjoying their musicianship in the evening.

Performing the occasional job along the way—guarding a wagon train, mending a storm-ravaged fence or bridge, rounding up ruffians who found it easier to extort a village than to contribute to its well-being—had provided extra coin or accommodation in appreciation. More often than not, however, they kept to themselves, foraging in nature's bounty for food and shelter.

Half a dozen times, they encountered thieves on the road, and while Phatomar stood rooted in fear at their brandished weapons, his immobile stance backed by his bulk lent the impression of an intimidating guardian over the horses rather than a terrified man. Eamon and Jal quickly disabused the bandits of the thought of purloining what didn't belong to them as Phatomar stood locked in place by his lack of courage, trying to breathe and finding little comfort in it.

Eamon continued to instruct Jal on the finer techniques of sword work each evening, and Jal continued to help Phatomar learn various ways to cope with—and hopefully in time overcome—the helpless state in which the loss of his courage left him. Both men taught Jal their language. Eamon quickly allowed Phatomar to take the lead once he saw how it gave the larger man a sense of purpose. Having discovered something he could perform without fear, Phatomar took to teaching with enthusiasm, and Jal soon found her grasp of the Merveah tongue growing more fluent under his confident tutelage.

The days grew warmer and the weather more temperate the further south they travelled. The air grew heavier with humidity and the brine of the sea became more prevalent until Jal could scent little else. She kept waiting for the narrow ribbon of blue-brown water that she had once crossed to appear on the horizon.

When Jal had first made the sea journey from the desert lands to Merveah, she had used the Randa Ferry where one could see either shore without straining. She had stood upon a raft capable of holding thirty people, but that day, it had only held ten, plus the two men who worked the pulley system that bridged this narrowest gap between the continents.

A corded rope the thickness of Jal's wrist spanned the sea, its lower portion threaded through bronze loops which topped shoulder-high poles attached to the lashed planks that made up the base of the craft. Its upper section, held taut on each shore by sturdy posts, remained unencumbered. One of the ferry men grasped the upper portion of the rope at the front of the raft and walked it to the back, the second repeating the motion when the first had reached about half way, thus keeping their movement constant as they propelled their passengers slowly across the water.

Though the sight of so much water in one place had awed Jal, she had found the experience pleasant, if slightly tedious. The thought of recrossing the sea from a different port didn't intimidate her. Even when Eamon explained that they would board an entirely different type of craft (something he called a sailboat) and traverse a much wider expanse of salty water—one that would take them away from the sight of land for more than a day—she believed herself undaunted. She knew about waters bigger than an oasis, and she knew about the dangers of travel into the unknown. She had conversed with gods, survived the rigours of Hada, outwitted bandits and thieves. Legends walked beside her, teaching her, drawing her into their world as an equal. *I can handle anything that comes my way.*

Then they reached the port town of Danvers during the middle of a furious storm, and she realised just how far out of her depth she stood. Jal stared in dismay at neither a narrow channel, nor a village nestled comfortably in a small bay. Despite the driving rain limiting sight, she had no impression of even a smudge of land visible across the grey and white water, only a vast tract of nothing save tumultuous water beneath low leaden skies and vicious winds. Her confidence shattered

A row of large disparate boats, strange vessels to her unpracticed eye, bobbed sickeningly within the sheltered confines of the harbour—yet another new concept for the desert girl. Ferna only had a collection of fishing vessels that didn't necessitate more than the shore of the bay to keep the little boats from floating off. Here, a system of ropes and cushions that she didn't understand somehow held these boats, larger than even the largest communal tent of the tribes, secured to spits shooting out from the shore without causing damage despite the seething sea. Her stomach roiled as she watched the open waters beyond the harbour churn into frothy waves under the onslaught of punishing winds and lashing rain.

"The storm will pass soon," Eamon assured her. He clapped Jal and Phatomar on the back, his grin beneath rain-drenched brown locks more a barring of teeth than an expression holding any real mirth. Phatomar stared with equal horror out at the vicious waves as the pair stood next to their horses, who continued to shake the rain from their coats even as it continued to drench them. "Let's find some shelter, then I'll see about arranging passage for ourselves and our soggy mounts."

***

Phatomar *knew* he had travelled aboard a sea vessel before. His hands remembered the feel of lines as they pulled square sails taut; his back recalled the strain of pulling on an oar to maintain speed when the winds slackened; his legs and feet knew the sway of a deck slicing through waves. Yet the thought of boarding the merchant ship with its canted tanja sails terrified him.

Even the captain and his crew made him nervous. The Marany men themselves—their skin duskier than Jal's, their eyes darker and almond shaped, their tongue more musical with its lilting cadence—didn't bother him. But he didn't know *them*, had never interacted with this particular group, and that unfamiliarity kindled his aversion to the unknown. Breathing deep, allowing Jal's gentle instructions to roll through his thoughts, he tried to master his trepidation, though his knees wanted to lock and hold him in place, and his muscles tightened as he fought the urge to flee.

He stood on shore waiting until the crew loaded the last of the cargo—said cargo including their three mounts, blindfolded and quietly led by Eamon up a sturdy plank into the hold. One might mistake his statue-like stance for that of an aloof passenger, refusing to offer his aid yet wise enough to keep out of the way until final boarding. In truth, he seriously contemplated the idea of putting a blindfold on himself and asking Jal to lead him by the hand as Eamon had led the horses. But the thought of walking unseeing into a dark hold, nothing between him and a fall into deep waters but the firm grip of a young woman half his size sent a spike of panic racing to his already strained heart.

He growled to himself, hating this constant state of fear yet unable to free himself from its grasp. When he found the being responsible for crippling him so, he would...

Would what? a cynical voice taunted him.

Even knowing that voice came from within, he blinked in surprise. What did he suppose would happen when—*if?*—they reached the end of this quest? Why should the goddess who appropriated his courage simply hand it back? If she truly believed he had somehow wronged her, Phatomar had to find some way to either appease her or defeat her; he likely couldn't simply wrest his courage back without a fight. Similarly for the god who had usurped his memories. Phatomar needed some way to win restitution or victory. So how did one lacking courage gird himself for battle with a goddess and a god?

Start by getting on the ship, he thought. *One step at a time.*

Still, the thought of taking that first step, of actually moving toward the swaying vessel, terrified him enough that he found himself gasping until his lungs hurt. His fingers ached from being wrapped into tight fists for so long, and he couldn't stop trembling.

Curse this weakness!

"I've never seen anything so big," a quiet voice confided next to him. Phatomar glanced down at his companion, but Jal's wide eyes—visible with her helm clutched in her hands instead of covering her face—stared up at the ship, not him. Despite the larger Merveahian coastal runner docked three slips down from the Marany merchant ship they would take, Phatomar understood her trepidation. They wouldn't sail aboard *that* boat, but this one, and a girl raised in desert sands had no real experience on the wide waters. *Any* such ship would look big, and this one filled her vision as it placidly rode the wavelets after the storm. They didn't have long before the tides would turn and the captain would demand the presence of his passengers or leave without them. Soon, Phatomar would have to face his baseless fear.

Perhaps if he concentrated on helping Jal overcome her concerns, he could ignore his own. With that in mind, he forced himself to speak.

"Have you ever seen a pod of dolphins play in the wake of a boat?" he asked. She tore her tawny gaze from the ship and stared at him, desperate for any distraction. He smiled, and his tone grew softer. "Some call them messengers, guiding sailors in times of trouble and keeping them safe.

Sleek and beautiful creatures of the sea, their presence often brings luck."

"What do they look like? Do you think we'll see any?" she asked.

"Not if we stand about here," he said. "They're best seen from the prow of the boat." He pointed to the front of the ship and found that the hope of seeing such a creature balanced out his fear of having to take that first step.

Is that the secret? he wondered. *To find the hope in a situation rather than dwell on the dread? Cling to the light and wondrous and not on what might go wrong.*

"Come," he said just as Eamon's head appeared on deck. "Perhaps we can find a safe place to watch for them."

Phatomar held out an unsteady hand and Jal took it with her own shaking fingers. Together, they walked toward the boarding plank. Eamon waited at the other end, and Phatomar kept his eyes focused on his friend as he moved forward, tugging Jal behind him.

We can do this, he thought as the crew drew in the plank and made ready to navigate out of the harbour.

Dolphins gathered to lead them into the mysterious waters beyond.

***

Navigating out of Danvers presented no difficulties, and their first day passed without incident. Jal had stood by the prow at the outset, hands wrapped tight around the guardrail, her features pale and pinched as she watched the harbour, then gradually the land, fade from sight. The frolicking dolphins helped distract her for a time, but eventually Eamon had shown her where she might lie down and tend to a stomach unfamiliar with true ocean travel.

Phatomar felt for her; first assaulted by mountain sickness and now by the sea, no doubt anticipating what other ailments might befall her on her unexpected adventure. He wondered what had prompted Jal to leave the Gobani and venture north, what had motivated her thirst for adventure. If she had revealed much of her past beyond her desert origins when she first joined them, Phatomar had missed the details, too wrapped up in his own shortcomings at the time. And now, he feared looking foolish by asking for details he perhaps should already know. Whatever her motivations, he admired her courage, her enthusiasm, and her ability to persevere despite adverse conditions.

Phatomar found that his memories of his own such adventures and travels—barring the forgotten feats that lay at the end of any such journey (and what had prompted his own foray into this life)—didn't lie. The mountain heights hadn't bothered him, and the swell of the sea as it rocked the boat held no horrors for him, his body absorbing the motion with ease.

The evening passed, and he and Eamon shared a meal with the crew in the mess while Jal tried to recover below. Night came and went, the soft pitch of the waves a soothing balm as they slept.

Calm seas met them in the morning. Reading the weather signs, the captain ordered out the oars rather than allowing the ship to stall. Phatomar surprised himself by his lack of fear at offering his aid to row. The captain studied the breadth of his back and shoulders, the bulge of muscles, and quickly agreed.

Rowing didn't require courage; only strength and endurance, and Phatomar, having lost neither of those, had plenty to spare, especially here at sea where he had nowhere else to go and nothing else to do. The ability to add his strength to the efforts of the Marany sailors quickly endeared him to the crew and gave him another sense of accomplishment.

Phatomar discovered something astonishing. Losing his courage and the memory of how one applied it only diminished him if he allowed it to. It had forced him to re-examine the other gifts he had to offer; gifts he only now began to appreciate. Yes, the theft had changed him, altered his perceptions, but it did not make him worthless, and now he knew to search for other means of defining himself, of making his life count. Little acts mattered as much—if not more—than grand feats of valour and prowess. After all, if the ship never arrived to shore, then the hero would have no tale. The gods had left him with the ability to carry out everyday actions, the tasks any person might accomplish—peasants, warriors, or nobles—and he would

63

make the most of those skills to go forward.

They made good progress that day despite the lack of any wind. Eamon also took a turn at the oars, and Jal made an appearance, enjoying a bowl of broth and a heel of bread. Her skin had lost its pallor, though she still moved with care whenever the deck shifted beneath her feet. Sometimes it took a bit to find one's sea legs, and sometimes someone afflicted only recovered when they reached solid land again. Jal might fall into the first category, though by her moue of distaste, Phatomar doubted that she'd ever truly enjoy riding the waves as he did.

Their third and final day on the ship made up for the peace of still waters by the ferocity of strong winds. No rain lashed the deck, and no lightning raged overhead, but it felt as though the gods of wind and air wanted them to experience all the other tempers of sea travel. At that point, Phatomar's ease on deck failed him, and he took refuge with Jal well out of the way. He could row, he could tend a line, but the vagaries of wind-swept waters funnelling a storm dried his mouth and locked his limbs. Better to cower in a corner than to cause any misfortune by hindering the crew.

Happily, the Marany well knew the temperament of wind and wave, and they navigated toward the southern shores, evading deadly shoals and the swarms of sea creatures that liked to hamper unwary sailors.

By mid-afternoon, they pulled into the protected embrace of Kemta Bay, docking at one of the long piers of Hamiqa Harbour. Sheltered from the worst of the winds, the crew set to unloading their cargo, bidding a jovial farewell as the three companions disembarked. Once their horses came ashore—Cosantoir and Onoir with anxious snorts of relief while Croga danced at the end of his lead once his hooves hit the land—they withdrew, following a muddy dirt road into the town supported by the harbour. One of two major ports servicing the northern shores of the desert, Hamiqa boasted several amenities, including taverns with decent food and overnight accommodations, and enough shops that dealt in the necessities for journeys into the sands to find the supplies they would require.

While Eamon took the horses to locate the first, Phatomar and Jal looked to the second. Not knowing where exactly to find the Faqadat Alqalb and therefore how long their trek into the deeper desert might last, Jal wanted to make sure they had enough supplies to last for a goodly while. Using funds Eamon had obtained from their factor in Danvers before they sailed, Jal procured desert garb, a variety of water containers, preserved foods, salt cakes, and fodder for the horses. And now, she intended to include camels.

"But we have horses," Phatomar said with a frown, not understanding Jal's insistence on the additional mounts.

"If we have to go into the deep desert, our horses won't fare well, despite their strength and heart," she said. She had donned her helmet again to keep her hair from blowing in her face, and while it shadowed her eyes, Phatomar had no problems hearing her voice. "Camels will endure the harsh conditions better with fewer provisions required. With their broader feet, they can also traverse the sand faster and easier than our horses."

"You want us to leave the horses?" asked Phatomar, horrified.

"Not yet," Jal answered. "Perhaps not at all. Even if we only have to get from one oasis to another, the less weight Croga, Cosantoir, and Onoir have to bear the better. Having camels now will spare our mounts some of the burden at the outset, but more important, we *know* we can obtain camels here. At the Fyum Oasis, where the tribes gather to trade goods and host travellers, while we might find the supplies we'd need, we risk losing out to competition, and we risk higher prices due to scarcity. Unless we have something besides coin to bargain with—something more useful to desert life than bits of gold or silver—we won't get a better price than here. The tribes enjoy trading for goods more than monies, and we don't have many goods that would interest the tribes."

"How far to this Fyum Oasis?"

"From here, I'm not sure," Jal admitted. "I only went once with Father, and we came from the Gobani in the west." She gazed at the brightly coloured stalls of Hamiqa, then looked back at Phatomar. "You and Eamon speak the desert languages; have you never travelled to Fyum?"

"Not that I recall," he said, frustrated that he didn't *know* where, or even whether, he had set foot in her homeland. He had vague memories of journeys along shifting dunes, but no knowledge of *where* those travels had taken place, nor what he had done there. "Perhaps Eamon will know."

She smiled gently, sorrow in her gold-flecked eyes.

"Not to worry," she tried to assure him. "Many here will know the route." She scowled, vexation crossing her features. "Assuming we even must head to Fyum. Without knowing where to find the Faqadat Alqalb, I'm only guessing our best course. If no one in Hamiqa can provide a better route, I think Fyum Oasis, being the closest and largest gathering spot that I know of, gives us the best chance of finding someone with the knowledge we require. But for all I know, it could take us in the wrong direction entirely."

"It's a start," a voice said from behind them. Phatomar started before recognising his shorter companion. He gave Eamon a playful shove, not sure whether he appreciated his friend's constant attempts to numb Phatomar to surprises or irritated that he still jumped every time. Eamon slapped him on the back, then turned his attention to Jal.

"I don't have any better ideas on finding our destination," Eamon went on. "So"—he clapped his hands and rubbed them together, examining the supplies already gathered, and studying the area where they had stopped—"what else do we need before we start?"

"Camels," Phatomar answered, keeping a straight face at Eamon's startled expression. He nodded at Jal's sudden grin and dared give her a conspiratorial wink. "To help share the load and speed our journey."

"And a map of the oases and watering holes," Jal added, heading toward a line of the humped beasts they hoped to acquire, the men trailing after her.

"Camels?" Eamon wondered aloud, just as Phatomar had.

"No desert trek is complete without them," Jal called back over her shoulder. She pulled off her helm as she reached the camel merchant. His skin tone marked him as a desert dweller like Jal, and she no doubt wished to meet him face to face, no subterfuge to dirty their commerce.

The girl might not have had any experience with how to judge a decent horse, but she certainly knew the temperaments of camels. She also knew their worth, and she and the seller soon came to an agreement.

66

Only after monies had changed hands and she stood folding a map—one which, Phatomar noted, included the Fyum Oasis—did Jal ask the man their most pressing question.

"If one needed a way to find the Faqadat Alqalb, where might one start?" She kept her voice light, her attention on the creases of the parchment in her deft fingers. Nevertheless, the merchant tensed. Jal tucked the folded map in a pack and spoke bluntly to the man. "I have a bit of a familial problem, you see," she went on, building a tale. "My foolish younger brother has accepted a challenge from his betrothed to find the Heart Stone, and my elder brother, not able to leave the tribes, has sent me to fetch him back before he finds death instead, sending these brave guards with me." Her wide arm gesture included both Phatomar and Eamon. Phatomar, enjoying the tale she spun, tried to look the part, arms crossed over his chest and expression neutral.

"I am by far the better rider," Jal continued, "and my brother has only a couple of days head start, but I do not know where he heads." She sighed and shook her head, pushing a loose strand of her rust-coloured hair from her neck. "Unless you've seen him, then I fear I must find someone who can point me in the right direction."

The camel seller wavered, perhaps enchanted with her story, or the wide-eyed plea in her face. His lips twisted into a grimace.

"What does this brother look like?" he finally asked.

"He stands a hand and a half taller than me." She used her hands to demonstrate. "His hair is darker with curls that he keeps shorn short. He has a strong jaw and a crooked nose, and eyes the colour of a camel's. Wide shoulders but gangly limbs as he hasn't finished growing yet. Three years my junior. Traditional garb in tan hues, as any from the Gobani would wear, so I'm afraid that won't stand out."

Jal paused, staring expectantly at the man. After a moment of chewing on his lower lip, he shook his head.

"I haven't seen such a man."

Jal heaved a heavy sigh. "Then I shall have to look elsewhere. I just wish I knew where. My hope is that he'll start at the Fyum Oasis, but the longer I wander with no set destination, the greater the chance we will lose him

67

altogether." She growled, her brow creased in a frown. "I wish I knew whether his betrothed suffers from naivete or slyness, but whatever the case, I refuse to let her foolish whims destroy my kin." She blinked, glancing at the vendor with an apology in her eyes before she turned away. "Thank you for your time, merchant. I wish you calm winds."

Jal spoke to Phatomar and Eamon carefully in their language. "We will have to try elsewhere."

Eamon shrugged, his eyes danced merrily though he didn't smile, and he turned to lead her away, leaving Phatomar to bring up the rear. Before they had gone two steps, the merchant called to Jal. She stopped, looking back.

"I don't know the way to the Faqadat Alqalb," he said in a low voice. "But I know a man who might."

Jal returned to face him.

"Any help brings me hope," she said.

He studied her a moment, as though testing her resolve. "Look for a man at Fyum named Terek. He wears a purple turban and sells camel milk. If any can direct you, he can. Whether he will choose to do so, I cannot say."

Jal touched her forehead with the fingers of her right hand, pressed that hand to her heart, and bowed slightly.

"My thanks. May the god of sand and wind protect your herd, and may the goddess of water and the oases always smile upon you," she intoned.

The merchant smiled and echoed the hand gestures, though he didn't bow.

"May the deity of the hunt guide your steps and lead you to your kin before death takes him."

With that, Jal gathered her companions and their new camels, and retreated toward their accommodations in Hamiqa, following Eamon's lead.

"That went better than I'd hoped," Jal said. Eamon slowed to walk beside her, Phatomar lengthening his stride so that they all moved together.

"It was a good story," said Eamon with a grin. "Let's just hope this Terek can guide us further."

Chapter 6

It started as a smudge in the distance, a slight shimmer of hues beyond the dun of the sand dunes surrounding them, offering the hope of relief from the dry air and glaring sun. The haze resolved itself into the greens of tree and crop, the blue of water, and the domes of cream or brown tents adjacent to caravan wagons streaked with all colours of the rainbow as Fyum Oasis emerged from the desert.

Six days had passed since the travellers had left Hamiqa. A straight line across their map might seem like a shorter distance, but the sane followed the Water Roads, lest dehydration and exposure to the harsh elements leave them as nothing but bones to litter the dunes, swallowed and forgotten beneath the wind-scorched sands.

Eamon and Phatomar had deferred to Jal's experience, and they camped each night near an established water hole. The heroes might have trod upon parts of the desert lands in past adventures, but Jal had lived here for most of her life, and had seen what happened to the overly confident who thought to tempt fate.

Calling them the Water Roads implied a visible path upon which one might journey, but such a thing didn't exist in the desert, not with the god of sand and wind constantly changing the landscape. Only the oases and the wells remained constant, the first marked by tree-sheltered waters, the second by high flag poles and brick circles capped by stone to protect the precious liquid beneath the surface. Maps, such as the one Jal had obtained in Hamiqa, provided the only directions along these roads, and navigating based on shifting terrain and sun positions without the practised eye of one very familiar with the desert could bring dire consequences to the unwary.

To maintain the efficacy of Fyum Oasis, all travellers and merchants set their tents a respectful distance from the waters and the vegetation surrounding it. This gave the semi-permanent city around the Oasis a fluid and spherical appearance. The large pool of clear water gave rise to date and olive trees near its shore, small citrus plants benefiting from the shade of their taller cousins a little further out. A variety of local crops and those brought in over the years by visitors spread outward in a huge swath of green, yellow, red, and brown. Vendors who dominated the inner circle of domiciles kept a good two furlong buffer between themselves and the water's edge, some further, none closer, so that all might benefit from the bounty of the Oasis. These vendors had constantly migrating neighbours in a middle ring reserved for tents from the tribes, while the outer areas—some of which extended out into the sands—had space for caravan trains.

The closer Jal and her companions drew to the miles-wide Oasis, the more city-like it appeared, until tents and vegetation overtook the sand. One could almost forget that they stood in the midst of a desert, especially once the calls of birds, the skittering of lizards, the startling glimpse of sheep foraging, and the din of humanity surrounded them. Even having seen the phenomena before, this hive of activity in a sea of sand still managed to leave Jal breathless.

The trio dismounted as they drew closer to Fyum, leading both horse and camel behind them. Jal noticed Phatomar growing tense, while Eamon's eyes hooded with wariness. Fyum Oasis might run under a constant state of truce—no large gathering between the tribes could occur without guarantees of neutrality—but that didn't stop the anxiety of her friends given Phatomar's condition. And their quest to locate something most tribesmen only spoke of in guarded whispers, if they believed in the legends at all, might raise more than just eyebrows.

Jal tried to curb her enthusiasm at returning to the Fyum Oasis—the happy memories of her time here with Father no

70

doubt colouring her expectations—and keep a vigilant watch of their surroundings instead.

"There." Phatomar pointed with a jerk of his chin. Jal saw an area set aside as a large pen for pack animals. Mostly camels, some with bright blankets across their humps and others bare save for their bridles, but a few horses mingled in the mix and even a couple of shaggy oxen, though Jal had no idea how (or why) anyone could have encouraged the sluggish beasts to make a desert journey.

A similar enclosure rested at the western entrance to the Oasis, even if Jal couldn't see it from here. Travellers needed a safe place to leave their means of transportation while they conducted business without fear of theft or injury. Each compound had a shaded section made of canvas stretched across poles, a couple of central troughs for simple fodder, pails ready with drinking water, and several children assigned to watch over the animals. In addition to providing a safe place for mounts, these corrals kept the rest of the Oasis free from the bulk of the beasts (and their droppings) and more open for humans to roam.

Jal made arrangements for Croga, Cosantoir, Onoir, and the camels. The boy at the entrance handed her an intricately tied piece of cloth with yellow, blue, and dark brown tassels, which he quickly braided into six knots, tying its twin to one of the camels' bridles.

Eamon raised an eyebrow in question, and the lad spoke in a high, bored voice, giving an explanation he had likely repeated to countless others.

"So none take the wrong beasts by mistake, one knot per beast. Ifn you want to leave the saddles and packs, there's spot there." He gestured to a sheltered area with a series of woven shelves, mostly full of the gear of others, and dutifully watched over by another youth. "Knives is okay in Fyum so long's they don't draw blood, but long weapons stay here." Again, he gestured toward the shelves, and Jal saw three large racks bristling with swords, staves, and a mace. "Those you mark on your own ifn you want same ones back." He turned away, deeming his task complete. Jal stifled her grin as she turned to her companions. She spoke in the Merveah tongue as best she could.

"Do we leave packs here in hope of a fast answer, or do

we plan for a longer visit? We need to stay the night, but I don't know where best to camp."

Eamon frowned as he considered, and Phatomar stared with only a hint of visible trepidation toward the bustle of the Oasis.

"If we're here for the night regardless," Phatomar said, "we'll need to unsaddle the horses, but if we can leave our equipment in their care, Croga and Cosantoir will guard our packs better than any children."

Jal allowed her lip to form a half-smile.

"These children are trained to deal with trouble. They may look harmless, but no harm comes to those they watch."

"I have no doubt about the safety of our mounts," Phatomar said. "But the boy said himself that they don't care for the weapons or gear."

"No one steals from their fellow at Fyum," Jal insisted. "Rules make sure of it."

"Rules some might break," Eamon said, then held up a hand to forestall Jal's objection. "But no one has any reason to single us out." He glanced over at the storage shelves. "We'll leave the saddles and swords here, but take the saddlebags with us. The camels can hang onto our provisions, but I'd like our personal gear with us. If we are to stay the night, then let's find a place to set up camp before searching for our man."

Decision made, they left the pen with a bag each slung across their shoulders, heading into Fyum Oasis. A helpful sentry, identifiable by the black sash around his waist, pointed them toward an area for those who travelled with neither caravan nor tribe. As not many people made the journey without such escorts, they had different fire rings to choose from and soon had a tent set up, their gear stored within.

Back on the path kept clear for ease of movement, the three discussed their next step.

"The man we want sells camel milk," Eamon said. "So, where do we start to look?"

Jal nodded up the path as they walked. "The inner ring. Closest to the water. All merchants set up around its—" She searched for the word in Eamon's tongue, then scowled and gave up, switching back to her own language. "Sellers stay around the perimeter so that everyone going to the water will have to pass them, and hopefully purchase their wares in the process."

Eamon flashed a smile.

"Then lead on, mistress," he said in Merveah, then added quietly in the desert speech, "We're your guards, ignorant northerners who remain oblivious to the subtleties of the desert and its language. Hopefully an unnecessary precaution, but always best to stay vigilant."

Jal resisted the urge to plant a good-natured elbow in his gut, but only just. Instead, she raised her nose in the air to affect a northern haughtiness and strode out in front of them. Both men chuckled as they trailed behind.

***

Jal shimmied between pedestrians and potential buyers into spaces that at first glance seemed too tight for her to squeeze through. Eamon and Phatomar had no difficulty following in her wake, other shoppers either warned by her passage or simply cognisant of the approaching bulk of Phatomar. Everyone jockeyed for position while the flow of commerce remained fluid, turning a crowded and sprawling market into a kind of dance. Jal could imagine Phatomar's tension, boxed in with so many strangers, but she forced herself to continue their search, leaving her large friend to Eamon's subtle care.

Like the market at Ferna—like most markets she had ever visited—Fyum Oasis tried to keep similar wares together, some set out in the open on tables or shelves, others enfolded by tents which the owner could secure at night. Of course, the constraints of space between the vegetation of the oasis, and sometimes the confident aggression of a vendor, might cause disparate items to appear side by side.

In general though, food stuffs—both local sustenance and delicacies brought from afar—sat near stalls of prepared dishes and drinks. High quality gems worked into necklaces, bracelets or rings often appeared next to baubles and broaches incorporating simple glass beads, stone, or bone. The intricate works of gold- and silver-smiths, along with wonders fashioned from bronze, clustered near steel works offering daggers and swords (such weapons carefully wrapped and held at stalls near the entrances to the Oasis to await the departure of the buyer).

Jal hunted through the stalls set aside for camel blankets and saddles, camel-hair cloth, and other camel-based accessories, but they had yet to find a man in a purple turban offering camel milk. As the shadows stretched long, she feared they might not find their quarry before nightfall.

"How can no one know this Terek?" Phatomar griped as they stood in an aisle between a tack shop and a seller of meat pies. He sounded as frustrated as Jal felt.

"Perhaps he's moved on, and that merchant in Hamiqa simply didn't know," Eamon ventured. "Or he goes by a different name now."

"Or he made it up," Jal muttered. She shook her head, trying to quell the disappointment and frustration at her failure. She studied the market, some stalls already beginning to tidy up their wares and shut down for the night. She forced some levity to her voice. "Or our man sits just around the corner. We've only covered about three-quarters of the market. My feet can handle a little more abuse before the dark steals our chance of locating him today."

"As long as we have light to see, I'm game to keep going," Eamon said.

"Will we have enough time to get back to the tent before it's too dark to see?" A quaver in Phatomar's tone betrayed his unease.

"Lanterns line the main arteries of the Oasis," Jal told him. "Lit at dusk and extinguished at midnight. By then, everyone will sit at their own fire or sleep in their shelters. The stalls close when the lantern lighters come through, so we have until then." Jal studied the length of shadows, judging they had under an hour until dusk stole their chance of finding Terek.

Phatomar took a deep breath, then nodded. "Let's use the time wisely then."

Jal pushed back into the throngs of people, her eyes sharp as she examined each stall. If it contained neither camel milk nor a man in a purple turban, she moved on.

It took another half hour before she caught a glimpse of purple. She nearly cried out in relief, and just managed to keep herself from dashing forward. The dark-skinned man with the purple turban had soft bristles of steel and black adorning his chin and upper lip, and he seemed ready to close his tent for the night. When she reached him, he raised a hand to the folds of the canvas, a flash of ruby and the glint of gold outlining the ring on his index finger.

"Forgive me, master Terek," she chanced, hoping they had found the right man. "But a merchant in Hamiqa bid us to seek you out. Have you a moment?"

The man regarded her from nearly black eyes, a frown folding his face into a forbidding aspect. His gaze turned to Eamon and Phatomar, and his glower deepened.

"I have sold the last of my milk this day." The deep rumble of his voice reverberated in Jal's head.

"The merchant said you might have information that we desperately need," Jal said softly.

His eyes narrowed further. "I don't deal in information." The man turned his back on her, pulling one side of the canvas down.

"Please," she said, surprised at the pleading tone she forced into that one word. She opened her mouth to spout off the story she had told before of her errant brother's search for the Faqadat Alqalb, but the lie froze in her throat. Instead, as the man's shoulder hunched, ready to shrug her off, Jal remembered another pair of dark eyes that had bored into her.

Should you ever encounter a Kursak in need, she heard Cleo's voice. Jal fumbled at the pouch tied to her belt and reached inside, her fingers closing around a small cloth bag. She hadn't thought about the package since the crone had produced it—had forgotten to ask Eamon what she meant by *Kursak*, a term unfamiliar to Jal—but she suspected she looked at one now. Did it refer to his race, his religion, or something else entirely? It mattered not, not with this overwhelming desire to gift this stranger with Cleo's leaves.

"Please," she whispered, holding out the bag. "A merchant may have provided your name, but I believe someone more powerful wished us to meet."

The man spun to face her, the irritation in his gaze quickly turning to surprise at her outstretched hand and the offering therein. She had loosened the tie just enough so that he

75

could see the odd speckled leaves within. Whatever he saw there seemed to placate him, for he held open a flap of his tent and ushered them inside.

"Where did you come by those?" he asked as he closed off the tent to the darkening passage outside. A row of empty shelves and a cloth-draped table stood within his tent, along with a stool in the corner, but he moved no further than the entrance.

"A wise woman on a high mountain gave them to me," Jal said. "For a Kursak in need."

The man jerked as though she had slapped him. "And did she tell you my tale?" he asked acerbically.

"Being overly fond of riddles, she told us nothing beyond the phrase I just gave you." Jal responded. She saw a slight smirk of acknowledgement from the man and a sense of relief in his eyes. "As I said, a merchant in Hamiqa suggested your name." Jal hesitated. "Are you Terek?"

He stared at her, then her companions, and considered his response. Finally, he nodded. "I am."

"You've journeyed to the lair of the Faqadat Alqalb," Jal stated. "And you returned with your life. This tells me you possess both honour and caution. I hope it also means you can help us."

Terek shook his head. "That journey will kill you, child," he said in his deep voice. His looked to her friends again, then back to her. "It will kill you all. Glory and honour have little meaning once you're dead."

"We seek neither glory nor honour," Eamon said, his easy command of the desert tongue startling Terek. "And we do not quest for riches."

"Then what do you seek?"

"Answers," Phatomar whispered. "And the chance to regain what was lost."

Terek frowned, his streaked beard somehow making the expression more severe.

"Explain." He stared at Jal, waiting for her, rather than the men, to speak.

"The gods of the north have sent us on a journey." Although not sure why she felt compelled to reveal so much, she knew it important to offer this man the truth. "They forced Phatomar's hand when they stole his courage, along with his memories of himself. To restore his identity, we sought the advice of an Oracle. She told us: *'in a cavern beneath the sands far to the east, you will find the Faqadat Alqalb, the Heart Stone.'* I come from the Gobani, so I know the legends, but I do not know how to find it. Which brings us here, to you. Will you show us how to find the Heart Stone?"

His dark features grew sallow, his eyes haunted and sad.

"I cannot return to that place," he whispered.

"We don't ask that you do," Eamon assured him. "Only that you help us find the path." He pulled the folded map that marked the desert's water holes from his belt. "Where do we start?"

Terek stared at the paper, eyes clouded. He blinked away some terrible memory.

"The path leads to death," he warned.

"Nevertheless, it is the road we must take," Jal said, though Phatomar's deep frown gave her pause.

Terek reached out with reluctant fingers to take the map from Eamon. He unfolded the chart on the table and studied the markers. Finally, with a heavy sigh, he stabbed a finger at a barren area in the east, deep within the arid sands.

"The caverns lie within a rise of rock, two days from any water source," he said. "But more than killing sands and leeching heat guards Kahf Alramal. Beware of the Thueban Alnaas, for they do not tolerate intruders. More, I cannot say, not because I wish you ill, but because *any* further warnings are prohibited. Should you survive Kahf Alramal, you will understand."

He raised troubled eyes to Jal. "Your Oracle has set you upon a dangerous journey, child of the Gobani," he said. "Travel with a light tread upon the sands."

"Thank you." Jal handed him Cleo's bag of leaves, wondering what properties they held, but afraid to ask. Terek stared down at the gift for a long moment, then spoke without looking at her.

"If my cursed journey to find the Faqadat Alqalb hadn't included a vow to aid the one who bore cantas leaves, you might save yourself great trauma. As things stand, your wise woman gifted you not only with the means to locate a deadly place, but with a curse of your own, for any who reach the Faqadat Alqalb will find themselves burdened with terrible knowledge.

"My advice, to all of you," he said, drawing himself up in a manner both regal and regretful, "is to forego this leg of your quest. Some things are better left unknown." He shook his head. "Choose as you will. I can only wish you better luck than I endured."

With that, he moved to the tent's entrance and swept aside the drapes.

"May the gods guard you," he intoned, fastening the tent closed once they all stepped outside.

"Thank you for your guidance, master Terek," Jal said. "And for your warnings."

Terek huffed out a resigned breath, and walked away.

Men had begun to light the lanterns along the way. Jal turned toward the path that would take them to their tent, Eamon and Phatomar following behind, each sifting through their own thoughts in silence. She hadn't gone more than a dozen paces when a voice interrupted those thoughts.

"Well, if it isn't the little run-away," someone sneered from the side of the road. Jal faltered, staring in shock at the brown-haired tribesman who stepped toward her, two companions at his back. Eamon moved to block his path before Jal found her voice, sorely missing the anonymity of her concealing helm.

"It's hardly running away when the head of the family casts you out," she finally retorted, her voice level and calm. Jal took a step to stand beside Eamon, Phatomar a looming presence behind her. She stared up at a man she had not expected to ever see again. "I made my choice, Olbaehn, and I don't regret it."

Chapter 7

Jal quickly counted the months since she had left the Gobani, and then cursed her lack of foresight. She had never dreamed she might encounter her brother at Fyum Oasis, but she should have made an allowance for the possibility, given her tribe's annual excursion to the famed oasis. The leaders spent at least a month here after several days travel, conducting trades and alliances in neutral territory. Elders from the whole of the Gobani would filter into Fyum over this month and the next, including Olbaehn as least of the five elders of his tribe.

Jal had focused so much on their quest that she had lost track of the rest of the world. She didn't anticipate any harassment from the other tribes, and now that she knew others of her people might roam the oasis, she would plan to avoid them—but Olbaehn enjoyed making her life miserable. The faster she could extricate them from her brother's presence, the better Jal would feel.

"Peace of Fyum, Olbaehn," she muttered, pushing past him.

"That's all you have to say to your brother after disobeying him and running off?"

She should have known he wouldn't let her walk away so easily, for he fell into step next to her, shouldering Eamon out of the way without any thought toward courtesy.

Jal stopped and turned to face Olbaehn, signalling Eamon not to make a scene. She gave an exaggerated sigh. "I neither disobeyed you nor ran away. You cast me out, remember?"

"I remember a girl who had a tantrum because she didn't get her way," Olbaehn said, ignoring Jal's derisive snort. "I gave you time to cool down, and instead of finding a reasonable scion of the house ready to obey her leader after some time to think, I found only an empty tent." His brow drew down over honey-coloured eyes in a fierce scowl, which still looked to Jal more like a petulant child than any sort of leader. "Do you know how long it took me to placate Terandor?"

"Perhaps you should have thought before promising him a wife he would never have," Jal said. "You gave me a choice, Olbaehn: marry that odious man, or leave the tribes."

"Yes, but I didn't think you'd be foolish enough to actually follow through with that," he growled.

"Which just proves how little you know me, Olbaehn. You knew Father's wishes, and you knew mine. Why you would believe that your own petty desires and ambitions should overrule both of those, I can hardly fathom."

"I stand as one of the tribal elders now, Ajala—"

"And I would never interfere with that."

"You made a mockery of my first edict!" Anger turned his skin an unhealthy shade of burgundy in the fading light. Jal rolled her eyes.

"Shall we remove him for you?" Eamon asked in his own tongue. He almost sounded bored.

"He might wear himself out soon," Jal replied in the same language, proud of her increased fluency. "If we start to walk away again, he might stop speaking."

Olbaehn regarded her companions with a narrowed gaze.

"I see you've taken up with northern savages," he said, spite lacing his words. "You'd forsake your own people for such pale reflections?"

"Does he seek to bait you by insulting us?" Eamon asked.

"Yes. He thinks that if he can force me to show anger, he proves I'm unfit to live my life without the firm hand of a tribesman to keep me in line."

Phatomar leaned close. "He doesn't know you very well, does he?"

Jal gave a dry chuckle. "No, he doesn't. And he never did."

Olbaehn watched the interchange with suspicion. A malicious gleam lit his eyes.

"Have you taken one of these savages as a lover, then?" he smirked. "Or perhaps both? Bed a brute in exchange for safe passage through foreign lands? Tell me, little sister, how soon after you ran away did you whore yourself out?"

"Wow, he really *doesn't* know you." Eamon kept his tone light, but Jal saw a dangerous glint in his hazel eyes, one matched by the steel in Phatomar's stare. Olbaehn wouldn't know that Phatomar's fine tremble came from fear at the confrontation, not an eagerness to cause violence, despite her friend holding his ground.

Eamon addressed himself to Olbaehn in the desert tongue, his easy tone belying the rage that vibrated in his muscles. "We're not Jal's lovers. We're her brothers."

Olbaehn gaped at the slightly shorter man for a moment before he found his voice again.

"She has brothers. She doesn't need you."

"Well, she certainly doesn't need you, either," Eamon said. "Jal is her own person, and with *your* decision to cast her out, you have no further say in her life."

"She is my sister, and she will obey the commands of—"

"Enough, Olbaehn," Jal snapped. "We share blood, but by your own edict, we no longer share the tribes. You will cease to fault me for your arrogant belief that I should bow to your selfishness. You gave me a choice, and I took it. As you for some reason continue to think you have any say in my life, let me make this painfully clear." She stepped so close to him that a strong inhale would have them touching. "I am outcast, clanless. Ajala of the Gobani desert no longer walks this earth. I am Jal, warrior, sister to warriors, and of no concern to you."

She pushed past him again and marched into the deepening twilight, following the lantern-lit path away from the Oasis' core. Eamon and Phatomar paced quietly at her side.

She should have known Olbaehn wouldn't let her leave it at that.

***

Jal's brother dogged them like an angry shadow, his two guards striding at his heels. Eamon didn't know what Olbaehn expected of Jal, what he hoped to gain by pursuing her, but he did his best to follow Jal's lead and ignore the man.

Jal had never spoken much about the family she left behind, nor what had prompted her to leave the desert, but Eamon had a pretty good idea now of a part of that story. He couldn't blame her for choosing exile over staying anywhere near this pompous man with delusions of self-importance. Eamon knew more than he wanted to about such men. He himself had chosen a life of wandering rather than service to some petty ruler who allowed his own ambitions to blind him to the welfare of others. That had led him to Phatomar, a hero who did good wherever he went; a man worth following.

What would Jal do to Olbaehn if he wouldn't leave her alone? Her shoulders inched up toward her ears, her gait grew stiff and annoyed, but she didn't give Olbaehn the satisfaction of dictating her actions. Eamon found it amusing how Jal's refusal to further acknowledge Olbaehn's presence irritated her brother more than any insult could, until the desert man exploded into stupidity. Olbaehn shoved forward, trying to push between Eamon and Phatomar to reach Jal. Neither man budged. Despite his lack of courage, Phatomar held his ground, lightening Eamon's mood when Olbaehn growled his displeasure.

Undaunted, Olbaehn dodged around Eamon, hoping to get in front of Jal to continue his tirade. But Jal slid her foot deftly into Olbaehn's path without breaking stride, causing him to stumble and sprawl out onto the sand. Jal calmly stepped over him and continued along the lantern-lit road.

"Take the hint," Eamon said as he passed by. "She's done speaking with you."

Olbaehn, of course, didn't. He staggered to his feet and lunged after them again.

"Ajala," he called out, equal parts frustration and pleading. "Wait, please."

Perhaps the *please* made Jal pause, or perhaps the embarrassing spectacle of Olbaehn begging for attention. She turned to face him, hands on her hips as she scowled at Olbaehn. Eamon and Phatomar smoothly flowed to either side of the girl, showing solidarity by standing shoulder to shoulder with their companion.

"Give me one reason to continue wasting my time listening to your vitriol, Olbaehn." Jal said in a dangerously soft voice. Olbaehn opened his mouth to answer, the disdainful light in his honey-coloured eyes quickly morphing into caution as he noted Jal's unforgiving expression. *How often has he tried, and failed, to cow his strong-willed sister?* Eamon wondered. Did he finally realise the futility of trying to bully her?

"Does family mean nothing to you anymore, sister? Do you not even wonder how our siblings fare?" he asked.

"Clanless, Olbaehn," Jal replied in an even voice, although Eamon detected a hint of pain in her. Would Olbaehn recognise it as such or would he fail to understand even this much of his sister? "I knew when I accepted your decree of outcast—unintended or not—that I must forsake *all* ties to the Gobani, including family. I have no right to inquire after the well-being of those who are no longer part of my life."

Olbaehn stared at her for a moment, surprise writ plain across his features. He glanced at Eamon and Phatomar, loyal compatriots flanking her, then looked back to Jal, contemplation kindling in his gaze.

"Was it worth it?" he finally asked. All trace of animosity suddenly vanished as he truly tried to understand her decision. Eamon saw Jal's face soften just a fraction.

"Yes."

Olbaehn shook his head, not in negation but in consternation.

"I don't understand," he admitted.

"I know," Jal said. "But you've always wanted the role the tribe set out for you. Just as Zania and Teagan could find contentment as wives and wives-to-be. Even Nolbaehn fits the role of warrior and guard, assuming the imp has continued to practise. Father knew I would never find satisfaction as a wife, and he suspected you wouldn't adhere to his wishes to name me a guardian. You never look beyond yourself and your own notions of what role others should fill because you can't imagine someone wanting a different path than those offered by the tribes.

"Despite that, the choice you forced upon me hoping to strengthen your own position freed me as nothing else could.

Though I doubt you care for it, you have my thanks for that. Outcast and clanless, yes, but"—she met the regard of Eamon and Phatomar—"not without family, though we share no drop of blood." She turned to Olbaehn once more. "I have no business with the tribes here."

"Then why did you return?"

Jal blinked, startled by the question. "We merely pass through. Besides, this is Fyum, not the Gobani. We depart in the morning."

"Going where?"

Jal narrowed her eyes. "East, Olbaehn. Far from the tribes, so you needn't worry that I'll stumble across anyone you'd rather I avoid."

His eyes narrowed as he digested this. "What business do you have in the east?"

"My own," Jal said firmly, returning to the path once more. "And nothing that concerns you."

This time, Olbaehn didn't chase after them. Instead, another figure appeared on the path, waiting in the dusk. Jal's feet faltered, and she heaved something between a sigh and a sob.

Eamon studied this new person. The lack of light beyond the lanterns lining the path stole a degree of colour and detail from the man's face, but Eamon saw a youth bearing similar enough features to Jal and Olbaehn that he guessed they now faced Nolbaehn, her younger brother.

"First he didn't believe that I saw you," Nolbaehn said, a grin softening his strong jaw. "Now he won't leave you alone long enough for me to get a word in." Nolbaehn stepped forward, arms open in invitation. Instead of embracing him, Jal pulled back. A frown crossed Nolbaehn's face.

"You look good, Noll," she said quietly, her arms crossed as she held herself back. "But that's not how you greet a nameless outcast."

"*Outcast,*" Nolbaehn scoffed. "You're my sister, Ajala, and the best sparring partner I ever had. You know how hard it is to get a good workout with that lazy sod behind you?"

Eamon read pain in Jal's eyes. *Cares for this brother even as she chafes at the restrictions the other tried to enforce.*

"That's not an appropriate way to speak of a tribal elder," Jal admonished.

Nolbaehn frowned. "It's Olbaehn, Ajala. Taking Father's place hasn't changed his disposition."

"But it did make him an official authority, Noll. Lazy or not, he's head of your tent and you have a responsibility to uphold his honour as well as guard his person."

Nolbaehn snorted. "His honour. His stupidity, you mean. After all, he drove away his best defender."

Jal grimaced. "You're lucky I'm outcast, Noll, or I'd have to strike you for a comment like that. His best defender stands in front of me."

"No, she stands in front of *me*," he retorted. Then he grinned again. "And I can get away with stating such truths *because* you're outcast. No harm to the tribe means I'm safe from any sisterly chastisement."

Jal didn't return his smile, but Eamon thought he caught the glint of unshed tears before she blinked them away.

"Outcast also means you no longer have a sister."

He waved a hand, dismissing her concern. "Bah. A word doesn't change what my heart knows, Ajala, and nothing Olbaehn decrees will alter that simple fact." This last he said over Jal's shoulder loud enough for Olbaehn to hear as he waited, a silent shadow at the edge of the path. Eamon heard a snarl from the elder brother, but Olbaehn made no other response.

"However," Nolbaehn continued. "In deference to the peace of Fyum, and as a way to actually speak with my *sister*, I shall greet you more properly. One warrior to another." He slapped a fist to his chest in a salute. "By what name shall I address you, clanless outcast?"

Although he kept his tone light, a serious weight had stolen across his features. Jal hesitated before returning the salute.

"I have taken the name Jal," she answered. Finally, a small smile played at her lips. "And that's the proper way to greet one such as myself."

"Pfft," he mocked, widening Jal's smile. Eamon felt his mouth quirk at the lad's irreverence. Nolbaehn turned to him and Phatomar. "And your companions? Who are these brave men who travel with a desert outcast?"

"Eamon, son of Branon, and Phatomar, son of Gordukah, I present you to Nolbaehn of the Gobani," Jal introduced. Eamon saw Nolbaehn's eyes widen at the names—or rather, at Eamon's name. With Phatomar's identity stolen, only Eamon's name might spark any sort of recognition, though he didn't know what sort of tales had reached as far as the Gobani. Jal hadn't said much beyond that she knew some of their adventures borne by tinkers and traders. Obviously, her brother knew something of those stories too.

Nolbaehn repeated his salute for each of them. "Peace of Fyum, brother warriors." Then he paused, slanting a concerned look at Jal. "I did hear at least one of them speak to Olbaehn, didn't I?" he asked. "They can understand me?"

"We can," Phatomar replied.

"Then let me express my appreciation for making my—" he bit his lip and tried again. "For making Jal's exile count for something. I don't know what she's up to, but I can see that she's found a purpose. If you're accompanying her, I can only assume that you share that purpose."

"Don't, Noll," Jal warned.

"Don't what?" He sounded far too innocent.

"You can't come with us, and I won't tell you what we're doing."

His eyes narrowed. "Then it's a good thing you have *someone* to guard your back." Nolbaehn stared hard at Eamon and Phatomar. He chose to keep eye contact with Eamon, perhaps as the man closer to his own size and the less physically intimidating. "Whatever takes you into the east," he said, proving that he'd stood close enough to overhear at least some of their exchange with his brother, "make sure she stays out of trouble. Or at least—" he spared another cocky grin for Jal. "As out of trouble as she'll let you."

"This one understands you," Phatomar said in an aside in their own language.

Jal smiled. "Yes, he does."

Eamon managed a mostly solemn nod to Nolbaehn, trying to smother a laugh.

"We'll do our best," he assured the young man.

Nolbaehn stepped forward and clapped Eamon on the shoulder. "Good. Let's find some food and drink, and you can tell us unbelievable stories of what Jal's done these last few months."

"Nolbaehn," his brother growled. He finally moved forward,

placing him next to his brother, his two guards joining them. "She's outcast."

"And we're at Fyum," Nolbaehn responded with a shrug. "Nothing forbids travellers gathering for refreshments, regardless of their origin."

"A quick meal," Eamon said with a glance to Jal to gauge her reaction. She nodded.

"But none of your *special* wine," she said with a stern wag of her finger. "We have an early morning and no need of a sore head."

Nolbaehn shrugged, a mischievous spark in his eyes. "Suit yourself. You don't know what you're missing."

"Oh, yes I do," Jal said with a laugh.

"Well, *they* don't," he amended, indicating Eamon and Phatomar.

Eamon smiled, then turned his attention to the scowling Olbaehn. "By your leave," Eamon addressed himself formally to the tribal elder. "Lead on to your tent."

Olbaehn hesitated and Eamon wondered whether he'd take the olive branch his brother wanted to extend. Finally, grumbling, he motioned to Nolbaehn.

"You know the way, little fiend."

The youth spun and led the group back toward the tent city ringing Fyum Oasis.

Chapter 8

They spent a surprisingly enjoyable evening with her brothers, Olbaehn relenting enough to stop shooting Jal querulous scowls as they shared a simple meal in his tent. She, Eamon, and Phatomar took their leave shortly before midnight, finding their way back to their camp as the lamplighters began to extinguish the guiding flames along the path.

When the first hints of dawn began to swallow the pinpricks of the vast multitude of stars, the trio packed up camp and retrieved their camels and gear, adding several soft-sided flasks filled with water to the saddles. The horses stood restless as the humans led the humped beasts away, but slightly wizened apples appeased them, and they settled. Jal felt a pang of foreboding to leave them behind, as though they abandoned their loyal mounts, but she pushed it aside. They *would* come back.

Assuming they succeeded at what Terek had called the Kahf Alramal—Jal refused to believe they might fail in their search, lest her nerve abandon her completely—they would have to return to Fyum before continuing to the Blackened Fields. According to the map and Terek's instructions, no other significant shelter crossed their route. Keeping the horses in the oasis' corral made the most sense.

Noll had promised to care for the animals for up to three weeks—the length of time Olbaehn and the tribal leaders planned to stay for the annual gathering. Giving Noll a reason not to follow her eased Jal's mind somewhat. Not that her brother would actually abandon his duty to the tribe for her—despite his youth, Noll would do his best for the people—but giving him a task that Olbaehn didn't disagree with helped ensure that her brother would leave his curiosity unanswered.

They turned the camels toward the rising sun and set off into the desert.

Several hours later, the hot sun glared down from a cloudless, unforgiving sky. Scorched sands released waves of unrelenting heat, and the air hung still and dry. No breath of wind provided even the illusion of relief, yet Jal found herself enjoying the journey from Fyum. She wore a damp length of fabric wrapped around her head and trailing over her shoulders, and a loose desert garment covered her arms and legs. Her camel carried the burden of her and her supplies across the dunes, leaving her free to navigate.

According to the area signalled out by Terek, they would pass three wells before having to venture into the deadly desert, devoid of further access to water. Another hour's ride this afternoon would see them to the first well for the night.

"What's wrong, Phatomar?" Eamon's soft voice carried in the still air. Jal glanced over her shoulder, noting Phatomar's frown as he glanced back the way they had come.

"I'm no expert on the shifting sands and mirages in this heat," Phatomar said, hand held over his brow to shield his eyes. "But I keep thinking I'm seeing something behind us. It disappears in an illusive wave, but I swear it reappears more than it should."

Jal looked back while she continued to guide her camel forward. She watched the horizon, as did Eamon and Phatomar, and soon, she saw it too.

"Someone's behind us."

Eamon shaded his eyes and peering in the distance. "Another traveller?"

Jal shrugged.

"We are heading to the nearest water source. Just because we haven't encountered anyone else doesn't mean we travel the desert alone." She considered the way ahead. "We haven't really run the camels hard today. We can give them a bit of a push, reach the well a little quicker, and wait to see who else might join us for the night. I don't imagine they mean us any harm, though."

Still, in the back of her mind, Jal couldn't help wondering: *did Noll find a way to follow me anyway?* She hoped not, for Olbaehn's sake at least. Her elder brother got himself into less trouble when watched over by the younger.

The three urged their camels to a faster pace, reaching the watering hole with plenty of time to set up camp. They had a small fire fuelled mostly by dried camel dung prepared in one of the three fire pits and a modest meal shared between them by the time the rider following in their wake came close enough to make out any details. The sun sat low on the horizon behind him, shading his face and stretching his shadow long from where he sat atop his camel. With a jolt of shock, Jal recognised the colourful blanket stretched across the camel's hump.

Noll hadn't followed them; Olbaehn had.

She rose to her feet, Eamon and Phatomar also standing, as Olbaehn came to a stop and dismounted. They stared at one another in a silence, interrupted only by the brief sigh of relief from Olbaehn's camel. Jal had never felt so unbalanced in her life. She couldn't find any words. Luckily, Eamon could.

"Why did you follow us?" he demanded. A simmering anger had replaced Eamon's jovial tone. His fingers curled atop the pommel of the sword sheathed at his side in undisguised hostility. Olbaehn hesitated an instant, perhaps sensing the threat, but he didn't retreat. Instead, he held Jal's eye.

"I know what you're doing."

"I doubt you do," she replied.

"Leading a couple of foreigners to the east?" Olbaehn raised an eyebrow in disbelief. "Unless they've a keen interest in the colourful basket weaving of the Krokos, or a desire to expanding this tiny herd of camels from the breeders at Anrabi, then only one thing would hold any interest for them in the far eastern sands. You're chasing legends of glory and wealth."

"We're not looking for glory *or* wealth, Olbaehn," Jal said. "And as I told you before, my business does not concern you. So I'll repeat Eamon's question: why did you follow us? And how are you here alone?" she added as an afterthought.

"Where are your guards?"

"They're watching over Noll, keeping my sibling out of mischief while he deals in my name." Olbaehn's brow creased. "The same thing I'm doing, actually. You may have scorned the tribes, Ajala, but you're still my sister. Believe it or not, that makes you my concern."

"How many times must I remind you," she retorted. "I am outcast, and you are absolved of any responsibility of my actions."

"Being outcast doesn't mean I stopped caring about you!" Olbaehn shouted, checking himself from grabbing her shoulders only because Eamon's sword edge suddenly caressed his neck. Olbaehn froze, his eyes wide, reflecting a mix of temper, wariness, and some other emotion Jal couldn't identify. She just stared at him, not fully believing his impassioned outburst, yet not able to dismiss it either. Olbaehn had always had a strange way of showing *any* depth of feeling, making it difficult to discern where his mind lay. Yes, he cared about his family to a certain extent, but he had never known how to show those feelings beyond expected platitudes, nor how to disassociate his own desires from what anyone else wanted.

Olbaehn held his hands out to his sides, taking a half step away from Jal. Eamon allowed the move, lowering his blade without resheathing it. She heard a sigh of relief from Phatomar, noting the large man trembling, though he held his ground. Lack of courage might still his hand and freeze his thoughts in times of peril, but real concern for her had kept his feet planted despite his instincts screaming at him to retreat.

"Listen," Olbaehn said. "I know the stories as well as anyone, and heading into the deep desert of the east alone will get you killed."

"Then it's a good thing I'm not going alone," she replied, feeling her lips twist into a snarl. She wouldn't let Olbaehn insult her friends so casually.

"These aren't desert men, Ajala," Olbaehn tried again. "I'm sure they're fierce warriors in the north, but no amount of swordplay and soft living can prepare a man for the dangers of the sands."

"Soft living?" Eamon quipped. "Is that what we've done?"

Jal snorted, glad to see his levity reasserting itself. He still stood at the ready, but she no longer felt the imminent possibility of bloodshed looming overhead.

"I don't think he'd have fared any better than I did at Hada," she said. "But then, he knows the desert, not the snows." She returned her attention to her brother. "We know the dangers and have prepared as best we can, Olbaehn, but we won't retreat from our quest, no matter your warnings."

"Who said anything about retreating?" Olbaehn asked.

Jal frowned. "You can't come with us."

"You can't stop me."

Eamon's sword rose again. This time, Olbaehn just stared at him, then made to push the blade aside. When it didn't waver, Olbaehn growled and ducked under it. Eamon whipped a foot out, tripping Olbaehn, then followed him to the ground. The northerner's knee on the tribesman's chest pinned him as he lay sprawled in the sand. Olbaehn turned a deep shade of red as he spluttered against Eamon's hold.

"Get off me!"

Eamon let him struggle for a moment. He looked to Jal, who gave a small nod. Only then did Eamon release Olbaehn. The desert man rose slowly to his feet, brushing sand off his leggings and straightening his long tunic.

"As you can see," Jal murmured. "We most certainly *can* stop you if we wish. Save yourself the embarrassment and go back to Fyum. The tribe needs you; I do not."

"Don't do this, Ajala," her brother pleaded. "Don't throw your life away so that strangers can add another story to their boasts. The curse that follows anyone who survives the search for the Faqadat Alqalb isn't worth your life."

"As I said, Olbaehn, we're not looking for glory or wealth, and we're certainly not doing this to make a story," she said, oddly touched by his concern.

"Then why?" he asked, anger and frustration colouring his tone. "Did being made outcast addle your brains? Why risk everything for something you can't possibly obtain?"

Irritation now overrode her previous sentiment. "Some things are worth risking your life for," she said. "Friendship, for one. Giving a good man a chance at redemption. Righting a wrong done by those who have power over the weak. We follow a course to restore something stolen, something beings greater than ourselves have bid us to seek out. To do so, we must head east."

Olbaehn's eyes narrowed.

"Beings greater than yourselves?" He barked out a laugh. "You *are* addled. You think the gods have set you a task? You? An outcast girl who threw a tantrum? And you wonder why you need a brother's hand to guide you!"

Jal felt her face darken, not a blush of humiliation but the flush of fury. She bit off the curse that leapt to her tongue and instead turned her back on Olbaehn.

"I hear empty words from one not worthy of my time," she announced with cold precision, cursing Olbaehn in a different way. "This man is a stranger whom I do not see."

"You're ostracising *me*?" Olbaehn scoffed. "You're already outcast, Ajala. No one but you will even know of your attempt to shame me."

"We know," Phatomar said, his deep voice reverberating despite how quietly he spoke. "And there is no one here named Ajala, only Jal."

"You have no connection to Jal, stranger," Eamon added, at last sliding his sword into its scabbard. "And you have no voice here either. The well is neutral territory, but you will find no welcome in our camp. If you have any brains, you'll return to Fyum in the morning and forget about the sister you once had."

"You can't do this!" Olbaehn said. Jal ignored him and moved to sit by their unlit fire. Eamon and Phatomar joined her. Eamon got a flame going as the sun's rays began to stain the sands in streaks of gold and red. They did their best to pretend that the irate man who had once stood as her blood brother didn't stomp around nearby. Olbaehn made it difficult to ignore him, but Jal had declared him a stranger. As of this moment, Olbaehn didn't exist to her.

With that thought firmly in mind, she followed what had become their evening routine.

Rising to her feet and moving a few paces away from the fire, she discarded her thin outer cloak so that she stood only in a light tunic and loose leggings. She reached behind her shoulder to the sword at her back, drawing the weapon with a hiss from its sheath. Eamon gave a small smile before he stood and moved opposite her, his own desert garb left by the fire, his sleeveless vest revealing the firmness of muscles on torso, arms and shoulders. He pulled his own sword free once more and with a grim nod, they saluted one another. Then they began to spar.

"What are they doing?" Olbaehn asked Phatomar. The large man who had kept his seat by the fire continued to ignore Olbaehn, his focus trained on Jal and Eamon. Phatomar had taken to studying their moves and even on occasion offered an opinion on technique, though he had yet to join them in their practice. Phatomar's body knew how to flow through the moves Eamon taught her, even if the large warrior's mind reeled from the thought of holding a weapon with lethal intent.

Jal still had hopes that he might come to see their training bouts as something more like a game or a form of exercise, something that he would not see as a task tied to courage. He had shown promise on previous nights, and would go so far as to circle Eamon and Jal in their martial dance to better observe them, in a way adding his own steps as he evaded them. On this night, though, Phatomar wouldn't leave his place by the fire, not with Olbaehn there as witness.

Again, Jal pushed Olbaehn from her mind, concentrating on matching Eamon's fluid motions. The sun slipped away beneath the world, bringing an explosion of stars into the night sky, thousands of ethereal pinpricks sparkling against a pitch backdrop. The goddess of the moon still slumbered in her ebon cloak, hiding her face in the early hours of the night. The snapping light of the fire painted Eamon's figure to Jal's eyes, and the mingling of both stars and flames provided enough illumination for the duellists to whirl across the sands of their camp without misstep.

Jal soon found herself in a kind of trance, engulfed in the motions of her own body and the sword in her hands as it met and countered Eamon's blade, and yet aware of her surroundings beyond the man facing her. She smelled the smoke from the fire, pungent in a different way than the wood flames in the north. Sand shifted beneath the soft soles of her light boots as she flowed from one move to the next, forcing her to compensate for the less sure footing of an ever changing landscape. Sweat beaded on her brow and dampened her tunic, quickly leached away by the dry air.

94

Though the night had stolen the warmth of the day, Jal's exertions kept her from feeling the chill, and she would find comfort from the raw cold of night in the sheltering walls of their tent when they finally retired.

The clang of metal on metal echoed around the well as they sparred; the soft *shush* of displaced sand made an arrhythmic counterpoint to their harsh breaths. Eamon pushed her hard tonight, perhaps sensing her need for diversion. The camels gave the occasional bleat or groan as they settled, and the fire hissed quietly to itself. Otherwise, no sound disturbed the camp.

Then Eamon gave a mighty shout intended to put Jal off her guard. He rushed her, ready to sweep a leg out from under her and declare a victory. But Jal turned her surprise into a deft block, leaping over Eamon's lunge and unbalancing him in the sand. He teetered for just an instant; all the time Jal needed to twist herself around his body as she released her sword.

Eamon spun as he fell, sword raised to catch Jal's attack but meeting empty air. She followed him down, pinning his legs with hers, and laid the edge of her palm rather than the length of her blade gently across his neck. His weapon would have caught hers and turned it aside had she still held it, but her hand had slipped past his guard. This move she had learned in the desert, and she doubted it would fool Eamon twice. Right now, though, she chuckled through her heaving breaths at the wide-eyed astonishment of the man now at her mercy, his own lungs fighting for air. Unwrapping herself from him, Jal stood, offering her hand to help Eamon to his feet. Behind her, she heard a low, deep voice speaking quietly.

"She's really quite good, isn't she?"

Jal spun in surprise, but Olbaehn had turned away from Phatomar and went to his camel, where he took out a small shelter, setting it up on the opposite side of the well. He said nothing further before disappearing inside it.

Jal shook her head, truly not knowing what to think.

When she retired for the night, having cleaned up and changed from practice, she still remained uncertain what to think of Olbaehn—his presence or his words. She knew only that she couldn't allow him to distract her from their quest.

The Oracle had sent them on this path to restore Phatomar to himself; neither Olbaehn, nor anyone else, would hinder their progress.

Chapter 9

"Run!" Jal yelled. The brown haze of cloud streaked with flashes of purplish lightning roared toward them across the increasingly rocky landscape.

Phatomar finished tying a damp cloth about his nose and mouth and crouched low over the back of his camel, urging the beast to even greater speed. With a bleat of protest, the camel dredged up extra strength from somewhere to comply, trying to outrun the sand storm that chased the riders across the desert. He silently thanked whatever gods might listen for Jal's foresight in this matter. Despite the nobility and loyalty of their northern mounts, the sands would have defeated horses, stranding the group in inhospitable terrain long ago.

The past five days had given Phatomar a greater appreciation for the stubborn hearts and incredible fortitude of these awkward southern beasts. The sure-footed and strangely fluid motions of the camels over the sand, even under his weight, impressed Phatomar, as did their ability to conserve water. The amount of water alone that they would have had to transport for horses would have weighed them down unreasonably. The humans needed far more liquid than the camels and quenched their thirst often, while the camels made do with filled bellies from the last watering hole.

Although the wind had sometimes brought a swirl of sand to hinder their vision for brief moments, this current storm posed a much greater threat than anything they'd faced so far. He remembered Jal's warnings of the capricious temperament of the desert: the scorpions, spiders, and snakes that might surprise the unwary; the biting and crawling insects that sheltered in the shade of boulders where one might hope to find a hint of comfort in the high heat of they day; and the vicious bursts of wind which pulled loose sand into violent vortexes, deadliest when accompanied by the warning of thunder, for that could bring rain. The rare occurrence of rain in the deep desert did not mix well with sand, creating the very real possibility of floods, especially in lower areas like the depression they currently traversed.

Terek had pointed out the rise of rock that led to the caverns they sought on the map, but the path to that rock lay through a valley. Should a storm break, and they didn't reach the higher ground at the entrance to Kahf Alramal, they faced the horrifying prospect of drowning in the desert. Equally terrifying, the whipping sands that now stole sight would ensure they never saw the arrival of that death until too late.

Phatomar clung to his mount, trusting the beast to see what he himself could not. Already, his friends had disappeared in the onslaught of sand and wind. Where a moment before he had seen Jal quickly protect her face with a cloth as she shouted her warning, he saw now only a cloud of yellow-brown. Eamon, a solid presence next to him, no longer presented even a shadowy outline. And Olbaehn, following in stubborn silence behind like a bad omen, yet also providing an oddly comforting rear guard, had vanished from Phatomar's sight. Only the camel beneath him, its straining neck barely visible as it raced through the tempest, held any sense of reality to him.

He grasped the reins in a painful grip and squeezed his eyes shut, tears of terror threatening to choke him. His heart pounded more fiercely than the camel's legs. Dread strangled him in an inescapable embrace. He could only pray that they reached the end of the trail together, but part of him feared that their path would lead to the underworld.

It took a moment for Phatomar to realise that the voice of the storm had changed and that the whipping sands had ceased to lash his skin. The roar of the wind became an eerie whistle, no longer ripping at his loose clothing. His camel slowed, then stopped with a groan, its lungs heaving between Phatomar's stiff knees. Phatomar sat there panting, hearing his own whimpers over the wind and hating that he couldn't make them cease. His muscles cried in agony as he tried to gather his resolve, searching for any hint of comfort as Jal had tried to teach him.

It didn't occur to him to try and open his eyes, the blackness just another arm of dread he couldn't banish. He longed for the comfort of courage even if he couldn't remember what that felt like.

Surely better than this mind-numbing state of paralysis.

Something touched his leg. "Phatomar."

Phatomar screamed and wrenched away, tumbling from his saddle onto the rocky ground before his mind translated that touch into the knowledge of a hand. The voice, he realised too late, belonged to Eamon.

Phatomar forced his eyes open. Eamon crouched beside him, concern and compassion visible in the dim light. They had reached the shelter of a cave, the storm blocking out much of the day as it raged across the nearby entrance, but not sucking away all sight. Phatomar's camel looked down at him with mild curiosity, Jal holding its reins and stroking its nose. She pulled the wrap from her face and offered him a tight smile before checking on the other mounts. Olbaehn's shadow stepped closer, an air of menace about him. Phatomar cringed.

"What's wrong with you?" the man demanded, disgust plain on his shadowed face.

"Leave off," Jal snapped, the first words she had spoken to her brother since she'd ostracised him. Olbaehn started, clearly surprised. He looked over to where she stood, then scowled and pulled back, leaving Phatomar alone with Eamon.

Eamon quirked a smile and stood, offering a hand to Phatomar. The larger man took it and stood, leaning a bit on Eamon, both amazed and grateful that his companion didn't see it as a weakness.

"Assuming we haven't followed false directions," Eamon said, "and thanks to the incredible navigational skills of Jal, I believe we've found our way to the cavern beneath the sands."

"Now we'll see what great task the Oracle envisioned when

she sent us here," Jal added as she joined them.

"Oracle?" Olbaehn asked. "What's this nonsense about?"

Phatomar realised they had spoken the desert tongue, unwittingly adding Olbaehn to the conversation. The man still believed they searched for treasure and glory, or at least that they followed a trail of folly. Ignoring Olbaehn hadn't turned him aside; leaving without informing him of their departure hadn't dissuaded him; forcing him to fend for himself hadn't put a hitch in his stride. But what good now leaving him in ignorance? Olbaehn might have scoffed when Jal mentioned higher beings; that didn't preclude their existence. And the Oracle herself had said they would find help and hindrance along the way. Until now, Phatomar—like Eamon and Jal, he suspected—had thought of Olbaehn as a hindrance. What if he, in truth, also represented help?

Either way, continuing to ignore him might put their quest in jeopardy. According to Jal, those seeking the Faqadat Alqalb for selfish reasons would find death. If Olbaehn continued with them in the belief that they sought wealth, he might inadvertently doom them.

"On the day we met Jal," Phatomar told him now, "the gods stole something from me." He went on to explain Jal's intervention in the fight, looking for answers in Grandon, and hearing the words of the Oracle as they followed the advice of a god. He didn't embellish anything and left out details unimportant to Olbaehn's understanding, but he also stressed that their need of the Faqadat Alqalb didn't lie in the lust for glory or riches.

"That's ridiculous," Olbaehn scoffed after a moment of silence, then surprised Phatomar with what he said next. "You've come to find the Heart Stone in order to bargain for your life back. How do you *not* see that as a lust for glory and riches? Perhaps you don't seek financial gain, but you can hardly call this so-called quest selfless. If you do this, what you gain only benefits you. Your courage, which, given your stature, would allow you to dominate most men. And having knowledge of your past deeds restored? What is reputation but another form of currency to barter with? I'd call those very selfish reasons."

The three stared at him in shock. Outside, a clap of thunder shook the skies and the heavens opened up, drowning the earth in a torrent of heavy rain.

Jal spoke quietly, barely audible over the rain and wind. "If we only sought a solution for Phatomar's quandary, I would agree that we had selfish motives." She sounded contemplative. "But we have a larger goal than merely restoring one man's courage and memories." With the daylight dimmed by the storm and muted by the cave's walls, Jal's tawny eyes had taken on an odd reflective glow, her intensity evident even among the shadows.

"Whether you believe me or not," she said to Olbaehn, "I heard the voices of *gods*. The god of warriors sent us to an Oracle, who in turn set us upon this quest. Do I believe we have a chance to restore what *gods* took from Phatomar? Yes. Do I believe that's the sole purpose of what these gods and Oracles expect of us? No."

Phatomar blinked in surprise at the conviction in her tone. He had thought himself alone in his questioning why gods would signal him—them—out. Had the gods a deeper purpose for what they had done? Had they chosen Phatomar because they knew Eamon would make sure he followed through on the course the gods set? Phatomar wanted his courage and his memories back, true, but that alone hadn't driven him. The desire—the innate *need*—to understand the will of the gods played a large part.

But then, why take so much away in the first place? He and Eamon would have tackled any quest the gods asked (or so Eamon's stories of their past deeds suggested); why then cripple Phatomar, send him to perform these tasks with part of himself missing? Unless that lack had some significance.

He regarded Jal's serious expression. *Or perhaps the sudden loss of my courage would bring forth someone also necessary for our fated journey.* He recalled Dearn's words in Grandon: *"It is for you three together to walk the path that might restore a warrior to their rightful place."* Jal had a role to play in their saga, and for some reason, so did his lack of courage. The first step meant finding the Faqadat Alqalb; not for himself, but because the gods demanded it.

It sounded arrogant to Phatomar, presumptuous, but it also felt *right*.

"We began this journey to help Phatomar," Eamon said, his thoughts obviously following a similar line. "And while

101

retrieving what capricious gods stole remains high on my priorities, Jal's right. It's not the sole purpose of our journey. If whatever guardians who oversee the well-being of the Heart Stone deem our presence selfish and overlook those who sent us here, then we'll have to find a way to change their minds."

The smaller man rested his hand on the hilt of his sword. Phatomar frowned, wondering whether, with his courage intact, he might also resort to might before words. He didn't think that, in a place where to seek wealth brought death, and the search for glory resulted in awe and horror, the threat of violence would impress any who safeguarded such treasures. A sword wouldn't help them prevail; they needed clearer minds if they hoped to fulfill this task—whatever it truly entailed. *Less courage and more foresight.*

"Let's find the Faqadat Alqalb first, see who or what guards it"—Terek, Phatomar remembered, had called them the *Thueban Alnaas*—"before we make any rash decisions. I'd rather not have to fight for the Heart Stone, and I don't believe it's a lack of courage alone that prompts that feeling." He turned to Eamon, saw his friend hesitate, then nod as he pulled his hand from his weapon.

Olbaehn shook his head. "You're all crazy," the desert man said. "But you also truly believe you have a right to stand here and demand what countless others have failed to obtain." Then, to their surprise, he grinned. "I'm glad I followed you, if only to witness the wonders these gods expect of you."

Although Olbaehn likely meant the statement as a taunt, Phatomar couldn't help but shiver at such a weighty portent. What *did* the gods expect?

***

They left the camels sheltered at the entrance to the caverns. Jal retrieved a bundle of torches from her pack and lit one, its light outlining the cave formation surrounding them.

With water skins strapped to each belt, the group moved deeper into what Terek had called Kahf Alramal, a complex series of natural caves and tunnels etched into the rock. In some places, sand had swept in from small fissures above to coat an array of rocks and boulders. Other areas boasted sculpted stalactites and stalagmites, some fused into towering columns while others still reached toward each other in an unfulfilled yearning to embrace. One section glittered in the glow from their lit torch, a huge swath of crystals jutting at odd angles to paint the cavern in prismatic shards of colour. In the next chamber, flecks of shining stones reflected from the walls—minerals, metals, or gems, Jal didn't know.

At each junction, they took the right most path, Eamon smudging a mark on the wall to trace their progress. If they found nothing before the tunnel branch petered out, they would retrace their steps, try another route. Equally important, they could find their way back to the entrance with their camels and supplies.

They entered a rocky cavern that brought with it a startling scent; the smell of water. Jal thrust her torch forward, amazed to see the edge of a pool outlined in her flames. The slow yet steady *plink* of water dropping from high above to feed the pool echoed in the cavern.

"Did you hear that?" Olbaehn demanded in a harsh whisper. His gaze focused into the dark recesses they had yet to explore, hearing something beyond this life-giving source.

"Hear what?" Eamon pitched his voice low, barely making a sound.

Then they heard it too, the dry scrape of something dragging over rocky ground accompanied by a hiss.

"Snake," Jal warned. Her eyes swept the chamber for the source. "Watch your step." While snakes generally avoided humans, they would defend themselves if startled or threatened.

"That's no ordinary snake," Olbaehn said. Jal wanted to chastise him before his panic spread to her companions, but she feared he had it right. Another sound accompanied the slithering which echoed in the chamber; the light tread of feet and a strange sibilant communication. Jal heard at least two different hissing noises, and to her distinct discomfort, could have sworn they made up a conversation. *Do snakes talk to each other?* she wondered.

"We tolerate no outsssidersss here," a voice hissed from

the darkness in the desert tongue. She heard Olbaehn's gasp and Phatomar's whimper as a figure stepped into the light of her torch. She could only gape at the creature revealed, a bow held drawn and steady in stubby fingers, nocked arrow levelled at her chest.

It had the highly muscled arms and bare torso of a man, long pale legs partially obscured by a knee-length skirt made of narrow strips of some kind of skin, and bare webbed feet splayed wide in a fighter's stance. Behind him, a long serpentine tail twitched in agitation, thick and strong and dark. The flat head and flaring hood of a cobra extended from its dense neck, pearly iridescent scales at the shoulders morphing into ebony swirls the higher they climbed. His wide lidless eyes, pools of midnight bisected by a slash of gold, reflected in Jal's flame. That sinuous neck turned an otherwise six-foot creature into a towering nightmare that loomed an extra foot above even Phatomar's head. A red forked tongue so dark it appeared black flicked between pebbled lips, as though tasting the air. Or perhaps the quality of the intruders.

A second figure, only a little shorter than the first, stepped up beside his companion, his bow levelled at Jal's companions. Other shadows further back, accompanied by the dry *shush* of serpentine tails, told of yet more beings waiting beyond the blush of light.

"There's more back here," Eamon murmured as he pressed his back against Jal's, ready to defend himself, though willing to take his cue from others before drawing his blade. Jal suspected Phatomar's words earlier advising caution had stayed Eamon's hand as much as the strange spectacle before them. After all, Eamon had seen many bizarre things in his adventures; perhaps half-men half-snake creatures seemed normal to him. Jal found herself somewhere between terror and fascination.

Surprisingly, Phatomar inched forward. He visibly steeled himself, straightened his broad shoulders, and stared up at that flared hood, the flickering tongue, those unblinking eyes.

"We—" His voice broke and he cleared his throat. "We wish you no harm." His arms trembled and Jal reached out to lay a hand on his shoulder, offering what strength she could. He gave her a slight nod, then forced his attention back to the snake-man. "The Oracle at Hada guided our steps to your door. We would not have intruded elsewhere."

A chorus of hisses filled the cavern, quickly silenced by the nearest creature, who swung his neck around to stare down his fellows. His head moved back, the torch again glinting in black eyes as he regarded them. But he didn't speak. Jal felt Phatomar's quiver grow more violent as the silence stretched.

"She instructed us to find the Faqadat Alqalb," Jal added, helping Phatomar hold tight to his resolve. "That in doing so, we might hope to find a motive for what we've endured." *Three tasks you must accomplish,* the Oracle had said. *One will give you motive; one a location; one an identity.* Jal prayed those words would aid them now, that they might somehow sway these snake-people, lessen their aggression. Because Jal didn't think her small group stood a chance if it came to a fight.

One of the creatures from behind Eamon pushed forward.

"Liarsss," he hissed. Fangs the length of Jal's outstretched hand unfolded to glisten in threat. "Thievesss. Come to take what doesssn't belong to you." He held a honed knife steady in his hand, a bow strapped across his back.

"Halt, Garnda," the snake-man who had first spoken commanded. "You will not belittle the wordsss of thossse we've waited for."

"We haven't waited for sssuch as thessse," Garnda spat. "They will bring only ruin."

"Perhapsss they fight chaosss," said another being sliding up beside Garnda, this one female. "If prophecccy bringss usss thessse humansss, we dare not reject them ssso quickly."

"Prophecccy, bah!" argued Garnda. His dark gaze turned to the snake-man in front of Jal and Phatomar, glaring over the heads of Olbaehn and Eamon. "Wordsss carved on a wall long ago to keep the Thueban Alnaasss captive to the whimsss of fate. Falssse promisssesss meant only to defang our people. Wordsss blindly guarded by zealotsss like Haassss." He sliced a hand dismissively across his chest to indicate the one who first confronted them.

"Enough, Garnda. I'm hardly the zealot here," Haass sneered. He stared down at Jal and her companions, a quizzical tilt to his great head. Suddenly, he thrust that head close. Jal and Phatomar drew back in surprise, Jal biting off a curse under her breath as her head met Eamon's. The creature, Haass, held them with an unflinching gaze. "What did you lossse?" he asked.

Jal didn't know what to say, but Phatomar did, though he couldn't raise his voice above a whisper.

"Courage," he breathed. "And the memory of what I once did with it."

Haass reared back so fast that Jal flinched again, her heart pounding painfully in her chest.

"If he keeps doing that," Olbaehn muttered in a low voice, "I might throw up."

"Certainly keeps a man awake," Eamon whispered lightly, but Jal knew he forced the levity into his tone.

"You will come with me." Haass turned in an arc that startled Jal with its gracefulness. She didn't quite understand how he could so seamlessly coordinate those human-like limbs with the supple twists of a serpentine body, neither interfering with the other.

"You cannot take them there!" Garnda snarled, his sinewy arms vibrating with tension, the knife in his hand dancing in a white-knuckled grip.

"I can and I will." Haass turned just his neck until his head looked backward, while the rest of his body continued on its way. Jal swallowed hard. "Remember your ssstation, Garnda," he warned, heading deeper into the caverns.

Jal glanced at Phatomar, who stared at her with huge eyes. A quick shrug from Eamon and a vigorous head shake from Olbaehn told her enough. No one particularly wanted to venture into the dark with these potentially hostile beings, yet they didn't have much choice in the matter. Jal took Phatomar's sweating palm in hers and followed Haass, pulling her companions in her wake.

They had come this far. She would continue ahead and see what came next.

Chapter 10

Eamon kept careful watch of these strange beings surrounding them as they progressed deeper into the darkness of Kahf Alramal. Ahead, Jal's torch bobbed in her hand, but light also came from behind. These Thueban Alnaas had their own unique source of illumination in the form of glowing globes which three of them had attached to a ridge atop their heads, leaving their hands free. Although most had secured their bows over their shoulders, each still had some form of weapon near to hand; a knife, a dagger, or a short sword strapped around the waist. They obviously planned to take no chances with their prisoners.

He had to admit that this race of people unnerved him. When Eamon had first heard Terek give name to the Thueban Alnaas, it had taken him a while to translate it to something akin to S*nake People*. Even then, Eamon had assumed these people worshipped snakes, or perhaps had a treacherous nature, or bore some other attributes that would earn them such a name.

The images of gorgons, hydras, and dragons had flitted through his mind, of course. He and Phatomar had dealt with both a hydra and a dragon in the past, but Eamon had never encountered anything quite like this, people human in body yet with full snake heads and tails. Although he kept his expression bland, Eamon's senses strained as he tried to keep his disquiet tamped down.

As they passed from the chamber with the pool of water, Eamon reached out to mark the wall as he had at each juncture. A blunt-fingered hand grabbed his wrist to stop him.

"No more marksss," the snake-woman said to him, her flared head boasting dark blue scales in the odd light. She didn't wear one of the glowing globes, but another stood close enough to offer some illumination to the area. Eamon looked up at her unblinking stare. Like the others, she wore only a skirt made of thin strips, leaving her torso bare, but Eamon felt no urge to glance at her exposed breasts despite how close she stood in the narrowing confines.

"You expect us to walk blindly with you, giving no recourse to find our way back?" he asked, more to see her reaction than in expectation of any answer.

"If you passss Haassss' tessst, we will lead you back to the daylight realm oursssselvesss. You won't need any markingsss."

"And if we don't pass this test?" Olbaehn asked in a tight voice.

"Then we eat well tonight," Garnda snarled from where he had slithered close behind Jal's brother. Olbaehn jerked away, which only made Garnda laugh, a dry, hissing sort of chuckle.

Eamon shrugged. He nodded his understanding as he pulled free of the woman's cool hand. He caught up with Jal and Phatomar. Olbaehn hurried to keep pace, preferring the company of those who shunned him to that of the possibly hungry serpentine race. Eamon hadn't missed the man's aversion to all things snake-like. Perhaps now that he couldn't retreat, Jal's brother regretted following them into the deep desert.

Haass and his people led them deep into the caverns, their path descending into lower sections of the cave structure. They encountered various branches in the path, none of which the snake-woman allowed Eamon to mark, until he had lost track of the turns they had taken. Time stretched into irrelevance in the oppressive tunnels and light-devouring caverns through which they passed. Like it or not, Eamon and his companions had to rely on their captors to guide them back to the surface again.

Assuming the snake people granted that freedom at the end of this long trek.

Eamon itched to draw his sword and force some real

answers (and perhaps some respect) from these Thueban Alnaas, even knowing the futility of such an act. He willed himself to patience. Getting them all killed now because of frayed nerves wouldn't help Phatomar, or help them reach their mysterious destination. So he forced his feet to follow where the Thueban Alnaas led without complaint while his mind searched for solutions to their possible captivity.

At last, they paused at the edge of another chamber. Black nothingness swallowed any indications of what lay before them. Jal's torch barely touched the inky void that stretched beyond. Haass came to a halt, then raised his legs like a rider in the saddle, leaned forward and glided with a strange grace using only the massive muscles of his tail to disappear into the darkness.

Eamon realised with dread just how quickly the Thueban Alnaas could navigate through their tunnels without the hindrance of their human limbs. Or perhaps, he amended, glancing at the bulk of arms and shoulders on the creatures ringing them, those powerful arms would pull them around corners and speed them along straight corridors, giving the snake people an even greater boost of speed. If it came to a flight to save their lives, Eamon didn't like their chances of outrunning the Thueban Alnaas. He met Jal's troubled gaze, and saw she had reached the same conclusion. He stepped forward to stand beside her and Phatomar, tried to give each a comforting grin, though he didn't know if he succeeded.

Suddenly, the chamber started to glow a soft blue, not unlike the globes the Thueban Alnaas wore, revealing an enormous cavern. Haass slid back to them, his cobra head tilted as he regarded the gaping humans.

"Welcome to the Alnawa." His arm swept wide as he gestured toward the treasures of his home. "The centre of Kahf Alramal."

Wealth beyond measure greeted their sight. Gold and gems lay in piles around the vast chamber. Silks and boldly coloured textiles lined the walls, draping from rocks like waterfalls. Weapons and armour from every age lay in orderly rows amongst the rest of the glitter, and statues and vases stood out like pieces on some giant game board. The hoarded glory of a dozen lands lay before them, a carpet of incredible history and power, stretching farther than Eamon could see. Indeed, the pale light gave the suggestion of even more rooms lost in the far shadows from which additional treasures spewed, waiting for someone to claim them.

Eamon shook his head. No, not waiting for a claimant, for this trove already had owners—or at least caretakers. And chief among this treasure, the Faqadat Alqalb.

Eamon pulled his gaze from the seductive sight of mind-numbing wealth and turned to regard Haass.

"So it truly exists," murmured Olbaehn, standing next to Eamon. Eamon saw the wonder of a childhood tale proven real in his eyes, then brought his attention back to the Thueban Alnaas.

"You wanted to know what I lost," Phatomar said to their guide, his pale grey eyes looking blue in the strange glow that emanated from whatever light source Haass had activated. Haass turned to the large warrior. To his credit, Phatomar held his gaze without flinching. "How did you know I lost anything? Why bring us here? I'm not likely to find courage in your fortunes."

Haass' lips stretched in a thin line, and his tongue flicked forward. It took Eamon a moment to read that expression as a smile.

"Wealth doesss not lie in gold alone," Haass said. "Often knowledge holdsss a greater value than gemsss."

"More than sometimes," Jal muttered, frowning at the cavern.

"Oh?" said Haass, swinging his cobra head her way. "You find no value with our gemsss?"

Jal wrenched her gaze up to the looming snake-man. She flushed. "Please forgive my interruption," she said, bowing her head.

"No, I wisssh to hear your thoughtsss, asss, no doubt, doesss Garnda."

Jal glanced to the creature behind Eamon, then back to Haass. She swallowed, but finally ventured her opinion.

"Only when gems pass from one hand to another do we give them any value. Otherwise, you only have a pretty rock sitting on the floor. Knowledge of how to find that rock, how to shape it into something someone will find worthy holds a greater value than the rock itself, and those who sell that polished stone hoard the knowledge to increase its value.

Yet without that gem, how does the merchant feed himself? For he has no knowledge of how to produce food, only wealth. You can't eat gems."

"Gems can buy food," Haass argued.

"To a camel herder at the edge of the desert, a blanket in exchange for milk holds more worth than a shiny stone. Trade for goods, not gold, dictates life in the tribes. Knowledge of weaving, of farming, of the herds outweighs trinkets that only burden the pockets."

"Wealth can buy knowledge—"

"But not understanding."

"*Ah-ha!*" Eamon jumped at Haass' exclamation (though not so badly as Phatomar). The Thueban Alnaas' tongue flashed out as though to taste the air in triumph. "And that realisssation essscapesss Garnda."

"Ussselessss philosssophissing," Garnda spat. Anger, and something Eamon couldn't read, danced in the man's slitted eyes as his neck arched in threat. "You wassste time with thessse intrudersss."

"You'll have to forgive Garnda," the female said. "He growsss impatient with Haasssss' posssturing."

Haass sighed, the sound turning into a drawn out hiss.

"Thalia hasss it aright, I fear," Haass said. "And though ssshe will not come right out and sssay it, ssshe remindsss me in her sssubtle way that few of my kind will tolerate the indulgenccce of outsssidersss for long." He looked back to Phatomar. "Knowledge hasss itsss own value, and we guard sssomething worth more than all the richesss you could carry from the Alnawa. The wordsss of a propheccccy that tell of a man without fear."

Phatomar stared at Haass, waiting for more information. When Haass remained silent, Eamon's friend hesitantly ventured his thoughts.

"A man without fear doesn't lack courage," he said. "So I fail to see how learning I've lost mine would prompt you to bring us here."

"Indeed," Haass agreed. "But the propheccccy pointsss to a motive, asss your female sssaid. A motive sssought when courage isss lossst."

The three companions exchanged looks while Olbaehn watched quietly from the side. Finally, Phatomar spoke again.

"What is this prophecy?"

"Come," Haass said, leading them down among the cavernous wealth of Kahf Alramal. "Let usss sssee if your anssswersss lie in the wordsss we have long guarded."

"Pray that they do," Thalia said ominously as she, Garnda, and a dozen others slid behind them in near silence. "Elssse you'll not leave the Alnawa alive."

***

Haass led Phatomar and the others deeper into the treasure trove that made up the Alnawa, past mounds of gold and gems, tables not unlike altars stacked with the wealth of ages, but he looked neither left nor right. Phatomar couldn't discern the source of the soft blue illumination. The light seemed to seep from intermittent veins crawling across the high ceiling, swirl down the walls, and hinted at rivers of iridescence on the floor, though their feet never trod on any obvious source of light. It revealed plenty of details about their surroundings, however, helping to keep Phatomar's dread of whatever unseen horrors lurked nearby at bay.

The flickering flame of Jal's torch, still gripped in her firm hand, painted additional colours and shadows upon each display as they passed between sparkling heaps of beauty and wonder. Phatomar wondered if the snake-man tested their resolve by forcing them to walk so close to uncounted riches, or whether he simply took them via the most direct route to their destination.

Prophecy the Thueban Alnaas had said, and the word shivered like shards of ice down Phatomar's spine. Did the concept set him on edge because he had faced such before and lost the memory? Or did the thought of such strange beings adhering to something written so long ago, yet somehow applying it to him, make him skeptical?

A part of him, a small, almost hidden part, fluttered with excitement that he might find the answer to why the gods would single him out. Why put such effort into erasing someone rather than just killing him? Did watching him flounder without courage amuse them? Why would such celestial beings deign to notice him in the first place? Surely such paltry entertainment lay beneath all-powerful gods.

But someone had altered Phatomar's path, and without Jal's witness and Eamon's loyalty, Phatomar would have fallen to the crushing weight of fear and doubt long since. His friends—his family—had kept him strong, kept him moving, helping him to reach this point, and perhaps that, the gods had not envisioned. After all, the memory of Phatomar had disappeared from the minds of men and gods alike; only Jal and Eamon remained immune. Why these two had escaped the spell, Phatomar didn't know. He wondered if Haass' prophecy might enlighten him about that as well.

They moved in near silence, relieved only by the slight scrape of scales pushing along stone floors, mixed with the quiet whisper of booted feet, both quickly swallowed by the vastness of the cavern through which they traversed. Finally, Haass veered away from the rows of riches and brought them to a dark chamber deep within the Alnawa.

Haass turned, staring at each member of Phatomar's party with those flat black eyes slashed by gold, his reptilian features impossible to read. His dark tongue tasted the air as he uttered a soft hiss. The Thueban Alnaas who had followed fanned out, some turning to leave, others planting themselves between the humans and the passage they had taken to reach this point. None made an overt gesture of threat, but Phatomar had no doubt that the only path for the humans lay forward, into that dark chamber.

Only eight snake people remained visible, but he didn't want to risk a fight should they need to flee. From the subtle hissing he could perceive in the darkness of the Alnawa, Phatomar knew others waited beyond sight, ready to slay the intruders should they fail Haass' expectations.

For a moment, fear of the unseen threat paralysed him. He forced in a breath, then another, listening not for whispered hisses, but for the beat of his own heart, the measured cadences of his body, and strove for that sense of calm Jal had help him find. Beside him, Jal did the same, and he took comfort from the fact that he didn't stand alone with his fears.

"Through here lie sssacred wordsss we have guarded for cccenturiesss," Haass announced, holding Phatomar in an unyielding stare. "Few beyond our people have read what

113

liesss beyond, and none have yet dissscerned the truth of the riddle. May you become the firssst to reveal its meaning."

It sounded like a ritual phrase to Phatomar, and he found himself worried that the Thueban Alnaas didn't guard a key to his problem at all, but rather followed a religion that doomed all interlopers to a fate of awe and terror like that displayed by Terek back at Fyum Oasis.

The path leads to death, Terek had warned, to which Jal had replied, *Nevertheless, it is the road we must take.* Phatomar remembered the claws of dread that had skewered him at the time, and felt them anew as he stood poised on the threshold of the unknown.

At that moment, Dearn's words also surfaced as to where their path would lead. *Into the unknown, as many paths do.* Phatomar would learn nothing by balking now, and potentially much if he but forced himself forward. Both Eamon and Jal waited on him, Phatomar sensed.

With a firm nod, Phatomar took that first step, his friends matching him.

The light from Jal's torch danced along the carved angles of words etched on the wall above a low stone altar. Curiosity lent Phatomar strength, and he moved to read the prophecy of the Thueban Alnaas, written in an archaic form of the desert tongue.

> *Death to the steadfast who takes up the Faqadat Alqalb, for it will avail him nothing but pain.*
>
> *The man who fears nothing has nothing to gain, though he above others might restore the Heart of Order.*
>
> *Only through acts of courage remembered can She whom Chaos slew rise to push the darkness away.*
>
> *Yet darkness must remain lest light fades forever.*

Phatomar read the words again. They didn't make any better sense the second time. He turned to Jal. A deep furrow had appeared between her eyes as she scowled at the wall, her lips gently moving as she read. She shook her head.

"I don't understand," she admitted.

"A stupid riddle," Olbaehn said in disgust. "Vague and contradictory. Words that will bend to fit any interpretation you want."

Jal tried to quiet him before his disapproval upset their hosts. Phatomar noted then that Haass hadn't followed them in. The four humans stood here alone for the moment.

"Stupid or not," said Eamon, "intelligible to us or not, the Thueban Alnaas put a great deal of stock into these words. Perhaps we should consider them a little more before we dismiss their relevance."

"What's to consider?" Olbaehn demanded. "Death to all thieves. The fearless man will bring order. Courage will defeat chaos. Darkness and light must co-exist. Just a bunch of meaningless platitudes."

"Haass asked what Phatomar lost," Jal said quietly, looking to the writing rather than her brother. "Something about lost courage prompted him to bring us here, to tempt our resolve to learn the truth by first trying to blind us with riches."

"Wealth can buy *things*, but knowledge can bring understanding," Eamon said, stepping away from Olbaehn to stand next to Phatomar and Jal, the three studying ancient words on a wall.

"A motive sought when courage is lost." Jal pointed to the third line with her torch. "*Acts of courage remembered.* That could refer to Phatomar regaining what was stolen."

"Or that only the brave will prevail," Olbaehn scoffed. "The brave that will die if they touch the Faqadat Alqalb, the Heart Stone."

The others ignored him, studying the prophecy again.

Eventually, Jal spoke.

"If only the fearless man can restore Order—and why is that capitalized? Does it represent a person, or a concept? —yet the steadfast will die if he takes up the means with which to restore that Order, then something must happen to make that fearless man fearful."

"Exxxactly," hissed a voice, barely an arm's reach away behind them. Phatomar cried out at the unexpected nearness, and slammed his shin on the altar as he stumbled away in fright. Jal and Eamon didn't fare much better.

Eamon's sword half-leapt from his scabbard as the man whirled, hand to weapon. Jal thrust her torch before her as she crouched, her breath coming in laboured gasps. Olbaehn had staggered to the side, eyes wide.

Haass chuckled, obviously pleased at having surprised the humans. But instead of gloating, he raised his eyes to the words on the wall. "Interpretationsss vary, asss your companion sssaid, but I believe the female hasss it correct. The fearlessss can only prevail if he hasss losssst hisss courage."

"Who is *She whom Chaos slew*?" Phatomar asked. He did not like the thought that *something* long ago had foreseen someone like him existing to start a chain of events beyond his control. He believed in fate, but seeing her hand at work so acutely made him uneasy.

"The goddessss of Order," replied Haass. "To whom the Faqadat Alqalb belongsss."

They stared at him, their eyes as unblinking as his.

"Many of the gods follow the ways of either order or chaos, light or dark," Eamon said. A frown lined his face. "But surely those are ideologies, abstracts, not other gods."

Haass said nothing, his expression neutral. Then he pointed at the altar beneath the carved words. Phatomar looked down, but saw nothing unusual. Haass' finger touched the stone, triggering a hidden light. Its golden glow revealed a page torn from a manuscript, well-preserved beneath a pane of glass. With some surprise, Phatomar realised that he recognised the text as Old Merveahian.

"What's this?"

"A hissstory of godsss you have forgotten. And a key to that which you sssseek."

Phatomar leaned close to read it aloud, feeling the heat of the others as they pressed close to listen.

> When the Elder gods of Earth and Sky brought into being Order and Chaos, they sought to fashion a balance among all creation. Beings of both war and peace, Order and Chaos complemented one another even while they competed for attention.
>
> In times of war, Order revelled in the logic

of battle plans, the structured layout of an encampment, the discipline of well-trained soldiers, while her counterpart Chaos enjoyed the uncertainty of an ambush, a melee without rules, mercenaries who knew how to stop and camp anywhere with little regard for structure or command. She encouraged humans to learn new and better ways to forge swords, fashion and fletch arrows, carve and caress supple boughs into stronger bows and spears. He encouraged the art of improvisation; scavenging the fallen weapons of another, imagining other uses for the bounty of nature, using fists and feet and gnashing teeth when no other device came to hand.

In times of peace, Order taught farmers how to plow and sow their fields efficiently, hunters how to read game trails, set traps and follow their prey. She instructed weavers how to fashion baskets to gather food, blankets to ward against the cold, shelters to protect from the elements. Chaos whispered the secrets of foraging, which wild plants and insects to consume and which to avoid. He pointed out how one could bend bark into a makeshift carrier, pile the leaves and deadfall of the forest—or burrow into the sands of the desert, the snows of the mountains—to escape frost and storms and predators, where to find caves and hollow trees that nature had already provided for shelter.

She liked to plan for the future; he preferred to bask in the moment, two sides of the same coin, benefiting humanity equally.

"Wait a minute," interrupted Eamon, baffled. "Benefiting humanity equally? I thought the forces opposed each other. This suggests they somehow work in concert, accomplishing similar goals using different methods."

"Order has rules," Olbaehn said. "Chaos improvises. They might start with the same objective, but their solutions will

117

have vastly different outcomes. The unpredictable nature of chaos makes it seem a darker force to us. Imagine the atmosphere of Fyum Oasis if we abandoned the rules that kept the peace, allowed everyone to act without any regard to consequence. Instead of order, we'd have chaos. Fighting, theft, and unrest would run rampant, as they do in many cities in the north. But because we all acknowledge and respect the neutrality enforced there, things run more or less smoothly."

Phatomar found himself impressed with the man's insight.

"The choice to follow certain moral precepts versus seizing the moment to advance oneself," Jal said. "Perhaps even selfless motives versus selfish gain. It sounds like Order embodies learning what benefits many, while Chaos finds strength in empowering the individual."

"Making them seem like opposites, though they really aren't." Eamon nodded. They thought they knew how the world worked; now Phatomar watched Eamon struggle to incorporate this new understanding. His eyes troubled, Eamon looked at Phatomar. "What else does it say?"

Phatomar turned back to the manuscript, found his place, and went on.

> Each had their followers, both mortal and immortal, servants to the ways of Order and Chaos. Yet some grew jealous of their counterparts, whispering half-truths and lies, spreading stories like cancer until the line between reality and falsehood became blurred, growing into cruelty and hatred.
>
> Order and Chaos did not stand immune to the rivalries between their factions, nor the lies that devoured the balance they once shared.
>
> Even knowing the animosity and competition brewing between the pair—gods who stood as a bridge between the Elder and Younger gods—and the influence of those who served them, the Elder gods did not anticipate the actions which would shape their world, and so did nothing to chastise their children.

Order strategised how to evade plots to steal her power, how to keep her followers safe as they fouled the plans Chaos conjured, while Chaos, in a pique of temper, took a more direct route.

In a towering rage, he committed the ultimate sin and struck Order down. He ripped out her heart and cast it into the desert to sink beneath the hot dunes—

Phatomar heard Jal's sharp gasp, and he paused, swallowing the dryness in his throat. The Heart of Order, cast into the desert. Foreboding pressed hard on his shoulders. He continued reading.

Her body he rooted into the molten slag of a mountain's wrath as it bled across barren slopes. He thrust her spirit into the blackest ocean, anchoring her anguished scream deep where he believed none would notice his crime. Alas, Chaos soon learned the error of his actions.

When his ire cooled, he felt the pain of remorse, the near-crippling weight of guilt, and he thought to hide his face from the world until his despair passed. The Elder gods found him thus and, mourning the tragedy, scorned their son.

One chance remained for Chaos to salvage his place among the gods, to escape the same fate he had bestowed upon Order. He had but to stand aside when Order found a champion and sought rebirth—

Had any other words existed, they had long since faded into history, for the page now lay ripped and incomplete. Phatomar took a shuddering breath.

"Take the Faqadat Alqalb to the Blackened Fields where ancient death engendered a tree of starry night," Jal quoted the Oracle in a hushed voice.

Haass focused his attention on her, and Phatomar found

119

himself grateful not to receive the full weight of those depthless eyes.

"Where did you hear that?" the snake-man demanded.

"From the mouth of the Hada Oracle," Eamon said when Jal remained silent.

Haass regarded each of them, his gaze at last resting upon Phatomar.

"Then the time hasss come for the Thueban Alnaasss to fulfill their dessstiny, and for the fearlessss man who hasss lossst his courage to take up that which will change the ssshape of the heavensss."

With that remark, Haass led them from the dark room back into the light of the Alnawa.

"Time growsss ssshort," he said to those waiting beyond. "The Heart Ssstone mussst make itsss final journey."

The Thueban Alnaas swayed in an odd dance, then followed their leader as he guided the four humans deeper into their lair, toward a distant altar atop which Phatomar could see something flash red.

The Faqadat Alqalb. The first part of an answer to a question that Phatomar wondered if he understood at all.

***

"Thessse humansss profane our hallsss," Garnda hissed to his companions. "Haasssss allowsss them to tramp through our home, read our sssacred wordsss, and now he will permit them to touch that which they mussst not touch."

"If they take up the Faqadat Alqalb without opposssition, all our plansss come to naught," the woman to his left snarled.

"Kissstawna hasss worked too hard to fail now," Garnda said, dark eyes sweeping his two dozen followers. "The humansss *mussst* not leave with the Heart Ssstone."

"If they fulfill the prophecccy, how will we ssstop them?" another cried.

"The dead cannot fulfill prophecccy," Garnda replied disdainfully.

"Haasssss will defend the fearlessss man to the death," observed the female. "Asss will thossse guarding the humansss."

"I can live with that," Garnda said. When his meaning took

root, the rest of those who followed the gods of Chaos thinned their lips in anticipation.

With bows strung and quivers ready, swords loosened in scabbards, Garnda's followers slithered into position near their unwitting brethren, waiting for the right opportunity to strike. The time had come for the Thueban Alnaas loyal to the goddess Kistawna to make their true allegiances known.

Chapter 11

Eamon suspected the Thueban Alnaas knew more about their prophecy than just the words etched on the wall. Haass put a lot of weight into the phrases and actions of his companions—especially Phatomar—in a way that didn't make sense to Eamon. It hadn't become much clearer after having read the prophecy and the startling history of the origin of Order and Chaos. He didn't particularly care for Olbaehn, but Jal's brother hadn't lied when he said those words would fit any interpretation one wanted.

However, something about the whole encounter had encouraged Haass to bring them now to the Faqadat Alqalb, a huge step toward their goal of restoring Phatomar to himself. That the prophecy hinted at the nature of their greater task—dealing with the powers of Order and Chaos sounded both dangerous and daunting, beyond anything they had faced before, even when Phatomar stood whole—Eamon would worry on later. Right now, they had a priceless treasure to obtain, and many dark tunnels to traverse before they saw the light of day again.

"The sssteadfassst may not touch the Heart of Order, lessst it ssseduccce them with power," Haass intoned, his dark gaze turning to Phatomar. "But he who fearsss her embraccce hasss a chanccce to ressstore what wasss taken. Do you dare touch the Faqadat Alqalb, human?"

Phatomar's throat bobbed in a hard swallow, the motion caught by the light of Jal's torch. Somehow, the soft blue luminescence surrounding them didn't touch the object they had come to retrieve. The blood red stone in a nest of black fabric repulsed the eerie glow rather than absorbed or reflected it, as the other nearby gems did. This added to the otherworldly feeling that swirled around Eamon now.

"If the gods have indeed set this plan in motion, for whatever reason casting my friends and me in the role of harbinger of this prophecy, then I have little choice but to try," Phatomar said. Only his hushed tone and deep breaths gave away just how much this task unnerved him.

"You alwaysss have a choiccce," said a dark scaled Thueban Alnaas next to the altar. This one, smaller than Haass but with a deeper voice, had twin streaks of copper lining his hood. His long tail curved into a coil, his mass settled upon it as though sitting or kneeling. Eamon hadn't noticed his presence until he spoke. *Careless to so easily miss a potential threat,* Eamon scolded himself.

A quick check of his surroundings revealed no other surprises, but then, the Alnawa had so much space, and contained so many things, that any number of unpleasant surprises might still hide in the shadows. *Best to keep vigilant,* he affirmed, stretching slightly to check for the feel of the knife in his boot, the dagger at his belt, and finally resting his hand on the hilt of his sword. Phatomar would deal with the Faqadat Alqalb; Eamon would keep his attention focused on their surroundings.

"Then I choose to see this task to its conclusion," Phatomar said, setting his shoulders in determination, a gesture he had once used in preparation for battle. Now, Eamon suspected he unconsciously mimicked a ready fighter's stance to bolster whatever strength he could in light of the frightening unknown before him. "With your permission and blessing, I will take the Faqadat Alqalb to where it must go."

"You do not require my permissssion, human." The copper tinged Thueban Alnaas waved his hand. "If you can touch it, then you may return it to where it belongsss."

Phatomar took a deep breath, held it. With trembling fingers, he reached forward until his hand hovered over the red stone. He paused, squeezed his eyes shut, and dropped his hand to wrap his fingers around the Faqadat Alqalb. The stone pulsed once, then became quiescent. Phatomar gasped, and his eyes flashed open as he held the Heart

Stone in his palm. He turned with a nervous smile to Eamon, and Eamon grinned in response.

"Ressstore the Heart of Order, human," Haass said, new respect colouring his words. Then sorrow weighed his next sentiment. "Make thisss sssacrificcce of the Thueban Alnaasss worthwhile."

In punctuation to his statement, the first arrow shot through the darkness to impale the snake-man beside the altar through the neck. A second thudded into the back of Olbaehn's shoulder, dropping him to his knees with a cry of startled pain. Jal pushed Phatomar to the ground, shielding what she could of him with her body. Eamon already had his sword out, his dagger to hand, and he leapt in front of the pair. The blades wouldn't do much against arrows, but just having them ready gave Eamon a sense of calm.

"Traitors!" Haass shouted as the glow suffusing the Alnawa disappeared, leaving Jal's torch as the only source of light; a source that now clearly outlined the humans amidst the turmoil of writhing snake people. She stared at it in dismay, eyes wide, before she tossed it aside, plunging the cavern into darkness.

The whistle of arrows reached Eamon's ears. The dry *shush* of serpentine bodies flowed around him amidst the hiss of startled exclamations, but his eyes saw nothing in the utter darkness. Only the press of Jal's hand against his back let him know where she and Phatomar lay, and Olbaehn's harsh breaths placed the injured man nearby.

We can't stay here. Their attackers knew the configuration of the cavern too well, and knew exactly where the humans currently cowered. Yet aside from their unfamiliarity of the Alnawa, they had the added disadvantage of blindness. *How can I get everyone to safety without leading us into the jaws of death?*

A blunt-fingered hand, dry and cold, gripped his wrist. If not for her accompanying words, Eamon would have taken Thalia's head with his sword.

"We mussst get you out," she hissed. "But Garnda guardsss the tunnel too well."

Haass' voice slithered from the nothingness to her right. "Take them via the Mamaru Almawtaa."

Thalia gasped. "I cannot passss there."

124

"Take my key," Haass insisted. "Garnda will not sssussspect sssuch a bold essscape. It will buy you time. Light an orb onccce free and make all hassste."

"What of you?" Jal asked.

Eamon sensed Haass' movement as a displacement of air, though his eyes felt only the weight of pure night pressing on them.

"Follow Thalia," Haass said, avoiding the question. "Ssshe will get you out. I will dissstract Garnda and hisss followersss."

The sudden absence of Haass' presence registered only as a void next to Thalia. Right now, Eamon worried more about their vulnerability as they delayed than where Haass had gone.

"Let's go," he urged.

Thalia needed no further motivation. She pushed something at Eamon, which he clutched in his hand next to the hilt of his dagger.

"Link up; keep clossse," she instructed. Only once they started inching forward together did Eamon realise he held a piece of Thalia's skirt as his guide. Jal had her hand wound in Eamon's tunic, and Phatomar and Olbaehn had presumably chained themselves together in a similar fashion.

Eamon wondered how well the Thueban Alnaas could see in the dark, and how much they relied on touch and memory. If their eyes could pick up motion without the need for light, surely their little group would soon draw attention. Yet somehow, they made their way through the warren of the Alnawa unhindered, hoping that Thalia would not betray them as she hurried ahead.

After an unnerving dash along a twisting route with the sound of battle rising and falling behind them, Thalia paused. Eamon heard what sounded like stone grating on stone, then she pulled them ahead again. After another few dozen steps, she stopped a second time. Suddenly, a faint blue glow outlined Thalia's hand. She held one of the glowing globes and raised it to her head, setting it atop the ridge behind her eyes.

Eamon studied the narrow tunnel they now stood in with a watchful eye. Just wide enough that he could touch either wall if he reached out, the ceiling hovered close to Thalia's head as she arched her neck forward. The passage stretched into darkness ahead, and disappeared around a slight bend behind. The air held the tang of disuse, a hint of a dry sort of muskiness and decay that tickled his nostrils.

"The Passssagesss of the Dead," Thalia hissed. "We will follow them until we find a sssafe route beyond the Alnawa. Garnda will have hisss zealotsss guard the way back to the Well, but if we hurry, we may beat them to the entrancece where you left your beassstsss." Her dark stare latched on to Phatomar, who stood bent over with hands on his thighs as he caught his breath and tried to control the shaking in his terrified limbs.

"Do you yet hold the Faqadat Alqalb?" she demanded, a quiver in her voice. Phatomar glanced up, straightening, then nodded. Thalia inclined her neck in acknowledgement. "Then perhapsss we have not lossst all." She swivelled around and pushed herself forward with her tail. "Hurry," she said, setting off at a fast pace that pushed the humans into a run to keep up with her light.

"What happened back there?" Phatomar asked.

"Garnda hasss played hisss hand," Thalia grunted. She kept them moving, and just when Eamon thought she'd leave that unhelpful response as her only reply, she spoke again. "Sssome among my kind want to keep the prophecccy unfulfilled, preferring Chaosss to Order. I had thought Garnda a malcontent, eager to challenge Haasss' authority, but I know now he isss a traitor. He followsss Kissstawna, like asss not."

"Kistawna?" Jal asked.

"A goddess who loves chaos," Eamon explained. *Or one who follows Chaos,* he amended, the disturbing revelation of Order and Chaos being true gods ringing in his mind, making him question what he thought he knew about the hierarchy of the gods.

"And one who hasss no desssire to sssee Order rissse again," Thalia added.

Eamon suspected Jal's thoughts had gone to the mysterious voices she'd heard take Phatomar's courage, wondering if one of those voices belonged to Kistawna. He still didn't understand why the gods had chosen to torment Phatomar, but perhaps they now had an idea of which deities to blame.

They ran through the twisting tunnel for another stretch of time, passing the occasional side chamber. Eamon could make out long shadowed shelves carved to either side of the entrances as they rushed past, shrouds and rotted fabric laid over stone ledges, housing the remains of the dead and the trinkets which accompanied them in their long rest. The Passages of the Dead, sacred catacombs entrusted now to humans who had unwittingly added to the numbers who would soon rest within these narrow walls.

Olbaehn's pained grunts grew worse as he struggled behind them. Whenever one of them slowed to check on him, Olbaehn would just shake his head and wave them on, but Eamon feared the jolt of the arrow still embedded in his shoulder would drain his strength before they could reach safety.

Finally, Thalia made them stop. She took the globe from her head and handed it Eamon.

"An interssssection liessss ahead," she whispered. "I will check it. If the way liessss clear, we will leave thessse confinessss and make better ssspeed."

As Eamon's legs and lungs already burned from their prolonged run, he couldn't imagine how much faster she expected them to go. He nodded anyway, then rejoined his companions as they leaned against the rough stone walls to await Thalia's return.

Jal turned to Olbaehn, her strong hands holding him still as she examined his wound. He looked gaunt in the light of the globe, his features pale and drawn. He tried to wave his sister off, but Jal refused to back down.

"We need to at least snap the shaft," she said. "Though I fear removing the arrow while we have nothing to bind the wound with." She glanced at Eamon, as though seeking confirmation. He nodded in agreement, but feared the worst, seeing the odd colouring at the edge of the injury—trickles of yellow-green mingled with the red of blood spread around the wound, evident even in the blue glow from the orb in his hand. Did he tell Jal her brother fought poison as well as pain? A subtle look from Olbaehn pleaded for silence. Eamon frowned but gave the desert man a nod.

Jal braced Olbaehn, took Eamon's offered dagger, and

swiftly cut the protruding end of the arrow as near to the back of Olbaehn's shoulder as she could. Olbaehn hissed, but made no further protest. He tried to smile at Jal, but his lips instead pulled into a sickly rictus that failed to bring solace. Jal offered him a grim nod, her eyes pinched with worry. *Did she suspect her brother's death lay near?* She must, but she also clung to hope.

"Thalia will get us to the camels," she said. "I brought medicines."

Olbaehn studied her, slightly dazed.

"I might not get that far," he whispered.

"You will," she insisted. "We'll help you. You just have to hold on." She kept her voice low, calm. Eamon suspected she held on to her composure with stubborn will and desperation, fearful of speaking any louder lest she break. He saw the trail of a tear etch Phatomar's cheek before he brushed it away with his shoulder.

"Come," came an urgent hiss from the darkness. Thalia moved just close enough to the orb for them to see her outline. "We have a brief opportunity." Somehow, the snake-woman managed to twist herself so that she faced the opposite direction again, leading them forward. Eamon watched her right hand tremble slightly as the blade she held dripped something onto the ground. Had he not hurried to catch up, he would have missed this indication of what it had cost her to create this opportunity for them.

Make this sacrifice of the Thueban Alnaas worthwhile, Haass had said. Had he known of this price even as he guarded prophecy and Heart Stone alike? Eamon suspected he had.

***

By the time they stumbled at last into the chamber with the pool of water, Jal's legs felt so unsteady that she feared that, if they stopped, she wouldn't find the energy to start again. Fortunately, Thalia had no intention of slowing down.

Unfortunately, the sound of slithering and the hissed exclamations coming from the tunnel they needed to follow demanded caution.

"Hide the globe," Thalia whispered to Eamon. Though Jal

feared the inevitable darkness, she understood the necessity. She grabbed Eamon's tunic ahead and Olbaehn's damp palm behind as their light disappeared.

Only then did she realise that this room had its own source of illumination. The water from the pool gave off a soft radiance, echoed in shimmering patches on the walls and ceiling. The light staved off total darkness and allowed them to pick out objects. They could still see, but so too could the two Thueban Alnaas who slid from the passageway ahead, bows drawn and black eyes glinting despite the distance separating the two groups.

Thalia's distressed hiss confirmed that these followed Garnda, and Jal and Eamon took action. Almost in unison, they drew their swords and swept forward in silence, the chamber giving ample room to maneuver. Jal heard the snap of a bow string, and felt air rush past as she threw herself to the floor. She rolled as Eamon had taught her, and came up into a smooth run to leap for the nearest surprised snake person. He managed to nock another arrow, but her downstroke struck the place where scales met the flesh of his neck before he could fire.

His mouth gaped in shock even as glistening fangs lunged for Jal's face, his throat bulging, preparing to spit venom at her. Jal didn't give him a chance, ripping her sword out and bringing it around in a vicious backhand that bit through his shoulder and struck the centre of his chest. He crumpled, his weight nearly taking her blade from her hand. Jal twisted and pulled her weapon free, a brief fountain of thick red arcing in a semi-circle from the corpse at her feet.

Eamon stood panting over their second foe. Thalia crouched nearby as she wiped her blade clean of blood. With shaking hands, Jal bent to retrieve an unsullied piece of cloth from her enemy's skirt, wiping it along the flat of her weapon, trying not to throw up.

She knew how to fight, had killed her share of game for the fire, but never before had she taken the life of a person. She understood the necessity—he had attacked, she had defended—yet the act had shaken her, and it took all her might to keep from retching on the foe at her feet.

Mustn't think of him as a person, a being of intelligence, with desires and aspirations. It's a vanquished foe, not a person who only moments before had drawn breath.

A hand gently gripped her elbow. Only then did she notice that she had squeezed her eyes shut. She met Olbaehn's feverish gaze and nearly cried, seeing such pain in his eyes, yet amazed by something deeper. Something that looked like pride.

"Come, little sister," he said, voice rough as he fought not to cough. "You're almost out." The slightest tug got her feet moving again, bringing her next to Eamon, Phatomar, and Thalia.

"Humansss," Garnda bellowed from behind, closer to the Alnawa. "Thievesss." Sibilant curses from at least two others rose to join his.

Thalia stared hard into the darkness behind, then grabbed Eamon's shoulder, pulling him toward the tunnels he had marked earlier.

"Follow your marksss, human," she said. "Take the Faqadat Alqalb to where it mussst go. Essscape. Help your friend fulfill the prophecccy. I will buy you time." She gave Eamon a shove, turning to block the narrower entrance with her body, intending to hold Garnda and his ilk at bay as long as possible.

Olbaehn gave Jal a shove of his own, then surprisingly turned to put his shoulder next to Thalia's, a sword taken from one of the fallen Thueban Alnaas gripped in his hand. Jal stared at him, her head shaking from side to side at what her brother intended.

"We have to go, Olbaehn," she said. "I have medicine—"

"It's too late, Jal," he said without looking back. The shock of hearing him use her chosen name instead of her birth name silenced her. "I can feel the poison coursing through me." His next breath held the hint of a rattle. "Let me do this," he whispered, his eyes growing a sheen of tears. "Let me finally be the brother you deserve, my sister."

"But I am outcast," she wiped at her own watering eyes, wanting to save him, knowing she couldn't. "You have no obligation to me."

He managed a gentle smile.

"Always my stubborn, wilful, beautiful and brave sister. I'm sorry it took so long for me to truly see you."

He turned back to the cavern, to where Garnda and three

130

others slithered into view.

"Get her out of here," Olbaehn ordered, his voice suddenly firm.

"Thank you," Eamon said, taking a step deeper into the tunnel.

An arrow flew from Thalia's bow before the snake-woman hastily pulled back, using the slight curve in the wall to hide her. Strong arms wrapped around Jal as Phatomar hoisted her into the air, holding her tight and running after Eamon.

"No," she breathed, but didn't fight. Jal wrapped her arms around his neck for a brief embrace of shared sorrow, then demanded he put her down.

Together, the three sprinted toward freedom, leaving behind unimaginable courage and sacrifice. Jal's heart bled as she accepted this last gift from a brother who had never really understood her, yet had defended her with his life.

Jal wept for opportunities lost.

***

The distressed bleating of camels woke Jal from the numbed daze of their flight. Although her body had stumbled after Eamon and Phatomar through the long shadowed tunnels, her mind had retreated to a place of stillness, unthinking, unaware of her surroundings. Now, as they neared the last stage of their retreat, everything snapped back into focus, her senses alerted to potential danger.

They rounded the final corner cautiously, Eamon slowing them to an inching crawl. He held the globe cupped to his chest to mute its glow. His sword sat comfortably in the opposite hand. Jal reached to the hilt of her own weapon, ready to draw it again if needed. Eamon took a measured pace into this last chamber before the sands and open sky beyond, Jal and Phatomar right behind him. Phatomar's fierce trembles vibrated against Jal's side, and his harsh breaths held the trace of a whimper as he fought panic.

Jal smelled the tang of blood before she saw the bodies. Eamon's camel lay sprawled in an undignified heap of its own offal, the other three beasts huddled as far from it as possible, bleating their distress. Two snake people—one male, one female—curled around their own mortal wounds, the tracks from both their webbed feet and serpentine aspects smeared in blood and sand across the cavern, speaking to a prolonged struggle. Whether they had fought with or against each other, Jal couldn't say, but no other combatants lay in sight. Eamon made a hasty search of the entrance cave before beckoning to Jal and Phatomar.

"They slashed two of the saddlebags, but the others remain intact," he said. "Let's redistribute the supplies and get out of here."

Jal looked to the star-streaked sky she could see past the entrance, clear now of any storms or the sheltering warmth of clouds, but she understood Eamon's desire to leave as soon as possible. She wondered whether they would find any moon glow to help guide their path, or if she'd have to rely on the stars alone to light their way. She wouldn't have advised travel by night across hostile and unfamiliar terrain, but couldn't remain here when an enemy might come at them unawares.

Hurrying to Eamon's side, the trio made hasty preparations. Jal tried not to notice the colourful blanket draped across Olbaehn's camel, the pattern well remembered from previous travels with her family. A blanket she must now return to a younger brother, now head of the household and tribal elder. Olbaehn had chosen to follow them out of concern for her safety, but Jal had failed to protect him. How could she expect Noll to forgive her for that?

The sound of scale scraping along stone grabbed the attention of the camels, their throats rumbling ominously as wide eyes searched the darkness. Jal and Eamon swung around in a defensive crouch and Phatomar held himself rigid, all three poised to meet the threat.

Laughter hissed from the darkness, followed by a wet thud and the awkward rolling of something into the faint light of Eamon's globe. Jal stared down in horror at the sightless eyes, once warm with the colour of honey, of her brother's severed head.

Garnda pulled himself into view. His left arm hung useless; a gash dripped red down his chest; a vicious blow had crushed the left side of his cobra's face; and his tail lacked its tip as it dragged behind him, leaving a bloody trail. But the spear he held levelled in his right hand remained surprisingly steady.

"Death to intrudersss and thievesss," he spat.

"Intruders, perhaps, but not thieves," said Eamon, holding to his crouch. "Your people brought us to the Alnawa, gave us the Heart Stone. We have taken nothing not freely given."

"The goddesssss punissshesss your blasssphemy and violation, and that of the foolsss who ssshowed you what they ssshould not have revealed." Garnda's tongue flicked out as though to point toward Olbaehn's lifeless head. "Do you think to essscape Kissstawna'sss judgement?"

"You're in no shape to stop us, Garnda," Eamon answered. "Crawl back to your hole or I will end your life where you stand."

Garnda laughed.

"I need only ssstop one," he hissed. The massive muscles of his arm bunched as he hefted his missile and aimed it at Phatomar. Jal and Eamon both leapt to their friend's aid, knowing they stood too far away to save him with swords alone. Garnda twisted with a roar to stare at the blackness behind him.

And Phatomar threw his dagger.

The spear left Garnda's fingers. It dropped and rolled with a clatter to Phatomar's feet. Garnda ripped his gaze from whatever apparition approached from behind to stare in disbelief at the blade piercing his heart. His fingers moved to touch the hilt, then the snake-man toppled to his side.

A laboured grunt as another Thueban Alnaas dragged himself past Garnda's body, his sword wrenched from the remains of Garnda's tail on the way. Jal recognised Haass' scales through the gore of blood marring his head and body. She wondered how much came from him, and how much from those who had once stood at his side. His right leg ended in a jagged stump, tied off with a piece of his skirt; one long fang dangled crooked from his jaw, the other gone entirely. Something had left deep slashes from his shoulder to his waist, and a broken arrow quivered near his collarbone. She didn't know how he could see anything through the tear in his left eye, its companion now an empty socket weeping blood, but he swung his head in their direction.

"Our thanks for your distraction," Eamon managed to say.

"I didn't even hesitate," Phatomar whispered in wonder, staring in amazement at his empty hand. He looked first at Eamon, then Jal, then finally to Haass. "I didn't have time to think, just to react. My body seemed to remember what to do." When he turned to stare at the dead Thueban Alnaas beside Garnda, his eyes turned sorrowful. "But it didn't stop the bloodshed. Our presence brought death to your people."

"It only hasssstened itsss inevitability," Haass said, his words heavy with pain and regret. "The prophecccy alwaysss sssspelled doom for many of our people while it brought hope to yoursss, though few underssstood our purpossse." He sucked in an unsteady draught of air. "And I have lossst the time to explain." His marred eye seemed to regard Olbaehn's decapitated head for an instant before trying to find the living again. "Know that it takesss death to essscape the Kahf Alramal," Haass managed, his breath growing more ragged. "The pricccce of freedom. Beyond thessse wallsss, you may not mention what liesss within. The treasssuresss, the people, the prophecccy, all musssst remain sssecret, elssse you forfeit your friend'sss offering for your livesss and will join him in death. Do not sssquander what we have entrusssted to you."

Haass fell to his elbows, no longer able to support his own weight. All three leapt to his side, trying to give what comfort they could to the dying man. His hand reached toward Phatomar, and the warrior took it with a gentle grip.

"Do not let Chaosss win." Haass' strained whisper barely rose above the grunts of the camels, his chest heaving with the effort to breathe. "Guard the Faqadat Alqalb with your life. *Her* life dependsss on it."

"Whose life?" Phatomar asked, glancing over at Jal, but Haass had no answer for him. Haass' chest rose once more and his mouth gaped as though to speak, but the spark of light left his vision and his breath hissed out in one final long sigh, taking the secrets of the Thueban Alnaas with him.

The three companions sat with him a moment longer, sharing sorrow and victory, concern and relief. Finally, they rose, and without saying anything further, took up the reins of their camels and turned to face the dark night.

"We have a long way to go yet," Eamon said. His words came on a puff of mist in the cool night as he stared up at the bright stars encircling the heavens.   "And much yet to accomplish."

"Let's hope we find the strength to bear whatever else the gods demand of us," Phatomar said, his eyes downcast. "Because the cost so far feels too great."

Jal studied him for a moment in silence. She understood Phatomar's dejection. How could they measure the lives of so many against the restoration of one man's courage and memory?

But that alone no longer drove them. They had stumbled into something larger, something the gods themselves had set in motion and positioned the three of them to find the answers. Jal just wished she knew what they struggled to achieve.

The Oracle's words echoed in her mind: *Three tasks you must accomplish.   Each will reveal part of the answer required to solve your riddle.*

This first task had gained them the Heart of Order. The slain heart of a goddess, if Jal understood correctly. And now they must take it to a tree of starry night where limb and Stone would point to a watery grave, or so the Oracle had said. The implications of these tasks, combined with the words of the snake priest, left Jal shaking.

Restore the Heart of Order...

Did gods expect mortals to restore a goddess to life?

Chapter 12

Although Kistawna could will her surroundings into whatever shape she desired, today she had chosen a tent of the nomadic tribes to confound her guest. Granted, a tent with far more luxury and amenities than any tribe could boast; no need to deny her own comfort just to put her visitor in his place.

Plush cushions of crimson and scarlet graced the burgundy silk floor. Gauzy lengths of sheer gold fabric waved in a gentle breeze from the open canvas flaps, the tent walls veined with streaks of pitch night against red a subtle display of her hatred interwoven with anger. Shadows gathered in the corners at the edge of sight, though few cavorted with any predictability in the flickering lantern light. Among her other titles, Kistawna bore the name Mistress of Shadows, the darker places hers to manipulate as she saw fit. One power among many that the goddess owned with pride.

She lay draped seemingly at ease upon a low divan, long raven tresses pinned back from her perfect golden face by a diamond diadem. A shimmering gown of bronze wrapped about the lush lines of her body, her feet bare. A gold bowl of red fruit sat on a small table at the end of the divan, and a silver goblet rested lightly in her long fingers tipped by nails painted a red so deep they looked almost black. One might mistake her lounging as a sign of tranquility, until one noticed the hard glint at the core of her flashing emerald-rimmed violet eyes, betraying the depth of her ire.

What should have continued a glorious road of victory for

her Lord and Father, the great god of Chaos, had somehow become the potential path of his downfall, and Chaos did not take well to failure. Kistawna had much to answer for if her plans continued to backfire, and she had no intention of allowing fate to continue to cloak her actions in ignorance, nor of suffering any punishment alone. If she fell, so would her co-conspirator, Dolanis.

To avoid that ignominious fate, they had to find a way to turn the situation back to their advantage, which required better information than Dolanis had yet provided.

How had Phatomar, a mere mortal, who by all rights should have died a mewling coward under an unnamed thug's sword months ago, not only manage to survive, but find the Faqadat Alqalb? Worse, how had his journey and its subsequent deed remained hidden from her for so long?

Dolanis had better have answers.

Delaying no longer, he swept in to her tent. The dark copper tone of the deep desert dwellers gleamed from his deceptively charming visage. Only the slight furrow between his sable brows as his umber eyes took stock of his environment, and the briefest hitch in his step, hinted at his disquiet at the nomadic setting. Dolanis didn't like to recall his humble origins. A trickster god, yes, but one who had won his place through cunning and deceit rather than birth.

His first squalls in this world had rung out from a tent far more humble than this, but they had come from weak, mortal lungs. Kistawna wanted him to remember that before thinking to use his cunning on her. Always anxious to prove his place among the pantheon of the gods, Dolanis understood that what one god had granted, another could take away. And though Kistawna might not have such power to quell Dolanis, Chaos did.

Kistawna regarded her companion over the rim of her goblet as she took a delicate sip. Dolanis opened his mouth to speak, hesitated at the narrowing of her eyes, then waited until she lowered her drink and gestured to a nearby cushion.

"Sit," she commanded, a second goblet appearing next to the cushion. Dolanis scowled, but sank gracefully to lounge on the offered pillow. *How much does he really know?* she wondered, taking careful note of his every expression.

"It has come to my attention," she said, her tone carefully

measured, "that our little ploy has failed to eliminate the threat."

Dolanis regarded her in silent perplexity. *Do you feign your ignorance, or does this revelation come as a surprise to you, too?* How could she find the answer to that question without giving him leverage over her?

"Tell me what has happened," Dolanis asked in that honeyed tenor voice that had gained the confidence of so many. No inflection to reveal his inner thoughts, no change of expression or quiver of a hand as he drank from his goblet to betray anxiety or trepidation—just a simple supplication for information.

"Did you follow Phatomar's progress after we crippled him?" she asked instead.

Now Dolanis frowned, his earthy gaze flicking briefly across Kistawna's face.

"A man with no name and no memory of his past deeds bears little of interest to gods."

"I thought as much," Kistawna said, the base of her goblet thunking harder than necessary on the small table. She sat up and put it aside. The shadows in the corner swirled as a shred of her ire escaped. "*A trifle, soon forgotten in this world,* I believe you said. But how, Trickster, did you manage to include *our* world in your little scheme to forget a hero?"

Dolanis' features revealed nothing, but Kistawna focused on the colours of Chaos swirling around him. She saw a flash of confusion, a spark of dread, but interestingly, she saw no deceit at the moment.

He chose his words carefully. "While I would very much like to take credit for such a feat, I suspect such vanity at the moment would serve me ill." He gave a slow blink, no doubt trying to order his thoughts. "Do you mean to tell me that, in trying to circumvent prophecy, we have somehow instead granted invisibility to the instrument of Order's return?"

Kistawna sighed.

"Enough riddles," she decided. "After our little foray in Ferna's market, where Phatomar should have met his fate, he and his companion survived long enough to reach Grandon, whereupon he faded from my awareness. *Soon forgotten.*

"So imagine my surprise when my adherents among the

Thueban Alnaas warned me of four intruders in their land, one of whom matched the description of the very person who had, until that moment, ceased to exist in my mind. Adherents who have since perished, their duty to keep the Faqadat Alqalb out of the hands of Order's champion a dismal failure."

"What?!" Dolanis lunged forward on his cushion, his goblet falling from startled fingers to spill a wash of crimson wine on the ground. A wave of Kistawna's hand erased the offending mess from existence. Dolanis didn't notice, his mouth working through several silent snarls before he found his voice again. "How?" he asked, his eyes grown dark and dangerous. "*How* could he even know to look for Order's Heart, let alone where to find it?"

"That, my little Trickster, we must find out, and quickly. Because if he knows about the Faqadat Alqalb—which, ominously has also vanished from my sight—he may also know about Natt Tre. We cannot allow him to reach the Formorket Enger and reunite the two. If you value your life, She whom Chaos slew must remain imprisoned."

He narrowed his gaze, his eyes speculative slits thick with cunning.

"You don't know where he travels now?" he asked, suspicion crawling through his voice.

"I do not. I can see neither him nor his companion, whom we did *not* erase from memory and *that*, Dolanis, should terrify you, for it means that Chaos no longer plays this game alone. We may not even hold a winning hand unless we can gain more tricks."

Now Dolanis smiled, the grin that had won him so many concessions along the road to godhood. That smile had led to the downfall of many, and Kistawna felt something loosen in her chest to see it now. She had the Trickster firmly in hand. Now to keep him there.

"If you discover who seeks to thwart us by masking Phatomar's steps," he said, "I will make sure our forgotten hero runs afoul of something unexpected and unpleasant before he ever sets foot upon the Blackened Fields. We will yet hold the ace, Kistawna."

She smiled, even as she felt a sense of foreboding. They didn't know where Phatomar travelled, nor who stood at his side, or what secrets he had learned on his journey thus far. Equally disturbing, she didn't know how the mortal had managed to survive this long without his vaunted courage, nor how he continued to move forward when every day should bring him incapacitating terror. But now, having set a challenge the trickster god couldn't resist, Dolanis, and not Kistawna, would bear the brunt of any future failure.

"Good hunting," she bade, leaning into the softness of her divan. A tendril of shadow curled around her lithe form in a playful gesture before whipping back to the darkened corner to merge with other embodiments of Kistawna's will. Dolanis nodded, then gained his feet and swept from the tent, his attention already elsewhere. Only then did Kistawna dismiss the image of the nomadic dwelling, frowning thoughtfully at nothing in a grey landscape of nothing.

"Now to learn who has intruded on our little game, and deal with them accordingly."

The daughter of Chaos vanished to trace the steps of her enemy.

Chapter 13

Jal grit her teeth, clutching the sides of her swaying hammock in a white-knuckled grip, and decided the tossing and turning of the ship in this latest storm reflected well the miseries of her emotional state over the last month or so.

If she closed her eyes, she saw the bloody image of Olbaehn's head rolling across the cavern floor; the poorly masked devastation of Noll's face when she returned to Fyum to give the news that her youngest sibling now led the family until Olbaehn's child came of age.

She remembered the endless days of trudging through the desert (first to Fyum, then north back to Merveah), followed by tracts of grasslands and forests swirling into the astonishing colours of autumn—a dramatic change of season she had never imagined, despite Eamon's descriptions—as they turned west. She endured days of sympathetic glances from Eamon and Phatomar even as they tried to resume some semblance of normalcy.

Jal trained hard to take her mind off the loss of one brother she hadn't thought she'd miss, and the forced maturity of another who had his freedom stripped away by an unlooked-for responsibility. Only exhaustion allowed her to sleep in those first few days, and nightmares often intruded upon that slumber.

Eventually, they had reached the western coast of Merveah.

"Formorket Enger stretches as far as the north-western coast," Eamon explained, studying both ocean and vessels in the setting light of the sun. "As I said before, I've never wandered those wastes, but I believe we stand the best chance of finding what we need if we swing down from the north, rather than up from the south."

"How much territory do these wastes cover?" Jal wondered.

"The volcanoes span several miles of the Tasor Mountain Range, six slumbering giants nestled among their quiescent neighbours, marching east from the shore. Legend puts the dark tracts of land that I suspect inhabit the Blackened Fields at the base of the two central-most volcanoes. Few venture inland from the north shore, which suggests to me that's where we're most likely to find the tree of starry night and whatever secret it holds."

"Right." Jal nodded in agreement, her face grim. "Where it's hardest to get to. Of course that's where the Oracle would send us."

Sound reasoning or not, they had booked passage on a ship heading to the Anstore Islands, an archipelago some days sail west from the north-western tip of Merveah. The *Swelling Tide* would pass near enough to where Eamon's map hinted the trio should go, and the captain and crew declared themselves willing to help them make landfall where no harbour existed.

Assuming they lived long enough to escape the fall storms that had barraged them near daily. Unlike the sea between Merveah and the desert, this *ocean* held little warmth. Given the nature of their quest, Jal half fancied that the gods now conspired against them, though she stopped herself from openly cursing them. No need to draw undue attention, especially when Eamon assured her that such storms simply followed the turning of the seasons, not the whims of gods.

That the *Swelling Tide* loomed larger than any vessel they had used before—a feature Eamon assured her would provide more stability in uncertain weather far from shore—gave her no comfort when waves taller than the masts threatened to drown them all, or when winds lashed at the sails until they wailed in torture. On the calmer days, Phatomar laughed with rare enthusiasm, his hands working the lines next to barefoot sailors, while Eamon grinned his delight at this unsteady mode of transportation.

Jal, meanwhile, spent most of her time huddled in silent misery below deck. She lay there now close to her companions, battling to ride out this latest tempest with at least a shred of dignity. The deep darkness, despite it being not long past midday, did nothing to alleviate her despair.

She heard the drumming lash of rain on the deck above, the heavy slap of waves thrown angrily against the hull, the cracking boom of thunder vibrating the air as the storm heaved the ship like a child's plaything, but she could see nothing. The captain had prohibited the use of lanterns until the waters calmed to limit any chance of a stray flame igniting tar-soaked wood, leaving Jal in blackness as she weathered the heaving deck in the crew quarters where the three companions had found welcome. Or rather, where Phatomar and Eamon had found welcome; the sailors tolerated Jal for the sake of her friends—and for the monies exchanged for their passage north.

"If we live to reach land," she gasped, trying to keep the latest meal of fish soup in her stomach as the ship lurched again, "I'm never setting foot on a boat again."

A low chuckle rumbled from the hammock nearest her. Eamon enjoyed her plight far too much, in her opinion. The scowl she threw his way had no effect in the dark, though she hoped that he imagined her expression anyway. *It would just make him smile all the more,* she acknowledged with a rueful grunt.

"Best not make promises you can't keep," Phatomar said from his swinging bed on her other side, the two men flanking her here as they often did outside.

"I will walk the breadth of Merveah and the Gobani together, over every mountain and volcano if I must, before forcing myself to endure this kind of torment again." But her vow held no power beyond her own fervent wish, and they all knew it.

The words of the Oracle pointed to a different fate: *Limb and Stone will point you to the watery grave; do not shy from its liquid embrace.* Should they find the Blackened Fields with its night-starred tree and accomplish whatever task then set before them, they still had to face this watery grave, which most likely involved boarding yet another ship. Jal prayed that the grave of the Oracle's riddle wouldn't belong to any of them. She had already lost one brother; she had no desire to lose any more, even if those brothers didn't share her blood.

"I believe the horses will share your sentiment," Eamon joked. They had left the camels at Fyum Oasis with Noll to do with as he chose, so they only had Croga, Cosantoir, and Onoir to worry about. None of the three equines had particularly cared for the blindfolds that ensured their complacency when Eamon had led them aboard a week ago, and the unsteady conditions through each successive storm had not, according to the shorter man, improved their disposition. Jal wondered whether the animals would refuse to risk donning the blindfold again when it came time to disembark, fearing yet more unknowns, or whether the beasts would leap overboard when they saw land and refuse to go near water again. She half wondered the same about herself.

The next crash of thunder made the whole ship shake, and the muffled yells of the crew above briefly rose to a pitch where Jal could almost hear their words. She discerned the tension in the shouts, quickly picked up by those taking shelter in the dark confines with her as a harsh bell clanged an alarm from the deck above. Even as she fought to twist her way to freedom from her swaying hammock, Jal heard the scrambling of bare feet slapping against the floor as sailors leapt from their hammocks and rushed from the quarters—somehow avoiding each other in the black.

"What's wrong?" she gasped as a large hand found her arm and steadied her enough for her to find her feet.

"Lightning strike, I think," Eamon said, his tone as serious as anything she'd heard from him.

Jal felt the blood drain from her face. Her stomach lurched violently at a spike of adrenaline-fuelled terror. "What do we do?"

"Get topside to see the damage," he said. "The bell is a call to all hands."

"Stay out of the way of the sailors," Phatomar added, the hitch in his voice and the trembling of his arm indicated his own fear as he pressed something into Jal's hand. She recognised the sheathed shaft of her sword and hurriedly strapped it into place.

144

"What about the horses?" Jal asked as the ship pitched with the rough waters again as the trio tried to navigate the invisible room. "They can't get to the deck."

"We assess the damage first," Eamon said somewhere ahead of her. "Then we make our next decision."

They reached the open hatch to the deck above and the spray of salty water splattered against her face. An orange glow outlined Eamon's silhouette as he hurried up rain-slick steps. He paused.

"Dearn save us," he said on a heavy exhale, a curse rather than a prayer. He pulled himself out into the open, turning in a crouch in the rain and wind to help his companions up. Jal followed, mimicking his caution by kneeling at his side. The wet plastered her hair to her head, and the rip of the wind tried to shove her off balance. She pushed the rust-coloured tendrils from her eyes and blinked at the mayhem she saw. With a swipe of her hand across her disbelieving eyes, she took in the horrifying image of a mast in flames, men trying to free burning lines, clear the rubble-strewn deck, aid a fallen comrade. Chaos.

Lightning flared across a sky heavy with charcoal clouds tinged with both green and purple, leaving a sweetly pungent odour in its wake. Again, lightning flashed, searing reddish-purple arcs across her vision, and thunder crashed with enough force to set her ears ringing. Thick rain pelted her like cold shards of glass, hard enough to sting. Dark, frothing waves soared overhead and plunged beneath the ship, tilting the vessel so that it became difficult to distinguish up from down. Jal clung to the edge of the hatch when the cant of the boat tipped them nearly sideways before briefly righting them, only to tilt them all back the other way. She swallowed hard, tasting both bile and salt water that she coughed out again.

Somehow, Eamon and Phatomar kept their balance enough to not tumble into the ocean. The former's gaze searched the horizon through blinding flashes of lightning, the latter looked everywhere, his eyes wide enough to show white in the orange glare of the thunderous fire.

A broad-shouldered sailor slid to a halt at Eamon's side. Jal recognised him as Inkorat, first mate of the *Swelling Tide*. The golden-orange flames flushed his pale face, turning the dark ink of tattoos that decorated his bald head into a frightening mask.

"'Fraid we're not gonna make landfall quite where we'd expected," Inkorat rasped. He didn't sound afraid, but Jal read resignation in his stance. "Lucky if we're able to salvage any of the *Tide*, but shore's thataway." He jabbed a thumb over his shoulder and Jal found herself searching frantically for any sign of land amid the churning waters. She saw only the storm. "Maybe a mile east. Doubt the longboats'll take kindly to the waves, but better 'n open ocean. Least until they reach the rocks. Last one casts off in three," he informed them. Two quick strides took him from view as he moved to gather the other sailors.

Eamon grabbed Jal's shoulder and gave her a shove that nearly sent her tumbling toward where the crew had begun to amass near the lifeboats.

"Go," he barked as he and Phatomar turned in the opposite direction.

"Where are you going?" she yelled over the howl of the wind.

"If we set up the ramp in the hold, the horses will at least have a chance to escape," he said. Jal pulled herself to unsteady feet and took a lurching step to join her friends.

"We stay together," she said.

"No—"

"Yes," she spat. "It'll go faster if we work together, then we will *all* make the longboat. Hurry." She pushed past them and raced toward the hold, knowing they would follow. While she feared for the horses, she dreaded the frigid water more. Jal didn't know how to swim, and she very much feared the prospect of the ocean's embrace. She wanted to give the mounts their opportunity at freedom before she surrendered her own.

A wave crashed over the rail, washing Jal's feet from beneath her. She yelped as her hip slammed hard onto the deck, the force of the water and the cant of the ship threatening to drag her overboard when her scrambling hands found no purchase. Strong fingers grabbed her tunic and belt, halting her movement. For a moment, Jal couldn't feel anything but overwhelming panic, couldn't hear anything past the frantic drumming of her heart. Then Phatomar hauled her to her feet, thrust her arm through some rigging, and indicated with a raised hand, palm out, that she should remain. She clutched the rope tight and nodded, but already the two men had disappeared.

How can Phatomar function in this chaos? she wondered, her own courage sorely battered by the terrors of the storm and the sickening sway of the ship. Perhaps his confidence in the ways of sailing somehow lent him strength.

"I didn't even hesitate." She remembered him saying that when he killed Garnda. If seeing to the horses took his mind off his own imminent peril, helping him act without hesitation, she had to admire his temerity.

Or maybe he follows Eamon blindly, not allowing his mind to truly see the danger.

Jal tried to will her body to obey her mind and release its death grip on the netting she clung to. Instead, another roll of the hull had her hanging on even tighter, until she no longer felt any circulation in her arms. Her teeth chattered and she thought she saw slight plumes from her gasping breath curling through the downpour.

I have more strength than this, d*ammit,* she berated herself. *Flames will soon engulf the ship, assuming it doesn't capsize first, and I stand here like a helpless babe instead of lending my aid.* She could at least render her assistance with the longboats.

Even as she disentangled herself from the rigging, a cry pierced the sky; the terrified scream of a horse. The sound of hooves clomping across the deck accompanied the next growl of thunder, and she saw three large shapes painted in flickers of orange and yellow by the flames on the mast. They headed for the railing, leaping over and into the waters beyond as the mast finally snapped under the heat and strain of the fire.

Jal, freed from her paralysis, threw herself in the direction the horses had taken. With a whoosh, the flaming mast smashed to the deck behind her, setting fire to the rigging she had so recently found refuge in. The mast tipped over the side as the ship rocked with its fall. Jal leapt to grab hold of the rail as the impact again took her feet. The swollen, angry sky briefly filled her vision before she found herself staring at the rapidly approaching ocean, the force of the ship's wild pitch lodging her hard against the rail with no

147

chance to escape.

Water closed over her head as she thrashed. Her lungs burned and the sting of salt water stole her sight. Jal suddenly realised she no longer held onto the ship. The ocean dragged at her and she panicked, arms and legs flailing.

I can't swim!

Breathing would spell her doom, but her starved lungs, not having had time to gasp in a final breath before the waters swamped her, demanded she draw in air. She fought the feeling for as long as she could, and then she lost the battle.

As darkness and despair came to claim her, something slid across her numbed hand. Reflex closed her fingers around a stringy mass before her consciousness fled, carrying her away into an uncaring embrace.

Chapter 14

Phatomar couldn't stop shaking. Only a small part of his tremors came from the cold slap of the waves tossing their longboat like a discus. Shock had set in, and it left him a quivering mess, barely able to coordinate as he hauled on the oar in the unstable waters, pulling frantically for land.

He and Eamon had manoeuvred a ramp out of the hold for the horses, freeing them from their restraints and urging the panicky beasts topside. They had grabbed their saddlebags, including Jal's, then had reached the top deck in time to witness the fiery mast snap and crash to the deck. He saw Jal's pale face as she escaped the crushing weight of the shattered splinters, then watched in horror as the next great wave washed her out into the ocean.

Eamon had echoed Phatomar's cry of disbelief, but while Phatomar's limbs had locked in horror, Eamon had found the strength to act.

Eamon loosed his hold on his bag and, timing the next roll of the ship, followed Jal into the lashing waters. Phatomar stood in shock for a moment, his mind refusing to cease its gibbering babble of dismay.

I can't throw myself after them, he realised, struggling against an all-encompassing sense of fear he couldn't reason past, even if such a reckless action might help save them. His head whipped around to where Inkorat and the other sailors struggled with the longboats. *But I can row.* With that thought, he found the strength to move, snagging all three saddlebags and lurching toward the rail and escape.

The last of the sailors (save a shadowy form at the helm) climbed aboard the final longboat, and only Inkorat still stood planted firmly on *Swelling Tide*'s deck. Four other longboats had already disappeared in the stormy waves. Hopefully they made for shore, but they might instead have fallen to the whims of Kordan, god of the sea to whom these sailors prayed.

The first mate glanced over his shoulder at Phatomar.

"Just in time," he grunted, then raised his brows in question. "The others?"

Phatomar shook his head. "They went overboard." He pointed out the location, though the constant sway of the ship made finding the pair impossible. "If we launch in that direction, we may yet reach them."

Inkorat jerked his head in negation.

"Lucky if we can haul toward shore," he said. "No way Kordan's gonna let us pick a direction and steer true. Don't worry, lad. They'll head for shore; that's their best chance."

"Jal can't swim," cried Phatomar, his chest tight with dread. A flash of sympathy softened Inkorat's face. He laid a hand on Phatomar's shoulder.

"Then pray that Kordan lets Eamon save her, and save yerself to see the miracle."

Inkorat nodded at the longboat meaningfully. Shoulders sagging in defeat, Phatomar put a hand to his abdomen, both to ease a stab of anguish and to check that the Faqadat Alqalb remained fastened beneath his tunic. Moving with the pitch of the ship, he stepped aboard the swaying longboat and tucked the saddlebags next to other small bundles lashed beneath the sailors' feet. Inkorat quickly followed behind.

"Lower her, boys," the first mate called.

Phatomar stared at him in surprise.

"The captain?" he asked.

"Holdin' the *Tide* to the end," Inkorat said, the grim set of his jaw suggesting his disapproval. "Either we come back once the ocean's settled to assess the damage under the flinty eye of Cap'n, or he goes down with the wheel in his hand and we got nothing to return to."

The sailors fore and aft released the lines holding the longboat in place and the smaller boat fell to the waves below. Somehow—either by luck or skill—they timed it so that the water cupped the hull rather than smashing the boat against the side of *Swelling Tide*'s heaving bulk.

"Pull," someone yelled, and the longboat slid away from its host. Phatomar added his weight to an oar, fighting his fear and straining with the crew to escape the storm's fury. He kept scanning the dark waters, hoping for any sign of Eamon or Jal, but the leaden clouds with their intermittent streaks of lightning and the heaving waters made it impossible to see more than a few feet. Rain and waves drenched him, washing away the tears from Phatomar's cheeks, but the stifling loss he felt made every shuddering breath an act of agony.

Phatomar couldn't recall the moment he had first met Eamon—in the midst of some brave feat of action lost to his mind—nor envision many of the adventures his friend had regaled him with since Ferna's market, but he well knew the camaraderie between himself and his companion; the sense of belonging, of kinship through shared experiences and beliefs, of having a brother as well as a comrade-in-arms.

In contrast, he remembered every day since meeting Jal; standing between him and a sword thrust meant to end him, daring to hear the words of gods and Oracles, trying to help Phatomar find ways to deal with his loss and discover his worth in other arenas. The way she eagerly soaked up lessons about Merveah—swordwork, language, customs—and combined them with her own knowledge encouraged both Phatomar and Eamon, her enthusiasm infectious. She had suffered from mountain sickness, seasickness, a troubling family reunion, and the subsequent death of a brother who had hoped to protect her, yet still she endured; still she tried to bolster Phatomar's spirits when her own so desperately needed strength. They had shared in boredom and fear, hardships and solace, smooth journeys and rough waters, and she had become as much a part of his family as Eamon.

And now both floundered beyond his reach, lost in the storm while Phatomar strove for the safety of land. Even knowing the truth of Inkorat's words—they would never find two people amid the violent waves in a boat that barely responded to the efforts of twelve men—Phatomar still felt as though he had abandoned his family. Here he sat, cowering in a longboat, failing to leap into action. He had instead taken the safe route, like the coward he had become.

"Brace!" one of the men shouted, jarring Phatomar out of his sour thoughts. He jerked his head up, trying to clear his vision of rain and sea water. The tearing of the wind had lost some of its vigour, the sky had eased its oppressive darkness with the green and purple hues having faded to swirling grey clouds, and the flares of lightning had subsided to only intermittent illumination. Enough light had returned to outline the rapid approach of land spanning the horizon. It also clearly defined the line of rocks rising from the thin strand of ocean lying between the longboat and the shore, too late to avoid the imminent collision.

With a rending sound that jolted the men from their seats, the boat ground among the rocks, jerking to a halt for only a heartbeat before a wave from behind swamped them, pushing the vessel free to eventually limp closer to the shore.

Without pausing to think, Phatomar rolled over the side, grabbing the edge of the longboat to steady it as his boots hit the water. His feet sank down to a loose rock base, treacherous with slick algae and unsure footing. On the other side of the longboat, two sailors had copied his movements, and the three worked to haul the boat out of the shallows, the others aiding with the oars. From the shore, more men suddenly waded into the water to help, crew from the other longboats who had made landfall before them. When oars bit into shale and shell, the men clambered out and they soon pulled the boat free from the grasping clutches of the ocean.

They secured the vessel next to those longboats that the rocks hadn't completely damaged, tallied their losses—one boat and its crew hadn't arrived, and a large tear in the side of another rendered it useless—and secured the meagre supplies they had brought.

Phatomar left them and strode to the water's edge to stare out to sea with a desperate hope that it would bring his family to him. Without them, he had no way to fulfill his quest, no purpose he could reasonably pursue on his own, and no heart to go on. Without them, any confidence he had found to replace his courage disappeared. He wondered how long he would stand staring into the dying teeth of the storm before circumstances forced him to give up all hope.

He heard the trumpeting call of Croga before he registered the sound of hoofs pounding along the rocky shore. With a shout of joy, Phatomar ran to meet his bedraggled chestnut stallion, who pranced up to him with a snorted whinny, dark mane and tail knotted, coat dripping wet. Phatomar flung his arms around his steed's neck, glad the horse had survived. He glanced around, but saw no sign of the other two mounts he and Eamon had freed.

"Oh Croga," he moaned, pressing his face into the horse's wet shoulder, caught between relief and despair. "At least you're here."

Croga whuffed, then pulled away. Phatomar stared at the horse, watched bemused as Croga danced back, lowered his head and threw it back again, tangled mane whipping with his motion. Croga reared and swivelled, galloped several paces, then stopped and looked back at Phatomar. He stomped a foot, glanced ahead, then back at Phatomar. Another trumpeted neigh.

Puzzled by this odd behaviour, Phatomar took a hesitant step in Croga's direction. The horse seemed to nod. Before Phatomar got close enough to reach him, Croga gave a half-rear and dashed away again. Phatomar found himself running to catch the beast.

They approached the shadowy hulk of a semi-circle of rocks. Phatomar suddenly realised not all those shadows belonged to boulders. One stood on four legs, his head lowered to nuzzle a shape lying supine just beyond the reach of the water. Another large hump sheltered a smaller shape.

Phatomar urged himself to greater speed, coming to a halt beside Croga as the horse joined his two companions, those two animals, in turn, keeping their human charges from being dragged back to the ocean. Phatomar dropped to his knees, not caring about the sharp bits of scree biting through his wet clothing, and wept.

***

"I didn't think," Eamon said, shaking his head. "I saw Jal go overboard and I just reacted. By the time I hit the water, I already knew my mistake. From the deck, I could at least

153

see in more than one direction. From the water, all you see is more water. Towering waves of it, ready to slam down on your head."

He shuddered, remembering the blindness, the suffocating pressure of wind and wave, the utter helplessness of finding himself entirely at the whim of a mindless storm. He had faced death before, but always with a sword in hand. How did one fight nature?

Even now, sitting before a fire made from deadfall the sailors had scrounged from along the shore and a copse of trees nearby, his hands stretched toward the shifting warmth in an effort to stave off the shaking after-effects of his ordeal, Eamon could barely grasp his escape from disaster. The circumstances of his rescue had a wholly surreal quality to them that he now feared he dreamed.

Please, Dearn, let me truly sit here, not flounder, overcome by hallucinations, drowning in the ocean. But he had to trust his senses—the heat of the fire, the sense of security he felt despite having no idea where they had landed, the deepening dark of true night following a brilliant sunset of blood red and golden clouds.

All this available to him thanks to some incredible luck, and three astonishingly devoted horses.

He remembered the shock he felt at hitting the cold water, how it sucked him under one moment and threw him high the next, threatening to smash him against the hull before tossing him out to sea.

Salt had stung his eyes, his nose, his lungs. He couldn't get enough air, couldn't find his bearings. Did the shore lie ahead or behind? Too consumed by his own peril, he couldn't spare a thought for Jal. The dark depths of the storm stole his sight, ripped away his breath, sapped his strength. Cold, terror, and fatigue took a toll on his strength, numbing his body. *Such a fool,* he thought, just as something grabbed the neck of his tunic.

He flailed out of instinct, trying to escape his captor. Images of deadly sea creatures flashed in his thoughts, leviathans or sirens eager to steal the lives of mortals, dragging them far under the water, never seen again. Did he even now lie in the grasp of a monster of the deeps?

Reaching back, his arm met the bulky warmth of flesh

instead of the cold of scales. He tried to clear his mind enough to understand. Had Phatomar followed him into the deadly waves? Had Jal found him? One of the sailors?

His sluggish fingers encountered a long soft nose, flattened ears further back, a powerful neck matted with a wet coat mixed with long sodden hair. Eamon turned himself enough to make out a dark equine eye, rolling wide with fright yet filled with a strange determination. He swung himself until he could throw an arm around Cosantoir's neck, freeing the horse's teeth from his tunic. Cosantoir forced his way through the heaving waves with powerful kicks of his legs. Eamon helped as best he could, clinging tightly to the horse's mane though he had lost most of the feeling in his fingers.

How had Cosantoir found him? Why would the beast stop his own flight to freedom in order to rescue Eamon? He well knew the loyalty animals could have for their owners, but this seemed somehow different. Eamon pushed these thoughts aside and concentrated on not hindering the horse's advance, wherever he took them.

Eventually, he felt a change in Cosantoir's struggles, a slowing of their motion. Certain the animal had come to the end of his endurance, Eamon silently thanked the beast for trying so hard, and wondered what death would feel like. But instead of the cold embrace of oblivion, Eamon felt something scrape against his dragging legs.

Opening eyes he hadn't realised he'd closed, Eamon blinked at his surroundings. A wave engulfed him and, when it retreated, he sputtered out the water, coughing hard to clear his lungs. He crouched on trembling hands and knees, staring at a rocky shoreline.

Hands and knees?

He stared in wonder at his shaking limbs, mostly free of the ocean, then wearily raised his head enough to see Cosantoir shake himself on dry land a few paces away. The horse turned to look at him, neck bowed in exhaustion, and exhaled a loud sigh over the rush of wind.

Another wave pushed Eamon forward, then threatened to drag him back into the waters. With an effort, he crawled from the sea onto dry land, barely cognisant of the sharp stones beneath his knees, still amazed to find himself alive.

Did my horse really just rescue me? he wondered as he

coughed out a spill of briny water. He stared hard at Cosantoir, watched the mighty beast turn and stumble a couple of paces. Eamon cried out in dismay, though nothing more than a strangled croak escaped his lips. But the horse only moved as far as a grouping of boulders before dropping his head again.

One of the boulders shivered and turned its head. Eamon stared in shock before his brain translated what his eyes showed him. He scrambled to his feet and hurried forward on weak legs toward Jal, sheltered from the decreasing fury of the storm by Onoir's bulk curled around her. His strength gave out as he fell next to Jal, his hand reaching out in a desperate search for life. He felt a hint of warmth, but no breath.

"No," he rasped, his vision blurring. Then, guided by unseen hands, he dropped his palm to her chest and pressed hard once, twice, thrice. Following instructions he feared he imagined, he lowered his mouth to her parted lips and shared his breath. *Clear her lungs, return her breath.*

Again, he pushed against her breastbone, gave her air from his own lungs. A shudder came as she coughed, water bursting from her lips. He turned her onto her side and she vomited out a surprising amount of the ocean before settling back with a sigh. Curling her back into Onoir's warmth, she lay without moving save for the soft rise and fall of her renewed breathing.

Eamon let out a sigh, then dropped in exhaustion. Blackness swept over him and he lost all sense of time.

When Phatomar found them, apparently led by his own horse to the duo and their incredible mounts, Eamon found only enough strength to turn over, then fall unconscious again.

When next he awoke, he found himself beneath a shelter of salvaged canvas stretched over tree limbs to block out some of the wind and remaining drizzle—one of four such pseudo-structures the sailors had erected. Jal lay next to him, unconscious and wrapped up in the blanket from her salvaged saddlebag, the wool only slightly damp. A half-dozen sailors shared their shelter, others huddled beneath the remaining protections or gathered around the fire. Eamon wrapped his blanket around his shoulders, dragged

156

himself out and now sat side-by-side with Phatomar before the flames, ringed by bedraggled sailors, shivering and amazed at having survived. The three horses stood sleeping nearby, seemingly content now that their riders lay safe and the worst of the storm had passed.

Eamon shook his head at their inconceivable luck.

"Better to have waited and taken the boat," he muttered with a glance to Phatomar, who already had a protest forming on his lips. Eamon didn't give his friend a chance to berate himself. "We would have both died if not for the horses," he said. "You were right to take the longboat, give yourself a hope of survival. Jumping into the teeth of a storm should have killed me. Taking to the oars provided a chance at life."

"Perhaps, but I felt so helpless, leaving you to the caprices of Kordan," Phatomar said, eyes downcast. "Fear kept me from following you, not sound reasoning."

"Fear kept you alive. If I had stopped to think, even for a second, I might not have jumped." Eamon shivered again, and not from the chill in the air. "Courage helps you face your fears, but throwing away all common sense and reacting to situations instead of considering the repercussions only invites death. Having courage doesn't make my choices right, not if I don't use my mind too."

So often in the past, when faced with problems needing instant solutions (like a friend falling overboard), Phatomar would come up with a reasoned solution, and Eamon would follow his lead. In hindsight, Eamon could even imagine one or two himself: loose planks of board to help them stay afloat; a rope to keep them close as they searched for Jal; something (anything) less reckless than tossing himself into the jaws of a tempest with no forethought.

Another approach might have worked, or it might not have, but Eamon hadn't even paused to consider. Phatomar had always come up with such plans, tempering Eamon's impetuousness with clarity of thought. Eamon hadn't fully appreciated until now how much he had always relied on Phatomar's quick wits, and how broadly fear that froze his thoughts affected his friend. With but a moment's consideration, Eamon could have spared both Phatomar's anxiety at watching his companions disappear into storm-churned waters, and his own terrifying battle with the sea.

With an effort, Eamon pushed aside the hollow churning of his gut and shook off his dark thoughts. Night had fallen and he could see little beyond the dancing flames of the fire. He gazed around, taking in the sailors as well as the beach.

"So, any idea where we've landed?" he asked.

"We're well south of where you wanted to go," Marn, the navigator, said. The short, blocky man who sat next to Phatomar had long graceful fingers, and he pushed irritably at a lock of curling hair that had escaped the tie he usually wore at the nape of his neck. "Cap'n made for land when we still had some choice on direction, but 'tis still 'bout a hundred miles afore the foothills of the mountains, and that on the wrong side as you wanted." His hand gestured northward, the mountains he indicated invisible in the darkness.

Eamon had no idea whether he'd see any sign of their dark peaks in the light of day or if they yet stood too distant to make out even a smudge. A hundred miles encompassed quite a distance, but from what little Eamon knew, the fiery heights which spawned the Formorket Enger towered above the surrounding lands. What lay between here and there that might help or hinder view, he simply didn't know.

He remained equally ignorant as to where in the vast stretches of the Formorket Enger they might find the mysterious tree of starry night. And now that they must approach from the south, he feared a much longer and harsher journey. Why he thought this, he couldn't say; just a sense that their goal lay on the far side of the mountains, the same feeling that had led them to take passage on the *Swelling Tide* to begin with. If fate proved him wrong and they found what they sought without having to traverse the dangers of the mountains, he would rejoice, but he wouldn't stake his life—their lives—on it.

Eamon regarded the sailors sitting dejectedly nearby. "What are the chances of the *Tide* sailing again anytime soon?" he asked, although he felt sure he already knew the answer.

Inkorat snorted from where he sat next to Marn, poking at the fire with a long stick.

"Ain't good," he said, staring into the flames. "Don't know the full extent of the damage, or even if we'll see a ship on the waters come morning, but she sure ain't goin' far in a hurry until she gets a new main mast. Don't know as any trees 'round here will do for rigging up something to limp for the nearest port, but I'm not holdin' my breath." He raised his gaze to Eamon. "Barring a flamin' miracle, you'd get where yer going faster on horseback than on the *Tide*, even having to go bareback."

"Where is the nearest port?" Phatomar asked. "How far would the *Tide* have to limp?"

"Trandee's maybe fifty, fifty-five miles off," Marn said. "Not huge, but she'd have somewhere for us to berth and enough supplies to make more serious repairs. If, as Inkorat says, there's anything left of the *Tide* to sail, let alone mend."

"And without a main mast, we'd as like find ourselves reduced to rowing to make much headway," a third sailor muttered. "Long way to limp."

"Ain't no good dwelling on it now," Inkorat said. "Until we know the *Tide's* fate, 'tis all speculation. Maybe we have a ship to fix, maybe we have a long walk and few supplies to split between four dozen men. Won't know 'til morning, and frettin' won't change the facts. Best to conserve what energy we got."

The first mate looked over their strange little camp—surely seeing nothing more than darker shadows against the night—before taking in his men. "Those as can sleep, now's the time. Standard watch. We don't know what dangers these shores hold, so let's not survive the sea only to have some wild animal whittle the rest of us away."

A muted chorus of laughs followed this, and most of the sailors left the warmth of the fire to curl up beneath the canvas shelters. Eamon stayed sitting next to Phatomar, though he often glanced to where he had left Jal. None of the men had approached her, at least not that Eamon could see. Inkorat and Marn sat with them still, and the two sailors presumably assigned first watch had settled slightly apart, so the dwindling fire didn't impede their vision

Phatomar spoke so that only Eamon would hear him. "What'll we do?"

"Let's see what the morning brings," Eamon answered in kind. "If we can help with any repairs, we'll do that. If we can take someone ahead to Trandee to get supplies, I'd not turn that chance away." He sighed. "If the *Swelling Tide* has gone down, removing three mouths to feed will aid these men best, and we could ride ahead and alert anyone who might offer them better aid."

"And if Jal doesn't wake in the morning?" Phatomar asked, a catch in his voice. "What do we do then?"

"She'll wake," Eamon said with far more confidence than he felt. "She has to."

Chapter 15

Jal remembered the panic she felt plunging into the ocean. The strange sense of peace which had descended in the instant after her lungs demanded breath that contained sea water, the feel of a wet yet silky tail gliding across her fingers, the blackness which had overwhelmed her.

She also remembered the voices, or at least, a dream of voices.

"Hold fast your lifeline, little warrior," one had said, tone resonant with power. *"Help approaches."*

Agonising moments later, after sensing the numbed glide of her body dragging through resisting water and the tug of her unresponsive form over the scrape of pebbles, she thought she had felt a hand on her chest, quivering lips pressed against hers, both following the guidance of a soft murmur.

"Clear her lungs, breathe for her, ignite the spark that lies fading." A different voice, more feminine and somehow reminiscent of Cleo from the Oracle, though perhaps only because it offered healing.

A burning sensation had torn up Jal's throat as the painful pressure in her chest lightened. Then, even the voices had faded, leaving Jal in darkness.

When she finally gathered the strength to open her eyes an untold number of hours later, pale light greeted her from beyond a canted canvas drape as the sun contemplated announcing the day. She blinked, raising a weak and weary hand to her pounding head. She moaned quietly as thirst assailed her.

A brief rustle of blankets beside her announced the presence of another. A head with tousled hair leaned over her, swallowing the dim light.

"Oh, thank Dearn," Eamon said in a thick voice. He reached forward and hauled Jal into a tight embrace.

She gasped, trying to get a full breath, but a second pair of arms engulfed them both, stealing what little air filled her lungs before she managed to draw in a gulp of life.

"We thought we'd lost you," Phatomar said, resting his chin against the top of her head, his shudders shaking them all. Or perhaps they all trembled; Jal couldn't tell. She only knew that their relief warmed her. And worried her. Just what had happened after her fall into the water?

"What—?" she managed to croak before a dry, wracking cough forced her to stop.

Phatomar reached for something beside him, guiding a flask of water to her parched lips. She greedily gulped at the precious liquid that soothed the fire in her throat, though the large warrior ensured she didn't drink too quickly, and her friends helped fill in what she had missed. Neither mentioned the voices, and she wondered whether she alone had heard the words. *Just like at the market in Ferna.* Thankfully not the same voices that had stolen from Phatomar, but still ethereal. Jal didn't know what to think of the possibility of higher beings interfering on her behalf. Movement nearby distracted her before she could share this potential encounter with her companions.

The sun had just crested the horizon behind them, bringing a fuller brightness to the sky. With it, a group of men from the *Swelling Tide* gathered at the ocean's edge, staring out into the calm waters. They spoke together, some pointing, others gesticulating around the shore, a mix of excitement and anxiety painting their motions. Finally, they broke off into three groups. One gathered around the longboats Jal could now see nearby while a second began preparations for a fire and, she thought, a meal. The third group, four men in total, came to Jal, Eamon, and Phatomar. She recognised the bald pate and inked face of Inkorat leading the way.

Eamon and Phatomar rose to meet him, and Jal struggled to her feet as well, clutching her blanket tightly and trying not to lean too heavily on the men at her side as her limbs still shook.

"The *Tide's* out there, but she's listing to port," Inkorat announced, raspy voice tight. "I'm sending a party to assess the damage and see whether—" He paused to clear his throat. "See what Cap'n has in mind." He shook his head. "She won't go far in a hurry, that much we can tell from here, and I guarantee there ain't no way to get your beasts back on board even if we get her to limpin'."

"You have other things to worry about than us," Eamon said. "But if we can lend a hand, we will."

"You brought us this far," Phatomar added. "If getting someone to Trandee for supplies will help, the horses are better on land than water anyway."

Inkorat gave a small smile. "The offer's appreciated," he said. He glanced out to sea as the first group of sailors dragged the least damaged longboat toward the water.

One of the men standing with the first mate—tall and rangy, dark of hair and light of skin—spoke. Jal struggled to remember his name.

"Likely a long list of supplies we'll need to fill," he said, his voice a light tenor. "If I can get the chandlery appraised of our needs afore *Tide* reaches port, mebbe we save some time in dry dock." *The quartermaster?* Jal wondered, but no name came to mind. But then, she hadn't needed to know many names. She had spent most of their time on the ship either ill or trying to keep out of the way.

Inkorat nodded absently to the man. "If she's salvageable, put that list together."

The man gave a sharp nod, then headed to the longboat just as the sailors launched it. Jal understood then that Inkorat had hoped for such an offer from them—the possibility of taking someone ahead to help refit the *Swelling Tide*. She also recognised by the first mate's rigid stance and how he leaned toward the sea that he longed to join his scouting party to assess the full fate of their oceanic home. Instead, he stayed on land, coordinating the remaining crew.

Jal wondered how far away Trandee stood, and whether their horses would appreciate the burden of two to a mount, especially without saddles. From what Eamon and Phatomar had told her, their remarkable beasts had performed quite the feat, dragging Jal and Eamon to shore amid the storm. She hoped Trandee lay nearby, for she feared they didn't have much fodder, if any, and the horses would need their strength to bear multiple riders any distance. She tossed a worried look toward the animals, who stood not far away upon the rocky shore. Some trees and other greenery grew further inland, she noted, perhaps enough for them.

"We'll stay through until tomorrow's dawn," Eamon said with a slight nod to Inkorat. "By then, we'll all have regained our strength and know what assistance we can offer before we depart. Until then, direct us as you would your own crew, Inkorat. We'll not shirk our duty to repay your help and hospitality."

Inkorat snorted and slashed a hand across his chest.

"You paid for passage; not your fault the storms defeated us. You get some of ours to a supply depot right quick, and that's good enough for me. However, you want to put those muscles of yours to work to distract from our current conditions,"—he glanced pointedly at Phatomar's bulk—"I'll not turn away the offer. Scrounging for food and firewood seems our most dire need on land."

"Aye aye, sir," Phatomar said with a little salute. Inkorat snorted again, then left to see to his men.

They spent the day assisting where they could—exploring the immediate area so they had a better idea of what resources lay nearby, gathering deadfall and old leaves to sustain a number of fires, setting snares for what small animals might frequent the region, and gathering edible plants under the supervision of the ship's cook.

Phatomar fashioned a couple of spears from sturdy branches and used them to spear fish to augment their food supply, aided by a sturdy ginger-haired sailor named Halvern, who had taken it upon himself to keep Phatomar company. The pair had stripped down to their underwear despite the chill bite to the air, and waded into the water, standing patiently with spears raised until prey swam past. In short order, they had added a dozen plump fish to cook's stores.

Other sailors mended the rents on the longboats and shaved off bits of bark from tree trunks, slathering them in a sticky resin that one of them mixed up to ferry back to the *Tide* to patch up the worst holes until they could make more permanent repairs.

Although the *Tide* had taken considerable damage, first in the storm and then against some of the rocks which blocked easy access to the beach, the crew had found some relief in discovering their Captain alive, though injured. Inkorat had taken their medic out in the next longboat upon hearing the news. He'd stayed aboard to oversee the more minor repairs and determine the most critical supplies needed from Trandee.

Jal felt some relief herself knowing that she and her brothers-in-arms would help speed the *Tide's* repairs by taking some sailors ahead for any supplies not readily available, for she knew no other way to offer her assistance to these brave men.

While the men did what they could on shore, Jal curried the horses with the comb in her saddle bag, then went on to care for their weapons. Eamon and Phatomar didn't want her exerting herself too much given her ordeal, and though she didn't think Eamon had fared much better than she, she acquiesced to their coddling, mostly because it eased their minds and allowed them to focus on their own chores. By mid afternoon, she found herself exceedingly tired and had to admit that perhaps the men had recognised the toll the sea had taken on her better than she.

Taking time to rest, Jal noticed something about her companions. Phatomar, dried and dressed once more, performed any requested labour without being startled at every noise—such tasks didn't need courage so much as strength and endurance, and he only betrayed any concerns when checking to ensure that the Faqadat Alqalb remained secure. When he couldn't keep it hidden (like when he had gone spearfishing), he would entrust the Heart Stone to Jal, carefully wrapped in a pouch otherwise well-fastened beneath his tunic.

Eamon, on the other hand, kept glancing out over the water, a subtle tightening of his shoulders belying his trepidation. At first, Jal thought he merely displayed concern for the well-being of the ship and her crew, but as she studied his reactions, she came to a different conclusion. The ocean had stolen a portion of Eamon's courage, just as the gods had taken Phatomar's. While they stood a chance to restore

165

Phatomar's magically stolen bravery, she worried that Eamon's anxiety would haunt him for some time. Having nearly died in those unforgiving waters herself, Jal could sympathise with his newfound agitation.

She hoped he could overcome this aversion, perhaps mirror Phatomar's attempts to conquer his fear, for she well knew Eamon's previous joy on the open waters. She certainly didn't share that joy, but she recognised how it fuelled his adventurous spirit. This new and unwelcome distrust had shaken Eamon, and Jal worried that it might affect his judgement. She prayed it didn't change his usually boisterous nature.

They had at least one more journey ahead of them that led somewhere across the waters. The Oracle had referred to a 'watery grave' and warned: *do not shy from its liquid embrace*. Had the Oracle seen this possibility; where not just Jal, but Eamon also, would balk at what their quest would require of them?

Half a year ago, she would have laughed at the thought that anyone could truly know the future. Since then, she had spoken with gods and creatures previously beyond her ken, and experienced the unlikely rescue of both her and Eamon by animals thought no more than beasts of burden. A being capable of seeing into the future didn't seem so far-fetched now.

She wisely held her tongue as both Eamon and Phatomar swayed over the stew the cook had prepared that evening, exhaustion finally beginning to overtake the stubbornness of her friends. She had rested some; they had not.

When they bedded down for the night, with perhaps a quarter of the crew remaining on land—including the quartermaster Tolik, Marn's assistant navigator Jast, and Halvern, the three sailors who would accompany Jal's group to Trandee in the morning—Jal forced down most of her disquietude over what the following days would bring. Sleep came quickly, her dreams untroubled.

***

They didn't dawdle, but they didn't push the horses too hard either, keeping to a fast walk with the occasional trot.

They gave their mounts plenty of time to rest, both by dismounting and walking next to the beasts for a while, and by allowing them ample time to graze. The fodder they had brought onto the *Swelling Tide* had not survived the storm, which meant that the only food available for the horses for the next two days existed solely in what the animals could forage. While the sailors had salvaged the saddles and bridles from the cargo hold, each horse now bore the burden of two people plus their limited supplies. Croga, Cosantoir, and Onoir needed all the sustenance they could find, and Jal didn't begrudge them the extra time spent filling their bellies.

Their expanded group had left shortly after daybreak. Phatomar and Jast—combining the largest and leanest members of the party—led on Croga, followed by Onoir with Jal and Halvern—again an attempt to match size ratios—while Eamon and Tolik brought up the rear atop Cosantoir. The horses had needed some convincing to accept the additional weight, but soon enough, they had set out from the beach, trusting Jast's skills at navigation to lead them in the right direction.

Trandee lay on the coast to the north fifty or so miles away, and although they had to move inland from the water to avoid the loose rocks of the shoreline and various marshy sections, the terrain thus far remained gentle enough: brush and trees (though nothing as vast as the forests Jal had encountered elsewhere), meadows and grassland, small rocky areas where the shoreline swirled inward.

Jast, though a year younger than Jal, assured them he could find the ocean again quickly from their uncharted path, keeping them on track toward where Trandee should lie. They had yet to find any semblance of a road beyond the occasional game trail, but both Jast and Eamon bade Jal not to worry.

"We'll see the occasional fishing village further along," Jast said at one rest stop. "But any roads lead east, deeper into Merveah, not along the shore, as that's where most trade'll happen. If folks here want to visit the other fishers, they take their boats, not a trail."

So they travelled that first day without seeing another person. Wildlife, however, they found in abundance, and they had no difficulties finding fresh meat for their evening camp.

Jal didn't know how the others felt, but when they did finally stop for the night, she let out a great sigh of relief. Though Onoir obviously carried the greater burden, her riders hadn't ridden in comfort. With Halvern pressed so close behind her—his bulk nearly as great as Phatomar's (*why did they pick such a large man to ride with us?*)—Jal had little space in the saddle and less room to breathe with ease.

A sailor with little experience on a horse, Halvern tended to tense up, his arms squeezing Jal as he fought for balance or some reassurance from clutching at the reins. Jal had given up on trying to quiet his unease with soft words after the sixth time he nearly unseated them, resorting to gritting her teeth and digging her fingers hard into his arms whenever he panicked or overbalanced. That physical reminder seemed to work to calm him for a time, but it left both of them stiff and moody by the end of the day.

She imagined Phatomar must have suffered similar discomfort. The few times she had spared a glance in his direction, she had noted Jast's white-knuckled grip around Phatomar's midsection and the tight grimace on her friend's face. Eamon and Tolik hadn't looked quite as miserable—she suspected Tolik had some familiarity with horses—but two men filling a saddle only meant for one still led to strained relations.

When the group settled for the evening, Jal finally managed to unclench her jaw. She made sure to pay extra attention to grooming Onoir while working out the knots in her muscles.

"We'll reach Trandee tomorrow," Eamon said as they set up their shelters. He knelt before a patch of earth he had cleared, around which he arranged a circle of rocks, building a small fire in his makeshift pit from wood that Halvern and Tolik had scavenged. Eamon and Jast had ridden a perimeter around their camp earlier, exploring the lay of the land and determining their location. The ocean lay less than a mile to the west, and after some study, Jast had recognised the contours of the shoreline enough to confirm they had only about twelve miles left to traverse in the morning.

"Hopefully before noon, doubled as we are." Eamon sounded both resigned and relieved by that statement.

Resigned, Jal imagined because, while they didn't have that much farther to reach the small port town, they still had to ride double for the morning. She tried not to scowl as she cleaned and dressed one of the hares she had snared while they waited. Phatomar grunted softly next to her, his own attention on feathering the rock partridge he had flushed out. She felt safe in her supposition that her companions had enjoyed their journey from the beach as little as she had.

"We'll take turns on watch tonight," Eamon said. "I don't know how far we stand from any village, but we're more likely to encounter predators scenting the horses than people stumbling through the countryside. I'd just as soon not wake to a wildcat or worse sniffing around."

They all agreed, and Jal offered to take the first watch after an uneventful meal and a brief sparring session with Eamon. She took the sword from her back and laid the sheathed blade at her side within easy reach. The others settled around the dying embers of the fire, the night promising mild temperatures and little need for bundling beneath blankets. They left the shelters for their equipment and supplies, the canvas walls of the tents able to keep any condensation or morning dew to a minimum.

Before long, only the song of crickets and the occasional snuffle in the undergrowth interrupted Jal's silent night. That and the sound of Halvern's low snore. Stars bloomed overhead, the constellations soon familiar to the desert girl, including the ribbon wending its way across the sky like a soft stroke from a paintbrush. The moon kept her face hidden near the horizon, not yet willing to peer over the trees, but the stars provided more than enough light for Jal to keep watch.

Nothing presented itself in the few hours she guarded the camp. The most dangerous creature she heard hooted as it soared over the land, a threat only to the squealing critters it caught.

She finally woke Eamon to take his turn as the moon, waxing just shy of half full, decided to add her brilliance to the stars and push herself into the sky.

Jal curled herself into her blanket and settled near the slumbering men, sword at her side, and quickly fell into a comfortable and dreamless sleep.

That sleep broken some time later by a snort and an

annoyed whinny from the horses, followed soon after by the soft *shing* of a blade being drawn. Jal started awake, stretching her senses to find the source of trouble.

"We have a problem." Eamon's quiet statement chased any tiredness from Jal as she rolled to a crouch, sword in hand, eyes searching the clearing in the pale pre-dawn, trying to see what had alerted Eamon. *It's not his watch anymore,* she realised, noting the hints of morning light. *Where's Phatomar?*

Her eyes snapped to two figures lying very still by the remains of the fire, one a hulking shadow and the other long and lean.

"Where are the others?" she asked, her gaze sweeping the clearing. "What's happened?"

Eamon crept closer to the motionless forms once Jal had him covered. He reached for the larger form. *Phatomar or Halvern?* Jal wondered, unable to make out any features. Eamon drew his hand back with a hiss.

"Blood," he growled, the anger letting her know who lay at Eamon's feet. For a moment, Jal couldn't breathe, fear squeezing her chest tight. *First Olbaehn, and now—*

Phatomar moaned and shifted. Jal blew out a sigh of relief, one quickly quelled as her mind worked through the implications.

"Who's missing? What did they do?"

With a groan, Phatomar pushed himself into an upright position. His hand rose to the back of his head and pulled away, a dark stain on his palm speaking of blood. His other hand went to his torso to make sure that the Faqadat Alqalb remained secure. Only this time, his comforting motion turned frantic. Even in the dim light, Jal could see his panic, and tasted bile at the back of her throat.

"Dearn save us," he gasped. "It's gone."

***

Eamon tended the gash on Phatomar's head. Tolik had a similar wound behind his right ear, the flesh purpling as it rose in an ugly lump to frame his abraded scalp. That saved the quartermaster from Eamon's wrath, because unless this presaged some elaborate ruse to alleviate their suspicions,

Tolik lay as much a victim as Phatomar. Eamon suspected he and Jal had escaped such treatment only because they hadn't woken in time. That Eamon and Jal had both slept through whatever had occurred only added to Eamon's ire and frustration.

Eamon and Jal had positioned their injured companions near the rekindled fire as they looked them over. Unless Phatomar and Tolik had a story featuring an unknown adversary sneaking into camp and snatching Halvern and Jast, those two had much to answer for. And seeing Phatomar reduced to a victim (again) had Eamon itching to repay them for this cowardly slight.

"What happened?" Jal asked with a calm Eamon didn't share.

Phatomar shook his head, then winced and froze, the motion paining him.

"Halvern joined me at my watch, maybe two hours before daybreak. Didn't think anything of it, as he'd helped me before. We talked quietly for a while, then he went to relieve himself. I saw Jast stir and sit up to stare my way. Then blinding pain and I saw stars, so I assume Halvern hit me from behind. I lost everything after that."

Tolik snorted, squeezing his eyes shut.

"Kordan, that hurts," he rasped and raised his gaze to meet Eamon's. "Caught in a dream, I don't know what I imagined and what actually happened, but I think I started to rouse when someone pawed at my belt where I kept part of the monies meant for resupply. The rest I left nestled away in the shelter, which I can almost guarantee ain't there no more."

He leaned over and spat into the grass at his side. "I think I grabbed the wrist or arm of whoever sliced the cord holding the goods 'neath my tunic, maybe struggled a little, but sleep still muzzed my brain. Don't think I even thought to call out. Then something slammed into my head. I woke with my head splittin', my tunic ripped, and you two glaring down at me, money sack gone."

Eamon turned to Jal and saw his reaction mirrored in the scowl on her face.

"So it's theft, plain and simple," Jal said.

"They don't know what they've got," Eamon agreed.

"Probably didn't even bother to look before they took it off Phatomar."

"How did they know I had anything of value?" Phatomar wondered.

Tolik grunted. "You wanna keep something secret, don't keep checking to see if it's safe," the quartermaster said. "Looked like habit, but you checking by feel for whatever you had beneath your tunic a dozen times a day still screams *lookie here what I got*. Begs someone to wonder what you value so highly, and if mebbe they shouldn't have it instead."

He didn't ask, but his tone made it clear he'd welcome any kind of explanation. Given the treachery of his fellow crew members, Eamon didn't feel obliged to share their dilemma just yet, despite the man's injury.

"We need to go after them," Jal murmured as she sat back on her heels. "Sooner rather than later." Eamon nodded as he finished with Phatomar's wound. He studied his friend with a frown.

"She's right, but can you ride?" he asked Phatomar.

"If they open up the bag to see what they've taken, they're dead," Phatomar replied solemnly. "And that means only I can safely retrieve it." By not naming the Heart Stone, Phatomar shared his agreement that Tolik didn't need to know details at the moment. "I might have to grit my teeth and brace my head to keep from throwing up, but I'll ride."

With that settled, they doused the fire and broke camp under the full light of dawn.

Eamon wondered if they might have misinterpreted the warnings of the Thueban Alnaas. What if Halvern or Jast *could* touch the Faqadat Alqalb with little or no consequences? No one else had dared touch the Heart Stone once Phatomar took it up; but what if anyone could hold the jewel? The prophecy had said *Death to the steadfast who takes up the Faqadat Alqalb, for it will avail him nothing but pain*, yet would one name a thief steadfast? Bold, certainly, but hardly of high moral character. Would that protect them from the dire warnings of the prophecy?

And what if the thieves didn't pull the stone out of its pouch? Eamon shook his head at that thought. A bright, shiny red gem the size of his fist begged for closer inspection. Thieves would want to examine their prize and gloat over its apparent wealth. But would that kill them, or merely bring them pain?

The prophecy, as Olbaehn had pointed out, could hold more than one interpretation, which left Haass' belief in its lethality as their only assurance that Phatomar alone could safely bear its weight. Eamon trusted the conviction of the dead snake-man, but a small part of his mind feared that they had lost their only chance to restore Phatomar to himself, and of fulfilling the unlooked-for wishes of the gods. He grimaced as they picked up the tracks of Halvern and Jast and started out, heading north toward Trandee.

Helping Phatomar regain his courage and memories had taken on a new weight when their trio learned that this would involve restoring a goddess to life—assuming they had interpreted *that* frightening development to their quest correctly. To have to set aside their journey now, even for a moment, to track down a couple of petty thieves kept Eamon's temper stoked. The storm had already robbed them of time, adding unexpected delays to their trek, but at least this diversion headed in the right general direction. With luck, they would catch the men before they reached Trandee, because if Eamon had to hunt them down in all the nooks and crannies of a port town he had never visited before, Eamon's current mood didn't court leniency or forgiveness.

This whole situation soured his stomach, but any time Eamon hoped to ease his anger, he had but to glance at the blood staining Phatomar's tunic, and clemency failed to find purchase in his mind.

By the time they found Halvern's body a couple of miles from their campsite, Eamon's jaw ached from clenching it tight for far too long.

He didn't think the body of the large sailor had lain in the grass for any great length of time before they encountered it. Halvern had no visible wounds, but his right hand had clawed into a half-fist, as though he had gripped something, then had it pried away. Eyes wide, mouth gaping in a silent scream, it looked like Halvern had died in terror and pain, and that Jast had left him that way. Only Halvern's pockets turned inside out, and his hand devoid of its prize, spoke to Jast having stopped long enough to witness his companion's demise, and he then had promptly divested Halvern of anything of value

173

before continuing his flight. Jast's departing tracks spoke to a greater urgency.

"Do we bury him?" Tolik asked from his seat on Onoir behind Jal. Eamon glanced up at him, took note of the sailor's conflicted face. To leave a man in such an undignified manner sat ill with all of them, but the longer they delayed, the more time Jast had to evade them. Perhaps the wily thief counted on that.

"We don't have the tools," Jal murmured. *Or the inclination,* Eamon added bitterly to himself.

"At sea, we'd give him to the mercy of Kordan's waves, and a thief who turned on his crew wouldn't find much mercy with the god of the sea." Tolik stared down at the dead man a moment longer, then spat on the ground. "Don't see that we should afford him any either while his fellow traitor runs free."

Eamon silently rose to his feet and moved back to Cosantoir. As he mounted, he heard Tolik's whisper.

"Even a traitor don't deserve an invisible death."

Tolik hadn't missed the implications that what Jast carried could kill him. Eamon found himself impressed by Tolik's restraint in demanding answers.

Eamon looked at Phatomar, couldn't read his friend's expression as he stared down at Halvern.

"Phatomar?" he asked softly.

Phatomar raised his eyes. "I mistook his interest for friendship when he in truth searched for weakness and established trust." He gave a slow shake of his head. "Would I have so easily accepted him before?" he asked, holding Eamon's gaze. "Or would I have seen through to his real intentions?"

"None of us saw this coming," Eamon tried to assure him, but Phatomar's eyes didn't clear of doubt.

"Have we strayed much farther inland from the water?" Jal asked in a soft yet even tone, pulling Eamon's attention away from Phatomar. "Or does it still lie close enough that we might return a sailor to its embrace?"

He didn't want to leave a body to time and the elements, even one who had betrayed them, but Eamon chafed at wasting a moment more on the dead man. Saying so out loud, however, weighed like ashes on his tongue, and he regretted his earlier uncharitable thought. Jal offered him a

174

grim smile, and a solution.

"You and Phatomar go after Jast. Tolik and I will deal with Halvern."

Eamon blinked, surprised at so simple an answer. Phatomar nodded to show his approval.

"You'll follow behind?" he asked.

"As soon as I can. Shouldn't take long."

Finally, Eamon agreed and set out after Jast with Phatomar.

In the end, even a man exceptionally fleet of foot couldn't escape the pursuit of determined riders without a much better head start than Jast had enjoyed. Eamon pushed Cosantoir hard, Phatomar and Croga matching his pace.

The sailor's inevitable capture didn't slow Jast's mad dash, however, and Eamon had to circle ahead and cut him off, herding the thin youth back toward Phatomar. The third time, Jast veered in a different direction, refusing to cede defeat. Eamon snarled an oath and changed tactics. Instead of using Cosantoir to keep pace, Eamon kicked free of his saddle and launched himself at the desperate thief, tackling him to the ground. He rolled to his feet and drew his sword in one smooth motion, pinning Jast with the end of his blade.

Jast lay there panting, eyes wide as he stared up at Eamon. His hand curled protectively around a bulging sack at his belt, even now hoping to keep what he had stolen. Eamon shook his head at the man's temerity.

"Leave off, Jast. It's over, and this," he nudged Jast's hand away from the sack with the tip of his sword, "doesn't belong to you."

"Demon's work," Jast spat, lungs still heaving. "Enchanted to kill."

"Not exactly," Phatomar murmured as he moved to stand beside Eamon, hand bereft of any weapon. "But deadly all the same." He stared down at Jast for a moment, waiting for the man to catch his breath. "Why do you still cling to what you've stolen like you have any right to claim it?"

"It killed Halvern," Jast whispered, eyes wide.

"And you thought, what?" Eamon demanded, seeing the avarice in Jast's stare. "You'd try to sell it to some unfortunate bastard and hope such a curse didn't befall him until after he'd paid you?"

"Would have worked," he said sullenly, and Jast's youth suddenly struck Eamon. It didn't absolve him, but it lent an exasperated pity to his reckless actions. Jast, like so many others, wanted the easy pay off, not the clean effort of honest toil, and Eamon doubted he had truly processed the consequences of his theft. He wondered whether the initial idea to steal had come from Halvern or Jast, then decided it didn't matter.

"So you felt lining your own pockets worth the cost of leaving your shipmates to suffer the risk of starvation and death?" Eamon asked. "By taking the funds meant to rebuild your ship, you destroyed the hopes of nearly four dozen others."

Tears began to flow from Jast's eyes, doing nothing to lessen the harshness of Eamon's words. If anything, the youth's self-pity disgusted the warrior.

"Men you sailed with, men who took you aboard their home, sheltered you, fed you, taught you; men who risked their lives to save you. And you repaid them by taking the food from their mouths, the safety of their shelter, their home, their very livelihood. You spat on their generosity and trust for the sake of your greed. And you have the effrontery to take offense when the gods punish you for your hubris?"

Jast drew in a ragged breath, fear finally swimming to the fore and overpowering pity.

"Gods?" he wheezed.

"No demons guard the gem you took," Phatomar knelt on one knee next to Jast. "But gods do. And for whatever reason, the gods have chosen to allow only one person to lay hands on it and live." The large man reached his hand toward the bag holding the treasure. Jast whimpered, pressing a fist to his mouth, making no move now to stop the retrieval of the sack.

"Understand, boy, that even without the curse that felled your companion, we would have still tracked you down," Phatomar said as he pushed to his feet, staring down at the shaking sailor. "The crew of the *Swelling Tide* counted on all of us to make them seaworthy again."

"Be glad your fate won't echo Halvern's," Eamon said, his tone flat. He slid his sword back into its scabbard with a firm thrust. Jast curled onto his side, wrapped his arms around his knees, and wept.

By the time Jal and Tolik rejoined them, Jast had quieted, in turns morose and contrite. No one spoke as Eamon and Phatomar remounted, Eamon hauling Jast up in front of him none too gently. He caught Tolik's eye as Phatomar tossed the older man the bag of coins, the Faqadat Alqalb again secure in Phatomar's possession.

"He's your responsibility when we get to Trandee." The quartermaster nodded, his gaze flinty and unwavering.

Eamon turned them north once again and advanced, anxious to reach the port town, more than ready to leave it, and their passengers, behind.

They crested a hill a couple of hours later and saw a town in the distance, the cove at its western edge glittering with the sparkle of the sun on gentle waves and dotted with boats. Eamon heaved a sigh of relief. He almost grinned when he heard the sigh echoed by both Phatomar and Jal, but the tense form of the thief sharing Cosantoir's saddle sullied Eamon's mood.

Sooner there, sooner gone, he thought. Cosantoir's whicker seemed to agree as the gelding bore them toward a road that stretched inland from the eastern part of Trandee. Nothing seemed to lead north.

Eamon found himself looking forward to the prospect of just the three of them—himself, Phatomar, and Jal—travelling without the possibility of encountering others. At least for a while. Perhaps once they reached the unknowns of the Formorket Enger, he would long for the security and excitement of a crowd. But right now, he only trusted two people, and he took comfort in the thought of his chosen family standing at his side.

Chapter 16

Chaos had many children. Few had the status or powers of actual gods, relegated into the minor ranks of the immortals: demi-gods, numen, sprites, even demons. Kistawna had half-siblings who could do little more than snarl a knot, snuff out a flame, or trip the unwary. Imps who moved objects or stole from mortals, goblins who haunted caves and caverns, demons who whispered nightmares. Each brought a little chaos to the world, but beyond a vague awareness of that infinitesimal contribution, Chaos ignored them all equally as beneath his contempt. This suited the minions of Chaos well, for none desired the weight of his regard even while they gleefully forwarded his goals.

The few offspring worshipped as lesser gods and goddesses of Chaos had more power and leeway, but needed to remember to step lightly when they schemed to escape their father's notice, for those who claimed godhood always bore watching.

Kistawna had managed to keep her difficulties with Phatomar and his unexpected achievements quiet...until she started asking questions.

Now Chaos had turned his eye toward her, his anger a palpable thing. The ire of Chaos pressed a suffocating mantle on Kistawna's shoulders, bowing her low and refusing relief. He did not, however, deign to bring her into his presence. Instead, he allowed his voice to thunder inside her head from afar. She counted that as a small mercy in her favour.

'Why does a daughter of Chaos confront an agent of Order?'

Kistawna tried not to cringe at the daggers shooting through her skull as his words reverberated in her brain. This intimate invasion of Chaos, however, didn't allow for subterfuge. Knowing she could hide nothing that wouldn't arouse further suspicion, Kistawna opened her mind, letting Chaos see what she and Dolanis had attempted, yet failed to achieve. She had no other way to explain why she had sought a meeting with the youngest son of Wisdom, Perception. While his twin sister Insight might have eventually responded to Kistawna's questions (she did lean more toward the precepts of Chaos than did her brother), past experience suggested Perception occasionally succumbed to a pleasing figure. If Kistawna had distracted him long enough, she might have learned which Younger god aided Phatomar and continued to shelter him from her sight. That Perception hadn't given an answer didn't dissuade Kistawna from asking her questions.

It did, however, draw the attention of Chaos.

'Foolish child,' Chaos chided her, the venom of his disdain clawing behind her eyelids. 'You seek to circumvent the Cycle without the benefit of forethought.'

Kistawna didn't dare suggest that she thought she *had* considered all the ramifications before she and Dolanis had acted. They had clearly missed something, or Phatomar would lie dead and forgotten, and those who sought to bring the influence of Order into prominence frustrated and disgraced. Now, she could only offer her contrition and desire to thwart Order's goals as her defence.

'By trying to turn prophecy, you woke Order's champion to his true purpose!' Kistawna clapped her hands to her ears with a whimper of pain, convinced she would find ichor draining from her head from the shards of Chaos' fury. 'Mewling infant!'

Kistawna scowled, pulling her hands from her head with an effort. If she wanted her father to give her another chance, he had to take her seriously, and a cringing, whining godling did not inspire confidence. She drew herself up and pushed against the weight of his presence to assert what she could of her own.

"An infant, maybe," she said, holding her voice firm. "But one willing to take action. I can yet turn this mistake into a triumph, snatch victory out of the very hands of Order. We have only to remove Phatomar from the board. But the proponents of Order hide him, and until I know who holds that shield, we work in the dark.

"We know where he must go next, Father, but unless you can tell me which god protects Phatomar, I have no guarantee of stopping Order's champion before he walks into the void of Natt Tre."

Kistawna imagined the fierce frown of Chaos in his distant palace, but she also fancied she felt the gossamer tendrils of approval briefly caress her mind.

'You cannot circumvent them,' he finally said. *'But you can work around them.'*

Kistawna froze. "Them?" she whispered, a blossom of triumph unfurling in her heart.

'Them,' confirmed Chaos, blowing their names into her thoughts. *'Do not dare to confront them directly, daughter,'* he warned, *'I cannot interfere on your behalf.'*

Cannot, not *will not.* Chaos seldom chose his words imprecisely, and this too must carry a message, one Kistawna had to remember. The Elder gods had placed restrictions even Chaos dared not contravene. By slaying Order so long ago, he had created ramifications not intended, consequences which forbade him from ensuring that Order could not rise again. Leaving it up to Kistawna, and those like her, to maintain the rule of Chaos.

She wondered if his disgust at her 'lack of forethought' might not refer only to her own actions. After all, Chaos had made a mistake those many ages ago. He himself had created the loophole that made the return of Order possible through her champion.

As though reading her mind, his next words lanced like hot irons in her head.

'Do not fail again.'

And with that, the god of Chaos turned his regard elsewhere.

***

Dolanis didn't know how much sleep, if any, other gods required. Immortal beings, yes, but not inexhaustible from what he'd witnessed. He himself still fell into the occasional mortal pattern of lying down to close his eyes from time to time. A brief restorative meditation to recharge his creativity, or a contemplative walk through fantastical landscapes intended to engineer some crafty thoughts brought a sense of refreshment. Yet still, taking the opportunity to close himself off from the world and fall into a heavy slumber did more to revitalize him than drinking in the adulation of mortals, something Kistawna assured him provided the ultimate high to the Chaos goddess.

Dolanis had never felt comfortable broaching the question with Kistawna or any other deity of what gods found commonplace. It would too easily remind his fellow immortals of the upstart godling who had joined their ranks through cunning and trickery; the mortal raised to godhood. Asking after the daily habits of gods would only remind them (and him) of his humble origins. Even after so long within the pantheon, his ignorance of how gods lived day-to-day irked him, but better to mask that ignorance beneath a confident bluster than show any weakness by admitting what he didn't know. That did, after all, define his nature.

That said, he didn't know if the others slept as he did. Which meant Dolanis also couldn't say whether other gods dreamed, or what might wake them from oblivion. But after a moment of intense concentration, he knew exactly what had woken him now.

Someone had revealed the Faqadat Alqalb; someone other than the man whose identity he'd stolen. The Heart Stone hadn't graced the realm of mortals for long before disappearing again beneath whatever strange shield that had enveloped Phatomar. But it had shone long enough to wake Dolanis now and allow him to see its location.

He sensed death and terror, then determination and resolve, and finally relief as the Faqadat Alqalb returned to Order's agent. Each emotion had coupled with an image: a young man with sandy hair watching as the Heart Stone's curse killed another; two men on horseback following the pair—one of whom should not have even possessed the courage to trust a horse, let alone ride it. And finally, a hand

181

reaching for the bag holding the Faqadat Alqalb while the point of a sword stayed the hand of a thief.

More importantly to Dolanis even than the face of Phatomar's companion—whose image Kistawna had lost as other gods slipped into their game to protect the pair (and if she had learned how many of the higher echelon, and who specifically, stood against them, she hadn't yet revealed it to Dolanis)—he saw a place in the mind of the thief. The small port town of Trandee, an insignificant little place south of the Tasor Mountain Range. That Range whose fiery mounts dominated the Formorket Enger.

Dolanis smiled, though no one could see the spark of mischief and satisfaction that flashed in his umber eyes. He now had confirmation that Phatomar did indeed travel toward Natt Tre. More, the Trickster knew *where* Phatomar and his brown-haired, sun-kissed companion stood in Merveah at that very moment, and the route they must travel to reach the Formorket Enger.

Time to set his own game in motion, and thwart the ambitions of those who would disregard a mortal-turned-god.

Chapter 17

The mountains which sheltered the home of the Oracle had stretched with sharp angles and craggy faces high into the sky, capped with the frigid glare of snow and ice. They had intimidated Jal from a distance, challenged her as she tromped almost blind up their slippery slopes with drifts up to her thighs, and nearly defeated her with their air-stealing heights. Yet she felt a kind of nostalgia for them now as they silently sat on their mounts, staring north toward the Tasor Mountain Range. Their hazy heights had steadily risen the closer they had ridden, growing sharper, more pronounced, and more daunting.

Trandee lay a day and a half behind them, leaving Tolik and Jast to their own devices. The quartermaster had grimly imprisoned the thieving assistant navigator under his own watchful eye until the *Swelling Tide* could find its way into the little port, as the militia there seemed inclined to act only if wealth might line their pockets. In their estimation, with Tolik's property already retrieved, they needn't deal with Jast, citing that he'd found punishment by getting caught. Jal had shaken her head over such lax measures and lack of order, disgusted by authorities who didn't look beyond their own self-interest. But with no one to curb their corruption, all too common according to Eamon, they had little recourse but to trust Tolik could deal with the thief.

Jal felt relief that they had so quickly and easily relinquished themselves of the burden of the sailors, even if the circumstances felt less than satisfactory. She had a lightness in her heart now as she rode again with only Eamon and Phatomar for companionship.

The intimidating peaks of the Tasor Mountains threatened to quell that lightness. No, not the peaks, she thought, but the strange and uneven craters left behind by the fury of fire, as though a god had reached down and scooped off the top of some of the mountains. *Volcanoes*, Phatomar had called them. Four had softer edges defining their cones, glistening fingers of white streaked with greyish-brown barrenness painting the tops where clouds didn't obscure the heights.

But the two central-most volcanoes, ringed by cloud yet rising above those white collars, trailed smoke into the sky from rugged lips of black. A haze of red and orange peeked around the rim of the larger of the two, spilling a thin line of fire down its side, just visible from where they waited. They saw nothing but black rock and rubble around the base of these mountains and spilling into the valleys and foothills; the build-up of years of activity solidified into a massive field of death.

"The mountains expel their fury," Phatomar said. "And each time their tears dry, they leave behind darkness."

"The Formorket Enger," Jal said in awe and apprehension. "The Blackened Fields."

"More like the gateway to the Formorket Enger," Eamon corrected, taking in the scene before them. Although the line of mountains and volcanoes stretched across the horizon, they still had a lot of ground to cover before they reached the towering spires, and the closer they rode toward the Tasors, the less defined each mountain would appear. Eamon searched now for the path they would take that would safely lead them to their goal.

"We'll find no trees of note on this side of the volcanoes. At least, I don't think we will." His uncertainty put Jal on edge even as it eased her mind, for he travelled as blindly as the rest of them.

The Oracle hadn't given them specific directions or instructions. *Find the tree of starry night* might sound simple, yet when presented with the vast reality of the Formorket Enger, it left them more than a little intimidated. The god of warriors had sent them to the mountains at Hada, to the home of the Oracle. The Oracle, in turn, had sent them to the caverns beneath the sands to retrieve the Faqadat Alqalb. Both tangible, physical destinations they could map, even if they had had to hunt for directions. *Blackened Fields where ancient death engendered a tree of starry night* left a great deal of territory to explore, with only their own senses to rely on to find it.

First things first. They had to find somewhere in the Blackened Fields that supported trees. Then they could locate the specific tree, and figure out a way to retrieve *a limb freely given*.

How does a tree freely give a limb? she wondered. Her mind conjured up an image of a person pulling off his arm and handing it over to Phatomar. She didn't know whether to laugh or cringe at the idea. *Does this tree of starry night walk and talk like a person?* Would they encounter strange beings like the Thueban Alnaas amid an equally strange forest? Perhaps tree people instead of snake people? Or did they merely search for a branch already fallen from the right tree?

What task will we face here? And what new revelations will we learn? The Oracle had said that each task would reveal a new answer to their riddle. Not the riddle of what had befallen Phatomar; not only anyway. Phatomar stood as the catalyst to a greater quest, and while they could speculate, none of the three truly knew what the gods expected of them. And yet, it had all started when Phatomar had his courage and identity stolen from him.

What would have happened had I not gone to Ferna market that day?

She shook her head, overwhelmed by that thought, and turned her mind back to the words of the Oracle, hoping to find some new insight into how they should proceed, though why she would think she'd determine anything new now, she didn't know.

The Oracle had said of their three tasks: *one will give you motive; one a location; one an identity.* Jal had thought those referred to Phatomar's dilemma. A motive for the theft, where to go to retrieve his gifts, and the identity of those who had stolen from him.

But the Thueban Alnaas had set them thinking along different lines. *Restore the Heart of Order,* Haass had bade them. *She whom Chaos slew*, the goddess of Order. Did that tie the motive into the death of a goddess? Did someone steal Phatomar's courage so that he could become the man who could safely touch the Faqadat Alqalb, or did the theft not take into account the unintended consequences? What location would they learn when they reached the Blackened Fields? The whereabouts of the watery grave? The place that held Phatomar's stolen gifts? And what identity would the watery grave unveil? Those who had stolen from Phatomar or something else entirely? Surely not Chaos, who had destroyed a goddess, for that, they had already learned.

Did anything the Oracle had said actually pertain to Phatomar? Or had they all made an assumption based on their own desires?

Again, Jal shook her head, staring out toward the Tasor Mountains with their vast skirt of black destruction.

"A grain of sand hidden in a dune," she murmured, citing an old desert proverb.

Eamon grunted with a nod. "And a long way to go to find that grain." He drew in a deep breath, as though to steady himself. "Shall we see what kind of a pass might lead to the other side?" he asked with forced cheerfulness.

"Do you think we'll find a pass?" Jal asked. "Or have those fiery monsters burned any that might have once existed?"

"We'll find a way," Eamon assured her with a wry smile. "I doubt we'll find an easy path, though."

Phatomar gave a small laugh, equal parts amusement and apprehension. His pale grey eyes wide, his jaw clenched and his lower lip quivering just a bit, the warrior nevertheless managed to hold his fear at bay.

Jal wondered what thoughts he used as a distraction to cope with this latest trek into the unknown. Her own thoughts kept swirling, trying not to dwell on the dangers they would surely encounter once they resumed their journey; what must Phatomar feel without his courage to bolster his resolve?

Thankfully, the gods didn't steal his strength.

Phatomar's will, and his firm belief in Eamon—and herself, Jal realised with surprise—would keep him moving where a lesser man would have faltered. The loss of his courage might have made Phatomar reassess how he dealt with situations, but his strength of character, his fortitude, his conviction, would all allow him to go where he must.

The thought made her sit a little taller in her saddle. Shoulders squared, heart lightened by shared resolve, Jal found an honest smile for her friends.

"Then lead on," she said. "Find us a forest in a field of death, Eamon."

He grinned and nudged Cosantoir on his chosen path toward the foothills of the Formorket Enger.

***

They had spent the night at the edge of a swath of green, the point where volcanic residue met the hope of life and choked it off. With bellies and canteens full, a decent night of sleep behind them, and well-rested mounts, the three set out again with the light of dawn, crossing into the charred landscape birthed by untold years of eruptions.

Eamon plotted a course in his mind that he hoped would take them to a pass through the mountains, between the smoking volcano closer to the west and its quiescent neighbour. He very much wanted to avoid the anger of the larger volcano further east.

Although he had never ventured close to any of the restless behemoths which dotted Merveah and the lands beyond, Eamon had heard stories of what one might expect near their fiery base. Scalding rivers of crimson and gold pouring from the mouths of volcanoes as they moved with unyielding force over the unwary. Air so parched and deadly that it seemed like the furnaces of Hell had burst open, leaching moisture from the body, poisoning the lungs. Punishing waves of brutal heat burning without flames, peeling exposed flesh to boil the blood beneath.

Each a horrible fate that Eamon hoped to avoid at all costs. If this pass did not prove true, he would lead them further west, back to the ocean if he had to, before he dared move one step closer to the living fire licking at the biggest volcano.

As the horses picked their way along ground boasting a mix of fine black sand, scattered shards of stones, baked earth, and barren rock—they would have to pay extra attention to the care of their mounts' feet along this leg of their journey—their riders chatted amiably, trying to keep their worries at bay with a semblance of lightheartedness.

Eamon assumed Phatomar and Jal shared his suppressed dread at this crossing. He had a feeling they each worked to cheer up their fellow companions in an effort to distract themselves from what loomed ahead. At least the sun shone from a mostly blue sky, the few light clouds prone to gathering around the tops of the volcanoes.

"...so there we stood, shoulder to shoulder, blades bare and ready for trouble," Eamon continued his latest tale. "When this noble woman in a brilliant yellow gown runs in, screaming about the basilisk that just froze her lady-in-waiting, and how someone had to stop the beast before it struck again." Phatomar's deep laugh joined his own. Jal's lips twitched as she tried to hold her own mirth. "And before we know it, in walks her husband, sword in hand, eyes wild, tunic in disarray. He stares at us, then at his wife, and he says—"

Eamon pulled Cosantoir to a halt with a startled oath as they crested a moderate rise, his mouth agape at the sight revealed. A chasm stretched across their path, too wide to jump. Eamon raked his gaze along its length, seeing no end to its serpentine sprawl.

"How in Dearn's name did I miss this?" he hissed.

"Miss what?" Jal asked, but Eamon barely heard as he dropped from his saddle and moved to the edge of the cliff, glancing down to determine the depth of this new obstacle. The sluggish crawl of molten rock, red and livid, heaved like a river as it pressed against either side. An incredible heat blasted him, stirring the hair that had escaped its tail into an agitated nimbus about his head and stinging his nose with its fetid breath. Eamon pulled back, dread churning in his gut. Phatomar joined him, staring with too much white showing around his eyes into the abyss.

"How, by the gods of the underworld, do we cross this?" Phatomar didn't bother to mask the hitch of dread in his voice. "Maybe a narrower stretch somewhere along the way?"

"I don't know," Eamon groaned, thinking up and discarding ideas in his head. Without knowing the full perimeter of the obstruction, how could he make any plans? Should they try east or west in search of some way to cross? Would they find what they needed, or would the land block any attempts to escape? Did the cliff's edge have enough stability to keep them from tumbling into a fiery death? That thought prompted a hasty step back, mirrored by Phatomar.

"What's the problem?" Jal moved to stand next to him, her voice low and soft. Her tawny eyes swept across the landscape, looking for dangers beyond the great rent blocking their way. Eamon appreciated her caution, leaving him free to come up with an idea of how to press forward.

"Do you hear that?" Phatomar squeaked. He nearly stumbled with the haste of his spin as he turned back the way they'd come.

Eamon's hand flew to his sword. A strange howl echoed, seeming to emanate from everywhere and nowhere at once. If whatever throat had uttered that challenge lay beyond the chasm, it had far less chance to affect them than if it came from behind. A second, then a third cry rang out, followed by a roar issuing from an untold number of beings. Definitely from the direction they had come. The chasm now held the three of them at the mercy of whatever beasts approached.

"Can you see what's making that noise?" He forced his tone to remain even, confident, even while his heart galloped against his ribs. "Where are they?"

Jal gave him a peculiar look, glanced with equal concern at Phatomar, gazed with mounting apprehension across the land. When Eamon drew his blade, Jal copied his action, albeit more slowly.

"What do you see?" she asked.

Phatomar cried out like a frightened child. "There!" He pointed, his back pressed against Croga's flank, his hand fumbling for a weapon, but shaking so violently that Eamon feared he'd drop his defence.

And then Eamon saw them too, dark shadows bounding forward with impossible speed, bearing armed riders so monstrous in nature that his mind fought against any sane description.

"Dearn save us," he managed before the abominations swept up the rise. Beasts before them, a molten chasm at their backs, and no room to retreat. Eamon brought his sword to bear and prepared for one final battle, but he would by Dearn take as many of them with him as he could.

189

***

The sand and rock and barren earth reminded Jal of the Gobani, yet the dark cast to the landscape and the less intense heat of the sun shining down despite the brilliance of a blue sky made the land seem somehow more foreign. The dichotomy weighed on her shoulders, pulling muscles tight with tension the closer they rode toward the volcanoes and, hopefully, a way to the other side. Eamon kept the mood light by recounting tales of past exploits. Whether true stories or exaggerated fancies, Jal appreciated his efforts. Judging by his laughter, Phatomar welcomed the distraction as well.

"...when this noble woman in a brilliant yellow gown runs in, screaming about the basilisk that just froze her lady-in-waiting, and how someone had to stop the beast before it struck again."

Glancing over to Eamon as the horses navigated the rocky surface, she saw his eyes crinkle in merry remembrance. Phatomar, riding on Eamon's other side, let out a deep laugh that made Jal smile. "And before we know it, in walks her husband, sword in hand, eyes wild, tunic in disarray. He stares at us, at his wife, and he says—"

Eamon's tale bit off with an oath. Jal's eyes snapped back to the path.

"How in Dearn's name did I miss this?" he gasped.

Jal followed his incredulous stare and frowned. She saw more of what they'd pushed through for the last several hours; black sand and rock, bare earth, undulating hills heading to the distant peaks ahead. Nothing to cause undue distress.

"Miss what?" she asked.

He didn't answer, just dismounted and strode a few paces forward, staring down. She couldn't see his face from here, but tension tightened his stance as wisps of loose hair blew back from his face in a breeze. Phatomar also slid from his saddle, focused on whatever Eamon watched. With rising dread, Jal dismounted and gave Onoir a gentle pat. The horse responded with a contented *whuff*, oblivious to the distress of the others. Jal joined her companions, scanning the area and still seeing nothing amiss.

190

"How do we cross this?" Phatomar asked, his voice raised in undisguised alarm. Jal nearly growled *Cross what?*, but the very real anxiety from both men stilled her tongue. What did they see that she did not? They obviously saw something. "Maybe a narrower stretch somewhere along the way?" Phatomar's head swivelled quickly left then right, searching for what, Jal didn't know.

"I don't know," Eamon murmured, his hazel eyes bunching in furious thought. Jal turned a slow circle, forcing herself to breathe deep and ignore the pounding of her heart as she searched for trouble, finding nothing. The lack of obvious danger contrasted with the dismay of the other two warriors only added to her tension.

Eamon took a step back, Phatomar imitating him.

"What's the problem?" she asked, holding her voice steady, hoping to hear an answer that made sense. Her circle brought her even with them again and she met Eamon's troubled gaze.

About to demand an explanation, Phatomar whimpered, sending her heart tripping faster. Her breath sped up despite her efforts as Phatomar spun, terror edging his words.

"Do you hear that?" he cried out. Jal and Eamon both turned, Eamon with a hand on his sword. Jal's fingers quivered in anticipation, but she still saw nothing, heard nothing.

"Can you see what's making that noise?" Eamon asked, his clenched jaw belying the calm he tried to convey. "Where are they?"

She stared at him, then at Phatomar. Eamon jerked and pulled his blade free, staring back the way they had come. Jal felt the first trickle of sweat dribble down her back. She reached for the sword at her back, sliding it free of its scabbard. *What by all the gods is going on?*

"What do you see?" she asked, still seeing nothing out of the ordinary. *How can I fight an invisible enemy?*

"There!" Phatomar pointed ahead even as he stumbled back, pressing tight to Croga's side as he groped at his belt for his knife. His stallion snorted in surprise, but the animal held firm, supporting his master.

Jal frowned, studying each horse in turn. Although they had picked up their riders' nervous tension, it didn't appear to

Jal as though they sensed any danger. She wondered what that meant.

"Dearn save us," Eamon moaned, his words full of despair. In a panic, Jal whipped her attention to her friend as he brought his sword up in a fighter's stance. Then she watched in astonishment as he lunged forward, his blade awhirl as he fought for his life...against nothing.

Jal blinked without comprehension. Eamon danced amid unseen foes, scowling and shouting defiance. He moved quickly, efficiently, with a ferocity that dropped her jaw in awe. At Ferna, he and Phatomar had held off their assailants with ease; when dealing with the thieves between Hada and Danvers, Eamon and Jal had mostly used intimidation as discouragement. During their training sessions, Eamon had sparred with enviable grace and skill, drilling her in various ways to move as one with the sword. Deep in the Kahf Alramal, she well remembered his swift defence each time he drew his weapon.

All of those times paled to his economy of movement now. She couldn't see what he fought, but she saw the skill behind it. More disturbing, she saw resistance against his blade. *Something* stopped his strokes, even if she couldn't see what. And he kept the *whatever* away from Phatomar's trembling crouch, the larger man's tenuous grip on the hilt of his knife causing the weapon to shake in an alarming manner.

A slash of red—three slashes actually, as though from some kind of claw—appeared on Eamon's arm. He grimaced and brought his blade around in a backhand slash that would have taken the head from an opponent, perhaps *had* done so.

The welling blood, visible consequences of a fight she couldn't define, snapped Jal out of her indecision. With a roar of anger, she pressed close to Eamon's side, sword held ready though she saw nothing to fight. In desperation, she swept her weapon in an arc before her, finding no resistance though Eamon grunted with exertion as his sword bit into something inches away from Jal.

Frustrated and furious, Jal searched the ground, finding their footprints but no telltale marks that might belong to something else. Phatomar cried out, falling to his backside, knife held defensively in front of his face. Something slashed through his tunic at his waist, a line of red dampening the torn edges of the fabric. Eamon threw himself sideways, trying to aid Phatomar despite his own struggles.

Not knowing what else to do, Jal stepped in front of both of them, placing herself between her brothers and this baffling enemy. She pulled a knife from her belt with her left hand, the hilt of her sword in her right. Spreading her arms wide, she bellowed out a fierce challenge, then brought both weapons into a guard position, balanced on her toes as she tried to stop anything from reaching those behind her, uncertain whether her actions would have any benefit.

Whatever had halted their progress toward the mountains—for neither Eamon nor Phatomar seemed willing to cross that point where they had gazed down at nothing—still held the men at bay, effectively trapping them. If Jal couldn't see what attacked them, she could at least make of herself a barricade, buy Eamon time to keep Phatomar safe, perhaps find a way to cross the unseen barrier. At the least, she could force the enemy to fight a little harder to reach her family.

The harsh breath of Eamon and Phatomar echoed from behind her, and the roar of her pulse throbbed in her ears. After a long moment, when nothing else penetrated Jal's senses, she slowly turned her head, trying to see both in front and behind her at the same time. Eamon pushed up to his feet and stumbled to stand beside her, staring in perplexity, first at her, then at the deserted spaces beyond her.

"What," he gaped in disbelief, "did you just do?"

She could only offer a troubled shrug in reply.

Behind them, the three horses whickered softly at each other, unfazed by the bafflement of their riders. None of them seemed to know why they had stopped so suddenly, and standing around in a place with no food or water simply made no sense. Better if they just moved somewhere more hospitable, somewhere with a little sweet grass to nibble on.

**

The half-hound, half-horse creature launched itself at Jal, black claws extended, vicious yellowed fangs nearly as long

193

as his fingers glistening with saliva reaching for exposed flesh. Jal bellowed a challenge though her weapons didn't move past guard position. It leapt for her throat...and disappeared, and every other creature vanished with it.

Eamon stared from Jal to the empty landscape beyond her, then back at Jal. Her hair lay damp and limp, pulled back from her face by a simple tie. Sweat dappled her golden skin, but not a trace of blood marred her. She held her knife in one hand, her sword in the other, her eyes raking the area for the enemy, and yet had not a scratch on her.

Considering that just a moment before, as he crouched in front of Phatomar, he had watched death aim for Jal, she looked remarkably healthy.

Eamon fought to control the painful slamming of his heart against his ribs, the sudden lack of anything to fight leaving adrenaline coursing through him with no outlet. Regaining his feet took some effort, but he reached her side without tripping despite the trembling of his limbs.

"What did you just do?" His voice sounded ragged to his ears. Jal shrugged, her shoulders tight, her eyes troubled.

He heard the horses whinny behind them. Eamon turned. If any of the creatures had attacked the horses—

"What happened to the chasm?" He wiped the back of his wrist against his eyes, careful not to stab himself, but when he looked again, no yawning abyss of crawling lava blocked their path. In fact, nothing met his gaze save the undulating hills of rock and sand that lead to the volcanoes.

Phatomar pushed himself to his hands and knees, crouched on his heels, and shoved to his feet. He held a hand to the wound in his lower torso. Confusion darkened his eyes as he searched the battlefield. The field with no bodies lying upon it, and no trace of a fight save for their own footprints.

"What in Dearn's name is going on?" Phatomar asked. A thread of anger overrode his fear.

Eamon had no answer. He looked at Jal.

"You stopped us and dismounted," she explained slowly. "Both of you stared down at something I couldn't see."

"A lava flow through a rift in the ground," Eamon said. "Hot enough to blast fumes up at us." He frowned. "You didn't see it? Or feel its raging heat?"

Jal shook her head, her tawny eyes reminding him of the molten rock that had held them trapped.

"I only saw what lies before us now." She gestured at the unbroken land. "Or what I think lies before us now," she half-whispered to herself. "Assuming you now also see the same barren landscape we've seen all day.

"Then you started fighting against nothing. Or something invisible." She sheathed her dagger behind her belt. Her hand reached out, fingers hovering over three bloody gashes on Eamon's arm. "Whatever attacked clearly had an effect, but I couldn't see it." She growled, her brow drawing down into a fierce expression as she slammed her sword back into the scabbard on her back. "I couldn't help, couldn't join in the attack, couldn't even see the enemy." The last came out in disgust and frustration. "Less than useless."

"But you did help." Eamon remembered how she'd placed herself between him as he shielded Phatomar and the snarling creatures with their hideous riders. "You blocked them from us."

"I couldn't *see* them," she spat through gritted teeth.

"Yet you put yourself in their way nonetheless," Phatomar said. He fingered the rip in his tunic, thoughts marching across his face almost too fast for Eamon to read. Almost.

"What is it?" he asked.

Phatomar turned his head to regard the horses with a thoughtful expression, then looked back to Jal.

"How did Croga and the others react to the attack?" he asked.

Jal shook her head. "They didn't. Croga seemed almost surprised when you pressed up against him, though he stood firm. None of them shied away from whatever attacked you. It seems they didn't see anything either." Her eyes flashed. "So what could hide itself from most of us? Why could you two see, but we didn't? What would have happened if they had fooled you, too? Who's trying to kill us?"

"I don't think that's quite the right question," Phatomar's upper lip curled and his eyes crinkled in distress. "I think we need to ask who has the power to send such an authentic illusion, and why it didn't affect Jal."

"Illusion?" Jal choked off an incredulous laugh that lacked all humour. "You're both bleeding. I watched those wounds appear even if I couldn't see what delivered them, and you certainly didn't cause them yourselves. How is that an illusion?"

Eamon stared at Phatomar. "Power of the mind?" he asked, wondering whether Phatomar recalled their encounter with that sorcerer several years ago. Probably not. "Could someone have fashioned an illusion so powerful that we experienced *every* aspect of it?"

Phatomar shrugged, then winced as the movement pulled at his wound. "It's possible." Jal moved even before Eamon did, pulling apart the edges of Phatomar's tunic to examine the gash beneath. Phatomar's hand rose to check that the Heart Stone still lay secured at his waist. That fuelled Eamon's speculation.

"Halvern removed the Faqadat Alqalb from its pouch, held it in his hand," he said. He met Phatomar's stare. "What if that drew the attention of something we'd rather not encounter?"

"Something with the power to play with mortal minds?" added Phatomar. "To cast illusions so real that they can inflict damage."

"You're going to tell me we have some sort of trickster god against us?" Jal retrieved a clean cloth and water from her saddle bag to dress the weeping wound across Phatomar's gut. She wiped away the blood, and Eamon knew the claw hadn't cut deep.

"He has worked as an agent of chaos before," said Eamon, "and it seems those who benefit most from stopping us from restoring Order's Heart would side with Chaos."

Jal glanced up at that, baffled. "What are you talking about? He who?" Then her jaw dropped. "Wait, do you mean you really *do* have a trickster god, a master of illusions? That maybe the voice I heard at Ferna—" She shook her head hard, returning to patching up Phatomar. "I think I was happier only knowing about the five gods of the desert," she muttered. "Gods who don't interfere in mortal affairs."

"I don't think this quest has much to do with mortal affairs," Phatomar grumbled.

Eamon agreed. "But if the Trickster does work against us, I'd like to know why his illusions didn't affect Jal."

Jal finished tending to Phatomar and stepped back from him. "Dearn said I had a unique gift," she rasped in a soft breath touched by a slight tremble. "A gift his brethren must not learn about. Maybe he didn't just mean my ability to hear your gods."

Eamon didn't know what to say to that.

Jal took a steadying breath, then said in a firmer tone, "We should see about that too." It took Eamon a second to realise she meant the gashes on his arm.

She lightly bit at her lower lip as she applied pressure to his wound. "What did they look like?" she wondered. "What attacked you?"

"Monstrous shadows," he said, low and serious. "Great beasts like a cross between hounds and horses."

"Teeth and claws," Phatomar added. "And immense, terrifying riders."

Jal glanced at Phatomar and back to Eamon with a puzzled frown.

"But what did they look like? What kind of creatures?"

Eamon opened his mouth to answer, but paused. He saw the same hesitation in Phatomar.

"At the time, I mostly saw dark blurs. Talons and swords. They moved quickly." Phatomar nodded in agreement, though Eamon read the same realisation he felt dawn on his friend's features. "But now, with the distance of time, I can't bring to mind any details."

"Beyond terror and the knowledge of death," Phatomar added.

"Exactly," Eamon nodded with a disgusted scowl. "He flung up illusions to inspire fear, overwhelm our minds with sensation rather than details. And we stood helpless against it."

Phatomar's pale gaze rested on Jal. "Not entirely helpless."

She fidgeted under his scrutiny, tying off a bandage around Eamon's arm. "If it happens again, how do I fight an illusion that holds you captive but leaves me clueless? It's not like you explained when I questioned why we stopped. Do I have you describe everything you see and tell you if I see different?"

"If either of us acts strangely again, you have my

permission to smack some sense into us," Eamon said, winning the hint of a smile. "Otherwise, we continue with the assumption that *someone* can see through the Trickster's lies. If not Jal, then our horses. We see something to worry us, stop us, or seek to attack us, we check everyone's reaction first. Perhaps not efficient, but it's a start."

"If you didn't fall for his tricks this time, perhaps he doesn't know you're here," Phatomar suggested. "Whether an aspect of your gift, or someone working to keep you hidden."

"Someone working to—" Jal bit off her objection with an oath.

"Those who spoke at Ferna saw only Eamon and myself; though they concentrated only on me, so perhaps they *didn't* see Eamon."

"Anyone who knows anything about you knows I'm always at your side," countered Eamon. "Or they should have known, before they stole all memory of you."

"True," admitted Phatomar, his conviction of the truth of that assuring Eamon that although Phatomar didn't recall any courageous deeds, he remembered the brother who always stood at his side. "But they'd have no cause to know about Jal." He regarded her a moment. "So far as we know, of the higher powers, only Dearn and the Oracle have seen you. Given our quest, they're not likely to betray us. Perhaps that anonymity protects you now from the Trickster and his companion."

Jal's mouth worked as though she chewed on her next words, but it took a bit for sound to emerge.

"What if he learns of his oversight and finds a way to include me in his delusions next time?"

"Then we deal with whatever he throws our way," Eamon said in a firm and determined tone. "Whatever happens, we stick together. We guard each other as best we can, we reach the Formorket Enger and its tree of stars, we complete our quest, and we escape the scrutiny of those who seek to use us."

"Or we die trying?" Jal asked, a glint of humour finding purchase in her eyes.

"Let's hope it doesn't come to that," Phatomar said, a ghost of the cocky surety that Eamon knew from past adventures pushing past his fears.

"Nothing has changed," Eamon said. "We just, maybe, know something more than we did before."

"Then let's get going before something seeks to teach us something new. Enough lessons for one day." Jal turned to her horse, an eyebrow raised as she waited for them to join her.

Eamon couldn't disagree with that. They mounted up, more aware of their surroundings. Eamon couldn't speak for the others, but he prayed that what he saw (or didn't see) as they rode reflected reality. He didn't know what he could do about it if it didn't.

Chapter 18

The past three days had taken a toll on them. While Eamon had made sure to stuff the packs with plenty of fodder before venturing into the wastelands of the volcanic range, their horses still required a lot of food, and no one knew how long until they might reach land suitable for grazing. Water also became a problem, saved mostly for the beasts bearing their weight, leaving only the bare minimum for Jal and her friends. Uncomfortable, but not unexpected.

Yet what wore them down lay not so much in their endurance, but in the constant struggle to fight off attacks and disturbances, both real and imagined.

An earthquake had rumbled Eamon and Phatomar from their bedrolls on the night after the first illusory attack, lava and steam roaring out of new fissures cracking the ground. A landslide had forced them to alter course the following day, the horses taking extra care with their footing. The first had proved a false event, with Jal having to step into an illusory rent to dispel the vision; the second, even the animals had shied from, kicking up loose rock and dirt as they navigated around the blockage, revealing it as a true obstacle.

The horses had dealt with the imps who tried to sabotage their food, much to the surprise of both imps and humans. When the first squat creature had appeared last night as the group shared a cold meal beneath a starry sky, Jal had looked on in shock at the creature. She had never seen its like before; small, winged, tiny horns and long pointed ears. She had stared at the flitting being, wondering if the

Trickster's illusions had finally begun to work on her too. When she gathered her wits enough to point it out, both Eamon and Phatomar let out a weary curse, the former pushing to his feet while the latter scooted back.

"Bloody imps," Eamon said as a dozen others just like it suddenly swarmed the nearby saddle bags, eerie chirps calling out what sounded like derision and obscenities.

Before Eamon had taken more than a couple of steps, Croga let out an annoyed neigh, matched by Cosantoir's harsh snort. Onoir pulled her lips back and made a sound very much like a growl. Then Croga had lunged forward, stomped on one imp, kicked another, and snapped his teeth at a third.

The imps had frozen at the unexpected attack, then rallied and focused on the horses. Cosantoir reared up and lashed out with his hooves; Onoir charged the small creatures, adding her large teeth to the fight; and Croga continued his irritated dance. By the time Eamon and Jal reached the animals, the imps—those not crushed or injured and whimpering—shrieked and disappeared, their fallen vanishing with them. Croga whuffed, somehow looking smug, while Cosantoir swept the area with a sentry's eye. Jal could have sworn Onoir rolled her eyes and dismissed the posturing males, pressing into Jal's hand with a contented sigh.

"Mischievous, but not dangerous," Eamon spat, examining the saddle bags for anything missing. Jal watched him, taking her time to thank the horses with gentle strokes. Phatomar joined her, and Croga sniffed his empty hand as though looking for a reward for vanquishing the foe. The stallion exhaled in disappointment when none of the humans offered more than a handful of grain and a withered apple in thanks.

Jal hadn't seen the giant scorpions, nor the harpies, only knowing of their 'attack' by Eamon's and Phatomar's actions and descriptions, but the swarm of ants the size of her hand had chased them a good four miles before they had escaped their snapping mandibles. Every attack, every obstruction whether real or imagined, took its toll, and the Trickster—or whoever kept taunting them—continued his onslaught even as they finally crossed the pass Eamon had found between the ominous smoking peaks.

Now, as they walked beside the horses down a slope of loose shale in the hour after the sun had reached its zenith, Jal blinked the dryness from her eyes and studied the area ahead as Phatomar pointed.

"Do you see that?" he asked through his exhaustion, voice thick with dread and resignation. He seemed prepared to endure another illusory attack, only this time, Jal feared they didn't face an illusion.

"If you mean the black smoke shaped like a little horned lizard rising on its hind legs with gold and red eyes staring at us, then yes, I see it."

Phatomar's sigh could have held relief or surrender.

"Do we fight it?" he asked with a fatalistic grimace, hand tightening on the reins.

She sensed Eamon's disquiet behind her. She slowed, then stopped, Phatomar and Eamon doing likewise.

"It's not attacking," she murmured. "Have either of you seen its like before?"

Eamon hooked Cosantoir's reins to the back of Onoir's saddle and stepped closer. "It's not familiar. If Jal didn't see it, I'd almost suspect that the Trickster had gotten creative."

"Maybe we're getting close to the tree, and this stands as one of its guardians."

Jal tilted her head to consider Phatomar's suggestion. "Like the Thueban Alnaas?"

"*You may find help along the way,*" he said, quoting the words of the Oracle. "*And you will find hindrances. Do not judge too quickly lest you lose an opportunity.*"

"We've certainly encountered enough hindrances," Eamon's tired voice lacked its usual lightness. "Though this would provide a great opportunity for another trick."

"How can we determine whether it means us harm?" wondered Phatomar.

"We could just ask it," Jal said, as weary of the uncertainty as they.

Eamon grunted, a sound that combined amusement and disbelief. He took two steps forward, hands held loose at his sides, yet within easy reach of his weapons.

"My pardon, little one," he addressed the smokey shadow. It stood about as high as Phatomar's hand, fingertip to palm, though wisps of vapour created an indistinct and trailing nimbus around the strange creature, distorting its true size. "Our apologies for intruding upon your lands, but we seek the Blackened Fields where ancient death engendered a tree of starry night. Do you know of such?"

"I guess we're out of subtlety," Jal said to Phatomar. He managed a small smile.

"Do you think it cares that an Oracle sent us?" the larger man asked.

"Do you think it even understands us?" she countered.

"Can't hurt to show some courtesy," Eamon called back at them, his gaze still on the creature. It blinked, swayed sinuously for a moment, then vanished in a puff of smoke. "Huh. Might not help either."

Jal laughed, feeling buoyed by even a pale reflection of Eamon's humour returning.

When nothing more happened for several minutes, they decided to continue forward.

"Keep a sharp lookout," Eamon advised as he regained his reins. "Friend, foe, or benign entity, we're not alone out here, despite the desolate landscape."

"Interesting to encounter something not trying to kill us," Jal observed. "Though perhaps a little disconcerting."

"Give it time," Phatomar grumbled. "I'm sure something will come along soon to break our peace and scare us witless."

They passed a second smokey lizard a short time later. Like the first, it watched them, but made no effort to communicate. It also didn't attack, so after a cautious greeting and another failed attempt to learn anything, the humans sidled past. Like the first, it disappeared, leaving no trace behind.

Three more times, they encountered their silent watchers with no reaction beyond a blink and a sway of smoke. Eamon made sure to give a polite smile and acknowledging nod to each small being, trying a different greeting each time.

"Civility costs us nothing," he said. Jal agreed. By the seventh sighting, she had begun to look forward to seeing them. The odd little creatures broke up the monotony as the adventurers descended to the black fields beyond the volcanoes.

She frowned, looking back the way they'd come. "Have you noticed that nothing dangerous has happened since we emerged from the pass?" she asked. "No illusions, no attacks; just our little lizard friends. Do you think they keep the Trickster at bay?"

"Them or the mountains?" Phatomar wondered. "Since we crested the range, we've remained unmolested."

"Doesn't mean he's forgotten about us," Eamon warned. "Whether the lizards guard us, or whether the Trickster has something up his sleeve for when we drop our guard, we're far from safe." With a nod of his chin to a group of boulders a few hundred paces ahead, he added, "We're also hungry. Let's break in the shadow of those rocks." Cosantoir nickered in agreement with his master.

The horses made do with water and a small portion of grain while the humans pulled out some hardtack to dull their hunger. After a time of silent chewing, Jal decided to address Eamon's distracted attention.

"What do you study so intently?" she asked. She saw nothing unusual in the direction of his gaze. Which meant little these past few days, and she worried he tracked something unseen to her.

He gestured with the last of his food.

"That one there," he murmured, pointing out a smoke-like lizard Jal hadn't seen until now. It crouched unmoving and well camouflaged against the grey rocks. It had positioned itself across the route they had followed, as though creating a barrier with its tiny body. Not that something so small and insubstantial could stop any advance by them. "Do you think it tries to warn us from our path, or has it just decided that makes a fine place to sun itself?"

In other circumstances, Jal might have laughed at the notion that such a slight animal could dictate their future actions, but they had encountered too many unknowns to slough off the possibility that the lizard wanted to send them some kind of message with its position.

"Do you think it's waiting for a signal of some sort?" Phatomar asked. "Some reaction on our part? A test, perhaps?"

"Maybe it's waiting for reinforcements," Jal suggested. "Keep us in place until more arrive?"

"It's smaller than my foot," Eamon said with a slight shake of his head. "We could walk right over it if we wanted."

"If you only look at size," Jal countered, "we also could have stepped over those giant ants. Didn't stop them from attacking. If this lizard waits for friends, I don't know that we want to encounter them."

"And if it's a guardian like the Thueban Alnaas, we don't want to insult them either," Phatomar refuted.

"Again, how do we tell?" Jal pressed. "How do we even know it's not just a native lizard? They haven't responded to our words." She paused, regarding the unmoving lizard narrowly. "Unless this posture stands as a response."

"What do you think it would do if we show it the Heart Stone?" Phatomar asked. Jal and Eamon stared at him in surprise. Phatomar pressed on. "The Oracle suggested a connection between it and the tree in the Blackened Fields. Perhaps we can use the one to find the other?"

"If we reveal the Heart Stone, it might draw the Trickster's attention," Eamon said, though not in negation.

"He didn't seem to have any problems finding us before," Jal noted, her gaze returning to the still lizard. It turned its head, red-gold eyes blinking once, then again. It flicked out a misty tongue, as though tasting the air. Or their words. Or simply acting like a desert lizard. A wave of exhaustion, born of uncertainty and frustration, pressed down on her. She breathed out a heavy sigh.

Eamon met her eyes.

"If we stand prepared for one of the Trickster's surprises," he said, hand wrapping around the hilt of his sword, "we might discover a better path. Even if this little being doesn't react to the Heart Stone, we'll at least have learned something. Right now, we're travelling blind. If revealing the Heart Stone might lead to locating the tree of starry night, I say we take it."

Not having any other ideas, Jal could only nod her agreement. Phatomar had already pulled the pouch from beneath his tunic. He waited until Jal and Eamon drew their blades, then carefully pulled back the wrapping that concealed the Faqadat Alqalb, not pulling the Stone free of its confines, but revealing the red jewel to the afternoon light. He squatted on his haunches to show the lizard what he cradled in the palm of his hand.

Jal thought the smoke being nodded before it disappeared on a breath of wind, but she might have imagined the motion.

***

"Well," Eamon said, surprised at the depth of disappointment that weighed on his chest when the little creature vanished yet again. He had felt certain that the lizard had some kind of message to impart, but apparently not. "I guess the Heart Stone didn't impress it." He glanced around, saw nothing ready to leap out and attack, and, praying that they hadn't alerted the Trickster by revealing the Faqadat Alqalb, slid his sword back into its sheath.

Phatomar made a sound at the back of his throat, seeming likewise disheartened. He rewrapped the stone and tucked it safely away, then rose to his feet and ambled to Croga's side, giving the horse a pat on the neck. More to comfort himself than his horse, Eamon suspected. Jal lowered her weapon, though she kept it in hand as she chewed thoughtfully on the hardtack she had plucked from her belt.

"Do you think they're real?" she asked. Eamon cocked his head.

"The lizards," she qualified. "They look like smoke; they appear and disappear at will; they leave no tracks. Yet we all see them, even the horses. Do you think they're really here, or some sort of manifestation set to watch over the pass? Like a scout, or a sentry."

He pondered that. If the lizards represented the eyes and ears of some other being, then perhaps they had no means of communication. Higher beings often used avatars, golems, or even animals to watch over and interact with mortals; could these lizards act on another's behalf? But if so, then whose? And to what purpose? Perhaps they stood as guardians of a sort, caretakers of some ancient prophecy.

Or, for all Eamon knew, the hazy animals simply dwelled in the shadow of the volcanoes, the only kind of creatures who could flourish in these barren lands.

If not for the insistent tickling at the back of his mind, Eamon might have dismissed these encounters as inconsequential to their quest. But he found that he couldn't put them aside so easily. He stared at the spot this latest lizard had sat, then turned his gaze in the direction it had faced. The large volcano, periodically belching up a plume of foul smoke and weeping hot red tears in the distance filled his vision.

Strange. He would have thought they stood too close to the mountains, too high between the peaks, to appreciate their size and grandeur. Yet he clearly perceived such detail as he followed the lizard's sight line. Perhaps a message lay there after all.

He frowned as he tried to put into words where his thoughts led him.

"You've thought of something," Jal stated.

"I don't know if I can explain," he hedged. Jal stopped him with a single fierce shake of her head.

"You've thought of something," she repeated, now sheathing her blade. "From what we've encountered thus far, I'm willing to believe intuition guides us as much as anything. Gods and Oracles have set our path, and at every turn, any resistance we've encountered has just led us closer to our goal. I, for one, trust that whatever you've thought of now will take us that next step closer to where we need to travel."

"As do I," Phatomar agreed.

"Even if it's following a nebulous path that little smoke lizards may or may not have set to a dangerous place I'd rather not go?" Eamon struggled to keep his tone light under the enormity of what he sensed building around him.

"Even if it takes us to the gates of the underworld," Phatomar said with such conviction that Eamon had to remind himself that his dearest friend had been robbed of his courage. He forced himself to swallow the lump in his throat. To see his fierce support and loyalty echoed now by others humbled him. He managed a sharp nod in appreciation.

"Then we head east," Eamon said. He took up Cosantoir's reins. "Toward the valley that surely joins this lesser mountain of fire with its elder brother. Let's just hope we don't have to go so far as into the actual belly of the beast, for that, I doubt we'd survive."

For the rest of the day, they headed east, slowly descending the treacherous slope. Eamon followed the barest suggestion of a track, though in truth, no markings outlined their steps. A sheltered ridge here, a section of rock swept clear of loose scree by wind there, a level stretch of ground elsewhere; all eased their passage when other routes presented greater danger.

What he followed, what truly guided their way, flitted in and out of sight whenever they had to choose a direction. The smoke lizards would show themselves, stare intently along the path that the humans should take, and otherwise bar their way, until Eamon had to admit that he obeyed their whim. If the Trickster had sent these elusive beings, then Eamon foolishly led his group toward a trap. He clung to the hope that these strange little creatures guided them true. *Guardians*, Phatomar had suggested, and Eamon would hold to that belief until forced to conclude otherwise.

They stopped for the night in the minimal shelter afforded by an outcrop of boulders near a bright blue-green pond, the last lowering light of a day growing red with sunset drawing the shadows close. The first water of any substance they had seen in days, but the stink of sulphur wafting from its crystalline surface barred any thoughts of quenching one's thirst in it. Steam rose from the ground a few dozen paces downhill beyond the pond, but the slight breeze combined with the obstruction of the rocks kept it from intruding on their little camp.

Night fell, and the shadowy fingers of the rocky, looming terrain cloaked the travellers in darkness. High above, stars danced among the clouds and the smoking drifts of the ire of the volcano that glowed angry orange and red. By day, Eamon could almost forget the troubling prospect of moving closer to the might of the mountain, but by night, the smudge of fiery fury that coloured the sky above them obliterated any illusions. They travelled on unstable paths, led by inexplicable spirits and a fervent desire not to walk into an ambush or worse.

Eamon shook off his misgivings and tried to settle in for the night. They had no fuel for a fire, so they sat their individual watches by the light of nature, each taking a turn to guard their sleeping companions. Compared to the previous few days battling the Trickster's games, this night passed without event.

As the sky began to show the first traces of dawn, Eamon,

having drawn third watch, blinked wearily around the camp. It took him a moment to register the presence of something unexpected, something he watched assemble just beyond the edge of the sheltering rocks.

That it didn't send a tingle of dread down his spine with its appearance startled him into full wakefulness.

Chapter 19

A lizard shaped from a puff of smoke had appeared before Eamon's eyes. A second joined it, then a third. They clamoured over one another in what Eamon mistook for play, or perhaps some sort of wrestling match. A fourth and a fifth appeared, a dozen; more, then more than he could count. Each swirled around the growing whole, until the myriad of little creatures formed a much larger...thing.

No other word quite fit what Eamon saw. The thing which combined the flowing, twisting, dancing bodies of the smoke lizards had a vaguely humanoid form; two arms and two legs standing upright, a head and a torso. Instead of becoming still in this alternate shape, it constantly moved. Or rather, the lizards moved, keeping up their frenetic dance so that one would imitate a finger, part of a foot, a section of chest, and in the next instant it would squirm into a new location and morph into a different body part.

Each piece retained an aspect of its lizard-shape while still being ephemeral and indistinct with a filmy smudge of smoke trailing its outline. Yet it also held a kind of solidity with the weight of so many bodies swarming together. Red and gold eyes flashed from the tiny faces of the smoke lizards wherever they roamed, like fireflies patterning the body, blinking amid the dark swirl of smoke. The whole experience left Eamon feeling faintly nauseated.

Its present form now topped Phatomar's height by at least three hands, and it stretched broader by half than the large warrior. Eamon nudged Phatomar and Jal awake without taking his attention from the being. By the time the billowing entity towered complete over them, swirling eyes made up of circling lizards peering down at them—the only two features that remained constant even as the eyes spun—all three humans stood silently facing the newcomer. A short distance away, the horses shifted about nervously.

"Why do you seek us out?" it asked, its voice the sound smoke might make if it could speak.

We didn't, sat on the tip of Eamon's tongue, but he held the thought back. He had no idea what manner of creature confronted them now, how the many disparate parts of the lizards could coalesce into the semblance of something almost human, yet his eyes beheld that reality.

A quick nod from Jal assured him that he *did* see this strange spectacle, or at least, that she shared the same delusion. How or why it came into existence—how such a thing *could* exist and interact with them—Eamon didn't know, but he *had* followed the lizards to this point. Perhaps, in attempting to communicate with them, he had urged the creation of this thing.

"Our apologies if we have intruded upon lands not intended for the tread of human foot," Eamon began, "but our quest has brought us in search of the Blackened Fields and the tree of starry night. If such a thing lies under the purview of your domain, then we did indeed seek you out in the hopes that you might teach us what we must learn."

He hadn't forgotten Haass of the Thueban Alnaas, and how the snake-man had sought to learn what lay in their hearts before revealing the prophecy or Heart Stone. If this being guarded the Blackened Fields, it might seek similar assurances. If it stood here as a manifestation sent from someone like the Trickster, then surely it already knew their purpose here, and Eamon had not divulged anything not already known.

The giant creature shifted, the smokey beings running their endless race through the massive body as they migrated. Its eerie eyes paused briefly before resuming their rapid whirl.

"Why do you seek Natt Tre?" it demanded.

Eamon stared in consternation. A glance at his companions showed Phatomar's fear held at bay, and a frown furrowing Jal's brow.

"Forgive our ignorance," Eamon said, turning back to the creature. "What is Natt Tre?"

"The tree of starry night," Jal breathed. Her frown had softened into contemplation, and a strange light shone in the depths of her tawny eyes. "Night's Tree."

"How do you know that?" Phatomar asked quietly, his eyes riveted on the hulking creature.

"It's like when I hear the voices of the gods," she said, equally low. "Like I can hear the meaning in both the fire spirit's language and our own." Her eyes narrowed. "That's not exactly right, but I don't know how else to describe it."

Although the fire spirit—whether Jal truly knew the nature of this being or merely guessed, Eamon thought she had named it accurately—seemed to follow their conversation, it neither agreed nor disagreed. Instead, it merely repeated itself.

"Why do you seek Natt Tre?"

"That we might forge Heart and limb together," Phatomar answered, voice trembling only slightly as he held himself against fear. "A task bidden by an Oracle, and watched both by those who wish us success and those who plot our failure."

The spirit gazed down at them for a time in silence. Just when Eamon feared it would offer no further words, it tilted its head forward. Eamon didn't know if it nodded or wanted a closer look at them.

"Do you bear the Heart?" it asked.

Phatomar glanced at Eamon, who gave a small nod. They had already shown it to one of the lizards, after all; might as well show it to the full gathering. Phatomar reached beneath his tunic for the secured bundle.

"I do," he said.

"Do you bear it of your own accord?"

Phatomar paused and frowned. Eamon had no clear idea on how to answer that. Dearn had sent them to the Oracle, who in turn had decreed their challenge. Both acts had followed the celestial interference in Phatomar's life. They had accepted the quest, but did they act of their own accord, or did they adhere to the whims of others? Perhaps it understood their dilemma, for it altered the question.

"Does the Heart permit your touch?"

Phatomar's eyes cleared and he drew forth the wrapped Heart Stone. Without taking his gaze from the spirit, Phatomar revealed the Faqadat Alqalb, the light of the day casting scarlet flares off its facets. Deliberately, the warrior tumbled the Stone into his right hand, cupping it naked in his palm.

"It does," he affirmed.

The fire spirit reached a hand forward, the lizards making up its arm squirming like trapped snakes. Phatomar braced himself as he held the Stone aloft. Eamon gripped his friend's shoulder, lending him what comfort he could.

Phatomar held firm, and though he felt stiff as a rock, tension vibrated along his body. When the spirit had drawn close enough to meet Phatomar's hand, a single lizard stilled its dance, stretched out, and touched Phatomar's finger, its tongue gently flicking out, stopping just short of touching the Heart Stone. It froze for a moment, then retreated back into the whole of the fire spirit, reintegrated into the morass of ever-moving parts. The spirit backed away a few paces, then stood still. Finally, it inclined its head, strange eyes swirling hypnotically.

"Follow," it instructed as it turned its great bulk and started to stride away. "If you can discern Natt Tre when we arrive, we will determine your worth."

Eamon exchanged looks with his companions. He read determination and resignation in their faces, much like he himself felt. Another test to ascertain their resolve. Together, they gathered their belongings and fell into step behind the fire spirit.

***

With every step it took, the fire spirit gained more substance, became more solid, less vaporous. Its little lizards still skittered about to substantiate its form, but they grew more defined, shedding their smoke-like ambiguity in favour of sharper details until at last, when the creature stopped and stood still—as still as continuously writhing lizards twining about themselves could become—Jal believed she might count each individual that created the whole, if only they would cease their nauseating dance long enough.

213

They had trundled along behind the lumbering form for a few hours, trekking through loose footing that reminded Jal of the Gobani. Her booted feet sank just a little into the black sand with each step, providing both traction and a hint of instability should she or her mount misplace a foot. The less-than-level surface they traversed across added another layer of distinction between here and her homeland, for the great dunes of the desert lacked the solid rock base of the Tasor Mountains. The sulphurous scent staining the air at this temperate clime also let her know she trod in unfamiliar territory, but if she closed her eyes and listened only to the sensation against her soles, she could almost believe they strode through desert sands. She almost expected to hear the groan of a camel.

Instead, she heard the surprised snort of Croga as she walked into his hind quarters. With a startled oath, Jal opened her eyes, bringing herself back to the present. Phatomar glanced back at her, and she gave him a sheepish grin.

The fire spirit had stopped while Jal had allowed herself to fall into an unmindful daydream. She berated her inattention. They might not currently walk in the direct sights of an enemy, but they certainly didn't move free from danger. Permitting herself to drift into any sort of lassitude spoke to a lack of caution they couldn't afford. The Trickster may not have interfered since they crossed the pass, but that didn't mean he had forgotten about them.

"You must wait here until the assigned time," the fire spirit said.

Jal swept her gaze over the immediate vicinity. It looked much the same as all the other areas they had recently walked; dark scree, sand, clusters of boulders, and the occasional wind-blown side of bare mountain. The whole presented a nighttime landscape defined by whatever sun penetrated the white cap of clouds.

Blackened Fields, Jal thought, *just like the rest of this area.* A wide chasm stood perhaps a hundred paces further up the mountain, a great crack in the earth from some quake long ago. Close enough to note its potential dangers, yet far enough that they needn't fear falling into its abyss. She didn't, however, see anything resembling a tree.

"What assigned time?" Eamon asked in a carefully neutral tone. Obviously, he held similar reservations.

"The time when you might reveal Natt Tre," came the less-than-helpful reply. "Take this opportunity to rest. None will come uninvited." When it became clear the spirit would say nothing further, the companions settled in to wait. For what, Jal didn't know. It seemed they had to solve this riddle on their own.

"Do you think we wait for more fire spirits?" Phatomar wondered. "Or something else?"

"The spirit said we wait for a time, not a thing," Eamon reasoned. "But what time?"

"It also said, *if we can discern Natt Tre when we arrive,*" Jal said. "Perhaps the tree of starry night only appears at a certain time."

"Like at night," Eamon agreed with a nod.

"And with help," Phatomar added. His hand hovered over the pouch beneath his tunic. "The spirit asked about the Faqadat Alqalb, whether it permitted my touch," Phatomar went on, his words aligning with Jal's thoughts. "Maybe we wait for both night and whatever powers the Heart might hold to show us what the fire spirit wishes us to see. Hopefully, Natt Tre."

Jal glanced up at the mantle of clouds tracing across the sky, noting the position of the sun. The bright orb hadn't quite reached its zenith yet. "Seems we have a bit of a wait to test out our theory."

Eamon's gaze swept over to the inert form of the fire spirit. "Do we all agree our best option lies in waiting for night to fall?"

Jal and Phatomar both nodded.

"Then I suggest we follow the spirit's advice and get some rest," Eamon concluded. "A bit of food, some sleep, and, if in fact we remain safe under the watchful eye of our friend here, we'll likely appreciate whatever strength a pause will afford us."

So saying, they shared a brief meal from their dwindling supplies, modified their tent into additional shelter against the ridge of rock, and settled in to find what rest they could.

Jal closed her eyes to the light of day, forcing her mind to stillness. Despite her exhaustion, it took some time for her thoughts to drift toward any semblance of slumber. As she hovered between wakefulness and sleep, she imagined she heard voices, though she couldn't determine from whence they came, nor did they rouse her from her lethargy enough to open her eyes and look.

"Why have you summoned me here, upstart?" an orotund voice demanded; deep, gravelly, sending tendrils of dread tingling down Jal's spine.

"Do you serve Chaos, or do you not, Epale?" a second man retorted. This tone, Jal thought she recognised. *From a market, many months ago.*

"I serve Chaos," grated Epale. "I do not serve you, Dolanis. Nor do I have any desire to become a victim to any of your tricks, rogue."

"Ah, but I didn't call upon you for my own benefit," Dolanis cajoled, the resonance of his tone begging for consideration. *Tricks,* thought Jal sleepily. *The Trickster god?* She found it difficult to hold the possible connection in mind. Dolanis spoke on, serious yet mocking. "Those who serve Chaos require the captivation of these mortals through your gentle ministrations."

"And yet you do not serve Chaos, Trickster," came the haughty response. "I well know you serve only yourself. By what misguided fantasy do you envision me obeying such an order?"

"I follow the plans of the Mistress of Shadows," Dolanis snapped, his voice suddenly a thunderclap. "Today, I speak to you on her behalf, not my own. She bids the god of nightmares to ply his trade."

A pause, in which Jal slipped closer toward true slumber even as a part of her struggled for wakefulness.

Eventually, a heavy sigh, almost a growl, escaped Epale's throat.

"What does Kistawna demand?"

Kistawna, Jal thought. *Where have I heard that name before?*

She remembered their companion Thalia from the desert caves saying that Garnda followed Kistawna, and Eamon's clarification that Kistawna loved chaos.

"Hold them until the beasts arrive," whispered Dolanis. The menace in his words swirled into a confused vortex just beyond comprehension.

Something dragged at Jal, weighing her down, capturing her in fingers of dread she felt helpless to escape. An image appeared in her mind.

They stood in the entrance to the cave. Laughter hissed from the darkness. The dull thud of Olbaehn's head tossed into the light. Garnda pulled himself into view, whole and hale.

"Do you think to essscape Kissstawna'sss judgment?" the snake-man snarled, gore encrusted sword catching the sunlight and sending glittering reflections of spilled blood across the walls of the cavern.

Caught now in a nightmare, Jal whimpered.

***

The grit of volcanic soil pressed into Phatomar's back, a reminder of days spent in the desert. Their tent displayed the muted radiance of the sun through its walls and held a comforting warmth, further enforcing the memory of earlier days. Phatomar folded his hands behind his head, allowing himself to relax into this moment of peaceful stillness. He took a deep breath, and settled in for some rest.

A sound from Jal caught his attention. It sounded strangely like a whimper. Phatomar raised his head and glanced over at the girl, then sat up quickly, his heart in his throat. Desert sand surrounded them, sucking at his companions.

No, not desert sand, quicksand!

Phatomar met Jal's panicked eyes, their tawny glow a mirror of the golden sands that tried to consume her.

"Help!" she cried out, but another movement stole Phatomar's attention.

On his other side, Eamon struggled futilely against the hungry teeth of the desert, his thrashing only serving to enmesh him further in the morass.

"Phatomar!" His free hand reached out, desperate, hopeful, despairing.

A sour taste slid down Phatomar's gullet. He looked from one to the other, unable to unlock his muscles to help either. Only a slim tract of sand supported Phatomar's weight; to move in any direction would ensnare him as well. But he couldn't just sit by and watch his friends perish. Jal had taught him ways to overcome his fear, to compensate for his shortcomings; he *knew* she had.

Every one of those coping mechanisms had evaporated from his memory.

A rope lay coiled near his feet. Relief swept through him. If he could secure that around his waist, hold the weight of his friends with his own bulk, they had a chance.

He shifted forward, his fingers stretching for that thread of hope. Suddenly, a golden viper raised its head, dark tongue tasting the air, scenting Phatomar's presence. Any sense of calm he had fled. His heart skipped and raced, bile flooding his mouth as fresh fear gripped him. Immobile in the face of this new danger, not daring to tempt the serpent to strike, Phatomar knew only despair. Help for his companions lay within his grasp, but it came with a cost.

A cost I'll gladly pay, he screamed in his head.

Yet he couldn't. He crouched frozen in the teeth of terror. His heart thundered painfully in his chest, the only part of him besides his harsh and laboured breath that produced any sort of motion. Fear lay laughing in his mind, and he cursed his lack of courage as the hot acid of scalding tears carved his cheeks.

"No, no, no," he moaned.

Jal sank deeper, the sand now up to her shoulders. She gasped in fear, her expression holding blame and resignation.

"After all we've done," she said. "After everything, you can't even stretch out your hand." She shook her head, the sand already tugging at her loosened hair.

"Hell with that, you coward," Eamon snarled. The vehemence in his tone snapped Phatomar's head around to stare at his dearest friend. In front of him, the viper hissed. "When it truly matters, you won't even try."

Phatomar wanted to deny that, but instead, he sat clutching his knees to his chest, weeping but otherwise silent, unable to even form words, let alone cry to the gods at the unfairness of it all.

If only the gods hadn't cursed me, stolen my most precious gift.

Phatomar paused, forced his mind to replay that sentiment; feel its falsehood. He had never counted courage as his most precious gift. Useful, yes, necessary, yet not most precious.

His most precious gift, what one could never replace, lay struggling for breath beneath desert sands, for now he could see little of his companions beyond the tufts of brown hair on one side, rusty locks on the other.

"Family," he whispered. "The gift of family far outweighs my lost courage."

With an effort, Phatomar squeezed his eyes shut and tried to remember how they had arrived in the desert with its quicksand traps. Hadn't they stopped elsewhere, far from the desert heat? His hand brushed against his tunic, finding the lump beneath of what they had taken from the desert cavern.

The Blackened Fields, he thought. *Haven't we reached the Formorket Enger? Where did this arid landscape come from? What's going...?*

"What's the matter?" a woman asked.

Phatomar opened his eyes. He gazed upon the dark beauty of a princess he almost remembered. She lay by his side, propped up on an elbow and draped in white silk, her black tresses sliding over a smooth brown shoulder.

Phatomar felt his heart slow to a gentle rhythm, wondering why it had thundered so alarmingly. The princess reached out long fingers the rich hew of chestnuts to brush against his temple, toying with his fair hair.

"Have you come to slay the monster?" she murmured, her breath carrying the scent of citrus and roses. "Have you come to save us?"

"Yes," answered Phatomar, unable to deny the plight of this exquisite creature.

"Such a brave man," she cooed, yet he sensed an undertone of mockery. *But why should she mock? I am one of the greatest warriors in the world.*

The princess rose to bare feet and stretched, arms high, back arched, a grin spreading across her face.

"Let's see just how brave." Her voice had deepened, grown more harsh. Phatomar frowned, uncertainty spilling into him. *Why can't I remember her name?* As he stared, her features lengthened, grew sharper. Her fierce grin now

219

showed needle-sharp teeth and her eyes transformed from a sparkling topaz into hard obsidian. A rough tongue like dried blood snaked out to caress her lips.

Phatomar leapt to his feet, back pressed into the nearby wall. His breath hitched in a painful gasp, his eyes so wide he feared they might pop from his face. He groped at his waist for a weapon, yet the thought of wielding a blade dried his mouth. He couldn't stop trembling. *Greatest warrior?* he chided himself. *Greatest fool,* he corrected, his innards turning to water.

Laughter fell from the princess' blackened lips, all beauty fading away. Her outstretched arms morphed into wings, and her legs stretched into those of a bird, wicked talons digging into the earth. *A harpy!*

"Come, brave warrior," the harpy cawed. "Come slay the monster."

Phatomar bolted from the room, terror lending greater speed to his long legs.

Barely aware of his surroundings, he reached a bridge. Two figures stood guard at the near end; Eamon and Jal. Weapons drawn, they urged Phatomar forward.

"Go," Eamon shouted. "We'll hold her here."

Phatomar slowed, not wanting his friends to stand alone against the monster that followed, but Jal pushed his shoulder, sending him stumbling to the middle of the bridge.

"You'll just get in the way," she admonished, turning her back on him to face the harpy.

The harpy rose high in the air, then descended with an ear-piercing screech, razor talons eagerly stretched forth to snatch at Jal. The desert girl swung her sword, but the harpy evaded, tearing into her tender flesh. Red arced across the bridge, stained with Jal's screams. Eamon cried out and leapt to the attack. His weapon scythed through the air, clipping the tip of a leathery wing, but the harpy spun and buffeted Eamon with wings and claws. He tried to defend himself, but the monster struck him down, his body crumpling next to Jal's.

Through it all, Phatomar had stood rooted in the middle of the bridge, shaking so badly that the structure swayed beneath his feet. Fear and anguish paralysed him. His pulse thundered hard and fast, making him dizzy with despair.

Tears streamed down his face, falling like chips of ice from his chin.

In a flurry of black wings, the harpy came for him next, her victorious shout echoing through the chasm. But instead of ripping him to shreds, the force of her attack knocked him over the side, and Phatomar fell into nothingness. Fear swallowed his scream as he tumbled...

The tang of salt water slapped Phatomar's face. He blinked to clear his vision, bracing his legs against the violent sway of the ship as it fought the storm. Phatomar watched as waves pulled Jal into the black ocean depths. His heart nearly stopped at the sight.

Eamon cursed, following the girl over the rail.

Phatomar silently wailed as his friends disappeared into the foaming maw of the sea again, his mind lost to yet another nightmare.

***

The sea tore at Eamon. Again and again, waves pummelled him, the uncaring arms of water lashed his face, squeezing his torso with punishing force, dragging at his limbs. Briny liquid inundated every part of his body. It seeped in through his mouth and nose, burned his throat, weighed like lead in his chest, making it impossible to breathe. It stole his air and sanity, taking all hope in its uncaring, unfeeling embrace. Sealing his fate.

Over and over, Eamon drowned. Sometimes crushed by the might of the ocean, sometimes swallowed by the enormous denizens that lurked in the deep. Leviathans tossed his screaming body down sinuous throats; tentacled monstrosities crushed the life from him in their unforgiving members; sharks tore him asunder in tugs-of-war. And every time, Jal's thrashing body lay just out of reach in the storm-ravaged waves before growing unnaturally still. Phatomar's hand ever stretched forth, a mere breath away, yet always too far, salvation a finger's width away, and untouchable.

He had vague flashes of memory: crossing deserted wastelands, riding toward flaming mountains, fighting off strange illusions. Each soon smashed by the return of suffocating waves. Had he ever escaped the arms of the

221

ocean, or did he wallow there even now, caught in an endless cycle of water and death? Had he dreamed of touching dry land again, or had he died when the sea took him, leaving him trapped in this nightmare forever?

Why would I dream of the Trickster trying to impede our progress? That must have happened, so I must have escaped the water.

On the heels of that thought came one even more disturbing.

Does it make more sense that I never left the ocean, or that gods have taken such a keen interest in our affairs?

He choked on salt water as he thrashed his legs in a furious attempt to stay afloat in the deep. *Who am I to think any deity would deign to notice me?*

He watched Jal again sink below the surface as Phatomar stretched out his arms to their fullest. He coughed violently, sucked in liquid he couldn't breathe. As he drowned again, one final thought penetrated the panic. *Not who am I, but who are we? For together, we have greater strength, the ability to restore a warrior to their rightful place.*

A god had told them that long before his plummet into the cold ocean. Eamon clung to the hope that he didn't struggle in vain as water rushed into his lungs, burning, tearing, searing...

Eamon gasped, barely able to draw in a clean breath in the arid landscape surrounding the volcano. The seared terrain parched his throat; no water in sight to quench his thirst. He stood at the lip of the great volcano with Jal and Phatomar. Molten lakes of red and gold swirled below, bubbling, steaming, bursting with lethal intensity. The heat burned his skin, charred his hair, melted the soles of his boots.

"You'll find Natt Tre down there," the giant fire spirit at his side said. Eamon stared at the scurrying lizards that formed the creature, his eyes wide in disbelief.

"You expect us to jump into a volcano?" Jal demanded, her voice high and frightened.

Phatomar trembled so badly that Eamon found it difficult to keep him in focus. "We'll die!"

"Take the leap, or suffer," the fire spirit said, no inflection in its tone to signify any emotion.

Eamon watched in horror as the scalding furnace of nature

reached up with shimmering fingers, taking hold of Jal's russet hair and turning it to real flame. Her tunic caught fire. She stared down into the bright depths as she burned, not uttering a word, as though oblivious to her own fiery death. Her blackened remains puffed into ash and blew away into the lava.

Phatomar, unaware of Jal's fate, continued to shake, his fright all-consuming. The more he shuddered, the less substantial he became, until he simply vibrated into tiny parts of himself, drifting out over the volcano's edge until each wisp singed into oblivion.

Eamon screamed, hands to his flushed head. He turned in shock to the fire spirit. It regarded him impassively. "How could this happen?"

"Take the leap, or suffer," the spirit said flatly. It pushed Eamon, tipping him over the edge. He fell toward the gaping maw of the hungry mountain, burning, burning...

Chapter 20

Ajala stepped from her tent into the glare of a cloudless day. The sun leached most colour from the desert sands, though hues of tan and gold, tints of blonde and white, suffused her vision. The heat—already fierce so many hours before noon—drew wavering illusions across the landscape.

A small boy clutched at the hem of her tunic, another child lay heavy within her. Her elder sister Zania had told Ajala that child rearing would curb her strange desires to flaunt tradition; that Ajala would come to accept, even enjoy, the role of wife and mother. Ajala had yet to find that fulfillment. What joy lay in a squalling babe, a domineering husband? What pleasure could she find in knowing her world of choices had narrowed to pleasing a man, bearing children, and providing sustenance?

"What else could a woman of the desert desire?" Zania wanted to know, still baffled by her yearning for anything more.

Ajala allowed her gaze to roam toward the men practising their spear work at the edge of the encampment before they set off on patrol. Once, she too had wielded a spear, swung a sword, held a bow. Now, her calluses had faded from warrior to wife; her use of a knife limited to preparing food and weaving. When Father had lived, he had permitted, even encouraged, Ajala's ambitions for becoming a guardian of the tribes. With his death, she still might have defied Olbaehn's ultimatums and pursued the ways of the warrior, save for the one threat she feared he would carry out.

If Ajala refused her brother's choice of husband, she didn't just consign herself to the fate of an outcast; she would condemn Noll as well. Ajala had not fully comprehended Olbaehn's ruthless cruelty until she looked into the hardness of his eyes. He would hold Nolbaehn's place in the tribes over Ajala's head, cause his own brother's exile should his middle sister fail to obey his edicts. Olbaehn hadn't always had such malice in him, but Father's death had broken something in their tribal elder. So Ajala had forfeited the future she had wanted so that Noll wouldn't suffer.

She hadn't told her younger brother—how could she? —and without that knowledge, Noll couldn't understand why Ajala had allowed Olbaehn to sell her into a life she detested. Why she didn't fight back. It had strained their relationship, but not her love of Noll. Better that he see her as weak than lose his chance to live the life *he* should have.

It rankled her, but at least she didn't have to see Noll's disapproval every day, nor Olbaehn's spiteful triumph. These remained the only consolations for having to live with her noxious husband's tribe and not her own. Small comfort.

No one hailed Ajala as she made her way to the cooking fires, the child traipsing after her, chubby little thumb stuffed in his scowling mouth. The other women saw her as ungrateful at best, sun-touched and incomprehensible, and felt no shame in shunning her and her oddities. Some had abusive husbands, unruly children, or jealous in-laws, but most found no cause for complaint within the cycles of the Gobani. Why should Ajala hope for a different existence? What manner of selfish vanity possessed the girl to believe she might have had a better life?

The patrol had set out an hour before, following in the wake of the hunters. That meant when the raiders came, none but the women and children—along with the old and the infirm—remained in camp. The assault swept out from the mirages of heat, the raiders riding sturdy desert mounts and bearing short spears. Ajala didn't know whether they intended capture or slaughter, and didn't wait to find out.

Pushing to her feet (an uncomfortable process under the burden of her swollen belly), she held her knife firmly in hand. Pushing the boy child at her side toward her nearest wide-eyed neighbour, Ajala lumbered as fast as her feet would take her to the tent which housed the weapons. Even with the men gone, a few bows and spears remained. Ajala took up a spear in her empty hand and strode back out into the bright day.

Forced into this life of domesticity, she still wouldn't leave it without a fight. Never let anyone say Ajala of the Gobani meekly accepted her fate.

Strangely, the day had grown dark, as though twilight had crept up on her unawares. It didn't disguise the bestial grins of the raiders, the brute strength of their squat yet muscular forms perched atop their mounts, nor mute the angry howls of the hounds.

Hounds? she thought, trying to reconcile that sound with the image of a rider bearing down upon her.

"Wake," a voice called as though from a great distance. A woman's voice, thick with resonance, one she imagined she might have heard before amid the fury of a storm.

Ajala braced her feet against the coming attack, spear held confidently before her. Her fingers longed for the hilt of a sword. *"Draw arms,"* the voice called again. Ajala blinked at her spear, her knife. What other weapons could she draw? *"Hurry. The enemy has found you."*

Ajala nearly laughed at the absurdity of that statement, countering the blow of a grim-faced raider meant to disarm her. Of course the enemy had found them. Did she not stand in the middle of a battle?

Then she felt a touch on her arm, a breath blown across her ear, the soft muzzle of a horse nudging her toward wakefulness.

"Throw off Epale's influence. Do not let Dolanis take you unawares."

The rumble of a fire spirit suddenly scalded across her dream.

"His minions have breached the boundaries," the spirit announced. "I cannot hold them back for long."

And with those words, Jal's nightmare shattered, and she opened her eyes to chaos.

***

Fire swept across the deck, engulfing the screaming

226

horses. Phatomar could reach neither them nor his friends as deep waters flooded his feet, dark tentacles wrapped around the ribs of the ship, and lightning seared the sky. He stood paralysed by fear, his heart caught in his throat as his rapid breaths threatened to pitch him into unconsciousness.

"Wake," he thought he heard. He longed with all his being to find an escape from this unending pain by the simple act of opening his eyes. He blinked water and heat from his face, not knowing how to wake when he clearly didn't sleep.

"Draw arms," came an imperious command. *"Hurry. The enemy has found you."* Phatomar shook his head. A sword wouldn't douse the flames, couldn't stop the storm. Nature merely existed; to call it an enemy gave it more power than it already claimed.

Then he felt the brush of something unseen, a heat with no substance, separate from the flames roaring before him. He *sensed* what his mind tried to hide.

The fire spirit, he thought, even as the being drew him from his nightmares into reality.

"His minions have breached the boundaries," the spirit said as Phatomar pushed to his feet, the shelter of the tent already pulled aside by Croga, who snorted at the approaching shadows, baring his teeth. The horse trumpeted a cry, and Phatomar again heard the scream of the horses from his nightmare.

Not screaming in terror, he realised. *Screaming a warning.*

"I cannot hold them back for long," the fire spirit told him, capturing his attention once more. "Use what others have gifted you to find Natt Tre and the hope it holds."

As the spirit finished speaking, Phatomar watched in stunned silence as the lizards disassembled, flowing down to the ground and spreading out. The individual reptiles fanned around them, creating a barrier. They grew less solid and more smoke-like as they moved. Once aligned under the first light of the stars, they burst into flame, forming a circle of fire. A circle to protect him and his companions from the approaching horde.

Phatomar gaped, caught up in dread at the sight of the huge black beasts with their glowing red eyes bearing down on them, yellowed fangs somehow glistening despite twilight's fall. Hell hounds. Did he face yet another nightmare or had he finally awoken? Would he watch his friends die again while he stood helplessly by, or could he find the strength to push past his fears?

He closed his eyes and drew in a deep breath, seeking calmness in the face of terror. He felt a moment of surprise when he succeeded. Phatomar opened his eyes and took hold of the bag containing the jewel beneath his tunic. The ring of fire surrounding them danced in the night, for the moment stymieing the beasts sent to hunt them, but Phatomar didn't think it would hold for long.

No longer frozen by his fears, Phatomar pulled free the Faqadat Alqalb. He held it aloft, revealing the Heart to the stars, firm in the belief that it would lead them to Natt Tre and whatever goal the gods wished them to accomplish.

An intense flash of light rewarded his belief.

***

The ground rushed up at Eamon. After an eternity of falling helplessly through water and fire, he almost welcomed the end, ready to embrace the sudden cessation of his own existence. Knowing the futility of it, he nevertheless braced himself for the pain to come, let out one final roar of defiance...

...and jerked into wakefulness, hearing the warning of the fire spirit: "I cannot hold them back for long."

Eamon rolled to his feet, sword drawn before he had fully opened his eyes. A ring of fire snaked around their group, created by the mystical lizards that had led them here. Two dark shapes soared over the barrier, trailing smoke behind them. Jaws wide, saliva dripping from snarling mouths and wicked claws, a pair of great hell hounds dared the flames with maddened growls.

"They're real!" Jal shouted.

Eamon nodded and brought his blade around to impale the creature that threatened him before it could land on him. The hound's weight on his sword nearly took Eamon from his feet. A flick of his wrist freed his weapon, dark blood dripping from the blade to speckle the ground.

A second hell hound sailed toward Cosantoir and Croga,

sensing easier prey. The horses reared, sharp hooves flashing. Croga's made contact, hurtling the beast to the ground. Cosantoir spun and brought his rear feet down with a sickening crunch. Onoir flanked Jal as the warhorses made short work of the enemy.

Meanwhile, the flames from the lizards rose high, momentarily halting the other attackers. Beyond their flickering light, Eamon could see a host of hell hounds, hear their frenzied calls as they scented their prey and fresh blood, just out of reach.

"What in Dearn's name?" he wheezed, too soft for the others to hear. Lingering fragments of nightmare still lurked at the edges of his mind, yet somehow, Eamon knew he faced real life now.

He nearly choked on a bitter laugh. Strange to find comfort in the knowledge that hell hounds—ferocious guardians of the lower realms—confronted them. *At least these I can fight.* Having even that much control—for he'd had none battling against oceans and living, molten rock—gave him a sense of assurance. They all might die in the next few moments, but not without a fighting chance.

Jal stood wide-eyed and ashen-faced as she watched the beasts beyond the flames, sword held in a white-knuckled grip. By the fine tremble of her body and the light sheen of sweat dewing her golden skin, he didn't think the hounds alone had drawn the colour from her face. He had seen her handle too many surprises with surpassing ease and grace to believe such monsters would give her much pause now. He suspected he hadn't suffered through endless nightmares alone. *The Trickster finding another way to torment us?*

And what of Phatomar?

His friend's visage showed a sudden draining of tension as Phatomar sought for calm. Phatomar drew forth the bag holding the Faqadat Alqalb, reached for the gem within, and raised it high. The sparkling facets of the Heart Stone reflected the light from the fire spirit encircling them and threw back shafts of crimson sparks.

Bright light pierced the night, fanning out from Phatomar's fist. It shone behind them, away from the hell hounds, illuminating...

A large island of basalt appeared within the chasm higher

up the volcano, invisible without the light from the Faqadat Alqalb to reveal it. Eamon could make out the outline of a narrow bridge granting access to the dark island, and the strange features which sprang up along it.

A small forest of skeletal trees rose from the island amid the rocky field, bare limbs stretching into the sky. The central tree, slender yet vast in the eerie light—its own and that of the Stone—thrust long limbs high above its companions as though seeking the benediction of the stars overhead. Bark blacker than night, dotted with pin pricks of light twinkling white and silver and blue, like stars.

Natt Tre beckoned to them.

The howls of the hell hounds reached a fevered pitch, frustration and fury combining into an ugly mix. All three horses laid their ears back, perhaps hoping to block out the unnatural sounds. They stamped and whickered, teeth bared and eyes wide. Eamon's jaw clenched as the noise grated against his senses.

The protective flames flared brighter, both barrier and guard sweeping clear the way to the bridge, but Eamon feared the fire wouldn't hinder the hounds much longer. The fire spirit had warned it couldn't hold the enemy at bay forever.

"To the bridge," he called out, sheathing his sword and reaching for Cosantoir's reins. Phatomar and Jal quickly followed suit.

A short ride made frantic by surging adrenaline, they galloped across the narrow span, the Heart Stone showing the way. Eamon dared not look down as they crossed, haunted by nightmares of endlessly falling into such trenches. The heat rising from below ignited an already over-sensitive imagination; he didn't need to *see* the flow of red-hot lava creeping past to fuel what his mind had already conjured. Nor did he want to know whether more than just a narrow bridge of stone held this island of rock aloft. Given the nature of their journey thus far, he feared he wouldn't like the answer.

The fire barrier followed close behind them, protecting their retreat. It halted on the far side of the bridge, gathering strength and height as the blaze fused into tighter cohesion, intense orange and yellow flames defending a smaller area.

The furious growls grew louder as the hell hounds pressed against the inferno, muzzles singed in their attempts to find a way through. Frustration rose in high-pitched yowls that echoed in Eamon's ears as the prey of the hounds remained just out of reach. Yet for all the impressive show of the flames, Eamon knew they didn't have long; the spirit would give them what time it could. Best not to waste it.

Not that Eamon knew what to expect from Natt Tre.

"What do we do now?" Phatomar asked, as though reading Eamon's mind. He slid from Croga's saddle on unsteady legs to stare up at the twinkling mystery of the tree of starry night, the Faqadat Alqalb still held tight in his fist. It bathed the tree in an eerie glow, lending hints of red to the brilliant sparks of white. Swirls of maroon shadows twisted across the black bark, seeming to both reflect and swallow parts of the Heart Stone's radiance.

Jal circled the tree, studying it from all sides. Her frown in the deepening night—only visible by the combined glow of Natt Tre and the Faqadat Alqalb—spoke to trepidation and bafflement.

"Nothing," she said. "No words, no hints, no loose branches offering themselves." She glanced over her shoulder, into the darkness beyond the copse of trees. "And no way off the other side that I can see."

"Trapped," spat Eamon, frustration and terror playing havoc with his nerves. "With no idea what the gods expect of us."

Phatomar gazed up into the boughs of the tree. "*With a limb freely given, you might win free of its mighty reach.* Does that make the tree sentient in some way? Could we just ask for a branch?"

Eamon shrugged, though neither of his companions saw it. A deep-throated growl drew his attention back to the hounds pressing against the bridge. They needed more time to decipher the riddle, and less interference.

Eamon moved closer to the bridge, cautiously studying the chasm it spanned. A good thirty feet of emptiness separated them from the main land and the slavering jaws of the irate hounds, a distance only accessible by the narrow bridge. Could the horses jump that space should the bridge fail?

Could the hounds?

A couple of the beasts ran along the edge of the chasm, red-eyed and whining, but none looked eager to attempt the leap across to the island. What if their only means of capturing the humans disappeared? Would they leave in search of easier sport? No doubt the Trickster, or someone of his ilk, had set these slavering creatures loose—hell hounds didn't escape the underworld without direction—which made the chances of them growing bored and leaving slim. But with only one point of access to their quarry, Eamon and his friends could more easily defend themselves. One or two at a time, they could defeat; the whole pack at once, they could not. Limiting their access seemed a good strategy.

Eamon dropped to his knees, keeping his sword close at hand. He studied the base of the bridge, as much as he could see in the light from the fire spirit. Solid stone made up the majority of the structure and, although a crack or two suggested itself in places, Eamon did not expect to remove the bridge with sword and strength alone.

He glanced up at the fiery blockade.

"Could a fire spirit destroy stone?" he asked of no one in particular, simply needing to voice his thoughts. "Can it break the bridge?"

The slight crunch of rock beneath a boot announced Jal's presence at his side. "It says it cannot remove the path," she said, brows creased, hearing things Eamon could not.

Phatomar joined them next. "What do you suppose will happen if I conceal the Faqadat Alqalb again? It revealed the way to the island and Natt Tre; might it not hide the land again now?"

"But what would that do to us, here on the island?" Jal asked, a hitch to her words betraying her unease.

Phatomar gave a fatalistic shrug. "The land lies solid beneath our feet now," he reasoned, his voice unsteady. "Either it'll stay solid, or it will vanish." He stared in the direction of the snarls. "Given the choice of falling to the flames below or waiting for the certainty of the rending teeth of hell hounds, I think I'd prefer the faster death."

Eamon pushed to his feet. "What happens to the fire spirit if hiding the Heart Stone makes us vanish from the sight of the hell hounds?" he wondered. "They won't like losing us. It

232

might make them attack our guardian. While no doubt some of the hounds will suffer, would the spirit escape the wrath of the survivors?"

He heard a strange crackle, like logs shifting in the snare of a fire.

"I think it's laughing," Jal said. "It sounds surprised by your concern."

"It's helped us," Eamon countered. "Of course we're concerned." He looked out at the flames of the spirit. Had they begun to dim?

"Spirit," he called out. "If you cross to this side of the bridge, we can catch you if something goes amiss." Although how Eamon expected to take hold of a being made up of fire, he didn't know. He just knew that he wouldn't leave *any* to the mercy of hounds, for they had none.

"And if nothing happens when I conceal the Stone?" Phatomar asked quietly, retreating a step.

Eamon readied his sword. "Then we hold the hounds here at the bridge for as long as we can."

Jal stood by his side. She glanced back at Phatomar. "If you hold on to Natt Tre when you extinguish the Faqadat Alqalb's light," she suggested, "perhaps you, at least, will find the way to the watery grave."

"I'm not leaving you behind," Phatomar said with firm conviction, his old self peeking through the crush of lost courage. "Together, or not at all."

"We're all a bunch of fools," Eamon said fondly. Jal gave a fierce grin, and Phatomar managed a nod.

Eamon turned back to the scene at the bridge. The hounds had worked themselves into a renewed frenzy, as though sensing the hope of the humans and trying to quash it. Eamon leaned forward slightly.

"Fire Spirit," he called. Its intensity had already begun to dim. "Thank you for your assistance. Come, preserve your strength. Join us here, if you can." He reached out his off hand, beckoning to the spirit, ready to reach into the heart of the fire should it prove necessary. A part of his brain screamed that he had lost his mind, thinking to take hold of the flames. The rest of him held firm.

"Ready?" Phatomar asked as the fiery barrier crept across the bridge, thinning and spreading so that flames still covered as much space as possible while also retreating. The hell hounds scrabbled at the other side, muscles bunching as they made ready to follow.

Eamon took a deep breath, his fingers warming as the heat of the fire spirit neared. When he felt the tingle of fiery fingers that approached his flesh grow into a crescendo of pain, he spoke through gritted teeth.

"Now."

Three things happened at once.

The fire spirit touched Eamon, its flames enveloping his hand, then evaporated and left the humans bereft of its illumination as it resolved into hundreds of little smoke lizards, Eamon's flesh unscorched.

Hell hounds howled in triumph and surged across the bridge, ready to leap at their foe.

And Phatomar quenched the light from the Faqadat Alqalb, leaving only the glow from Natt Tre to light the island.

An eerie silence descended as everything beyond the island—including the bridge with its heavy load of hell hounds—vanished.

Chapter 21

Dolanis had taken a risk summoning the Chuka and sending them across the wastes of the Formorket Enger. The Chuka, Hell's fearsome hounds, didn't often leave the gates of the underworld, and only by altering his scent to seem as if he'd spoken to Hell himself had Dolanis convinced some of death's guardians to stalk the land of the living to hunt for him.

His illusions had not worked as he hoped in foiling the progress of Order's champion. The imps had had greater success, though even they hadn't lasted long against Phatomar and his companions.

Perhaps most distressing of all, Dolanis could send his illusions and some lesser minions of Chaos to play with his prey, but found himself blocked from any personal interference. Watching from afar, he saw mostly shadows, hints of the events he wished to direct. While this allowed him to exert his influence into Phatomar's and Eamon's minds—strengthening into reality the results of illusion—it restricted his experience of his ploy, held him back from witnessing his efforts with any clarity. *Something* made him unable to watch (or experience) first hand the events he sought to dictate, obstructed somehow by another's subtle shield. It forced him to rely on manipulation from afar, leaving him unsure of the efficacy of his successes.

Worse, once his quarry slipped beyond the pass that brought them firmly into the realm of the Formorket Enger and under the protections of the fire spirit Salamander,

Dolanis could no longer sway their minds. That left him little recourse. Rather than try to follow the path Salamander set, Dolanis gathered his resources closer to the goal, prepared to stop Phatomar on the cusp of locating Natt Tre.

Salamander could guard against Dolanis' illusions, but had no power over Epale, god of nightmares. Convincing Epale to lull into a trapped sleep those whom Order ruled had taken some fast talking. But the Trickster couldn't hold the trio immobile on his own (a vexing frustration for the mortal-turned-god), and he needed them unaware of the danger that approached.

And where had this third companion, this desert girl, come from? Dolanis had only noticed her thanks to Epale's dark vision, and he wondered if even Kistawna would understand the import of this surprising presence.

Dolanis didn't know what finally allowed him to push through to the playing field, but he managed to manifest behind the hell hounds as Salamander blazed into a protective barrier, guarding the retreat of Phatomar and his companions across the bridge to Natt Tre.

"No," Dolanis swore, seeing his chance to win Chaos' game slipping away. He surged forward, goading the Chuka to test Salamander's teeth. The hounds bayed and lunged, but retreated each time Salamander slapped them back with his fiery whip.

Dolanis transformed himself into the semblance of one of the Chuka. Hell's guardians tended to follow the largest in any pack, and the Trickster fashioned himself into a hulking brute. In this form, colours became muted, and although he could see the vague shapes of the humans beyond Salamander's muted flames, their scent—the scent he had imprinted on the minds of the Chuka—drove him mad with the need to reach them.

He led the Chuka over the bridge as Salamander retreated, then stretched, thinned, and disappeared. With a howl of triumph, echoed by the Chuka at his heels, Dolanis pushed ahead, tensed his powerful haunches—

—and plummeted toward the blistering heat of the volcano's blood as the island sheltering Natt Tre vanished, taking the bridge with it.

Ripping his thoughts away from that of a hell hound and

morphing back into his own form, Dolanis halted his headlong drop toward death in a cushion of air   The four Chuka who had crossed the bridge with him had no such powers, falling with startled yips into the streaming lava.

Hell will want reparation for that, if he ever learns what I did, thought Dolanis in an oddly detached way. Dread should have crept through his gut at this, yet another set-back in a ploy that continued to deteriorate, yet Dolanis felt nothing, and that worried him. He pushed all thought of the future aside and concentrated on only one consideration: *What do I tell Kistawna?*

As though the thought summoned her, the Mistress of Shadows now stood at his side, both of them standing at the edge of the chasm that a moment ago had led to the island of Natt Tre. Dolanis blinked, wondering whether she had seen his latest failure, or if she had simply chosen this inopportune moment to appear.   Not one to believe in coincidence, Dolanis waited for the goddess to speak, to reveal the extent of her knowledge, and the direction of her displeasure.

"So they've reached Natt Tre," the goddess said, ice riming her words.

Dolanis offered a grunt in return, not meeting her emerald-rimmed violet eyes. What more could he offer?

"You've failed in your mission to stop them," Kistawna snarled, the weight of her gaze almost compelling enough to force Dolanis to meet her stare. He held firm against her influence. "I charged you with a simple task, Trickster. Stop them before they reach the Formorket Enger. Now they've danced right up to Natt Tre itself, unscathed, unhindered, closer to weakening the powers of Chaos than any in generations."

Dolanis narrowed his eyes and he finally turned to confront Kistawna, letting his own ire leak through.

"I failed no mission, Kistawna. In fact, I achieved all that we discussed. That Order still stands ahead of you in the game doesn't fall on my shoulders."

"How can you *not* call this a failure, Dolanis?" Kistawna demanded with a sharp wave of her fingers.

"As I recall, we struck a bargain." He created the illusion of that meeting in her make-shift tent, reminding Kistawna of their words.

"If you learn who seeks to thwart us by masking Phatomar's steps from us," Dolanis had said, *"I will make sure our would-be hero runs afoul of something unexpected and unpleasant before he ever touches foot upon the Blackened Fields."*

"Good hunting," Kistawna had replied.

Dolanis slashed the edge of his hand through the image, shattering the memory.

"Shall I list for you all that Phatomar and his cursed companions endured before they crossed the slopes?" he asked, a false sweetness dripping from his tone. "Their terror-filled days, their sleepless nights, the number of ways their own minds worked against them?"

Kistawna glared at him, but kept her silence.

"I even found a way around Salamander's protective presence, held them immobile for a time." He stepped closer to her, enjoying the way she tensed in an effort not to pull away. Dolanis stared down at her, using the advantage of his height to its fullest and lowering his voice to a menacing rasp. "And where were you, goddess, while I held your enemy in thrall? What have *you* brought to the table? By what right do you think to hold *me* accountable for achieving what you could not?"

Suddenly, Kistawna smiled. Dolanis nearly leapt back at the strange ferocity of her expression, so at odds with their conversation.

"You did achieve more than I thought possible," she purred. "More, I believe, than Chaos alone might have managed." His brow furrowed as he tried to decipher that comment, but she went on. "Just as we work on Chaos' behalf, so too do others work toward Order's ascendance, as we surmised. Your actions, dear Dolanis, have proven that Order's adherents cannot assure Phatomar's success." Her hand reached out to stroke Dolanis' face; he grabbed her wrist and jerked his head away from her touch, feeling as though he held the fangs of a viper from his flesh.

"Who stands against us?" he said, refusing to show any signs of weakness. "Who protects them?"

"The warrior god, and the goddess of horses and the hunt."

Her eyes flashed, and this time, Dolanis knew she aimed her vexation elsewhere. Dearn's intercession didn't surprise

Dolanis—Phatomar *had* once stood as the foremost warrior in Merveah, after all—but why would Cetain deign to involve herself in these affairs? Perhaps, like him, she merely sought some entertainment.

Kistawna's voice drew him from his speculation even as she drew her wrist from his grip.

"Chaos has warned me not to confront them directly. He did, however, imply that we might work around them."

"How?" Dolanis didn't like this Chaos goddess playing with him in this manner. *He* played word games with others, not the other way around.

"If the champions escape Natt Tre's sphere, they will find Order's grave. Instead of trying to stop them, let us find a way to bind them."

Dolanis' eyes creased in speculation, his tone turning cautious. "How?"

"To restore power to Order, Chaos can demand certain conditions. We have but to determine what Phatomar and his *friends*,"—she spat the word as though she spat poison—"cannot, or will not, do. Order will not permit outright interference, so we must twist any conditions into impossibilities without raising objections. So, what can we demand that will thwart their efforts, and how do we make sure the request seems benign enough that no one questions it?"

A smile spread across Dolanis' face as the Trickster god set his wily mind to the task.

Chapter 22

Jal blinked, her eyes adjusting to the dim light. She could still see after-images of the fire spirit as it flared in Eamon's hand, and a hint of red teased at the edges of sight as a reminder of the glow of the Faqadat Alqalb. Yet only the twinkling of Natt Tre behind them provided any real illumination. She wanted to turn to that light now, find some respite from total darkness, but Jal hesitated.

She thought she heard the growls and whines of hounds across the chasm, thwarted from claiming their prize. Did she see the shadows of their frenetic movements even now in the misty nothingness beyond this strange island, or did she just imagine them?

The voices, however, she did not imagine, and she closed her eyes to block out other distractions, concentrating on the reverberating timbre of conversing gods.

"It worked," Eamon breathed in relief and wonder.

Jal hissed and held up her hand, begging for silence.

"What is it?" Phatomar asked, his voice a whisper. Jal appreciated the effort, knowing her friends couldn't hear what she did. She didn't particularly like the fact that she alone heard the mutterings of these beings she hadn't even known existed a few months ago, but she would use every advantage she could to survive.

"Dolanis and Kistawna stand across the way," Jal said, following the conversation. "And neither seems happy. They're talking about Order and Chaos, and he wonders who protects us."

Both men waited quietly, though Jal knew they must burn with questions. She did as well, but she dare not shift her concentration for fear of missing some important detail.

When the gods fell silent, she loosened taut muscles and opened her eyes.

"Whatever lies at the end of this quest apparently also holds conditions. They plan to demand something we cannot or will not do."

"Of course," Phatomar said bitterly. "They started us on this journey, not expecting us to get this far. Why wouldn't they stand at the end and expect us to fail?"

"We'll just have to find a way to disappoint them," Eamon said, his scowl turning into an unpleasant grin. "Again."

Jal nodded, though her smile felt forced. They might have slept, but she, for one, had found no rest in her nightmares, and exhaustion weighed heavily on her shoulders. She sheathed her weapon and turned toward Natt Tre's beckoning light. The silhouettes of their horses waited near the mystical tree and Jal stumbled in their direction, Eamon and Phatomar at her side.

"We still have a puzzle or two to decipher before we reach the end," she sighed. "Maybe by then, we'll have a better idea of what obstacles the gods plan to toss our way."

The trio wearily approached Natt Tre, lithe and smokey lizards twining around their feet. Eamon let his curiosity speak.

"Dolanis thinks someone protects us. Did Kistawna say who?" he asked. "Besides the fire spirit," he added as one of the lizards scurried up his body to perch on his shoulder. Jal let out a surprised laugh at the sight, as did Phatomar.

"Other than Salamander here,"—Jal nodded her thanks to the lizard, whose red-gold eyes glittered briefly—"the warrior god and the goddess of horses and the hunt stand at our side. I presume they spoke of Dearn, seeing as he sent us to Hada, but who is this other goddess?"

"Cetain," answered Eamon. "I can't say why she'd find interest in us, but I'm grateful for any assistance she might offer."

At that, Cosantoir turned his head and snorted at his master. Eamon froze, staring at his horse. The deep and knowing eyes held more than a horse's mind behind them.

Slowly, Eamon raised his hand in a warrior's salute, placing his fingers over his chest.

"Forgive me if I offended," he said. Jal gaped, suddenly remembering a voice in a storm as Onoir dragged her to shore—*Hold fast your lifeline, little warrior; help approaches*—and after that, a woman instructing Eamon on how to save her life. Onoir now gazed down at her through dark, soulful eyes—the eyes of horse, or goddess?

Stunned at the enormity of the moment, her knees buckled, and Jal found herself sprawled at the base of Natt Tre, staring up at their four-footed companions. Onoir arched her neck to nuzzle Jal, then stepped back with a gentle *whuff*. Jal felt moisture on her cheeks, tears of awe mingled with fatigue.

"I cannot take much more of this," she whispered to herself. Phatomar's hand fell on her shoulder, his expression one of understanding. With a nod, she allowed him to help her to her feet.

"I don't know if it's more intimidating or less to know that so many have taken an interest in our quest," the large warrior admitted.

"They might lend us aid," Eamon said. "But ultimately, *we* must fulfill the tasks they set. Which means we need to figure out what the Oracle sent us here to find, and to determine how to escape from Natt Tre's land."

"With a limb freely given," Jal said, looking up into the bare branches of the tree, its ebony fingers stretching into the night sky. "Which brings us back to the question of whether the tree has some form of understanding, and how to ask it for a branch."

The stars held captive in the tree's bark flashed bright. Jal squeezed her eyes shut, though bursts of red and black lightning streaked behind her eyelids. When she dared open them again, a bough as long as Phatomar's leg and as wide around as Jal's wrist lay in front of them.

"Well, that seemed a little too easy," she said, staring down at it.

A deep chuckle answered her. Salamander had reformed itself into a single gestalt entity. It gazed at the three startled humans, whirling eyes holding them in place.

"With a limb freely given," it echoed Jal's earlier words,

then gestured toward Eamon. "A selfless act to save another. You willingly reached into fire to aid me. Her limb freely given"—it pointed at the tree branch—"to honour the sacrifice you offered to make."

Jal stared down at the limb again, as did Eamon and Phatomar. Finally, Phatomar crouched down, elbows on his knees and hands dangling between his thighs. He stretched his hand out to the branch, but Jal stopped him.

"Wait," she said. "Is it safe for him to touch that?" She looked into the whirling eyes of Salamander as best she could. It regarded her in turn, yet kept its silence. Hard to read the feature of a being made up of skittering smokey lizards, but she thought she detected a hint of approval in its stance. Or perhaps she simply saw a shift in the breeze, twisting tails of smoke. She didn't know. She looked back to her companions.

"The Thueban Alnaas and their prophecy made it clear that only Phatomar could hold the Faqadat Alqalb. I see no prophecy or riddles here, but Salamander told us *Eamon's* act granted the limb. What if only Eamon can touch it?"

"That would fit with everything else, wouldn't it?" Eamon said with a shake of his head. "Our three tasks, as the Oracle called them. One for each of us. The gods do love these kinds of quests."

Phatomar nodded. "Dearn said: *It is for you three together to walk the path that might restore a warrior to their rightful place.* We've already figured he didn't mean me, or at least not my plight alone. He might also have meant that each of us has an integral part in this. I hold the Heart, Eamon the limb, leaving whatever we find at the watery grave for Jal."

"I can hardly wait," Jal muttered.

Eamon snorted, then grew serious again.

"So if the limb permits me to pick it up, what do we do with it?" he wondered. "The Oracle said: *Limb and Stone will point you to the watery grave*. That suggests the two join somehow, or work together in some fashion. Which means Phatomar has to take out the Heart Stone again." He glanced over his shoulder to where the bridge had stood. "Will that reopen the way for the hell hounds?"

Jal remembered the haunting, tormented cries of the beasts. Their claws and teeth, the thirst for blood in their piercing gaze. She didn't want to encounter them a second time, yet they couldn't stay here either.

"One way to find out," she said, turning to where the bridge had stood, hand over her shoulder grasping the hilt of her sword. "You two work out how to fit limb and stone together. Find the map, or beam of light, or whatever strange pointer that marks the way to the watery grave. I'll stand guard against whatever the Faqadat Alqalb's light might reveal."

Jal moved away from the skeletal forest guarding Natt Tre, drawing her weapon and settling into a fighter's stance. She took a deep breath and prepared for battle, eyes scanning the darkness of the night.

She saw nothing, until an aura of red swept over her shoulder. The Heart Stone, throbbing among the stars. Jal braced herself, expecting the weight of a hell hound to crash into her at any moment.

***

Eamon stared down at the inky branch with the diamond points of light glittering on its surface. Or perhaps it shone from within the eerie offering at his feet. He rather wished Jal hadn't brought up the possibility of the branch having lethal properties. Better paranoid than dead, he supposed.

His hand hovered over the bough, though it took a concerted force of will to actually touch it. His fingers paused a hair's width away, and Eamon wondered if Phatomar always now felt this heart-pounded sense of dread, bereft of his courage. Eamon's muscles locked, refusing to obey him. Blood rushed in his ears, throbbing through his head, blocking out any external noise. Then, with a deliberate—if slightly desperate—gasp of air, Eamon pushed beyond his paralysis, closing his fist around the branch.

No spectre arose to steal the life from him; no power tried to stay his actions. Eamon breathed a hearty sigh of relief, echoed by Phatomar, who crouched next to him. Eamon met his friend's scrutiny and gave a reassuring nod.

"That's the limb, then," Eamon said, keeping his tone light, swallowing down his anxiety as he pushed to his feet, the bough held in front of him like a staff. "Now to see how it reacts to the Heart."

Phatomar reached into his tunic for the Faqadat Alqalb as Jal guarded the path from the bridge. Looking back to Eamon, Phatomar pulled free the Heart Stone. The gem flashed crimson.

Eamon tipped the branch forward and Phatomar touched the Stone to its black tip. Both strained their ears, listening for the approaching howls of hell hounds.

Only their ragged breathing disturbed the night. That, and the quiet nickers of the horses as their animals stood waiting in the dark.

"What do you suppose happens now?" Phatomar whispered.

Even as Eamon shook his head, lacking an answer, the stars beneath the skin of the branch pulsed and began to flow up the bough, tiny globes of radiance travelling across this minuscule slice of the heavens as they reached for the Heart Stone. Each twinkling sphere that gathered at the apex of Eamon's staff extended around the Heart, solidifying into darkness as they built some sort of web around the jewel, cradling it in a new growth of black bark. Phatomar yanked back his hand to avoid touching the filaments now wrapping the Stone. He cursed, ready to snatch the gem back from the layers ensnaring it.

"Wait," said Eamon, mesmerised by the morphing sinews of stars topping the staff.

As the last star climbed the limb and curled around the gem, Eamon found himself holding an ebony staff topped by a rough knob of fresh bark. A thin sliver of red peeked out from the knot, the only indication that the Faqadat Alqalb lay nestled at the centre of the bole.

"Well, I didn't expect that," Jal said from behind them. Eamon nearly leapt out of his skin, Phatomar cowering behind him. Jal had her hands raised and her sword sheathed.

"I didn't mean to startle you," she said. "But it seems revealing the Faqadat Alqalb didn't cause the bridge to reappear. Nor any portion of the land beyond this floating rock. The hounds can't get to us, so we have nothing to defend against." Her smile faded. "However, we also have no place to retreat to, nowhere to go."

"So this stick must hold the key to escaping Natt Tre's

245

island," Eamon concluded, staring at the dark staff in his hand, though he had no idea what to do with it now.

"So it seems," Jal agreed.

There followed a tense moment of silence.

"How do we use it?" Phatomar finally asked. Eamon shook his head in consternation. Like Jal, he had hoped for some kind of guidance for their next course of action—a map, a signal, a pointer—not this fantastical melding of two strange objects. He knew the staff must do *something* that would help; he just didn't yet know how to make it reveal its secrets.

"*Limb and Stone will point you to the watery grave,*" he quoted the Oracle. "Maybe..." Eamon shifted his hands so that he braced the staff with the knob facing forward and away from him, pointing it like a dowsing rod. He turned a slow circle. Jal crouched low to keep out of his line of sight, while Phatomar paced at his shoulder, searching for any reaction. When the staff came level with Natt Tre, Phatomar drew in a sharp breath.

"What?" Eamon asked, having seen nothing.

"Do the stars in the tree's bark look any different to you?"

Eamon squinted at the dappled trunk, but nothing had changed to his sight. He glanced to where Jal now stood, and a slight lift of her shoulders indicated that she saw nothing either.

"There," Phatomar cried out just as a star from a branch above Jal erupted, tendrils of black-edged filaments exploding outward. Jal backed away and threw up her arm to protect her head. Strands of starlight wrapped around her upraised forearm, darkening as they hardened into bark, very like the fingers which had webbed the Heart Stone. She tried to pull away, but the manacle held fast. She pulled a knife from her waist and slashed at the bark. The blade rebounded with a dull *thunk*.

"What in Dearn's name?" Eamon yanked the staff into a fighter's embrace. More stars burst along the length of the tree, bright flashes stabbing across his vision. With each, another curl of transforming bark shot forth, seeking new targets. One shaft wrapped around Cosantoir's left leg, another around Croga's neck, and a third encased the bulk of Phatomar's thigh. Onoir trumpeted and stamped, her eyes showing white all around as she tried to evade the one aimed

246

at her front right leg, only to have her rear leg snagged instead.

Eamon didn't wait for more attacks. He laid about him with the staff. Every time his weapon connected with a new growth, it melted back into starlight and retracted into Natt Tre's skin. But as quickly as he broke each bond, a fresh explosion occurred, until Natt Tre writhed with silver-white filaments streaked by black lightning, a storm centred around the ancient tree as it resumed its assault.

Strangely, no grasping fingers stretched toward Salamander as the fire spirit stood motionless, but the tree had a cunning mind and continued to evade Eamon's strikes. The staff could affect the supernatural assault, but they only had the one. Unless Eamon found a solution fast, Natt Tre would trap them all even more surely than did the confines of its rocky island.

"The trunk," Jal gasped as a starry arm snaked around her torso. Eamon smashed the staff against her newest prison, understanding her meaning. If the staff broke the burgeoning sprigs upon contact, what might it do against the parent?

As if reading his mind, Natt Tre spat a restraining star at his wrist, narrowly avoiding the shaft of the branch.

"No," Eamon spat, straining against the tree's hold. Phatomar's hand shot into view, reaching for the staff. Before Eamon could scream an objection, Phatomar's fingers made contact. Something jolted up Eamon's arms. With both of them now holding the staff, Natt Tre reacted.

White light glared along the trunk, pulsing in anger, or perhaps fear. Gritting his teeth and tensing the muscles in his arm, Eamon shoved the staff forward. Phatomar's biceps bulged as he aided Eamon's efforts, pushing the staff closer to the tree. Blood slicked Eamon's wrist as he fought his restraints, the bark digging into tender flesh, but he refused to give ground.

At last, the knot at the tip of the staff made contact with the trunk. A brilliant blast of red pierced the tree, stealing sight, and a violent clap of thunder deafened them. Eamon felt the fetters that held him crumble and he stumbled to his knees with a gasp.

Slowly, sight returned.

Natt Tre stood tall and proud, its midnight boughs

stretching high and, thankfully, immobile. The stars within, however, began a slow dance, gathering and swirling in a vortex of glittering light around the centre of the trunk.

"By the shifting sands, what's going on?" Jal asked, sprawled out next to Eamon, her tunic ripped and arms bloodied from the attack, staring wearily at the spectacle. Phatomar supported himself on one knee, off hand only now letting go of the staff. He shook his head, transfixed by the eddy rippling in front of them. A sense of resignation came from the large man, bracing for whatever crisis came at them next.

"You have calmed Natt Tre's ire," Salamander said from behind them, its deep voice startling Eamon. He briefly wondered why he could understand the words now. "She opens the portal in recognition of your desire to serve Order."

Desire to serve Order? Eamon thought, barely masking an incredulous snort. *So far, I've only felt a desire to save my friends and survive.*

"A portal to where?" Jal asked in a soft whisper, her eyes fixed on the swirl of stars. "Or to what?"

"To her watery grave," Salamander replied. "Where Order's spirit has lain trapped these many years by her brother Chaos, when he tried in vain so long ago to mask his foul deed."

"She whom Chaos slew," Phatomar remembered. "Who might rise to push the darkness away."

"Order and Chaos are siblings?" Jal leaned back on her knees to test the scratches on her arms, her gaze shifting between Salamander and the forming portal.

"Twins," said the fire spirit. "Once united by the shared cause of teaching humanity the many ways to survive and thrive in this world. Later prone to manipulation and rivalry, which led to suspicion and anger, and finally sororicide. The minions of Chaos have tightened their hold wherever they can while the agents of Order have clung to their mistress' ideals as best they could; the eternal struggle between the pair shifting the balance of the world the Elder gods created."

"And we're supposed to...what? Bring Order back into the world?" Jal asked.

"Order has had many champions throughout the centuries," Salamander informed them. "None have yet found a way to restore what Chaos wrought, to correct the unbalance of an act done in haste. Nonetheless, those who follow Order continue to hope, even when hope grows thin."

"And we're the latest fools thrust into a task no one else has accomplished," Eamon grimaced. "But no pressure or anything." A thought tugged at his mind. "What happened to previous champions?" He stared into Salamander's whirling eyes. "What became of those who failed to revive Order? What fate can we look forward to should we also fail?"

The fire spirit didn't shy from Eamon's glare, nor did it spare them from the truth.

"They all died with their task unfulfilled."

"Wonderful," Eamon muttered as Phatomar winced from the thought and Jal uttered a sound somewhere between a growl and a sigh.

"Making us nothing but playthings in the ongoing saga of your gods," spat Jal. "Now you know why we of the Gobani have nothing to do with them."

Salamander fixed her with an intense stare of red and gold sparks. "They are your gods too, child of the desert, though perhaps you knew them not before embarking on this journey."

"A journey taken in the hopes of helping Phatomar," Eamon rejoined. "We had no knowledge or desire to champion any god. We've always sought to help the people; gods get in the way of that, more often than not."

"And yet you all continued upon this venture even after you learned that the scope encompassed far more than the life of one man," Salamander countered. "You have known your cause served the gods for some time now. Do you say otherwise?"

Eamon looked away with a resigned shake of his head; he couldn't deny the guidance and assistance of celestial beings on this quest, but understanding that Phatomar's original predicament was predicated on an ancient struggle among deities only frustrated him.

Yet the only way forward lay ahead. To restore Phatomar to his former abilities, they had to restore a goddess to life, or die in the attempt. Nothing they had learned had changed their objective, only their understanding of that goal, and the consequences of failure.

"What happens on the other side of the portal?" Phatomar asked in a small voice, his body trembling.

"That, I cannot say," Salamander responded. "I have never set foot upon that rain-swept shore."

With those words, the churning of starry arms upon Natt Tre's trunk coalesced and the portal opened fully. Beyond it lay a stormy sea, its foaming waters dark with turmoil. At the edge of the water, a spit of land drenched by torrents of rain waited for the adventurers.

Eamon saw nothing that might indicate where in Merveah that shore might lie—if indeed the land stood anywhere near Merveah.

Jal rose to her feet. "Do we go through?"

Phatomar stood rigid at her side, and Eamon joined them. Eamon heard the horses nicker nearby and then, before he could utter a protest, watched as Onoir stepped through the portal onto the rainy shore beyond, followed by Croga and Cosantoir. He gaped at the beasts, who all turned to watch the humans with an uncanny intelligence.

"I suppose it's follow the animals, or stay trapped here," Jal finally said with resignation.

"The choice always remains your own," Salamander said, a pair of lizards sweeping across his brow in what Eamon could only describe as a frown. "Although in this instance, the choice does appear obvious should you wish to survive." Eamon could hear the disapproval in the fire spirit's tone, and he suspected Salamander did not agree with Cetain trying to force their hand.

Yet having come so far, and having reconciled their goals with the desires of the gods, the choice *had* become obvious, even without Cetain's silent plea.

Eamon turned to the fire spirit and offered a slight bow.

"Our thanks, Salamander, for your guidance and assistance."

The creature nodded in return. Turning back to Phatomar and Jal, Eamon nodded to the portal.

"To the watery grave, then."

Together, they walked through, leaving Salamander and the Formorket Enger with its fuming volcanoes far behind.

Chapter 23

Rain lashed at Jal's face and flattened her hair to her head and neck, snarled strands of rust plastered over a sheen of gold. Chill tendrils of water slithered with abandon beneath her tunic, washing the blood from her wounds and stealing what warmth she'd brought with her from the heated pit that had surrounded Natt Tre's island. She shivered, but only in part from the change in climate.

The waters that confronted them—black waves crested with white fury—reminded her all too much of the storm that had swept her from the deck of the *Swelling Tide*. Now the time had come to face what the Oracle had called the watery grave.

It didn't settle her stomach any to see these waters as beset by winds and leaden clouds as the ocean they had sailed amid autumn storms. The lack of any aquatic transport to leave this shore didn't help her peace of mind, and she recalled her moan of misery declaring that she'd never set foot on a boat again. Ironic, should that idle objection prove prophetic now.

Strangely, the heavy skies hinted at daytime, though they had left Natt Tre at night. No sun pierced the oppressive cloud cover, making direction impossible to judge. Jal had no idea where in Merveah they now stood. Assuming they stood anywhere in or even near Merveah. When it came to affairs of the gods, Jal couldn't take anything for granted; not even which world they currently inhabited. She tried to shrug off the chill weight of such uncertainty and ground herself in what she could understand.

Frothing waters lay in front of them, flat beach sporting black sands and tufts of dark grass behind, grey skies weeping above. Already, the portal from the Formorket Enger had vanished, taking with it what little colour Salamander and the lava had shared. Only shades of black and iron and white now met her gaze. No boats, bridges or islands presented themselves; just a swath of storm-savaged shoreline whipped by wicked waves beneath their feet.

"Where in this horrifying expanse do we find the watery grave?" she asked. She heard the quaver in her voice and did not care that it betrayed her trepidation. Eamon and Phatomar well knew how she felt about the sea.

Eamon glanced at the black staff in his hand, the knob at its tip pulsing a deep red.

"Limb and Stone will point to the watery grave," he said, holding the rod out vertically before him. Nothing happened, and he turned it horizontal so that the encased Faqadat Alqalb pointed across the water, sweeping it slowly from right to left. It gave a bright flash, and Jal blinked to wash the after-image from her sight.

"There." Phatomar peered over the waves, hands held above his brow to shield his eyes from the rain. "Where the water circles. Do you see it?"

Jal leaned forward as she tried to spot what Phatomar's sharp eyes had seen. She shuddered when she saw it; an eddy in the water, swirling much like the portal had. A whirlpool, sucking at the waves and spitting them out again. It lay at least a furlong from the shore. She felt her upper lip lift in a quick snarl. Under other circumstances, she might wonder why she should expect such an inhospitable location to mark their destination, yet where else did the portal point? Why not get sucked deep into the ocean to find a watery grave?

"How do we reach that?" she demanded. "We certainly can't swim to it, and I see no craft to take us there, even if we could push through this maelstrom."

"It does appear out of reach," Eamon noted, brows pulled low as he frowned out over the waters. Jal recognised the note of consideration in his voice.

"I hear a qualifier in that sentence," she said. "What have

252

you thought of?"

"I agree with Phatomar's assessment of the Oracle's words.   One task for each of us, though we must work together to reach the final goal.   This watery grave falls as your task, Jal.   Maybe the way in will only show itself to you."

He held the staff between them, not so much offering it to her as offering to share its burden.   Jal stared at the inky length of branch with its maroon-encased tip winking through the bark.   For a moment, she stood frozen.   Yet Eamon's words, echoing Phatomar's, rang true.   This third task had to fall to Jal to complete.   She had already risked much coming this far.   Everything led to this moment, this test of Jal's mettle.   To falter now would negate everything they had accomplished.

Jal firmed her resolve. *This will work.*   She stretched out her hand, wrapping cold fingers just below Eamon's upon the talisman.   At first nothing happened, then the staff throbbed beneath her hand, and an iridescent wave of light swept over the tumultuous waters.   She forced herself not to release her hold even as panic squeezed her chest.

Mist rose from the agitated sea, forming an odd path to the distant whirlpool.   It solidified while remaining transparent, distorting the air as it flattened the waves, carving a roadway for the trio.

"And there's our path," Phatomar whispered with terror and awe tinging his breath.

Jal slowly released the staff, rubbing her hand on her tunic to remove the memory of the bark pressing against her palm. The shimmering path remained and she breathed a sigh of relief.   At least she wouldn't need to keep hold of the staff while trying to maintain her balance.

The horses neighed behind them, dancing nervously, eyes wide enough to show white at the edges as they backed away.   She frowned.

"I don't think the horses will follow us onto the platform, let alone into the waters beyond," she said.

Eamon turned his head to study the beach, much as Jal had before.

"Perhaps best if we left them here," he answered, equally troubled.   "I see grass they might eat, and the rain will provide fresh water.   They might even find some shelter

253

nearby." He glanced back out toward the eddy. "Besides, I fear them becoming trapped beneath the waves if—" He bit off the rest of his words, but Jal knew their substance. *If we don't come back.*

Salamander told them that none of Order's champions had ever succeeded. Jal wondered whether they had all faced the same tasks, and in the same order, or if others had encountered different challenges. If every champion must hold the Faqadat Alqalb, then surely none had made it past Kahf Alramal, yet Salamander had recognised the portal. Did that mean other champions had found a different route, a different quest, all of which led to death anyway? How many of their predecessors knew the likely outcome of their journey and continued anyway? *How many like us?*

Eamon didn't voice any of that. Instead, he chose optimism.

"When we come back," he said, "we'll find the horses rested and fed, ready for a curry brush over their flanks."

"With Onoir in firm control of Croga and Cosantoir," Phatomar added, a grim smile on his face. Jal looked at him in surprise, proud of his attempt to mask fear with humour. If a man who had his courage stolen could put on a brave face, so could she.

They loosened the saddles and let the horses roam free, then turned back to the misty path. One by one, they tested their weight on what looked substanceless. Pressing against the battering wind, they made their way cautiously over the storm-swept sea. Although the waves splattered each step with salty droplets, the path remained firm, and they soon found themselves staring into the dark vortex of spinning ocean. Sea and sky met with charcoal menace barely delineated by a horizon, and the whirlpool that yawned before them surged with white capped blackness.

Jal's heart pounded a staccato beat behind her ribs as she witnessed the fury of nature staring back at them. She trembled, knowing her companions shared in her anxiety.

So when Phatomar suddenly leapt into the abyss, she could only gape in shock as his fair head disappeared into the depths. *Had he slipped? Lost his balance? Had the wind blown him over?* But no. He had taken a deliberate step.

She and Eamon stared at one another, equal parts dread and surprise. She saw terror in Eamon's eyes, though she couldn't know the full extent of his new-found fear of storm ravaged waters.

Do not shy from its liquid embrace, the Oracle had instructed of the watery grave. If Phatomar could so cavalierly throw off caution, so must she.

"Together," she whispered, reaching out a shaking hand. Eamon wrapped chilled and trembling fingers around hers, clasped them tight, and together, they followed Phatomar into the depths of the watery grave.

***

Smooth rock pressed into Jal's cheek, rested beneath her hands. She opened her eyes, and saw that she lay prone on a stone floor. Disoriented, she pushed herself to a kneeling position and looked around, trying to get her bearings. The walls of a cavern surrounded her, stretching overhead into a dome; some kind of grotto made up of brown-grey stone dotted with strange prisms of light which glittered as she turned her head. Eamon lay motionless beside her, Phatomar not far away. Although they also lay face down as she had, their chests moved rhythmically as they drew breath. Even now, Phatomar began to stir, and Eamon's hand twitched as his consciousness returned.

Jal climbed to her feet, looking in vain for some indication of where she stood. She remembered taking that step forward into the whirlpool, the terror that infused her, shared in the vice-like grip of Eamon's hand. She remembered the swirl of water grabbing her, spinning them in its mighty grasp, her desperate attempts to find enough air to fill her lungs.

And then, nothing, until she opened her eyes, finding herself here, whatever here meant.

A pool of crystal clear water gathered in a depression in the centre of the grotto. Four flames (perhaps to denote the cardinal directions) burned with no visible source, hovering at head height near the walls, though not attached in any way Jal could determine. Nervously, she backed away from one, not wanting to get caught in whatever magic maintained their eerie light.

A raised garden shaped into a semi-circle edged the left side of the pool, but nothing grew there, not even moss or lichen; only loamy soil bereft of life. On the right, a shaft of light distorted the air, motes of what she could only describe as energy dancing in its glow. Like the flames, she found no discernible origin for this light; no opening in the ceiling to allow light to filter in, no crevasse in the walls to suggest another room beyond this one. It lacked the warmth of fire or sun, yet Jal wouldn't call the light cold. Rather, it highlighted the presence of the shimmering motes swimming within it.

"It's almost as if the light points out the existence of air rather than providing illumination for the cavern," Eamon said quietly at her side, startling her. Only now did she notice how heavily silence hung in the grotto, the smooth stone having muffled Eamon's footsteps. He nodded at the features around them. "Water, fire, earth—" he gestured at the light, "—and air. The four elements of life."

Phatomar called to them, drawing Jal and Eamon back toward the pool. "What do you make of this?" On the far side from where they had awoken rose a slab of pale grey stone, an altar where a body might once have rested, though none lay there now. Instead, something else decorated the surface.

A stone-tipped arrow, a bronze helmet, an iron sword, all arranged precisely upon the slab. Leaning against the altar, they saw also an unstrung longbow, a damaged mace, a shield with its crest so marred none could identify its origin. Phatomar pointed silently to the side, where weapons and armour and clothing from many ages and lands lay in neat piles, somehow preserved as though time refused to touch these mementos of the past.

Then he indicated an area behind the altar. Jal saw the pyramid of human skulls encircled by tidy stacks of arm and leg bones. She wondered who, or what, had set out these artifacts—clearly gathered over many generations—with such care and attention to detail, and when they had last set foot in this sealed cavern. No dust or grime marred any surface, suggesting continuing care. Or perhaps some mystical form of preservation beyond her comprehension. They did, after all, deal with devotion to a deity.

"The watery grave doesn't just belong to a goddess," she

muttered.

"Looks like it belongs to her champions too," Eamon agreed. "Those who didn't restore Order."

"I wonder whether any actually made it this far," Jal said. "Or if something instead gathered them up from wherever they fell and brought them here to this shrine?"

"Whatever the case, I certainly don't wish to remain to contribute our own bones and weapons."

"I wholeheartedly agree." Jal shivered. "So how do we avoid that fate? What task do they expect us to accomplish here?"

"We have the Heart of Order," Phatomar said, his gaze going to the staff Eamon had brought through the vortex of water. "And a limb, which must symbolize the body of the goddess. What remains after heart and body?"

"Mind?" Eamon suggested. "Spirit? Soul?"

"Breath," Jal whispered so quietly that neither man heard.

Jal only vaguely recalled otherworldly voices during her ordeal at sea, but she remembered Eamon's awe-filled description of a goddess on the beach instructing him on how to breathe life back into Jal.

"The breath of life," she said now, drawing the curious stares of her friends. "Heart, body, and breath, united together to give life," she said. Their perplexed looks suggested they hadn't followed her thinking. But then Phatomar's frown told her they didn't question her conclusions; merely what to do with the information.

"How do you give breath to a stick and a gem?" the large man asked. Jal laughed as her imagination tried, and failed, to envision breathing life into the talisman that Natt Tre had created for them. Maybe it had a hole in the bottom?

"It's like a symbol," Eamon blurted, his hazel eyes widening as he raised the staff to shoulder height. "Like the elements of nature in this cave, here we have the elements of life." His enthusiasm dimmed as he stared at the branch in his hand. "But how does that help? As Phatomar said, how do we incorporate the element of breath when we have no true body to capture it?"

"Perhaps we need the elements of nature *and* of life," Phatomar suggested, though with little conviction. "A segment of the natural forces here—earth, air, fire, water—

woven together with heart, body, and breath?"

Jal shook her head even as she studied the elements anew.

"I think they're a distraction, aimed to misguide us. We don't wish to birth an elemental, but a goddess," she reasoned.

An idea formed of how to give birth through breath. As though in response to that idea, Jal heard a soft voice, resonant with unfathomable power.

Oh, well done, Daughter.

She shuddered and threw her arms around herself as goose flesh prickled her skin.

"What's wrong?" Eamon's gaze became alert and his fingers brushed against the hilt of his sword as he searched for the source of Jal's distress.

She shook her head, forcing her arms back to her sides. "Voices," she said with a small and rueful smile. Eamon nodded his understanding, though his stance didn't relax.

"What did they say?" Phatomar asked, his nervous gaze darting around the grotto.

"I think it applauds my thoughts," Jal temporized, uncertain whether she liked the implications of such approval, of giving her breath up to another. She blew out a heavy sigh.

"How did we come to this point?" she wondered, trying to steer her mind along less dangerous roads. "We set out to help Phatomar, to restore his courage and memory. Then we followed the guidance of other gods and oracles, servants to an Order we didn't even know had vanished, and now we stand trapped here, hoping to rebirth a goddess instead of healing our friend. How did our goals shift so much?"

Phatomar surprised her by answering. "I'm not sure they shifted so much as aligned. Had the gods not stolen those gifts from me, we would never have found ourselves here, with this opportunity to right an ancient wrong. Perhaps that theft made us the champions of Order, or perhaps we had always stood as champions, and Kistawna and Dolanis robbed me of these things to thwart Order's plans."

"Imagine their horror when it triggered those plans instead," Eamon snarled, clearly displeased at being a pawn in the gambits of the gods.

"Then you believe we might still succeed at our original

goal should we fulfill the will of the gods?" Jal stared hard into Phatomar's pale eyes, willing him to tell her the truth as he saw it. "If we rebirth the goddess of Order, restore the balance that Chaos shifted, do you think the gods will make you whole again?"

"I think if we don't act, we die anyway," Phatomar stated, his tone startlingly calm. "Order chose us and if we fail, we join those who went before." He didn't need to point out the bits of skeleton displayed behind the altar, yet Jal glanced at them nonetheless. "But regardless of that striking incentive, I say to you, yes. I do believe that if we succeed, I will regain what they stole. I just pray that I don't lose what I've learned since.

"But far more than that, I believe we have a duty to the world, not just to ourselves. How many innocents have suffered because of this imbalance between Order and Chaos? How much darkness has ruled in unlawful places because the light hid? How much illness has gone unchecked because no one offered aid? How many have fallen victim to the tyranny of Chaos because Order didn't have enough strength to fight back? Whether the gods restore me to my former self or not, we cannot let the opportunity to right a much greater wrong go unchallenged."

Jal's gaze fell to the altar again, her heart heavy. "Then I need to find a way to birth a goddess." Her fingers brushed against the stone slab. "I'm told that giving birth involves opening yourself to a whole new experience, surrendering a portion of your essence so that the new life you bring into the world might survive. I suppose breathing life into a goddess requires a similar surrender." She laid her palm flat on the altar. "A part of my life sacrificed on Order's altar."

"No," Phatomar said. The large man stared across the cavern to the empty space where they had first arrived. She had expected an objection or a counter to her conclusion, but he offered none. Instead, he expanded upon her hypothesis. "The altar signifies an offering, yes, but also hints more at death than life. Chaos has already brought death. We need life, and only life. No misinterpretations; no ambiguity."

"What do you suggest?" Eamon asked.

"A balance to counter Chaos. Like everything here already exists with its own counterbalance." He pointed to the water at the centre of the grotto. "Water as the focus bracketed by fire. Earth and air on either side. Here, the altar which hosts the shards of death. And across the water, opposite the altar with its skeletons and memories"—he extended his arm to indicate the vacant area—"an empty place, lit only by the fourth and final flame. If we study the cavern as a whole, that area feels incomplete, lacking some feature to balance with the rest."

"Lacking life to balance death," Eamon said with a nod, moving around the water to the empty space. Jal followed in his wake, though her legs felt leaden, her chest hollow with impending dread. While the men could speculate on their next action, neither Eamon nor Phatomar would pay the price for whatever sacrifice she would make. She hoped that somehow breathing life into the goddess would only involve a sharing of her essence, yet she feared it would cost so much more.

"I'm scared," she confessed in a small, lost voice.

A warm hand clasped her shoulder, and she looked at Phatomar's soothing gaze.

"I know. I understand such fear in ways I never could before." His voice offered comfort like a warm blanket. "A very good friend of mine taught me to hold to the light and wondrous in the world, not on what might go wrong. She also promised me that, no matter what else might happen, I wouldn't stand alone." He clasped her fingers in his.

Eamon took her other hand with a gentle tug. "You'll not stand alone here, Jal. Whatever happens, we're here with you; here for you."

"Together or not at all," she said, eliciting a grin from Eamon.

Phatomar nodded. "Exactly. Together or not at all."

Jal drew in a steadying breath, and gave a firm nod. She squeezed each hand in thanks before pulling away to stand on her own. *On my own, but not alone.*

"Okay, so what now?" she asked.

"Now you breathe life into the body and soul of a dead goddess, represented by a stick with a rock in it. What could be easier?" Phatomar drawled, and Jal found a laugh of her own. Some of her tension bled away, taking a portion of her fear with it.

She reached out her hand, and Eamon placed the black staff holding the Faqadat Alqalb into her palm.

"Heart, limb, and life," she said, her hands slowly rubbing up and down the talisman, wondering just how to accomplish this strange rebirth.

Going with her instincts, Jal flung her arms wide, staff in her right hand, left palm open to the air. She threw back her head, eyes closed, and offered her heart, her mind, her *self*, for lack of a better term. Jal opened herself to the universe and invited a goddess to find rebirth through her.

A goddess answered.

She didn't come alone, but Jal's awareness had already gone elsewhere.

Chapter 24

Eamon blinked to clear his vision, but the strange scene which had materialised before him didn't change. He stood with Phatomar, the pond at their backs, Jal in front of them with her arms outstretched, head thrown back, the staff grasped in her hand. A warm glow suffused her in an expanding halo, glitters of gold further highlighting her skin, her clothes, the rust of her hair. Yet this intense display of power paled compared to the seven incredible forms that had appeared to tower over the trio, forming a loose semi-circle.

They stood in four separate groups, each displaying varying degrees of interest in the proceedings. On one side stood a man and woman; she with long raven tresses framing cold emerald-rimmed violet eyes, and boasting a statuesque physique; he bearing the countenance of a desert man with sable hair and an umber gaze that shone with cunning. Both radiated strength and arrogance, their unearthly faces betraying contempt and a hint of hungry anticipation. Eamon suspected he looked at Kistawna and Dolanis, who had inadvertently started them on this journey those many months ago, and who now awaited the conclusion of their gambit.

Opposite these waited a warrior, a scar puckering the left cheek of his otherwise smooth face. His muscle-bound body overshadowed even Phatomar. He wore practical armour of burgundy and black fashioned of the finest materials; his sword and spear, secured to his broad back, appeared of superior quality. The woman at his side looked small, but only in comparison to the warrior. She wore a chestnut tunic the hue of Croga's coat which fell to mid-thigh, leaving a hunter's physique visible. A silver-tooled quiver hung at her hip, and an intricate horn bow hooked to its side. Yet her dark and soulful eyes caught Eamon's attention. He had seen them before, staring at him from Cosantoir's equine face. The goddess Cetain, surely, matched by the warrior who had championed them since Grandon.

Eamon felt the blood drain from his face as he glanced again at the flint-eyed warrior, knowing he stood in the presence of the god to whom he had served most of his life. He bit his tongue before Dearn's name fell from his lips in a reverent oath. This was not the time. The warrior god offered him a curt nod, as though he had heard Eamon's thoughts despite his silence.

Eamon next looked at the solitary figure standing deeper in the shadows, its features made opaque by the floating torch at its back. Chill fingers of dread plucking discordant notes against his soul. A dark and disturbing power vibrated around this being, the essence of chaos bound. Fury edged with...guilt? remorse? pain?...flowed from this creature, evidence of a reluctant participant in these proceedings.

The god Chaos himself? If so, no wonder his ire and torment, forced to relive his darkest deed as Jal tried to bring his sister back into being.

And finally, two indistinct shapes hovered furthest away, a magnitude of light that hinted at human form rather than revealing any defining features. Yet these, Eamon sensed, held the keenest avidity for the unfolding drama. Their identity he couldn't begin to guess, although something made him think of overly proud artists, waiting to unveil their latest masterpiece. What that boded, Eamon didn't understand.

He did, however, understand the malevolence he felt from several of the gods around them. He moved to put himself between Jal and the deities. He didn't fool himself into thinking he had any power to stop them, but he refused to stand aside and leave his sister-of-the-soul open to attack.

Though pale as death, eyes pinched tight in terror and a light sweat dewing his upper lip, Phatomar had mirrored Eamon's action, the two of them moving as one to shield Jal.

Dolanis snorted to his companion.

"Order's little toys think mere mortals might stand in the way of gods."

"Silence," a voice laced with daggers spat, though the word hadn't risen above a whisper. Dolanis quavered, mirth replaced by a scowl trying to mask the pain unleashed by Chaos' command.

Eamon heard a whimper escape Jal. He reached back, laying a hand on Jal's shoulder to let her know they hadn't left her. She didn't stand alone. Jal didn't open her eyes, but he *felt* that she appreciated his support.

And then, he sensed an urgent plea tug at his soul, imminent danger swirling from Jal through his connection. She needed help, and she needed it now. Without hesitation, he opened his mind and offered every scrap of strength he had to that need, even if he didn't know how to share that strength.

The grotto fell from his perception, and Eamon found himself floating in a deep void. An all-encompassing darkness surrounded him, his consciousness torn from his body, leaving his mind free to roam. The suffocating abyss stabbed at his awareness, and although he didn't have eyes to *see* it, he felt the lack of anything resembling light and hope like a physical weight trying to drown him.

Facets of brilliant sapphire suddenly shattered the blackness, surrounded by a swath of golden sparks. The blue cut through the whirling gold, tumbling the sparks askew even as they tried to corral the facets into a semblance of order. The gold began to diffuse in a wide sweep across the vast nothingness, overwhelmed and scattered by the uncaring strength of blue. Still struggling to hold its charge, the gold emitted a distress which drew the essence of Eamon close.

Sensing the gold somehow belonged to Jal, Eamon wrapped his splintered being around the scattered specks of light. Acting on instinct, he tried to hold her together. The gold strengthened, flared brighter, and deepened in places with hints of a greenish-brown flame. The champions Order had chosen tried to gather the blue into a being of ancient and unknowable power, attempting to draw a fundamental concept of the universe together and restore it to life.

But their efforts fell short, the task left incomplete. They

264

floated there, stranded, unable to find an anchor to the world they had left behind, corporeal bodies lost behind the veil of death.

Then a beacon of crimson flared in the distance, beckoning to them like a signal fire. Eamon stretched forth, and found the heart that would unite them and lead them home.

***

Jal came apart, every particle of her being splintered into innumerable shards and scattered across the ethos. Yet at the same time, her core shrank into a dense ball no larger than a single thought. Every substance in the universe suffused her, and the emptiness of oblivion crushed her. Life exploded all around her while death pressed in from all sides. None of these sensations made sense, yet Jal understood the dichotomy of this reality with a terrible clarity.

She stood on the cusp between two worlds. Both life and death existed simultaneously in this sliver of time, existence and extinction married in one impossible breath. Chaos had unwittingly trapped the soul of Order into this void of life with its absence of death. In this timeless moment dwelt the memory of a goddess, severed from heart and limb yet still connected to them by the thinnest thread. Here Order had waited in her confused state; conscious of the passage of ages, yet oblivious to aeons past.

And here, she confronted Jal.

"You do not belong here, child." Order's words rang with the crash of cymbals in Jal's head, although no voice reached her ears, for she had no ears to hear.

"Nor do you," Jal countered, somehow able to speak though lacking a mouth.

Thoughts span the distance, even when bodies do not. The concept did not come from Jal's mind, nor from the goddess floating with her. Jal had no doubt a deity had imparted the notion, though. She had no idea which, nor why they would offer even that sparse comfort. She didn't even know whether the deity had meant the message for her or for Order.

"Why have you come?" Order demanded.

Jal hesitated. Though true, *'I've come to help my friend'*

265

didn't comprise the whole reason of her sacrifice. Nor did *'some of the gods have bid us set you free'*. What could she say to honestly explain her presence in such a concrete and nebulous region? *'I hope to accomplish what no one else has'*? In a way true, and yet so far from her intention, and far too arrogant to voice.

"I've come to try to right a wrong," she finally replied. "More than one. I've come to challenge a theft; to answer for a life taken in rage; to understand what makes me different from others—why I should hear what others do not, remember that which only one other remembers. I have accepted the terrifying possibility that I might help champion Order's resurrection, and restore a balance to the world. I do this even though I barely comprehend these powers, of which I have stood in ignorance most of my life.

"Here I stand, offering to become the vessel that might birth you back to life, for the world needs your balance against the increasingly suffocating forces of Chaos. I offer this because I believe it the right thing to do."

For an eternity that lasted mere seconds, thundering silence roared in Jal's mind. The goddess spoke again, a subdued excitement burring with resonance.

"You offer to become a conduit? You offer this of your own free will?"

Jal forced her scattered thoughts to hold firm. *For Phatomar. For Eamon and for the future. For myself, that I might leave something worthwhile behind.*

"I do," she affirmed.

She felt a surge of triumph not her own, and then searing agony as the essence of the goddess flowed into her, tearing apart that which made up Ajala of the Gobani desert, Jal the warrior remade, and a frightened young woman bravely— perhaps foolishly—offering to suffer what no mortal should have to endure.

Jal felt her life slip away. Order subsuming rather than borrowing, claiming Jal's essence instead of sliding through her to reform what had once existed. No rebirth this, but a possession. With every scrap of will she could muster, Jal fought back, struggled to retain some small portion of herself. She had nothing but her mind, her will, her thoughts to fight with. *Thoughts which span the distance that bodies do not.*

As the last of Jal's fortitude battled the insurmountable strength of an ancient goddess determined to take by force a gift freely offered, Jal reached across the vastness of space, searching for strength. Another's will flowed into her instead, helping to hold her together.

'We're here with you; here for you.' She felt Eamon now as a source of power. Yet even together, they stretched thin around the torrent of Order. Too thin to hold to life while they struggled with the frantic efforts of a goddess to take form.

Tears would have marred Jal's cheeks had she the ability to weep, a body to reflect her pain. She had feared losing her life to this task, but the thought of taking Eamon with her wrenched at her soul. She tried to pull away, to spare him this end, but he held tight, stretching himself to the breaking point.

Then a third force joined them, mingled with them; a force that somehow held firm. Phatomar, stripped of everything physical, his essence free from fear, as strong now as he had once stood in Merveah. He unified them in strength and purpose, solidifying the three into one being. Jal remembered the Oracle—Aura, Rachel, and Cleo—merging into one body to deliver their riddle. *Is this how something like the Oracle came into existence?*

Phatomar provided an anchor back to the world, and Eamon the bridge that spanned the distance. Jal had but to cross that distance, bring the essence of the goddess with her. But if she faltered, Order would destroy them. So how did she follow the ephemeral trail of a human back to the world carrying a goddess, while losing neither?

The memory of Phatomar's words came to her. *'Breathe life into a stick.'* Faintly, as though held in phantom fingers, Jal remembered the sensation of the black bark of Natt Tre, the smooth texture of wood fashioned into a staff that could hold a Heart. She slid insubstantial hands up to caress the protrusion of the gem.

While her essence twirled in a vortex around Order, holding the goddess together while fending off her usurping clutches, her physical arms slowly brought the staff of Heart and limb to her lips in the grotto. She opened her mouth and warmed the staff with her breath.

Jal's eyes flashed open. Awareness slammed back into

her body as Order erupted like a geyser from her convulsing form. The goddess fled Jal's body with titanic force, throwing the girl to the ground as Order grasped Heart and limb unto herself. Jal crumpled, the weight of Eamon and Phatomar tossed with her, united here as on that alternate plane.

Jal slowly rolled to her side, pushed up to sit on the hard stone floor and stared at the reformed body of Order. Only now did she have the first glimmers of the ramifications of her merging with Eamon and Phatomar in a realm that spanned life and death. Of the consequences of succeeding as the champions of Order.

Numb from the ordeal of housing a goddess within her, even for so short a time, Jal had little surprise left to spare. Still, she did find it exceedingly strange to see so many gods for the first time, not with her own eyes, but through the thoughts of someone else.

Chapter 25

From the moment he'd had his memory and courage ripped from him, when every new and unfamiliar sound would petrify him, Phatomar had lived in constant turmoil. The frigid climb to snow-capped mountains, the sweat-inducing journey into the deep desert, the hair-raising travel through stormy waters and the lifeless wastes of the Blackened Fields—all of it paled against the immobilising fear inspired by the presence of these gods.

Phatomar had served gods, worshipped them, tried to adhere to their strictures, yet he had never expected to stand amongst so many. And now, trapped in this underwater grotto, mere strides separating mortal from immortal, Phatomar felt he couldn't escape, even if his muscles unlocked from their paralysis. Turning away from such implacable countenances, putting his mind to a different problem, made him feel less the coward, though he couldn't remember feeling any other way.

He could, however, brace Jal and Eamon in whatever struggle they now faced. He cupped Jal's arm in his right hand, Eamon's in his left, and an incredible force slammed through him. He felt Jal's fingers tighten around the staff as she breathed life into Heart and limb.

Suddenly, something tossed them aside like chaff in the wind, and they collapsed in a heap on the far side of the grotto. Phatomar felt the impact on Jal's back, Eamon's side, his own knees.

He tried to clear his vision, separate himself from this

strange power which had fused a part of his mind with that of his chosen family. He stared up into the triumphant smile of the Warrior, the relieved nod of the Huntress, the inflamed glare of Chaos, and the incomprehension of the Trickster and his Chaos-born Mistress of Shadows. Of the two indefinable beings haloed by power and holding themselves apart, Phatomar understood nothing, though he suspected they rejoiced more in creation than destruction, their glow having gained a measure of radiance at the arrival of Order reborn.

Phatomar's skin itched as though dozens of hidden eyes also bore witness to this event. Seven gods had chosen to manifest among mortals; that didn't mean other deities hadn't observed from the shadows.

Phatomar tore his attention from the torrent of emotions to see the newly formed body curled between gods and mortals. He felt Jal's attention turn with him, the sensation of two—nay, three—minds sharing one sight stomach churning. Eamon crawled to his side and Phatomar felt the stone floor beneath the smaller man's knees. He gulped hard, uncertain whether the bile burning at the back of his throat came from him or someone else. Eamon swallowed convulsively with him.

"I think that's me," Eamon said in a hoarse whisper, a hand pressed against his belly.

"What's going on?" Phatomar asked.

"Not what I expected," Jal admitted. He heard both her words and her thoughts. *How long will this last?* she wondered. Phatomar shrugged, and knew his companions felt the motion.

Do they know what's happened to us? Eamon wanted to know. Phatomar studied the gods through Eamon's perception. *Can we use this to our advantage?*

I wish we could control it better, Jal said/thought. *Trying to comprehend all of this in my own head and using my own eyes makes me nauseous enough. Trying to filter everything through two other minds at the same time just makes it worse.* She thought for a moment, Phatomar following the process. *Though interesting.*

Phatomar blinked again, felt two other pairs of eyes blink alongside his own. He directed his own eyes to see what *he* wanted, willing himself separate from the others. Shunting

270

their thoughts and sight to the back of his mind left him better able to reclaim mastery over his own body as he threw up a mental barrier.

Oh, that's better, he distantly heard from Jal as she mimicked what he had done, as did Eamon with a sigh of relief. Still together as one, yet more able to self-identify.

In the grotto, Order now stirred, shifted, sat up. Not a stitch of fabric concealed her perfect body, making Phatomar's cheeks warm as he averted his gaze. Yet she wore her nakedness with such unconcerned grace that he soon looked beyond to what made her even more astounding.

Phatomar had no idea what she might have looked like in her previous incarnation, but now, the goddess bore a striking resemblance to those who had returned her to the world. Eamon's hazel eyes peered out from a golden face framed by the same russet locks as Jal, although Order's skin had a slight pattern to it, as though the limb from Natt Tre had left its mark. As Order slowly gained her feet, Phatomar recognised his own height and breadth of shoulder in her build. He prayed she didn't also share their minds. Strange enough knowing his friends could sense his fears; the thought of a goddess so intimately conversant with his soul as well left him trembling.

Thankfully, when she spoke, he heard only her words, her emotions locked away from the trio.

"Well Brother, I seem to recall we had a small disagreement about the town of Atrus when last we spoke." Her voice held an eerie resonance that shivered through Phatomar, and he knew Jal had felt this every time a god had spoken near her. "Time passes strangely in the places between life and death, but I trust we can put that issue to rest."

Venom laced her sardonic comment, and given the sharp hiss of breathe from Chaos, it seemed Order had scored a point. *Yet what game does she play?* Phatomar wondered, completely ignorant of the town she had named.

"You had no right to transplant the entire population to the mountains," Chaos snarled, black eyes flashing with ire.

"I didn't; just those who listened to my suggestion that the hills provided better air that season. You can hardly blame me that Pestilence could only manage to infect those who

271

remained behind."

"Your accuracy in recalling the details shows an astounding gap in our agreement," Chaos charged. "As always, your adherence to your precious plans and strategies only lasted long enough to change your mind."

"And your frivolous disregard for structure, *as always,* sent you into your usual rage, only this time, you went too far."

Slack-jawed by the petty insults they continued to fling at each other, Phatomar began to doubt the wisdom of having returned this goddess to the world. They may have balanced some sort of cosmic scales, yet he couldn't help but think they might have become the unwitting accomplices of a kind of injustice.

By all the gods, it's like listening to two children bickering, Jal marvelled. He nodded in agreement.

With a sigh that shook the cavern and rattled Phatomar's bones, one of the nebulous beings hovering behind the other gods flowed forward, clearly sharing Jal's assessment. Order and Chaos fell silent, their heated gazes looking anywhere but upon this mysterious creature. By the shocked reactions of the other gods, Phatomar realised none but the humans had seen them here before this moment.

Who are they? Jal wanted to know. Phatomar shook his head, as did Eamon. Neither knew the identity of these beings, though clearly the gods recognised them. The reverent yet fearful air of obsequiousness told him that they stood in the presence of beings even greater than these gods.

When gods make a mark, mortals tend to suffer, Eamon mused, his thought a cross between bitter observation and simple resignation. Phatomar agreed with a sinking heart, anticipating some imminent peril. Panic locked his limbs, and a cascading quaver trembled through his body. He tried to push it aside as Jal had taught him, concentrating instead on the unfolding drama.

"Even after your time apart, you do naught but argue," the being commented, its voice the molten heat of liquid earth, evoking the greens and reds and yellows of a forest through the seasons, the unyielding solidity of mountains combined with the soft contours of desert sands and water-lapped shores. It had a feminine quality, but the vastness of ages

overrode any gentling notes. *"With your moment of redemption at hand, Chaos, can you truly only revisit old grievances, cling to a hope that your sister's act of will might overshadow your heinous sin?"*

Chaos cringed, a miasma of darkness swirling around him.

"Goading him to pique his temper doesn't relieve you of blame either, Order," the other nameless deity chided as it moved to join its partner, its voice deeper and more masculine. Vast stretches of space, the blues and greys and pink-tinged clouds of the sky blew through its words with the dampness of rain, the chill of a winter storm, the warmth of a brilliant sun.

Order now flinched, eyes downcast, accepting the admonishment with ill-grace.

"You'll forgive me, mother Earth and father Sky," Order murmured.

Phatomar felt a jolt of shock. He had never imagined any Elder god would inhabit the same space as a mortal. The Elder gods had long left this world alone. Now, two of the greatest stood before them, their disappointment in their children's quarrels an oppressive weight pressing down on Phatomar's senses.

Oblivious to the discomfort of her champions, Order continued.

"I had not intended to dwell upon what we cannot change. Yet seeing him here now in all his scowling majesty reminded me rather forcefully of our last encounter. I will not let myself succumb to diversion again. Let us instead move toward the future, and find strategies to rectify the balance skewed by my absence."

"If you seek to counter an imbalance, you need look no further than the disparity created by your champions," Kistawna suggested, her honeyed tone laced with malice. Fire flashed in her jewel-like gaze as she swept it disdainfully over Phatomar and his companions, though she concealed her displeasure when she turned to regard Order, her body poised into a conciliatory posture.

Order stared down at the daughter of her brother with narrowed eyes. "Speak plainly, child," she commanded, ice in her voice.

"Every generation, those who followed your mandates

273

spawned a potential hero to bring you home, and every generation, that champion failed. Your minions sought to circumvent the rules by bringing together *three* to champion your cause, not one. It seems to me that only by bending their own rules did your disciples manage to succeed."

"You see such adaptation as an imbalance?" Dearn demanded, the immense warrior god taking a threatening step forward.

"If you can only win by breaking the rules," Dolanis interjected, his arms crossed over his chest in derision, "then you've failed in your objective. Does it seem fair that the goddess who adheres so fiercely to rules and plans should benefit from the improvising tactics more akin to Chaos without consequence?"

"Consequence," Dearn chewed on the word as though tasting stale travel rations. Order nodded for him to continue. "What does an upstart little god who delights in flaunting the rules know of consequence?"

Phatomar wondered how much Order knew of what had occurred over the last several centuries. Did she know of this once-mortal Trickster god? Had she realised the efforts taken on her behalf through the years? The lives lost, as evidenced by the orderly stacks of bones and weapons of previous champions? Did she even understand how she had returned to this world?

Do we understand that? Jal asked in his mind, and Phatomar conceded her point.

"I know that Chaos can demand a price to allow Order to regain full strength," Dolanis said.

"And yet, you don't serve Chaos," Cetain said, her voice husky. "One might even say that you actively oppose both Order and Chaos, delighting in turning compatriots against one another."

"I'd rather say I delight in challenging others to use their minds," Dolanis countered. "To doubt their senses if the need arises. Perhaps even to learn to enjoy a certain discomfort if it helps them to grow."

"*Perhaps,* you say," Dearn spat. "Though you don't mean it. The Trickster god only works to benefit himself, to entertain himself, no matter the cost to others."

Dolanis shrugged. "None of that changes the fact that

Chaos can demand a stipulation for Order's return."

"And what stipulation would Chaos demand in light of the sin he caused?" the Elder god Sky thundered.

Chaos drew himself up, eyes flashing, but he didn't speak. Phatomar recalled the startling history he had read in the caverns of the Thueban Alnaas, the admonishment that Chaos must stand aside when Order sought rebirth or forfeit his own life. Chaos could request no stipulation to his sister's return without incurring dire consequences.

Kistawna, however, had no such inhibitions on her ambition. She smiled, and sprung her trap.

"Simply that Order hold but one champion, not three. That these mortals do battle until only one remains, in the true spirit and honour of the original intention of those who have purported to follow Order these many long generations. *Order's champion may free her from death,*" Kistawna said, as though quoting an old adage. "So let Order find her *one* champion."

***

Order studied Kistawna's jubilant expression with an air of indifference. Then the goddess turned to regard the trio of humans for the first time. She stared down as though from a great height, yet physically she didn't stand much taller than Phatomar, making her short among her peers. However, her awesome presence and confidence more than made up for the lack of stature, giving her an aura of equality among the gods.

She'll likely grow to match the overwhelming grandeur of these other gods, Eamon mused. His gaze met that of Order even as his thoughts tumbled in the minds of his friends.

A restoration that Kistawna hopes will only occur if we slaughter each other, Jal continued, her ideas merged with those of the men.

She rightly believes we won't harm each other, Phatomar joined in. *Not for the sake of beings who have done little but manipulate us.*

Eamon continued the stream of consciousness. *We didn't set out to forward the aims of Order, yet they all act as though that remains our primary purpose.*

275

We're here for Phatomar's memories and to restore his courage, Jal added. *That we restored Order in the process, brought a little light into a dark world, I count as a boon.*

The trio felt themselves grin as one, though no expression crossed their features.

We already stand as one, Phatomar said. *Kistawna has outwitted herself in demanding what already exists.*

Together, or not at all, they thought, using the mantra which had carried them from Grandon to this point.

Order smiled, satisfied with her examination of them. She turned back to Kistawna.

"I agree to your terms," said the goddess.

She knows, Jal realised.

The others don't, Phatomar said.

Dearn stalked close, whether to stand as Order's support or shield, they couldn't tell.

"Phatomar cannot fight," he said to Order, yet his glare pierced Kistawna, whose smug expression showed that she knew full well his objection. The Chaos goddess did not deign to reply. Dolanis, however, did.

"If he won't fight, he can die on one of their blades or watch his friends deal each other a mortal blow to save him."

"A man without courage *cannot* fight," Dearn said through gritted teeth. "The will to do so alone cannot overcome the curse that prevents his body from obeying."

"What curse does he suffer?" demanded the Elder god Sky.

Jal drew her sword and pointed it first at Kistawna, then to Dolanis.

"She stole his courage. He took his memories." The two gods stared in shock, wondering how she knew. Jal nodded to Eamon, who had also drawn his weapon. "We preserved his sanity until he learned to cope with the thefts."

"They say Order's followers broke the rules by finding three champions," Eamon said. "I say these two broke the rules by maiming one champion before he could even begin. And now they wish Phatomar to suffer more to cover up their failures."

"We won't allow that," Jal affirmed.

Dolanis merely chuckled with a scornful shake of his head, already thinking to gain the upper hand. The keen edge of a blade suddenly caressed Phatomar's neck as Kistawna emerged from a shadow at his side. He froze, briefly locking Jal and Eamon in paralysis as well. Eamon and Jal forced courage into him, unlocking his muscles.

So this is what it feels like, Phatomar marvelled, Kistawna's knife at his throat losing its full import.

The ghost of a smile brushed Order's lips.

How much does she see? they wondered. *How much does she know or guess?*

More than the Trickster, Jal reasoned, her eyes narrowing as Dolanis spoke, a certain venom in his tone.

"You have little say in the affairs of gods, mortals. I'd have thought you would have learned that by now. Your lives are our playthings. You either dance to our tune, or admit the wasted efforts of these last months; your quest doomed to failure. Either one champion of Order steps from this grotto, or Order herself falls back into oblivion."

"We will acknowledge your concern for dear Phatomar here," Kistawna purred to Dearn, her blade drawing a bead of red on Phatomar's neck. Phatomar held himself perfectly still, and she mistook his new confidence for fear. "Perhaps he cannot fight, but he can observe. Let these others fight for the right to belong to Order. If one remains standing at the end, then we can look to Phatomar's involvement."

This posturing grows tedious, Eamon thought. *Let's just get this over with.*

Should we give them a suitable demonstration of our skills? Jal asked.

Let's see what you've learned, desert warrior.

You two have fun, Phatomar thought. *I'll stand ready to shock the hell out of Kistawna when you wish to proceed.*

Sick of the gods' metaphorical sabre rattling, Jal and Eamon sprang at each other, swords singing, fingers, wrists, feet, and arms subtly moving in the dance of warriors. Already well conversant in each other's style from many long months of training, they now presented a beautiful display of prowess. Sharing their thoughts, their minds, their abilities, each knew the next move and flowed to meet it, the chosen pattern laid out clearly.

Step, lunge, parry, riposte. Jal's curved sword blocked Eamon's overhead swing near the cross guard, and the two spun in a simultaneous countermove that ended with another clash of blades. Jal's weapon flashed low, and Eamon leapt over it, his own sword a graceful arc which Jal evaded.

They flowed continuously, their dance mesmerizing, their battle breathtaking. With each fluid motion—limbs crossing in matched stride, weight held precisely on the balls of their booted feet—they circled the cavern and its occupants.

Kistawna moved with them, her dagger still at Phatomar's throat. She kept him facing the combatants, moving in her own little dance, her tension rising, as though she suspected some trick to free Phatomar.

The Chaos goddess had only half-guessed their purpose. Eamon and Jal didn't dance toward Kistawna; they aimed to reach Dolanis.

With a final wicked chime of blades that sent sparks exploding like a swarm of fireflies, the pair spun in graceful unison a pace from where the Trickster stood.

Each blade halted a hair's breath from either side of Dolanis' neck. With his courage fuelled by the others, and the synchronicity eerie in its precision, Phatomar reached up and grasped Kistawna's wrist. He wrenched the knife from her and placed it to her throat as he twisted her arm behind her back. Both Trickster and Mistress of Shadows went rigid, all movement ceasing as they stared with wide eyes and hitched breath at the audacious move.

Dearn, who had followed each action with avid intensity, let out a shout of satisfaction, punctuated by a single clap of his great hands.

"Marvellous!"

Chaos stared, his countenance dark, his manner indignant.

"You dare to threaten *gods*?" he thundered. The air in the grotto grew thick with his displeasure. "You, who stand beneath contempt, your meagre lives a blink of our existence, dare to dream of harming your betters? You think your mortal weapons can mar our flesh?"

Weapons steady, Jal and Eamon ignored the furious god, as did Phatomar. They turned their collective gaze instead to Order.

"Look closer, brother mine," Order suggested, a biting edge to her tone. "Let those who hoped to gain your favour look also. Look to my champion; see what I see."

Those gods supporting Chaos all gaped at the humans as Order revealed her vision.

I almost wish to see what has them so impressed, Jal mused. *Almost, but not quite. Bad enough to hear them when no one else can.*

Amusement threaded through their link.

"Impossible," Kistawna finally said in a strangled whisper as she tried to see all three humans at once.

"Not impossible," Cetain replied with smugness and satisfaction. "Only unlikely. A confluence that took generations to succeed."

"Explain this, Daughter," the Elder goddess of Earth challenged, but whether she spoke to Order or Cetain remained uncertain. The goddess of horses and the hunt chose to reply.

"Long ago, great Mother, you stipulated that should Order find rebirth, Chaos must stand aside and allow the transition. As you know, for Order to return, a mortal must open the door, but you did not prohibit those who sought Chaos' favour from trying to manipulate events to thwart Order's ambitions. Those champions who came before failed to achieve Order's restoration, the tasks beyond their ability. Order had to adapt.

"Those of us who would see the restoration of Order thus devised a new kind of champion. The world would still see the birth of one with great courage, steadfast loyalty, and the intuition to see the greater workings of life, but that soul would find its home in multiple hosts. Only the right set of circumstances would bring them together, and even then, they still needed to overcome every obstacle, make the choices that would lead them all to this time and place.

"Some generations failed to unite all parts of the champion; others failed to remain together, so it seemed at times that the champion of Order came less frequently into the world. Not so, though Chaos knew it not. Instead, the champion spanned age and gender, language and experience, continents and culture. Time did not bind the instrument of Order's champion. Each aspect of the soul chose when and where to find life. Circumstances then dictated how and if they would find one another."

Dearn next took up the tale. "This generation saw the

coming together of two great warriors.   A friendship cemented early in life, giving rise to legends, great achievements now masked by the trickery of Dolanis." The god of warriors scowled at the Trickster before he continued. "Phatomar's circumstances did not dissuade Eamon's loyalty, however. In fact, it made him more protective, more willing to see his brother-in-arms healed.   That, more than Order's plight, motivated him, yet that too worked in Order's favour, drawing two parts of the champion's soul even closer as they looked for answers.

"The third piece followed her own path, a set of circumstances that led her to stand in the right place at the right time. She had the greatest link to the gods, despite her ignorance of that fact. When Kistawna robbed the courage of who she thought as the sole champion of Order, loyalty and intuition remained to bolster him. When Dolanis pulled his identity and memory from the minds of the world—and even the minds of gods—his kindred in soul clung to the truth, uniting to preserve the whole, remembering what no one else could.

"From that moment, every choice they made brought them closer together, while any other choice might have driven them apart. At each juncture, they opted to remain together, to see this journey through. Together. Even when they discovered that gods both guided and barred their actions, they continued to follow the path that brought them here."

"That explains how they share a purpose," Chaos growled, both intrigued and perplexed. "But it doesn't explain what Order has shown us. How did one essence spread among three mortals, united and able to act in concert yet remain separate? For surely they did not stand thus when we arrived."

"Intuition led the girl to me, but she spread herself too thin," Order explained. "Loyalty led the other to reach across time and space to hold her together, but to do so, he lost his connection to this world. When he reached out for aid, courage, despite his supposed lack, responded without hesitation, enfolding loyalty and intuition in his embrace. At that moment, three became one, each aspect of the construct of *champion* fusing together.   Held fast by intuition, cushioned by loyalty, and led by courage, I found my way home, reborn through their efforts.

"You see before you my champion," Order concluded with a triumphant smile. "My *one* champion." She turned to Kistawna, still held at bay by Phatomar. "My champion who has fulfilled the stipulation laid out by Chaos. My champion standing here of one mind shared among three vessels. The culmination of aeons of planning. They move as one, act as one, have become one."

"Together, or not at all," they said in unison.

That took on a whole new meaning, one thought, and with a sense of disquiet, none knew which had expressed the sentiment.

Like the three aspects of the Oracle, they stood as one. That the one soul inhabited three vessels didn't lessen their strength. If anything, their combined experience made them stronger.

Still, if we can remain as separate people, I'll not complain, Jal confided. *I love you both, but I'd find* being *you forever just a little too unnerving.*

They shared a warm thought, weapons held unwavering and steady against gods who had unwittingly brought them to this juncture.

"You impugn them, brother," Order continued as she turned to stare at Chaos. "You dismiss their threat against your agents as childish outrage. Yet mere mortals do not stand before you, their knives at your cohorts' throats. You look upon the instrument of Order. And they dare as much because I allow it, their weapons those of a goddess despite their mortal origins. Weapons even gods must fear."

I thought we dared as much to prove a point, Eamon thought.

We may have proved a point, Jal considered, *but* she *gave us the opportunity to do so.*

She allowed Kistawna to set the terms of Order's return, Phatomar added, *knowing full well we had already fulfilled those terms. In that sense, she* did *allow us to hold the gods hostage.*

I grow tired of manipulation, Jal sighed.

"You cannot kill them," Order said, her voice casual yet with an undercurrent of warning. It took a moment for the humans to realise she had spoken to them, not Chaos.

281

"We did not intend to," they chimed together, voices holding a resonance.

This just gets more disturbing, they acknowledged.

Eamon pulled his voice from the others, though none dropped their guard. "We simply wish for these two to restore that which they took from Phatomar. That is why we began this quest. We may have grown into Order's champion along the way, but we didn't start out with that goal."

"Give Phatomar back his courage and his memory," Jal hissed, her lion's gaze fixed on Dolanis. "And then we *meagre mortals* will gladly withdraw, leaving you to your mighty machinations once more."

Do you want to bait them like that? Eamon asked with a thread of caution.

I want them to wonder about our resolve just enough that they leave us alone in the future.

Before they could put more thought into that, Dolanis sneered.

"Do your worst," he said. "Order has prohibited you from harming us, so your threats hold no power."

Jal quirked an eyebrow, disturbingly mirrored by both Phatomar and Eamon.

"You stand as the instrument of Order," Kistawna half-mocked, half-objected. "Let *Order* put you to rights."

A beatific smile stretched across Order's face, but a malevolence lurked behind it.

"You speak of a goddess of balance," Order said, her voice carrying the overtones of deep-throated bells. "And you have just given me permission to rectify your audacity in trying to thwart the will of the Elder gods." She looked to Chaos, ignoring the suddenly distraught countenances of both Kistawna and Dolanis. "You stand witness to their arrogance, brother. Do you oppose my right to seek balance?"

As one, three honed blades shifted just enough to trace an angry red scratch on the Trickster's desert-kissed neck and Kistawna's smooth complexion. The mortals stood immobile, uncertain whether the three had acted of their own volition, or if Order had just demonstrated her power by moving through them.

Chaos grew ashen, but he did not balk or shy away. "I so witness your right to answer their foolishness."

Order drew herself taller upon hearing those words, somehow more on par with her brother and the other gods.

Did he just shrink, or did she just grow? Eamon asked.

I think she took some of his power, Phatomar mused.

Or he restored it to her, Jal added. *Gave back what he had held while she suffered in that in-between place.*

Order offered them a brief grin, as though fully cognisant of and in accord with their thoughts. The three stifled a shiver.

"Father, no," Kistawna gasped.

"Failure carries its price, daughter." displeasure laced the words of Chaos with fire. "And I will not abide careless words."

"So be it," the two Elder gods chimed. *"Let Order recompense the offense given her champion so that this might come to an end."*

Order stepped forward, graceful and confident. She examined Dolanis first, then Kistawna. Then she turned her gaze to Phatomar.

"How long has it been since you stood whole, all your gifts your own? How long have you suffered this geas, my champion of courage?"

To hear himself so named startled Phatomar, yet he held firm under her scrutiny.

"Six months," he calculated.

"Half a year." Order's stare returned to contemplate the lesser gods in their midst. "A fair compensation for setting you on the path of fate."

Order made a casual gesture, and the companions understood her desire for them to sheath their weapons and stand aside. They did so and gathered side by side, at the edge of the pool, able to watch as Order confronted both Shadow and Trickster. Order's eyes sheened with an unnatural blend of gold and silver, like a warm star flashing on a cold night.

"Six months. You will suffer as he suffered," Order said, her hand passing over both Kistawna and Dolanis but not touching them. "You will wander, fearful of your own shadow, remembering neither yourselves nor your surroundings. I take from you your courage, and I take from you your memory. Your names and powers I shall hold against the completion of your punishment."

Kistawna and Dolanis shuddered. And then they screamed, huddling away from their fellow gods, ignorant of themselves, their plight, and lacking all courage.

Order glared at Chaos.

"Remove them from here. To where, I do not care."

Chaos nodded once and vanished, taking his daughter and her accomplice with him.

Order looked to Phatomar, her eyes still aglow. When she blinked, the eerie light faded. Phatomar gave a jolt, Jal and Eamon echoing it.

A sense of calm and well-being, confidence and surety suffused them all; the return of the warrior's courage, and with it, a flood of memories. Memories that were Phatomar's, and Phatomar's alone. He stared with wonder at the goddess who now stood before him.

"My champion, returned each to their own minds until such time as I call upon them again."

Jal heaved an immense sigh of relief; Eamon shook himself like a man awakening from a deep sleep. A smile blossomed across Phatomar's cheeks as he bowed to Order. Surely advocating for such a deity would have consequences, but at this moment, finding himself whole and yet able to retain the experiences of these past months, Phatomar mostly felt gratitude. He shared a smile with Eamon and Jal.

"We did it," marvelled Jal.

Dearn, the stern warrior god, gazed down at them with perhaps a hint of fondness. "You did." He then bowed to Order as Phatomar had done. "Welcome back, my lady," he said to the goddess, then vanished.

Cetain followed his lead with a quiet smile, leaving only the Elder gods and Order with the humans.

Still too many gods for my peace of mind, Jal considered, startled to have the thought to herself and no one else.

"We hope your exile has taught you the importance of listening to your heart, and not the malice and envy of others, daughter," Elder Sky said. *"And of the need to consider how your actions might affect the balance of this world you and your peers have fashioned."*

"Though you know it not, your brother has taken some of this message to heart," said Elder Earth. *"Help him keep the lesson in mind when his temper frays."*

"May your long thought-out strategies during your exile bear useful fruit."

Having given their parental advice and with nary a glance at the humans, the Elder gods departed the grotto.

One left, Eamon mused. Somehow, he felt more uncomfortable in the presence of just this one goddess than the overwhelming pantheon of celestial beings that had surrounded them. *Dearn's sake, I hope she doesn't leave us trapped here.*

Order regarded them in silence for a time.

"Well, my champion, though I did not devise your creation, nor guide your experiences and decisions, I find myself pleased by your actions. Stand ready should I ever have need to call upon you."

A horse trumpeted with excitement behind them. The three turned, feeling a spatter of rain. Croga danced next to Cosantoir while Onoir shook out her mane. A flat beach of black sand edged by tufts of dark grass stretched behind the horses as they trotted up to their masters. Startled, they turned back to the grotto, but it had disappeared, along with Order, leaving them upon the shore where Natt Tre's portal had deposited them.

Rooted in stunned silence for a time, they stared out over the churning waters. The weather began to calm and the sun soon peeked through dark clouds. Their horses, once placated by neck rubs and the assurance that their owners hadn't abandoned them, soon wandered back toward the grassy snacks.

Eventually, Jal, Eamon and Phatomar turned to regard one another. They had no need of words. Not yet. Though they no longer shared their thoughts so intimately, each knew the others' mind, or thought they knew. After travelling so long together, after so many adventures, a moment to catch their breath with no expectations of the future seemed like a luxury.

In due time, they gathered their mounts, looked to the heavens to get their bearings, and retreated from the shore, not knowing their location and not sure it mattered just yet.

"This reminds me of when we escaped the minotaur's lair, far from civilisation and lost in the night," Phatomar said with a small smile. "We found our way back then, and we will again now."

Eamon stared at him with relief and pride. He nodded in recognition of his friend's returned prowess and sense of self, then turned his face to the wind.

"Shall we go home then?"

"Where is home?" Jal asked, her voice small. She hadn't thought about what she'd do after the Oracle's quest.

"Wherever we want it to be," Eamon said. He gave Jal a penetrating stare. "Phatomar and I call no place home for long. We travel Merveah and the lands around it, looking for adventure, to help those who need it, occasionally trading our services with might and steel for money and goods."

"We would welcome your company, should you choose to continue to travel with us," Phatomar said. Eamon gave a nod in agreement.

Jal stared from one to the other, warmth searing her heart.

"I wouldn't want to break up the family," she said, and held out her hands. Phatomar took her left, Eamon her right.

"Together or not at all," she vowed, and they set out to find their next adventure.

Author of several fantasy novels, Kelly Peasgood has an Honours degree in English with a Minor in Classics, so she likes old stuff. When not writing, you will likely find her reading, playing the flute, or travelling. Perhaps gardening, if she gets ambitious. She lives in Ontario, Canada with her fantastic husband.

You can find her at www.kellypeasgood.com

www.ingramcontent.com/pod-product-compliance
Lightning Source LLC
Chambersburg PA
CBHW070311260626
47160CB00003B/805